ALSO BY PAUL GUERNSEY:

UNHALLOWED GROUND

ANGEL FALLS

A NOVEL BY

Paul Guernsey

SIMON AND SCHUSTER

new york london toronto sydney tokyo singapore

Simon and Schuster
Simon & Schuster Building
Rockefeller Center
1230 Avenue of the Americas
New York, New York 10020

SIMON AND SCHUSTER and colophon are registered trademarks
of Simon & Schuster Inc.

Designed by Eve Metz
Manufactured in the United States of America

1   3   5   7   9   10   8   6   4   2

Library of Congress Cataloging in Publication Data

Guernsey, Paul.
Angel falls: a novel/by Paul Guernsey.
p. cm.
I. Title.
PS3557.U355A5   1990
813'.54—dc20   89-29472
                                                      CIP

ISBN 0-671-67598-2

FOR MARYANN, WITH LOVE

AND FOR MY FRIENDS CHEDDY MORENO AND DAVID BROWNE,
con mucho cariño

PROLOGUE

I call myself Jimmy Angel. I have always been a Jimmy; Angel is a name I took shortly after my twenty-first birthday. I took it in an attempt to create an identity for myself out of longings and old memories. Before I was an Angel, I was a Teller, a name I borrowed from my mother's family. Some would say I borrowed it without permission. I was more than happy to give it back.

The name Jimmy Angel is well known in Venezuela, where I lived for several months before leaving at the request of the foreign ministry and a half-dozen police agencies. The other Angel, also an American, arrived in the country many decades ahead of me and made a large and lasting mark for himself. I never met him. As far as I know, he was never asked to leave.

Prior to my de facto expulsion from Venezuela, my name sometimes inspired astonishment and disbelief among people I met there. Sometimes even laughter, because of the fame of the other Angel. Outside of Venezuela, the name meant little to people, and comments were rare.

I once saw a picture of the first Jimmy Angel; I would not quarrel with anyone who wanted to call him the authentic, or the "real" Jimmy Angel. In the photograph he is wearing a white shirt with the top button open. He is a dark-faced, jowly man, and his ample stomach sags over the belt of his trousers. On his head he wears a

7

narrow-brimmed hat tipped back to expose a furrowed brow. He is not smiling.

The Jimmy Angel in the photograph reminds me of a stereotypical scowling Southern sheriff. He looks nothing like Hollywood's idea of an explorer; he probably would not have survived the first cut of a casting call for the role. But Jimmy Angel was not a sheriff. He was not a lawman of any sort. He was a bush pilot, and for many years he flew a small, single-engine plane over unexplored jungle and savannah in search of the raw riches of the earth.

I claim no relation to the real Jimmy Angel. He came about the name naturally, and I readily admit that I did not. Rather, my interest in the other Angel stems from a sentiment I have that something in his stubborn and dissatisfied explorations of jungle, plains, and mountains bears similarities to journeys I have made over a broken and desolate terrain all my own.

The authentic Angel's greatest discovery was that of the towering cascade that carries his name. Spurting from underground channels in the side of an imposing plateau called Devil Mountain, the waters of Angel Falls spill more than half a mile down a sheer cliff-face. The drop is fifteen times longer than Niagara Falls; twice the height of the Empire State Building. Much of the water scatters to mist before it ever reaches the river below. It is the highest waterfall on earth.

Jimmy Angel found the waterfall in 1935. He found it by accident. He had not been looking for a waterfall at all.

What Angel had been looking for was gold. His story, believed by all hearers who are pure of heart, was that an old prospector in that rugged and convoluted eastern Venezuelan jungle country had once taken him on a flight into land known only to the Indians, had shown him a river that flashed with the yellow metal. Afterward, after those fatal moments of temptation, he spent years wandering the mysterious territory between the Orinoco and the Amazon, trying to retrace that flight. But he never again found the river of gold. Instead he found Angel Falls.

I imagine him as he turns his little red monoplane into the dead-end canyon of Angel Falls. The canyon is full of shadows; the rippling shadow of the airplane is the only shadow that moves. At first he does not look up. He is scanning the river below, trying to match it to an old picture he carries in his head. He is scanning the ground, looking for a place to put the plane in case the striving engine should fail. He feels the vibration of that engine through seat and rudder pedals and joystick. Perhaps the sun makes him squint. Perhaps he feels his own sweat slick against the joystick as the little plane bucks in the wind. And then his eyes travel upward and he sees the long white plume leaping from the side of the mountain.

The real Angel's heavy jaw drops open. He forgets the gold. He trembles. It is as if God had suddenly spoken to him in a loud voice. I imagine him heading for the cliff, slipping the plane in close enough for water to form moving beads on the windscreen. Perhaps he even crabs it in as close as the pilots of the tourist aircraft from Canaima do today, but this is doubtful. He is too careful a flyer to take reckless chances.

Feeling like a lover whose time is precious for being short, Jimmy Angel stays with his waterfall until the fuel gauge tells him he has to go.

So there it is. The story of the real Jimmy Angel. He was a man who put his heart, his mind, years of his life into finding riches of a specific kind. Instead he discovered a different, an unexpected, richness, or at the very least discovered a personal moment of almost frightening beauty and purity and truth. In this, it is easy to see resemblances to my own lonely travels. At least, it pleases me to think so.

CHAPTER 1

Caracas, Venezuela, was disorienting from the start. When I left the States, the headlines in the newspapers had been screaming BRITAIN WINNING FALKLANDS WAR. But as soon as I stepped off the airliner at the Simón Bolívar International Airport, I was assaulted by an array of Spanish sixty-pointers that said ARGENTINA NEARS VICTORY. I was a professional newsman, and I paid attention to all headlines regardless of the language in which they were written; I scanned them with a mixture of hunger for the happenings of the universe and dread at the possibility of having been beaten at my best and only game. My first reaction to these Venezuelan headlines was anger at what I considered to be their arrogant dishonesty. Surrounded by the protective wall of my worn gray suitcases, I stood transfixed before the airport newsstand and tried to see through all that black boldface to some deeper window into the workings of this newest world.

I had come to Venezuela to try my luck as a wire service correspondent. Previously I had been more or less contentedly employed as a reporter for Mexican and Mexican-American affairs on an Arizona newspaper. I had gone to that newspaper directly from college and had been there for several years before Mickey Calderón, Caracas bureau chief for a large North American wire service, began to court me. Part of Mickey's reason for wanting me was that during a brief stint as a college journalism instructor, he had taught me a good deal of what I thought I knew about the newspaper business, and he felt a touch of proprietary pride in me because of it.

But his main motives in pursuing me were more practical than that. I made an excellent candidate not only because I spoke good Spanish, switching from the formal and the grammatical to the low and the coarse with less thought or effort than most two-tongued gringos, but also because I had fewer ties to the world than almost anyone and therefore would presumably not be subject to the familial longings and strange materialistic nostalgia common to overseas Americans. Mickey, the son of an American mother and a Cuban father, was well qualified to assess my Spanish as well as my aptitude for life as an alien.

"Look," he had said during the drunken party at which he had first cornered me and presented his proposition. "You don't have anything here. What have you got to tie you down? No wife. You don't even have a mother to worry about, do you?" I avoided his eyes by staring into my glass, which was full of melting ice and watery amber whiskey.

"I've got one," I said. "Someplace."

"No father, right?"

"Everyone's got a father." It did not occur to me to refuse to answer. I had not seen him in a while, and the party, after all, was a sort of homecoming affair in his honor.

"Who else? Who else have you got to hold you back? What the fuck are you going to do, be a beat reporter all your life?" I felt pressed to come up with some sort of evidence that I was not an emotional tumbleweed.

"A grandmother," I said.

"Hah!" he shouted, spraying me with whiskey and spit. He was a short, thick man with bowed legs and a round, fleshy face the color of rare beef. He was in his late forties, and although nearly bald, he possessed the hairiest body I had ever seen. The backs of his hands were thick with hair, tufts of hair like cat's whiskers stuck from his ears, and hair like the black legs of insects grew from his nose and twitched when he talked. Liquor had a way of making him emphatic.

"A grandmother!" Mickey said. "Back in Connecticut. You don't even keep in touch with her, do you? Bad blood, is it?"

"I've got a woman now, Mickey." My eyes stayed on my glass, and I could barely hear my own voice above the noise of the party.

"A woman?" Mickey laughed a laugh that was not entirely unsympathetic and gave me a thump on the shoulder. "Let's have a look at her, then. Is she here?"

I looked around and nodded in the direction of the woman in question, a blond, self-conscious wisp of a college girl, who happened to be talking to Mickey's wife, Beatrix. Beatrix had been raised in Argentina and was the daughter of a high-ranking German officer who had fled Europe following the war. Although she and Mickey had children, two little boys, she had never looked much like a mother to me. She was too attractive, and there was something wrong with her blue eyes, a wildness to them maybe, that made her seem miscast in the maternal role. In fact, she reminded me a little of pictures I had seen of my own mother, and the resemblance made me uneasy.

"Hmm," Mickey said after a moment. "Pretty." It was hard to tell whether he was talking about my latest woman friend, or his own wife. "And how long do you suppose *this* one will last?"

I had not answered just then. But two women later, during a spell of intense and solitary drinking, I had called Mickey and asked him if the job was still open.

On that first day in Caracas, a couple of hours after I had finally torn myself away from the confusing airport newsstand, Mickey Calderón handed me an impressive-looking laminated credential bearing my photograph and the seal of the agency.

"It's counterfeit," he told me, his nose hairs, which had begun to gray suddenly, moving as he spoke. "A friend makes them."

"What do you mean, counterfeit?" I said. "I work for the damn agency now. Don't I get a credential?"

His eyes slid away from me; he let them wander around the Colombian restaurant where he had taken me for my welcoming dinner. His hands moved nervously against his napkin; he seemed thinner, less cheerful, and jumpier than the last time I had seen him.

"Perhaps," he said, "I didn't fully explain your status as an employee before you came down here."

"Oh boy," I said, my appetite leaving me. "I'm screwed. I smell it coming."

12

"No, no," he protested, his eyes meeting mine for a second and then jumping away. "It's not that bad. It's just that to rate an authentic credential from the agency, you have to be a named agency correspondent. In other words, a direct hire of the New York office. See, the agency budget only allows for one named correspondent in this town, and that's me, son."

"And I'm . . ."

"Locally hired. Technically, an employee of the bureau rather than the agency."

"Oh, shit." I threw my napkin onto the table. "What the hell does that mean?"

"Not much. Not much at all." Mickey sent a big hand across the table to touch my arm, but I pulled away from him.

"Basically it just means that you'll be paid in local currency. But that's no real problem, because it's a strong currency, and there's no trouble about buying dollars if you need them."

"And that's all? That's the only difference?"

"Well, a couple of small things. Like, you don't get any health insurance, or any fringe benefits. But you're young and strong, Jimmy. You don't need that crap anyway."

"And if I get hit by a truck?" Mickey took a small loaf from the bread basket and broke it in half. He bit off a chunk and began to laugh. Wet crumbs flew from his mouth; I felt one hit my eyelid.

"Jimmy. Jimmy. You won't get hit by a truck. I mean, what are the chances of that?"

"And if I go out on assignment and get splashed by guerrillas? What's the agency going to do for me then?"

"No, no," said Mickey. "You'll hardly leave the office. Believe me. Besides . . ." He became intent on buttering the remains of his half loaf of bread. "There are no guerrillas." He took an enormous bite of the bread.

"None that are very *active* anyway." Another bite. "At least not yet."

"Oh," I said. "Oh, God." I settled back into my chair. I was stuck. There was no way I could return to the States with any kind of dignity or hope for the future until I had put in at least a year at this job. In fact, I had no money to make the return trip even if I wanted to. Mickey seemed to be reading my mind.

"You'll like it here," he said. "It's almost just like the U.S., only they speak Spanish. The girls are beautiful, too. Wait till you see them." The waiter came by and set a bowl of thick beef soup in front of him, and he immediately picked up his soup spoon and began digging in.

"As soon as you find a decent place to live, just let me know, and I'll float you a loan for the deposit. Until then, of course you know that my house..." He looked up at me then and said, "Hey, what's the matter with you, boy? Have another beer, for Chrissake."

Later, after we had eaten and had both drunk more beer, Mickey said, "Yeah, Jimmy. Very little practical difference between named correspondent and local hire. No difference at all in the job. Do a good piece of work, you get the credit. And when you screw up, and believe me, you'll screw up a few times, everybody does, they'll kick your ass from here to Bogotá."

"Great, Mick."

"Oh," he said. "And another thing I should warn you about." His face took on a look of fatherly concern. "Try to keep your nose clean with the cops and the government. The agency will only go to bat for someone who carries an authentic credential. Know what I mean?"

"You are un-fucking-believable," I told him. But my words carried no heat; the beer had chilled my anger and scattered it. Mickey seemed not to hear me.

"That credential you have? The phony one? Keep it in your wallet. It'll come in handy. Believe me. Believe me, Jimmy."

Still later, after we had removed to a nearby bar, Mickey began to laugh. He began to laugh as soon as I got around to asking him about Beatrix. The laughter was strained, almost manic; it seemed to be his way of avoiding the question. Then he began to taunt me.

"Local hire," he said. "Local hire. You know what we call local hires in this business, Jimmy?"

"No, I don't."

"You don't know?"

"What did I just say?"

"I'm a little deaf. Did you just say that you did not know what we in the wire services call locally hired help?"

"That's what I said."

"Local trash. That's what we say. Local trash. You'll hear that anywhere you go."

"Just call me L.T.," I said. "Say hello to Beatrix for me, Mickey."

I got up and made my way to the front of the bar and stepped through the door onto the sidewalk beneath the rounded awning. But in the end I did not walk away, because I realized suddenly that I had nowhere else to go.

Mickey had assured me many times that I could stay with him and his family for as long as I wanted. After I went back into the bar that first night and washed down his insults with another couple of beers, I allowed him to lead me home.

Mickey and Beatrix had a huge apartment in a fashionable building in a wealthy neighborhood called Altamira. Altamira was known for its high population of well-to-do foreigners, as well as for its plaza, at the heart of which stood a thin white spire that looked like a miniature of the Washington Monument. The apartment itself, with its two floors, four bedrooms, and huge dining room containing plush, ornate furniture that I thought was much too formal for a home where two small children lived, seemed like it had to be a bit above the most ambitious range of Mickey's wire service salary. But I just stared with wide eyes and said nothing as Mickey led me on a tour of the first floor.

He had begun to seem nervous as soon as we walked through the door, his voice taking on a strained quality like that of stretching wire. His nervousness infected me even as I tried to guess the reasons for it.

Then, suddenly, Beatrix appeared, and Mickey immediately barked some kind of endearment at her, surrounded the handles of my suitcases with his sweating hands, and disappeared with them, leaving me to face her by myself.

Blond Beatrix, with the feral eyes, squeezed the tips of my fingers and from between clenched teeth she said, "So nice to meet you again, Jimmy. I'm so glad you could come to visit us for a couple of days."

She spoke English with a mild German accent, saying "glat" instead of "glad," and her hand was cold to the touch. I became suddenly aware of the deep-throated ticking of a hand-carved grandfather clock that stood next to the dining room's false fireplace.

"If there is anything I can do for you, just let me know," I said, ashamed of the desperate edge to my voice. I had begun to feel naked.

Beatrix dropped my hand and studied me with eyes the color of Danube ice. "Um," she said finally. "Yes. Of course." Then she turned and walked lightly, floated almost, through the dining room doorway and out of sight. In a moment I heard her giving instructions in her harsh Spanish to someone on the other side of the apartment, to the maid, perhaps, or to a child.

Caracas was a large, modern city packed into a narrow valley choked with traffic and roiling with fumes. The press agency's bureau was located in a cramped and dreary rental office on the fourth floor of a building called the *La Nación*. This building stood in the loud, grimy, and ironically named section of town called El Silencio and it housed, as well as bore the name of, one of the largest and most well-respected newspapers in Venezuela. The bureau office sat at the rear of the fourth floor of the newspaper headquarters the way a tick rides the ass of an indifferent dog.

The walls of my office were the same gray-green color as the lichens you find growing on rocks in barren places. Near the entrance, close to the ceiling, someone had glued Styrofoam letters that spelled out the legend LA AGENCIA DE NOTICIAS MÁS PRESTIGIOSA DEL MUNDO. The most prestigious news agency in the world. All the letters were dusty and yellowed with age, and the *c* in AGENCIA and the *p* in PRESTIGIOSA were missing. Below the window there were slums. When you looked down, you saw the corrugated steel roofs that covered tiny, red-brick shacks of the type known in the country as *ranchos*. On any open space in Caracas, whether between tall buildings or on steep hillsides, little villages of *ranchos* were liable to spring up at any time like blemishes on a ravaged adolescent face.

The small hamlet beneath my window emanated a constant salsa beat that would begin softly in the morning, nearly inaudible above the whining and buzzing of the electronic teletypes and the metallic clashing of the single ancient telex machine. It would build throughout the day as more and more cassette players and tinny stereos joined in, until the office windows chattered like brittle teeth and my head vibrated with that Caribbean rhythm. Drums and horns and cheerful Puerto Rican voices. Sometimes it seemed as if all of Venezuela throbbed to that complex, sensual, violent beat.

Aside from Mickey, my only office mates were the quiet Colombian secretary, whose job it was to keep payroll records and handle Mickey's other paperwork, and Carlos, who was a combination office boy and photographer. Carlos, a round, oily-skinned young Venezuelan with thick eyelids that always seemed half-closed, had abandoned a job as a full-time photographer for one of the afternoon scandal sheets because he had grown weary of photographing half-naked murder victims. His duties for the agency were light; most of the time he could be found sleeping in the closet-sized darkroom. Mickey called him Carlos the Jackal, after the famous Venezuelan-born terrorist.

The choice offices in the front of the *La Nación* building overlooked a narrow side street that ran north toward sunlight and a plaza bearing the incongruous name of O'Leary. The windows of these offices offered splendid views of a coffee shop and lunch counter run by the family of a former Italian tank commander, as well as the pornographic movie house a few doors down from it. Every afternoon at four-thirty, *La Nación* reporters and editors who had nothing better to do would gather at the windows to study the queue of theater patrons waiting to buy tickets for the early showing of *Mujeres Calientes* or *La Garganta Larga*. This line usually spilled out of the theater, ran down the street in the opposite direction from the main avenue where I caught my *por puesto* microbus every evening, and turned a corner that led to a block of cheap hotels, greasy bars, and sudden death at midnight.

Sometimes, when I was ahead of my work, I would go down to the front offices with the *La Nación* boys and observe the daily procession. We would all watch in a brotherhood of somber silence, smoking cigarettes and drinking tiny cups of strong Venezuelan coffee. Then, when the men below us, young men and old men, mostly from the poorest ranks of the working class, had finally been swallowed up between the childish posters of naughty women that hung on either side of the ticket window, we reporters and editors drifted back to work. We walked slowly, singly, avoiding each other's eyes.

The agency thrived on stories of violence. A good plane crash or a mud slide that crushed poor people while they slept, or the kidnapping or murder of anyone wealthy or in any way important

17

was almost guaranteed a spot on the worldwide Triple-A wire. I once earned a few words of commendation in the morning messages sent by New York to all the Latin bureaus for a piece I did about an attack by killer bees on a Chinese restaurant.

But the important, ongoing, bread-and-butter Venezuelan story was the economy. Venezuela produced oil, and oil prices, oil demand, and oil revenues had all been dropping steadily while the government continued to spend money and give money away in the same carefree manner as always. Some Venezuelans were beginning to look around with a nagging sense of lost opportunity, wondering what the country had actually achieved during the years of prosperity. But most of them did not seem to be looking around; they seemed to be concentrating more than ever on earning and buying and spending, on eating and drinking and making noise to drive away the evil spirits.

There were rumors of a coming devaluation of the proud bolivar, the currency that bore the name of the Liberator of South America, but these rumors were considered semitreasonous, and they were generally spoken softly.

"It's a good time to be a journalist here," Mickey told me. "Every once in a while you get a whiff of panic in the air."

"What do you think's going to happen?" I asked.

"Change. *Rápido.* I think you're going to see the devaluation in less than a year. You're going to see this place go from oil rich to oil poor so fast, your head will spin. Food prices will go up like crazy, because they never arranged to start growing any of their own. In a few months you'll start to see stresses on the fabric of society, as the sociologists like to say. More violence. Things like that." Mickey laughed and rubbed his thick hands together in an exaggerated gesture of glee. "You might even see red guerrillas come crawling out of the woodwork again, dragging bombs and bazookas behind them. Shit! Wouldn't that be something, Jimmy boy?"

"Jesus, Mickey." He seemed to have forgotten telling me that the entire guerrilla movement was comatose.

"Don't Jesus me. It's the only way New York's gonna know we're alive down here."

"And who are the players? Who do I spend my time watching? The president?"

"The ribbon cutter? No. Forget him. Keep one eye on the finance ministry and the other on the Central Bank. I figure they'll be at each other's throats before you know it. And keep your third eye on the Ministry of Energy and Mines. They handle the oil, and anything coming out of there will affect everything else."

Despite his enthusiasm for the job, Mickey immediately began leaving me to work by myself a good deal of the time. He did not bother telling me where he went or why he was so often gone from the office. Frequently, when a message for Mickey came over the teletype from New York, I would have to punch out a vague answer on the telex and code in his initials at the end of the tape.

I went about hunting for my own apartment with an obsessive desperation, and within Beatrix's "couple of days" I latched onto the first place that seemed to meet my requirements. My new apartment covered the entire top floor of a house at the end of a cul-de-sac in the hillside section of Caracas called Sebucán. It was the largest and best-kept-up house along that dead-end street, and for a brief time it seemed perfect.

A lazy stone's throw from the small balcony where I drank my morning coffee rose a fifteen-foot-high white steel wall; it rose from asphalt and weeds and ran for several blocks in either direction, casting early-morning shadows on the low houses that had been built alongside of it. That wall reminded me of a prison enclosure, but it actually formed one of the four faces of a rectangular compound protecting the vast gardens of an estate on the other side. The dead-end street that ran past my house disappeared beneath a pair of huge steel doors that formed a gate in the wall. These doors were always closed.

From the ground below the wall, I could see the estate's leonine palm trees with their blond manes of dead fronds. And from the vantage point of my balcony, I could see orderly rows of fruit trees. I watched limbs grow heavy with mangoes and avocados, watched the fruit drop to the earth, unpicked like grains of sand in a celestial hourglass. The sight was comforting, almost hypnotic at times, strangely disquieting at others.

I set out to make friends with the neighbors, presuming to rediscover the same openness and warmth I found among the people when I had traveled in Mexico. Instead I encountered resentment.

Sebucán was a suburb of the rich; it stank of oil money. But because no one who was rich wanted to live beside the forbidding white wall, a pocket of the Venezuelan working class—factory technicians, auto mechanics, free-lance bus drivers—had hung on along my cul-de-sac. These people did not like me because I was an *extranjero*, a foreigner, and because I lived in the biggest house. I was threatened frequently, and occasionally came close to getting into a fistfight. Things were stolen from me.

Whenever I walked in the street near my house, the neighbors stared and openly discussed my shortcomings, both physical and social. They would even *point* at me in a startling Venezuelan manner that involved puckering the mouth and jabbing it in my direction.

"*¡Mira!*" I would hear someone say. "*¡Mira!*" And I would look up to find a long labial snout zeroed in on me like a bird dog's nose.

At first it was hard for me even to understand them; rather than speaking the slow, singsong Mexican Spanish I was used to, they spoke in the rapid-fire Caribbean fashion, sending each word careening into the rear of the word that had gone before. Before I understood them perfectly, I told myself I was merely imagining that they were talking about me. Later, when my ears had become more attuned to their rhythms and their slang, this convenient make-believe was no longer possible.

They cursed a great deal, my neighbors did. It seemed that nearly everything they said was punctuated by the words *coño* and *vaina*, which appeared to correspond roughly to the Mexican *chinga* and *pinche*.

The neighbors went so far as to send their children to climb the lone mango tree that grew in my tiny yard. The *chamos* scurried up the tree like monkeys even as I sat watching from the balcony, and they stripped all the fruit before it was ripe. I never got to taste a mango from that tree, and I always wondered what force it was, whether fear or superstition, that kept the neighbors from scaling the white wall and stealing the untended fruit on the other side.

Shortly after I began working, I was invited to a party. It was a birthday party for the daughter of the managing editor of *La Nación*. I had been told she was a student at the Simón Bolívar University, but I did not know her; in fact, I had never met her. The invitation came through the managing editor's secretary, who called me at the office and said the great man himself had asked her to get in touch with me. I knew the managing editor about as well as I knew his daughter.

"He thinks you might enjoy it," said the secretary. "You're quite young, aren't you?"

I was flattered that the M.E. was thinking of me, and I thanked his secretary profusely. But then she came out with the real reason for the invitation.

"Many of the guests are studying English. He thought they might enjoy practicing with you. Well, have a good time."

After I found out that I was being invited as some kind of un-compensated English tutor, I decided not to go. But it was a Friday evening, and I had just rented the top floor of the house on the cul-de-sac. After I got home and had cooked and eaten my dinner, the place began to seem oppressively large and empty. I felt like a solitary pea rolling around in a huge pod. For something to do, and in order to keep my mind off of women, I started to pace the house end to end. But soon I began to feel pursued by the echoes of my own footsteps. Finally I grabbed my jacket and headed for the party, which was within walking distance, at a house in Los Chorros.

I heard the party music while I was still a quarter-mile away. Strident rock 'n' roll. When I arrived, I found a big, brightly lit hillside home with a wide-open first floor. Squinting, I walked out of the darkness through the open front door and pushed my way into the throng.

At first I noticed only the women. I noticed their hands; the house seemed full of perfect feminine hands holding glasses of wine. Then, after a few minutes, my scope widened and I saw slender legs sheathed in jeans so tight they could have been painted on, and I saw loose blouses that softened lovely curves and angles. Because I felt shy, I looked at the faces last of all. Almost all of them were pretty, European-looking faces; some were as striking as magazine covers. I even recognized, off in a strategic corner of the room, the honey-colored face of a former Miss Universe.

I caught myself standing in the middle of the living room with my mouth ajar. I felt foolish even though no one had yet noticed me, and to give myself something to do, I pushed through to the bar to make a drink. There was good Scotch and whiskey and wine, but I settled for a rum and Coke and then leaned back against the bar to look around the room. I tried to guess which girl was the guest of honor so that I could go up and introduce myself, but I was unable to pick her out. A young man was walking past, and I asked him, but he only shrugged and kept moving.

I began to notice the men then. They all looked preppie in a Venezuelan sort of way. Smiling with impenetrable smugness, a few even wore shirts with crocodiles on the pocket; the sight set a little fire of annoyance burning in me and brought to mind some of the many smug and self-satisfied people I had known in my life. To stop those depressing thoughts, I quickly downed my drink and made myself another. Then I wandered out onto the back patio, where the band was playing and people were dancing.

There was something about the guitar player that made me study him closely. It wasn't that he was physically remarkable in any way; he was just a very thin, slightly grubby, long-haired young man with a small, heart-shaped white scar on the side of his head next to his eyebrow. The dramatic slant of his eyes told me that he had Indian blood in him and that he probably came from some country other than Venezuela, most likely from somewhere along the Andean cordillera. He did not meet my gaze, or even glance at me, but I continued staring at him just the same. He wore a white poncho, and he looked down at the strings of his guitar as he played, his face twisted in a perpetual grimace that changed slightly from chord to chord. High up on the neck of the guitar, a burning cigarette protruded from between the steel strings.

A bass player and a drummer performed on the patio as well, but there was nothing about them that drew my attention. The singer, however, was a huge, dark, curly-headed boy who obviously lifted weights a few times a week. For his size, he had a voice that was surprisingly high and delicate. Angelic almost.

During a break between songs, the dancers on the patio began to shout requests and comments at the Andean and the giant. The giant they called El Camión, or Truck; the guitar player with the funny scar they called Packy.

Packy was a competent guitar player, and El Camión was a

singer who was better than good. The other two band members were not bad either. But as a group they sounded awful. I don't know whether the blame lay with the acoustics of the wide and sloping backyard, or with the fact that they had not practiced much together, or with their choice of music, which was speeded-up late-sixties British rock. The sound they produced was anarchic.

The people dancing beneath the floodlights on the patio did not seem to mind, however. More preppies and beautiful, haughty-looking Venezuelan girls in tight pants. They smiled and posed and moved their hips to the beat of the bad music. I listened until Packy and El Camión and their friends began to mangle "Satisfaction," then I turned and went back into the house.

Inside, I made another drink and stood on the peripheries of several conversations. No one paid attention to me. I asked a few people where the managing editor's daughter was, but nobody seemed to know. I noticed that some of the guests were taking turns sidling off to the dark area under a stairwell to snort cocaine from the backs of their hands.

Then I heard someone speaking in English. A short, pretty girl with dark hair who was standing with four other people said, "Yes, California is where eet's at." Her accent was thick, but I understood clearly.

"That's very good," I said in English. Overly eager, I shouldered my way into the little circle. "Where did you learn English? I'm from New York."

"No hablo inglés," the girl said. She gave me an annoyed look and dropped her eyes away from me.

"What do you mean? Sure you do. I just heard you. You said—"

"No. I don't speak it." She turned quickly and left the circle. The others stared at me a moment, and then all but one of the boys turned away as well.

"You are from New York?" the remaining boy said in English.

"I used to be. Near New York. A little place called Connecticut." I found myself speaking rapidly, desperate to keep my audience. "Then I moved to Arizona to go to college and learn your language, and I was an exchange student in Mex—" The boy nodded curtly. Then abruptly, I was standing alone.

I made another drink. Out on the back patio the band stopped playing. Surrounded by the sudden murmuring of Spanish voices, I felt naked without the crash of music in the air.

Then a smiling Venezuelan with a crocodile on his shirt came up to me. "You're a North American?" he asked in Spanish.

"*Sí.* From New York. Near New York. I used to be, you see, but..."

He asked me some questions, and I started talking, telling him about my work and my impressions of Venezuela. His smile grew broader and broader, and he began to signal for other people to come over. Soon I was standing at the center of a small crowd. I was starting to feel good, accepted.

Then the smiling young man interrupted me. "*¡Coño!*" he shouted. "Listen to that *vaina.* This gringo speaks Spanish just like a Mexican!"

The entire group burst into laughter. I laughed, too, and when I had finished laughing, I saw that I stood alone.

I began to drink. I had three or four quick drinks before I took my glass and wandered back out onto the patio. The patio was nearly deserted now that the music had stopped; aside from the members of the band, who sat on the hillside holding glowing cigarettes, there were only a couple of sets of lovers hugging in the shadows.

"I heard there's a grin-go at this party," somebody said in English. "A mother-fucking grin-go." The voice came from one of the band members; I could tell he was drunk. I hoped it wasn't the big guy with the high voice. I faced the musicians.

"Me," I said in Spanish. "I'm the gringo."

"*¿Gringo? Coño de tu madre, gringo.*" A Mexican would have said *Chinga tu madre.* I did not know how serious he was; I knew that such mother-insults could sometimes be used almost affectionately.

"*Coño de la tuya,*" I said, responding with uncertainty.

I was relieved to see that it was the skinny guitar player who stood. A rum bottle dangled at the end of his arm.

"Packy, sit down," said one of the other musicians. "You're drunk." Packy ignored him; he advanced on me, his face stretched out ahead of the rest of him. He weaved from side to side as he walked.

"I'm from Chile," he told me. "The gringo *coño de madres* fucked up my country. Now I can't go back there."

24

Even through my drunkenness, I felt guilt. I held up my hands. "It wasn't me," I told him.

"It wasn't you? Tell me now it wasn't the Nazis who burned all those people. Fucking gringo *huevón*."

"The gringos had a little help," I said to the unsteady Chilean in front of me. "Your general wasn't born in Chicago, you know."

There was a stirring on the hillside; the big singer stood and went past us, toward the house. Packy looked up toward the patio floodlights, and I saw tears shining in his slanted eyes. His tone was more sad now than angry.

"Gringo. Haven't you heard? The presidential palace, how the gringo *militares* helped to bomb it? And the truck drivers? How the CIA paid them not to work? Paid them in dollars so the country starved?"

"The part about the truck drivers may be true," I said, my voice beginning to tremble. "But the presidential palace thing is just a myth. And what do you expect me to do about it, anyway? Do you think I have any more control over things than you?" He lifted the half-empty rum bottle then, and he stepped forward.

"I'll show you a myth," he muttered. I don't know if he would have hit me, but I put my hands on his narrow chest and pushed him. He was light, and he flew back and landed on the hillside and lay still.

Then suddenly I felt huge arms surrounding me. It was El Camión, and he lifted me off the ground and squeezed me. I tried to struggle, but he held onto me and he kept on squeezing until he had wrung all the air out of my body and I blacked out.

Later I felt someone going through my pockets. I somehow got the idea that they were trying to steal the phony credential Mickey had given me, and I began to thrash. I felt the big arms go around me once more, then darkness came again.

When I came to, I was lying on the broken sidewalk in front of my house. Someone was shaking me. I opened my eyes and saw that it was Séptimo, the neighborhood orphan. The sun was beginning its long climb into the sky.

"*Coño*," I said. "My damn head."

As soon as he heard me speak, Séptimo backed away and stood looking down at me. "Four men in a car dumped you here," he said.

"Friends," I told him. "Good friends." My head pounded as I struggled to sit up.

Séptimo was seven or eight years old, and he lived beneath a piece of corrugated steel that leaned against the high white wall opposite my house. His mother had apparently named him Séptimo because he was her seventh child. No one knew where his mother was or how he had happened to settle on the cul-de-sac. He was a strong-looking, if dirty, little boy, but his dark face was disfigured by several white spots the size of a penny. The spots had been left by a rash of facial blisters he suffered as a toddler.

I pulled out my wallet and went through it; nothing was missing, not my bogus agency credential or even the money. I decided then that they had gone into my pockets to find my address. An innocent motive. I felt Séptimo's dark eyes on me and I looked up at him.

"Did the *frutería* open yet?" I asked. He looked up the hill toward the corner where the fruit store stood.

"The Portuguese rolled up his door a few minutes ago," he said.

I took out thirty bolivars, a twenty and a ten, and handed them to him. "Run up and get me some juice. *Parchita*. Passion fruit. The big container."

Séptimo left and shortly returned with a plastic container of yellow juice and an *arepa*, a round white wheat cake, stuffed with shredded cheese. He handed me the juice, then he took a bite out of the *arepa* and grudgingly held out a handful of coins.

"No," I told him. "You might as well keep that." He slid the change into his pocket and began to back away without a word, the plump *arepa* clutched in his filthy little claw.

"*¡Epa!*" I said. "Hey, if you're hungry tonight, come by. I'll have something for you."

But Séptimo patted his pocket, making the change jingle. "I've got my dinner right here," he said. Then he walked down to his lean-to and crawled inside.

I sat on the sidewalk drinking the juice, which was tart and cold. The rising sun struck hard at the backs of my eyes, but it was beautiful, so I tried to watch it anyway.

Loneliness drove me to weather Beatrix's frostiness in order to try to reach her children. They were a pair of quiet little boys named Floyd, who was eight, and Nestor, who was six. Despite the fact that both their parents spoke fluent Spanish, the children felt out of place in Venezuela and would speak nothing but English. They met all attempts to teach them the new language with a stubborn, stony silence that could not be breached. I eventually learned that during the time they lived in Tucson, Mickey and Beatrix had spoken Spanish only when they did not want the boys to understand them. For Floyd and Nestor, Spanish had always been a dark tongue of adult and frightening things, a language of anger, secrets, and sex.

In Caracas the two brothers created a world belonging only to themselves, and they lived in this world most of the time that they did not spend in the American school they attended. Floyd had named this imaginary place "Home," and they populated it with people and things from their past: American things and people they had known during happier days. One of the leading citizens of Home was Miss Martin, a kindergarten teacher they had both enjoyed. Another was Bobby Oakes, a young Tom Sawyer from Tucson with whom they had shared splendid adventures in the desert. Miss Martin held class for the boys behind the closed door of an upstairs bedroom; as I passed in the hallway on my way to Mickey's bedroom office, which was my lone sanctuary in his apartment, I would often hear her voice. It was a voice that sounded very much like the voice of an eight-year-old boy speaking in falsetto.

Along with Miss Martin's classroom, the dimension called Home included a vast desert that occupied a certain barren portion of the Plaza Altamira, and Bobby Oakes was always there, ready to kill a rattlesnake or to stone a hated thicket of cholla cactus.

I spent many evenings after work and large parts of several weekends doing little but watching the boys, watching them and trying to sound the depths of their distress. I could not believe that Mickey and Beatrix were unable to see how far from happiness their little boys had grown.

But when I finally attempted to approach them and to join them on the sacred sand of the Tucson desert, they jerked that magic ground from beneath my unwelcome feet. Nestor, who was thin and blond like his mother and had a brown, crescent-shaped birthmark on the side of his jaw, turned his eyes on Floyd, who was a stout and hairless miniature of Mickey, and shouted, *"Air raid! Air raid!"* This was a signal, because Floyd nodded almost imperceptibly, and then the two of them made whining sounds that were supposed to resemble the scream of jet engines, and they bolted across the plaza toward their apartment building. I followed them under the unspoken pretext of going to Mickey's office, and as I climbed the stairs to the second floor of the apartment, I heard Miss Martin's voice coming from their bedroom. Miss Martin was cautioning the boys never to take things from strangers.

I had just begun to resign myself to working for days at a stretch without much of Mickey's help or companionship, when he appeared at the office early one afternoon and told me he was ready to reveal a secret that would make my job much easier.

"A secret, Mick?" I said, feeling a child's thrill of expectation.

"A secret for success. A source of news who is always happy to lend a hand. Here, let me introduce you." He turned away from me as if to address a third party in the room, and he said, "General Jorge, *le presento* Jimmy Angel. Jimmy, General Jorge."

Carlos and the secretary were both out to lunch, and there was no one else in the office. I looked around the empty room, and I shuddered.

"No, no, Jimmy. Down here. The general is *down here*."

I followed Mickey's eyes downward; he was staring into an open file drawer that contained nothing but a few empty manila folders, a bottle of glue, some loose elastic bands, and a condom. I decided I might as well play along.

"Okay," I agreed dispiritedly.

"He's an army man first and foremost," Mickey said. "But he is also a navy admiral, and a wing commander in the air force."

"Come on, Mick. What's the point?" Mickey lifted his thick eyebrows at me.

"I forgot, Jimmy. You haven't yet spent much time trying to coax even the most innocuous information out of the military folks here. Pretty damn impossible. Pretty damn uncomfortable, too, if you've got New York breathing down your back. But luckily, the good general is always on hand with a handy phrase or two."

"Of course," I muttered. "I should have known."

"Observe," said Mickey, with the greatest of cheer. He bent forward so that his heavy face hovered a mere foot above the drawer. "General Jorge. I wonder if you would be so good as to comment on the recent purchase of sophisticated F-16 fighter aircraft from the United States." Mickey now cocked an ear toward the drawer; he screwed his face into a mask of rapt attention.

"Yes? Yes? The powerful F-16s will not only defend Venezuela from all its enemies, foreign and domestic, but will also increase the motherland's status in the region? That's excellent, General. Just what we were looking for. I assume that we can quote you? Yes, only on background, of course. Thank you, General. You're so kind."

Suddenly Mickey slammed the metal drawer and turned narrowed eyes to me. He was not smiling.

"The General," said Mickey, "speaks only on condition that we always refer to him as a high military source who does not wish to be identified. Got it?" When I said nothing, he grinned and chucked me on the shoulder.

"God, do I love this business," he said.

After Mickey's impressive display of ethics, I began to wonder whether I would survive a full year of working for him and his agency. From then on I began to keep one eye on the local classified ads in case I found myself in sudden need of a temporary job in order to buy an air ticket back to the States.

One of the most intriguing offers appeared in the city's English-language daily. The unnamed advertiser invited American expatriates who spoke Spanish and Venezuelans fluent in English to apply for a handful of jobs that involved serving as interpreters for visiting American rock musicians. Persons hired by the advertiser would be placed on call for the intermittent but high-paying work.

So low did I feel when I first saw this ad that I almost dialed the telephone number at the bottom of it. But then I told myself that, no, I was a journalist and I should stick to journalist's work for as long as I could.

I did clip the ad, however, and I filed it with a selection of other emergency options that had captured my attention.

I had come to Caracas with expectations of the glamour and excitement that I imagined went with the job of foreign correspondent. But when Mickey told me I would never leave the office, he was not far from wrong. When you have one, two, or even three people to cover an entire country, you are spread impossibly thin: For the sake of efficiency, you end up relying on the local media to do your foundation work. You become a glorified filter, screening television and newspapers and radio for items of international interest. You make a few phone calls to give your own spin to these items, and then you punch them into a telex tape and send them through an underseas cable to another continent. I even covered a world-championship prizefight by viewing it on the office television while they played salsa music in the little slum beneath my window.

So it was not surprising that I spent a lot of office time watching Venezuelan TV. The newspapers gave you better information, but if you heard about something big for the first time in a newspaper, it often meant the other agencies had beaten you to the story.

There was a cartoon that came on following the afternoon news; I would watch it sometimes if there was nothing going on. In the cartoon a little Catholic boy owns a pet goldfish that frequently transforms itself into a large blue whale with the power of cosmic flight. The whale is always carrying the little boy into heaven to see Jesus. Jesus, who is larger, even, than the whale, talks to the boy and solves all his earthly moral dilemmas. This cartoon left me with a feeling of sadness and loss, but I continued to watch it anyway.

One day the station broke into the middle of my cartoon with a bulletin announcing a military action in the east. The excited announcer said the government was claiming that operatives of the national security force known as Disip, the Department of Military Intelligence (DIM), and the *Guardia Nacional* had surrounded and destroyed the jungle camp of a band of Marxist guerrillas. This was the last group of insurgents left in Venezuela; the only ones who had not come in from the cold to participate in democracy after the dictator was ousted, and now they were finished. No longer would they extort money from ranchers on the lonely eastern lands.

The announcer promised that more information would follow. Then the cartoon came back on; Jesus was beaming down at the little boy.

Mickey was in the middle of one of his frequent and unexplained leaves of absence, so I punched out a quick tape and sent it chattering through the transmitter. After that I got on the phone, but I could find out very little. The government had already released all the information it wanted to release for the time being.

Then Mickey appeared, drawn by the smell of blood; he called all his best contacts, but fresh news was elusive. He suggested that we summon General Jorge for a consultation, but I convinced him that we should wait for a day or two to see if the authorities would decide to provide a few more details.

The story was slow in coming, but luckily, enough of it trickled in over the next week for us to allow Mickey's little friend to remain slumbering in his file drawer. According to Disip officials, they had gotten a tip about a meeting at the secret camp; wearing jungle fatigues and carrying automatic weapons, they had thrown a noose around the site and gone in shooting. They killed twenty-five guerrillas, both men and women; the only survivors were two of the leaders, who managed to escape. On the way out the two leaders had abducted a captain of the *Guardia Nacional* and had disappeared with him into the jungle. One of the escaped guerrillas, Victor Rojas, had been the Disip's most wanted man for nearly twenty years; he was believed to be wounded. The other escapee was Enrique Mosca, Rojas's protégé.

When television crews were finally allowed on the scene, all that was left to be filmed was a bare patch of dry jungle covered with scattered clothing and blowing papers. The papers, the Disip said, were Marxist tracts that were being distributed to universities around the country. The authorities displayed a small collection of guns they said they had found in the camp.

In Caracas the congressional Socialists were outraged that not even one prisoner had been taken. They pointed out that most of the people killed were young university students and not serious guerrillas at all; they cried massacre. The Conservatives, on the other hand, were angry that the assault force had been sloppy enough to allow Rojas and his companion to kidnap an officer and then escape.

The story cooled after the mass burial of the guerrillas a week later. The authorities continued searching for Rojas and Mosca and their captive, but they weren't giving out the details. I turned my

31

attention to other stories, and Mickey returned to the mysterious preoccupation that kept him from the office. On the one occasion when I assembled the courage to ask him about his absences, he merely stared at me and gave me a smile that was both sad and angry; he seemed to be telling me that his life contained complications for which words were entirely inadequate.

Shortly after the massacre had quit making the news, I met a woman who called herself Orchid. Orchid was a tramp. By that I mean a person with no job, no home, no clothes, no future. A crawler in gutters, a smoker of discarded cigarettes, an eater of crumbs found on sidewalks near hot-dog wagons. At the time our paths first crossed, she was one of the most awesomely nihilistic of all those who live in doorways and beneath highway overpasses, a member of that small order that thinks nothing of falling asleep on hot pavement at the center of a busy intersection, or who maim themselves, divorcing themselves from a finger, an eye, an arm, so that someone takes pity on them and gives them enough money for a few swallows of *caña* or a couple of joints made from a cocktail of raw cocaine and marijuana.

The self-destructive ones had always fascinated me every bit as much as they revolted me. Each one of them was a reeking statement concerning the true market value of an individual human life. And some seemed quite aware of their importance to the rest of us as reminders of our own foolish arrogance. I could see it in their eyes, in the weird and frightening self-respect they showed when they came up and asked for money, demanding it almost, as if to say that my comfort, my soft bed, the roll of fat around my middle, did not belong to me by any virtue of my own, but had been won by me in a throw of the dice, and that I could as easily have lost my first wagers in the world and from the gambling table taken circumstances such as birth in a slum to a twelve-year-old mother or possession of a face half-covered by a hideous purple birthmark.

Orchid had not maimed herself in any way. I would not have been able to stand it if she had; it has been my experience that a weak stomach will always overcome a strong conscience. But she was so completely indifferent to any kind of danger or humiliation that she seemed to be inviting the world, goading it even, into doing the maiming for her.

The first time I met her, I was on a break from a slow day at the office, drinking coffee in the shop owned by the former tank commander for Mussolini. The Italians who worked in the shop liked me because I was an American. They liked all Americans. They called me Peter, and they joked that this was because all Americans were named Peter. The Peters had been very nice to them after the war, they said. The front of the shop was open to the street, and as I sipped from my plastic cup, I could see men beginning to queue up in front of the pornographic theater. Waiting, some of them read the blood-red headlines of the afternoon papers, while others stared absently into space. I was drinking my second *marrón*, far from *negro* but still darker than a *café con leche*.

I spotted her first from the corner of my eye; there was a movement down near gutter level, and when I turned my head to look, I saw an old gray mechanic's jumpsuit, torn and stiff with filth, moving along the street like the shell of an impossibly deformed turtle. I blinked and looked again, and then I saw the head of matted hair sticking out from the neck of the jumpsuit as well as the naked legs that rose from bare blackened feet. The jumpsuit was in such dismal shape that it failed to cover both the front and back of the body beneath it; the person had to slink along in a tucked and bent position much like an Indian hunter crouching beneath a buffalo robe in an attempt to penetrate the herd. If the wearer of the jumpsuit was a woman, and I guessed from the shape of the thin, dirty legs that it was, then by standing to her full height, she would expose nakedness of one sort or another.

Then the matted head rolled back. She had the features of a true *criolla*, that Venezuelan mixture of Spanish and black, with a trace of Indian. Dark eyes looked directly at me, and a thin mouth spread in a smile. The smile was of a whiteness that was startling, almost blinding, appearing as it did across a brown face stained black with road tar. It was a woman. A woman with awful, tangled hair and an inexplicably beautiful smile.

My chest went icy with panic. I was embarrassed because I had been staring, and I felt blood rush to my face. I turned back to my coffee and whistled softly through my teeth for Amedio, the tank commander, so that I would not be alone at my end of the counter if the creature decided to step up into the shop and accost me. Amedio started down from behind his gleaming espresso machine and reached me just as the woman appeared at my elbow and rested her cheek on the counter next to my cup.

"I saw," she said. "I saw you looking at me." I was freshly startled by the musical, even innocent, quality of her voice. Her unsoiled voice made her seem like a child dressed for Halloween in rags and black greasepaint. She spoke haltingly, dreamily as if *I saw, I saw you looking at me* were some childhood song she was trying to remember.

I glanced at her and then looked away, feeling a soft pulsing like butterfly wings in my throat. The woman appeared to be in her mid-twenties; her face had a scar or two on it, but life in the street had not yet broken her down to the point of irredeemable ugliness.

"Look here, *chica*," said Amedio, jumping in to defend me. "This is an American. He doesn't speak a word of Castilian, so it's useless to talk to him."

The woman did not even blink in his direction. "Yes, he does," she said with that pretty voice. "He does speak Castilian. And I saw him looking at me."

I decided to face the problem with a little humor then, and I turned to her. "Yes, I speak," I admitted. "And I was looking because I was admiring your evening dress."

She gave a throaty chuckle and her smile broadened. She slid her lips an inch closer to my arm so that she was almost touching me with them. Reflexively I took my arm from the counter and set it in my lap.

"*Sí,*" she said. "Looking at me. All the boys used to look at me, back where I come from. No one does it anymore, but one day they will again."

I stood to leave. A small hand came out from beneath her shell of cloth then, and it grasped the sleeve of my shirt.

Amedio was outraged. "Let him go," he said. "Get out of here, you worthless thing!"

She paid him no mind. She just rolled dark brown eyes at me, still smiling, and said, "I have nowhere to go. Nothing to wear. No friend anywhere. No food."

My chest was tight with embarrassment and guilt; I took a twenty-bolivar note from my pocket and held it out to her. But she made no move to take it.

"I could buy rum with that," she said, singing almost, and smiling up at me. "I could buy a *basuco* cigarette and fly up to the clouds for a minute. But then what would I have?"

I dropped the money on the counter and tried to pull away; she held me with urgent fingers. "My name is Orchid," she said. "Isn't that a pretty name? I need . . . I need . . ." she said, desperation making her voice go higher now.

Amedio could stand it no longer. "*¡Coño!*" he shouted, and he rushed around the end of the counter and gave her a backhanded slap across the face.

She spun away from me then; she stumbled back a few feet and landed in one of the plastic chairs that lined the wall. Her sad garment slid to one side, and for a second we saw one entire naked half of her; a small firm breast, the graceful curves of hip and ass, a sharp piece of shadow between her legs. She managed to cover herself again as Amedio advanced on her, his huge hands reaching for her shoulders.

"*¡Fuera!* Out!" he yelled. I grabbed his arm and tried to pull him back, but he was too strong and he towed me along behind him like a kite. He was so angry, he seemed not even to remember that I was there.

But Orchid was not afraid. She raised a smiling face at him, seeming to invite another slap, and she began to sing an eerie song of her own invention. She sang, "My Lord Jesus, they wounded him with a spear. They made him carry a heavy cross up a steep hill. Later they gambled for his robe. We are all children. We are all children of the Lord."

Amedio had been raising his hand, but he stopped then and crossed himself rapidly. He said with a hoarse voice, "*¡Loca!* Get out of my place. Don't come back here, crazy woman." He looked at me with wide eyes before he turned and lumbered away.

Then she was staring at me again. I swallowed hard and said, "Buy yourself a sandwich with that twenty." I headed across the street to the *La Nación* at a trot.

The gate in the white steel wall across from my house was seldom opened. In fact the first time I witnessed the opening of the gate, the neighbors reacted to it with an awe that could not have been greater had a vision of the Virgin appeared in the sky.

It was evening. Séptimo was eating his dinner at the top of the stairs that led to my front door. On the street in front of the gate the men of the neighborhood were drinking beer and laughing. The loudest talker, the most raucous laugher, was Adolfo, the plumber. Adolfo was a round, dark man who seemed to bear a special bitterness toward me. A Boston Red Sox baseball cap was turned backward on Adolfo's head. He wore no shirt.

Suddenly Séptimo looked up at me with startled eyes, and a moment later a strange rumbling filled the air. The men in the street gasped a collective gasp, and they looked upward to the top of the wall as if expecting to find an apparition hovering there. There was nothing to be seen but purple evening sky and the darkening tops of the palm trees. Women and children ran squealing from the houses to join the men in the street; two or three of the men turned to shush each woman or child that arrived. Then a two-inch split appeared between the massive halves of the gate.

"*¡Coño!*" the men said reverently.

The people began backing slowly away from the gate. They formed two silent groups on either side of it. When the gate had opened farther, I recognized the mysterious rumble as the sounds made by gears and pulleys and electric motors. Twentieth-century magic. The noise stopped completely when a wide breach had been opened in the white wall. For a moment I heard nothing but the cries of roosting birds in the trees on the other side.

And then a car shot out. It was a long, silver Cadillac limousine, and the window glass was darkened to such a deep shade that no human forms could be discerned from without; my neighbors moaned an anxious moan at the sight. The car passed through the trembling gauntlet of my neighbors, almost brushing a few of them with its chrome, and then it climbed the hill, turned the corner near the Portuguese *frutería*, and disappeared.

Adolfo and the others moved like dream walkers to fill the space they had made for the car. All eyes remained on the corner at the top of the hill where the Cadillac had turned and vanished.

Then the rumbling resumed. The people below me gasped and turned their heads to stare out into the grounds of the estate. I also looked. Through the open gate I could see long uncut grass and row after row of fruit trees. Unharvested mangoes the color of gold lay scattered everywhere on the ground.

When the gate had closed for good, my neighbors sighed and drifted sadly away. Even Adolfo walked with his head down.

CHAPTER 2

Watching the slow, uneven rain of wasted fruit falling on the estate adjacent to my house had a way of transporting me to places and times deep in my past. One place and time that I went to over and over was the backyard of my grandmother's house on a particular cool August morning in the middle of my childhood. I was waiting for a visitor. I wore short pants and a white T-shirt, and as I wandered my grandmother's broad lawn with a not unpleasant feeling of anticipation prickling in the pit of my stomach, the deep grass slid through my toes and tickled me. I was a thin child, blue-eyed and towheaded, a bit small for my age, and unremarkable to look at. A long, triangular piece was missing from the outer edge of my right front tooth, so that the broken tooth and the tooth next to it formed a V-shaped notch that reached almost to the gum. I had a nervous and frequent habit of exploring this notch with the tip of my tongue; it was a mannerism that gave my face a rueful expression.

Waiting, I amused myself by whispering the names of all the unseen birds that sang in my grandmother's yard and on the surrounding properties. I knew them all, from wren to vireo to red-winged blackbird. My gentle grandfather, an amateur ornithologist, had given that knowledge to me; it was the only fatherly thing he had known how to give to a fatherless boy, and I had taken it willingly, almost happily, always greedy for more.

"Song sparrow," I hissed to myself. *"Mourning dove,"* I muttered from behind the obstruction of my questing tongue.

The expected visitor was a man I knew simply as Tony. For many years he had owned one of the largest houses in the neighborhood; it was a house with a pair of stone turrets and lawns that rolled right down to the shore, a house in which my friend Tony lived alone. For as long as I could remember, I had seen him walking the beach with his frequent houseguests or playing baseball with the other boys on the playground adjacent to my grandmother's land. But it had only been a year or so since he had begun to seek me out, to speak to me and tell me stories. Although he told fabulous stories about wild Indians and lonely rivers full of carnivorous fish, my favorite had to do with the pilot, Jimmy Angel. I, too, wanted to explore, to discover. I wanted to show the world that it needed me.

As I waited, my eyes traveled constantly between the two most important places in my narrow little world. The first place was a certain section of a dense hedge of forsythia at the back of the property. A skeletal picket fence, gray for want of paint, stood buried in that overgrown thicket. I knew that at any minute Tony would come creeping through the forsythia from the playground on the other side, and that once he reached the fence, he would raise himself to a crouch, grasp a pair of staves in his clean, slender hands, and whistle his low, beckoning whistle.

The other place I watched was a particular second-floor gable of my grandmother's many-gabled Victorian house. From this gable a pair of her close-set, greenish windows commanded a complete view of the lawn. I was forbidden to have visitors of any kind; my grandmother was convinced that my mother's distressing precociousness and incorrigibility had resulted from her childhood associations with children and adults of mediocre backgrounds and upbringing. And so, as I walked, and waited, and danced my solitary childhood dance across the cool grass, I often turned anxious eyes toward those windows, checking for any hint of motion or telltale silhouette on the other side. Though from my perspective the panes were dark, the reflected sun shot out inquiring fingers of light as bright and hard as the molar-sized diamond my grandmother wore on her hand.

My tongue flicked nervously at my broken tooth. *"Catbird,"* I whispered. *"Crow."*

Tony was late. My faith was strong, however; my only worry had to do with the windows. Then a sudden loud thump from the direction of the dreaded gable startled me. I cringed, then turned to see a blur of red spiraling downward from the divided glass; the bird landed on the lawn with a soft *tick* and lay completely still save for a slow, unconscious extension of legs and toes. I bent over it looking for signs of life. It was a small and beautiful bird, entirely red except for black wings and tail, and I recognized it as a male scarlet tanager.

I gently picked him off the grass; felt the warmth of him in my hands. Recalling my Peterson Field Guide, I knew that this was a bird that had come for a brief stay from the unknown jungles of Venezuela or Colombia or Peru. If he survived, he would return there soon, long before the leaves began to fall, and holding him gave me a deep feeling of mystery and longing.

I was on my way to the back door to take him in and have my grandfather minister to him when Tony's whistle finally came from back behind the forsythia bushes. I ran to him, intending to ask him to wait for me until I had delivered the bird to the old man's library. But something profound and sad in Tony's face threw me instantly into an ancient worry and made the welfare of that small creature seem suddenly unimportant.

"Well, Jimmy," Tony said, and his voice was raw and rasping, as if it hurt him to talk. He had told me he was raised in South America, and the hoarseness seemed to bring out his fading accent, which was an amalgam of Italian and Spanish. He was wearing one of the exotic white suits that always made him seem even darker than he was, and he sat back on his haunches, holding fence staves in his hands. Forsythia branches touched him everywhere.

"Tony," I said. My voice was small.

"What have you got there?" He dropped his brown eyes to the bird in my hand, and he left them there, his dark lids fluttering a little.

"Bird," I said, almost whispering. "He hit the window. I think he's dead."

"Let's see."

I passed the bird through the fence; his dusky tail brushed the

40

staves, and Tony took him in his graceful hands. Then, with gentle fingers, he spread the two halves of the bird's bill and blew softly down its throat. I thought I saw the black wings twitch a time or two before Tony made the bird disappear into an inside pocket of his jacket.

Tony finally met my eyes and smiled. He made the kind of smile that seems to swallow up all the light around it.

"Birds," he said. "They're always hitting something. Then they get right up and fly away again. I think this one was just stunned."

I was already feeling lost, but an interior voice told me it was important to pretend I did not care about anything. I looked down at the ground and began arranging little pebbles I found near my toes.

"Jimmy," he said. "I have business to take care of. I have to leave the country. It'll be a while."

"Grandmother says you're a gangster. That you sell illegal things." My consciousness had suddenly become a tiny point, a little voice, buried deep in a dark corner in the back of my head.

"Not true, Jimmy." His voice was strained. "Not the way she says, anyway."

Then he said, "Here," and I looked up, and after a moment of hesitation two fingers came through the fence at me, scissored against the strap of the thin gold wristwatch he always wore.

"Turn it over," said Tony. I turned it over and saw his name engraved on the back. His last name, which I had never heard him pronounce, was long and very Italian.

"That's for you to have. Keep it wound; as long as it ticks, you can be sure I'm alive and thinking about you."

I said nothing, but was secretly pleased.

"Here. Give me your hand." His fingers came through the fence again. I wanted to pretend I was too angry to touch him, but I could not find the strength to hold back. I wrapped my entire hand around his two fingers, and then I forgot all about the watch as real grief shook me.

"What have I done?" Tony whispered. Then he said, "Jimmy, I wouldn't leave if I didn't have to. I'll try to come back sometime. I really will."

"I'm all alone."

"You're not. I'll always be with you. As long as somebody some-place cares for you, you're not alone."

He pulled away from me then, backed carefully out of the tangle of forsythia, and stood. Tears made spots on the front of his white suit.

"Bye, Jimmy," he said. "I'll miss you. I want you to be happy." He began backing away into the playground.

"Tony," I said. "Wait."

"I have to go."

"Wait."

"Good-bye. Be good."

"*Tony!* What should I do?"

He was moving steadily away, but something in my last desperate shout made him stop for a moment and turn. He smiled a narrow smile and opened one side of his jacket; he shook his creamy lapel, and the red bird shot out from his chest and headed into the sky on pumping black wings. I turned to follow that bird as it went up over my grandparents' house, over the telephone poles and the trees on the other side of the street, and became a blood-colored speck against the blue sky before it vanished altogether.

When I faced the playground again, Tony was gone.

I never saw him again, of course. But I didn't forget him, not even after his watch stopped running three or four years later. The jeweler I took it to said that it could not be fixed, because although the outside was gold-plated, the workings themselves were of poor quality and had already gone as long as they were meant to go.

My main motive for wanting to learn Spanish was that it was one of the languages Tony had spoken as he was growing up. And when I decided to give myself a name other than that of my mother's family, I seriously considered taking Tony's foreign-sounding and nearly unpronounceable name before finally settling on the sweet and simple name of the explorer he had introduced me to. I did not dream that I would eventually end up in the one land where that name would be recognized.

Throughout my life, when faced with some difficult choice or decision, I often tried to imagine how Tony would want me to behave, and by imagining, I would find my way through. We who were never given much learn to take what we can.

• • •

From the first days that I lived on the cul-de-sac, Séptimo came to me for food. At supper time he would climb the metal stairs to my front door, and he would wait there for me to bring him a pork chop, or a piece of steak, or a sliver of fish and a potato. He would eat standing up, one hand holding the plate in front of his face, the other clamped in a hard fist that grasped the fork and scraped the food toward his open mouth. I often watched him eat, but he always kept his eyes downward and did not look at me; he seemed to be avoiding my patronizing smile. He declined my repeated invitations to come in the house.

"I'm very dirty," he would say.

After a time, however, I began taking care of a dog, and Séptimo stopped coming around for a while. Séptimo did not like dogs; he had to compete with them for nearly everything.

I found the dog one night as he lay whimpering under a car. The car was parked beneath my bedroom window, and I heard the dog before I saw him.

I had been sleeping, and the dog's low, plaintive whine came through the open window and invaded my unconscious mind. For a confused minute or two before I was fully awake, the noise seemed a part of me; it seemed to be coming from somewhere inside of me. But then I awoke, wet sheet sticking to my back, heartbeat filling the room, and found that it was the dog. Only the dog. That revelation made me grateful to the animal before I felt any other emotion toward him, any emotion such as pity or love or betrayal.

I stepped into a pair of pants, the night chill brushing intimately, silkenly against my skin, and walked outside onto the top of my wrought-iron stairway. The dog fell suddenly silent then, and since I did not yet know where he was, I stood patiently, breathing the night and waiting for him to make his sad sound and give himself away.

Earlier in the evening the neighbors had held a raucous party on the street in front of my house. The men of the neighborhood drank beer and played salsa music on a car stereo and schemed in loud voices to win the lottery. One little group had even parked a pickup truck beneath the streetlamp and then sat in the bed, playing dominos. But everyone was gone now; the cul-de-sac was quiet.

Above the white steel wall I could see the pregnant branches of mango trees and the pure, sweet light of stars. The stars put my heart at ease for a moment. I knew that despite some differences in perspective, the sky was relatively the same for everyone a thousand miles around me; it made me feel connected to things to imagine other people looking up at the stars that very moment. People back in the States were seeing them, as were Brazilians, and people in Colombia. The night sky was so vast and so deep that it rendered insignificant the individual angles from which we viewed it. Somewhere, an artist was seeing my stars. And somewhere else, a pair of lovers. I chose a tiny red star for my own and watched it making a slow ascent from the top of a mango tree toward the dark zenith of the round sky.

Then the dog cried out again. He made such a pathetic whine that I thought he had to be a puppy. But when I went down the stairs and searched for him and dragged him out from beneath the car of my neighbor, Adolfo, I saw that he was full-grown.

He was small, yes. He was not much taller than my knee. And he was so skinny that his pencil-thin ribs rippled the short brown hair of his flanks. He had a narrow, pointed snout and triangular ears that stuck out stiffly from the side of his head. But he was an adult, and he looked at me with frightened eyes as I gathered him into my arms and carried him up the stairs and into my house. I recognized him as the street cur that Adolfo the plumber and his two hideous little boys had been smacking with sticks a couple of days before. The dog ate a hamburger that I fried for him as well as a little bread, and then he fell asleep snoring on the living room floor.

The next morning I awoke as usual to the sound of revving automobile engines and shrieking car stereos. Nearly every morning at about six, Adolfo, with his four-wheel-drive jeep, or Lola, who drove an old Camaro and operated an illegal beer dealership out of her mother's house, would park under my window for ten minutes or so and play the throttle like a musician, like a virtuoso of internal combustion tuning up for a recital.

I soon learned that complaints only increased the duration and frequency of these serenades. So, uncomplaining, I climbed out of bed and found the little dog lying in the middle of my living room. I had completely forgotten about him. I looked him over, noticing for the first time that his dull fur was badly stained with oil in places, and I almost regretted having brought him in. But he rolled his eyes at me, blowing air through his black button of a nose with a sound like a sigh, and I put a hamburger on to fry for him while I made my coffee.

The dog ate slowly, as if forcing himself, and then went back to lying on the carpet. He impressed me as a creature who considered himself to have stumbled into a period of impermanent and fragile good fortune and was prudently gathering strength for whatever new hardships lay ahead.

I covered three press conferences that day, the last one at the presidential palace. And during each of them I found my mind wandering to thoughts of the dog. I felt a weight start to settle inside me whenever I considered the responsibility of having him in the house. How would I take any of my infrequent trips to the beach? The beach was one of the few pleasures I had in this country. As the president was winding up his talk on the early preparations for the Pan-American Games, I decided that I would put the dog back out onto the street that very night.

When I got home that evening, however, he rolled his eyes up at me from his chosen spot on the living room carpet, and I went to the refrigerator and took out some leftover chicken. I carefully shaved the meat from the dangerous bones before I put it into a bowl and set it on the floor next to the gas range. The dog ate without looking at me.

That was one of the first nights since I moved in that Séptimo did not come by.

Within a week after discovering Max, the dog, I found myself coming home with a black leather collar and a leash for him. I gave him a bath, and when the stains that appeared to be motor oil did not readily come out of his hide, I bought a new, stronger shampoo that gave off eye-watering fumes and bathed him again. Max endured the baths with cold resignation. Later, when I tried to play with him, slapping his muzzle lightly with my hand, he crawled between the couch and the wall and stayed there until I found something else to do.

Max did not take well to going for walks on the leash. He probably had never worn a collar or a leash before, and he was constantly pulling away from me or sitting down and forcing me to drag him.

The first time I took him out, Adolfo was in front of my house, using the community spigot near the white wall to wash his jeep. He was always washing and waxing his jeep, making love to it in public. Adolfo wore plastic sandals and tight green swimming trunks that showed the lopsided bulge of his genitals. His bare belly was a taut brown globe rising smoothly from the straining waistband of the trunks. He slid his narrow eyes at me as I went past, towing Max up the street.

"*Extranjero,*" he said, freezing me with his tone. "That is the ugliest dog I have ever seen."

I turned to him, saw him standing with the green hose in his hand, and I wondered if he possessed the imagination to think of spraying me with it. I wondered, too, what I would do if he did spray me. Adolfo's lacquered fingernails gleamed like reflected moonlight; his left thumbnail was long and filed to a threatening point.

"His looks will improve," I said. "He's been starving. I've been feeding him lately."

Adolfo grunted and turned back to his jeep. "A street dog," he said to the white wall in front of him. "Full of disease. You would expect a rich *extranjero* to buy himself a German shepherd or some other animal of value."

I made no reply. I just pulled the reluctant dog, sliding him on the dry pads of his feet, and went up past Lola's house, where three men were waiting for beer on the enclosed patio. Lola was an unmarried woman of dark good looks, but she was rapidly arriving at an age where her prospects for rising beyond the cramped neighborhood of her birth were beginning to melt away. Many of her once-ardent suitors were already banking their fires, growing stomachs, and turning into customers. The frustration of fading possibilities did nothing to improve a disposition that had probably never been much sweeter than sulphur to begin with.

As Max and I went by, Lola was upstairs screaming at her ancient mother. Her words rather than the wind seemed to be causing the white curtains to stream out through the grillwork over the open windows; one of the many things Lola called her mother was a *puta huevona,* a lazy old whore. A green parrot hanging in a cage by the window added an occasional irritated squawk to the noise that boiled out around him.

Then suddenly Lola's head appeared in the window next to the parrot cage. She looked down at us for a moment before bursting into a laugh that sounded like breaking glass. When her laughter had simmered to a choking cough, she began to call her mother.

"¡Mira!" Lola said from behind my retreating back. "Mama. Look at this. You won't believe it."

Even on the days when he did not show up for work, Mickey would sometimes come by the office in the late afternoon and take me to his favorite spot, which was a private club with accommodating hours of operation. Theoretically, if you had the money and the time, you could enter Mickey's club at noon, install yourself somewhere within that humid atmosphere of blue smoke and red leather, and then sit there until six the next morning, drinking Scotch at eight dollars a glass and admiring the tastefully dressed young women who moved like tentative whippoorwills through the artificial twilight.

Drawn indirectly by the black nectar of the Venezuelan earth, these girls came from all over the continent, and every one of them was unfailingly polite. For the price of a drink, one of them would sit with you at the elegant bar and gaze at you with admiration as you talked. If you continued to buy drinks, you could hold her hand at one of the back tables, or even take her to a secluded booth to squeeze her. And if you had the money and were so inclined, it was not difficult to convince a girl to invite you for a visit to her room.

New girls were always coming into the club, veteran girls moving on. Mickey said you could tell by a girl's eyes whether she had just arrived from western Venezuela or Peru and was still fresh or had been around for two or three years and was on her way out. He said that with most of them, a dark shade seemed to come down somewhere in the backs of the eyes after a time, and shortly afterward their smiles became forced and their conversation brittle, and then they disappeared, to be replaced by someone from Medellín or São Paulo who did not yet have the darkness of the eyes. It was a predictable malady, Mickey said, and some got it more quickly than others.

But Mickey's favorite girl at this club was a Mexican woman who had been there for several years, and her gaze had not turned opaque. And it never would, Mickey assured me; Lulu was a rare woman who was actually cut out for and enjoyed the work she did. So that while she was plump, with tiny creases beginning to spread away from the corners of her eyes, she was perhaps the most valuable and pleasing woman at the club. Lulu always greeted Mickey warmly and then swept him away from me almost as soon as we were in the door.

He never forgot to buy me a drink before he disappeared, however, and I would carry my glass from the bar and find myself an upholstered booth where I could nurse my Scotch while avoiding the pointed looks of the maître d'. They had a couple of different pianists there who could do everything from Chopin to Scott Joplin, and I found it relaxing to sit with my drink in a haze of cigarette smoke, listening to the music and thinking my thoughts. Sometimes I watched the other clients. There were journalists as well as businessmen, Congressmen, and TV personalities. An occasional gringo would wander in and attempt to make light conversation with the women in his bad Spanish before letting one of them lead him away.

"For God's sake, quit staring," Mickey had hissed at me during one of my first visits. "Act blind; they know you're a journalist. Remember, there's a truce here, just like at an African watering hole."

I seemed to remember reading that plenty of blood was spilled at an African watering hole, but I didn't argue with him. Instead I sat in my booth, drank my drink, and thought. Sometimes a girl would sit down with me. I never sent her away immediately. I bought her a drink and looked into her eyes to see if I could tell how far down the dark shade had fallen.

They all told a story.

"This is not forever," a girl would say after seating herself on the other side of my booth and holding out the unlit cigarette that served as her pretext for approaching me. "It's just that I don't know anyone here, except for the other girls. When I get a little money, I'll look for a job, and I'll quit."

They all spun variations off this same theme. After a time I figured out that the girls who looked away when they told it and acted as if they no longer believed it were the ones who would soon be touched by the deep shadow at the backs of the eyes and then vanish, to be replaced by another hopeful girl from the frozen mountains or the baking plain.

Mickey would sit and drink with me after coming down from Lulu's room. He had a very short story of his own that he always told.

"That Lulu is great," he would say. "And I'm as good as I ever was." He would stare into his drink as he spoke, and his voice would be brittle. Later, when he finally lifted his eyes to me, I would see something in them that was difficult to look at.

Late one morning a couple of weeks after my rescue of Max the dog, Mickey quietly entered the office and asked Carlos and the secretary to take an early lunch break. When they were gone, he smiled his most paternal smile at me. He looked quite tired.

"I thought I ought to tell you that from now on, there might be quite a few days when you won't see much of me in the office." I did my best to choke back an angry laugh of disbelief.

"I know, I know," Mickey said, raising the palms of his hands in my direction. His palms were thick but creamy smooth, unmarked by toil, and they gleamed with sweat. "You must think I'm gone too much already. Isn't that right?" I nodded.

"Yeah. I guess it is. I guess you could say that." But I could not meet his eyes; he somehow managed to make me feel both petty and unreasonable.

"Well, let me explain something to you. This office doesn't run on news alone. There are subscribers that need to be dealt with. Potential subscribers who need to be wined, dined, and signed, and old subs who must be consulted, stroked, and made to cough up the money they owe us. Administration. I guess what I'm trying to say is administration. That's the other half of the job down here." I was livid, but I found myself nodding, as if I understood perfectly. When I spoke, my words and my tone seemed to drop into a no-man's-land between irritation and empathy.

"So that's half the job? Talking to these people? That's where you are all the time you're not here?"

"Well, Jim . . ."

"So you don't have time to do *any* news work at all? So all of it is my job, by myself?"

"Okay, Jim. All right." He was showing me his palms again. His hands were trembling a bit now; the sight of them shaking caused a cool burn of guilt to flare beneath my heart. "I'm not always with the subs, okay? I'm being honest with you now. I'm with subs a lot

49

of the time, but not all of the time. You're my friend, I can tell you this."

"So, the rest of the time . . ."

His eyes narrowed and went skittering around the room. A damp hand rose and rested on his smooth forehead for a moment. He said, "I've got a few personal problems I'm working out. I'm doing that during some of the time when I should be in here, I guess. Not all of the time, but some of the time." He gave me a pained smile that seemed to say I should consult General Jorge if I wanted further details. "But it won't be forever, what I'm going through. Someday I'll tell you all about it, but right now I can't." My imagination began to paint all the possibilities. Beatrix was a prominent figure in at least half of these imagined pictures. The image of Lulu the whore dominated many of the others.

I was trying to figure out a subtle way of eliciting a further hint from Mickey when he startled me by saying, "Now, if I were you, Jimmy boy, I'd probably consider complaining to New York about a boss who was never in the office. And I wouldn't blame you one bit if you did just that."

"Mickey! You're my friend . . ." He shut me up with a wave of his hand.

"I'd actually deserve it, too, I guess. But the sad truth is—and believe me, Jimmy, I'm only warning you for your own sake—is that when New York gets to the point where it has to ax a bureau chief, it also looks with a jaundiced eye at any local hires that particular bad bureau chief brought in during his tenure. Know what I mean, Jimmy?"

"Jesus! Are you saying . . ."

"I'm sorry, friend, but it's a fact of life. And you can't blame them, really. A bureau chief bad enough to get himself shit-canned . . . why, there's no telling what sort of riffraff he may have dragged in. Druggies, criminals, his own homosexual lovers maybe. Nope, better to kill the whole contaminated brood and start over again." I walked over and sagged against the wall and looked at the floor. I said nothing. After a moment Mickey came over and put his hand on my arm.

"Don't look so stricken," he said. "I'm doing my best to get all my shit in one sock. I really am."

"Yeah?" I was breathing quickly, as if fighting off suffocation.

"All I need is your continued patience." I stared hard into his wincing eyes.

"Goddamn it," I said in an unsteady voice. "Why did you have to haul me down to this country? Why didn't you just let me alone?" Mickey looked astounded.

"Oh, Jim. It just broke my heart to see you wallowing in the mediocrity of a small-city newspaper beat like that."

Before I could recover enough to respond with the outrage that this last remark deserved, he had turned and left the office, leaving me once more with nothing but the whining, cold-hearted teletypes for company.

Later that afternoon I found myself combing the help-wanted section again. It seemed like a prudent thing to do. Nothing caught my eye, however, so I pulled out the file of ads I had clipped over the past several weeks. Among that sad pile of clippings I spotted the notice from the nameless advertiser who had been looking for interpreters to accompany American rock stars. That ad had not appeared in the paper for quite a few days. My curiosity came to life, and after giving it only a second or two of thought, I dialed the number at the bottom.

A bored male voice answered on the second ring.

"Ballesteros Productions," it said.

"Hello," I said. *"Con el Señor Ballesteros, por favor."*

There was a long moment of silence, and then the voice, now tight and suspicious, said, "Who's talking?"

"My name is Jimmy Angel . . ."

"Jimmy Angel, *the pilot?"* The voice carried a heavy note of disbelief.

"No," I said, "Jimmy Angel, the English-language interpreter." He laughed then, all suspicion leaving his voice at once.

"Coño. I guess all gringo *coño de madres* are named Jimmy Angel, aren't they." He continued laughing.

"Listen, *is* this Señor Ballesteros, or isn't it?" If I had to endure laughter at my own expense, I did not want it to come from some office peasant.

"It is," he said, when he had finished enjoying his laughter. "And you called before, right? About the job."

"No, I never—"

"Well, there isn't anything yet. Maybe in a couple of weeks I'll know something."

"Thanks, well, I'll—"

"*Oye, gringo*, tell me, have you ever heard of a group of *roqueros* called the Prowlers?"

"Sure," I said quickly. "Yes, I have." I had heard the name, but I couldn't remember any of their music.

"Very big in Gringolandia. The singer is a tall creature that goes around in an earring and leather pants that have no seat in them so he can shake his gringo ass at the audience. Strange fucker."

"Yes," I said. "It's coming back to me." I now had a hazy picture of that singer in my mind. A scrap of his lyrics, sung in a seductive but overdone rasp, echoed in my inner ear: *I'm a night crawler, baby, gonna crawl on yooou, oh yeah.*

"Well, we may get them to come here, about three months from now. Call me in a couple of weeks, and I might be able to tell you more."

"Yes? Well, thanks, but three months won't help me much—"

"In fact, you better call earlier than that. I've had a lot of people get in touch with me about those jobs, and you're late as it is. *Ciao.*" Then the phone went dead in my hand.

I had almost forgotten about Rojas and Mosca, the two guerrillas who had kidnapped the National Guard captain, when I received the first telephone call from a friend of theirs.

"Mr. Angel," the caller said, "we have heard of your work." He spoke in English to disguise his voice, but his accent was thick, and he was able to answer questions only when I asked them in Spanish. As a further disguise, he choked his voice to a low croak; it was difficult to understand him.

"I am calling on behalf of my friend Victor Rojas."

"Jesus. Who is this?"

"*¿Cómo?*"

"*¿Quién es usted?*" He held a muffled conference with someone in the background before he spoke again.

"A friend. Of Victor Rojas." I opened a notepad and reached for a pen. My mouth was dry.

"How do I know this is authentic?"

"Rojas wants to surrender. He was wounded in the leg, and his leg has not been healing well. He needs to go to a hospital. We want you to help us negotiate the surrender with the government."

"You want me to call the cops, the Disip?" More muffled talk. Then: "Call them."

"How do I know—"

"Tell the Disip that the *guardia* is alive and wants to say hello to Alicia Flor. That's it." Then he hung up.

An angry cop was pacing my office less than an hour later. His name was Nelson Lugo Alvarado, and he stood as high up in the Disip demonology as anyone could get and still spend time on the street. Lugo Alvarado was a black man with a thin, brittle-looking nose and a face that was as narrow as a hatchet. He had light-colored eyes that reminded me of steel ball bearings. He was in his mid-forties, and built wiry and powerful.

"Alicia Flor is a civilian secretary the captain was fucking," he told me. "He's a married man, and if that *vaina*, that shit, gets out over the local wire, I'll cut your gringo *bolas* off."

"Hey," I said. But he grabbed me and pushed me up against the wall. Carlos the Jackal, who was clipping the wire, looked up and then quickly back down again.

"Hey, yourself," he said. "Why don't you tell me why they chose to call *you*."

"I don't know," I answered. My eyes would not meet his.

"You don't know." He let me go then. "Well, you better start thinking about it."

Lugo Alvarado stayed with me for several days, listening on the phone whenever the Croaker called me. He had the calls traced; each time they came from a different Caracas telephone booth. Negotiations went smoothly. Both sides seemed to want to end the standoff.

The local journalists were offended by the fact that Venezuelan guerrillas had the poor taste to use a gringo to help them negotiate with the police. But they were forced, for a change, to take their news from me. I was riding high, despite my uneasiness about Lugo Alvarado's dark presence in my office.

Soon a deal was struck whereby two priests and a Caracas TV crew would accompany the police to meet Rojas and the *guardia* at a designated spot. Rojas would surrender his weapon to one of the priests, and then the *guardia* would be free to go, and Rojas would allow the Disip to take him in. He was to be taken to a civilian prison, rather than the military prison, and the priests would be present to make sure he got medical treatment. He would also be permitted a visit from his mother, whom he had not seen in twelve years.

For many weeks afterward they played the scene over and over on the air. I have it memorized; I can close my eyes and see it all. From a distance I see two men standing in a field. It is one of the fields of the cattle ranch where Rojas had been hiding. The two men seem to be holding something together, holding a dark board or a stick or a farm tool that joins them, front to back. Then, as the bouncing camera moves in, I see it is a rifle that stretches between the men. Closer still, and I see that it is Rojas who holds the weapon, an M-16, and that the gun is touching the back of a uniformed captain of the *Guardia Nacional*. Rojas holds the rifle with one hand. His other hand grasps the homemade crutch that props him up on one side. The captain's face is pale and serious and a little frightened around the eyes. Rojas looks ill. He is pale as well, with black stubble standing out along his jaw, and he squints unblinkingly into the captain's back. A faint breeze lifts his dark hair. On his bad leg he wears splints that are tied on with white rags that could be pieces of bed sheet. His green pants and the pieces of bed sheet are stained in places, stained brown with what could be blood.

Then the camera shifts. Hand-held, it sweeps unevenly along, taking in empty field, and finally it focuses on the two priests, who are standing startlingly close to Rojas and his prisoner. They are dressed just the way you would expect priests to be dressed. One priest clasps empty hands in front of him. The other holds a rosary.

The camera moves again and shows me a group of twenty men walking across the field toward the priests and Rojas, and the hostage captain. Some of the men are in uniform. Some are not. All of them are armed. The only man I recognize is Nelson Lugo Alvarado. He wears a white shirt with no tie, and he carries a pump shotgun. Behind these men roll two ambulance vans, and behind the vans, a convoy of cars with their lights on; the black cars remind me of a funeral procession.

54

The camera lens lifts for a minute to show the military helicopter that circles overhead, then it dips back down to take in one of the priests, who has already begun moving toward Rojas. The priest looks frightened for his own safety. He moves with underwater slowness. But he does move.

There is commentary by an unseen television narrator throughout the surrender, but I do not listen. For me it is a drama that is always enacted in silence.

Rojas, who is lean and dirty and in pain, studies the priest for a moment. The priest is old and soft-looking. Effeminate almost. Then Rojas points the barrel of the gun at the sky; the priest winces as if expecting it to go off. But it does not go off, and Rojas gives it to him. The priest seems reluctant to take the gun, and Rojas almost has to push it into his plump hands. The priest turns, holding the weapon awkwardly, reminding me of the way my bird-watching grandfather once held a baseball bat. Then the police and the military men move past the priest quickly and surround both Rojas and the captain.

The captain is led to one ambulance, Rojas to the other. Rojas's leg seems very stiff as he moves, and they appear to be pushing him along faster than is comfortable. As he goes by the camera, he looks directly into the lens. I get the strange feeling that he is looking for me. Then they close him into the back of the van, and he is gone. The surrender is a success.

Two days later Rojas was dead. They said he tried to escape from the prison hospital, dragging his crippled leg behind him. They said he threatened a guard with a scalpel he had gotten from somewhere. Another guard had been forced to break all of his ribs with a nightstick and put two bullets into the back of his head.

The Socialists in Congress complained about the killing. Their complaints were aired on television for three or four days, and in the newspapers for a week. Then they faded away. The authorities went on searching for Mosca, but they did not find him.

After they killed Rojas, I was frightened. I was afraid Mosca and the Croaker and any friends they might have would consider me an accomplice in the death. I spent many days jumping at shadows and looking over my shoulder. I hugged Max the dog until he growled and snapped at my face. I even called Ballesteros

Productions again; I decided that if they promised me a job at a high enough rate, I'd quit the agency, lie low, and live on my meager savings until the Prowlers arrived, and then use my earnings as an interpreter to get home.

When I called, a female secretary answered the telephone, and it took some doing to convince her to put Ballesteros on the line. When the promoter finally picked up, he was very abrupt.

"Who are you?" he said.

"Jimmy..."

"*Coño*. Another fucking gringo. *Oye*, all the jobs are taken."

"Oh?" But I felt curiosity along with my disappointment. "They're coming, then? The Prowlers?"

"Ten weeks. But you're too late. *Ciao*, gringo."

"Wait!" I shouted in a desperate voice. "What if somebody quits?"

"*¿Estás loco?* Nobody gives up a job like that. Good-bye." And he hung up.

I was almost ready to quit my job and go into hiding even without the prospect of another job, when the Croaker called me again.

"You can tell them they didn't get all of us," he said. "You can tell them we plan to bring the war to Caracas. We'll be in touch, Mr. Angel." Then he hung up.

The Croaker's call reassured me that I was not marked for immediate death. But the day before I got that call, when I was still jumping at every sound, Orchid the tramp nearly scared me into my grave by appearing unexpectedly beside me. She had apparently been waiting in ambush outside the front door of the *La Nación* building, and when I went through that door at the end of the day, she spoke to me.

"*¡Americano!*" she said. I yelled then, leaping an inch or two into the air, and I threw my hands in front of my face. She stared at me and began laughing. Her laughter was amused rather than mean; it might have sounded quite pleasant under other circumstances, but I only lowered my shaking hands to glare at her for a moment before wheeling away and heading up the street.

She followed me, struggling to stay in step beside me. Her gait as she hunched along beneath her denim carapace was ridiculous; I looked around to make sure no one I knew saw me with her, and then I began moving faster, to escape. But she moved right along with me, quick on those dark, dirty legs, and she began to talk. She began to spew a stream of childish free associations in her soft, singsong voice; it was like an unending nursery rhyme with ever-changing and unpredictable lyrics.

I lived near a river it was a big river and there were mango trees every-where, so many we would eat them all the time and become sick and we got scolded. It was the Orinoco River and I lived in Ciudad Bolívar, named for the Liberator of our continent. All the little girls adored Don Simón, and in his pictures he looks so handsome. They say he was short, do you believe he was short, Americano. His boots in the museum are so tiny. I went to church in a mango-colored dress and I sang all the time, the padre said I had a voice like an angel, like a perfect angelito *and I was proud because my mother was and I had shoes, you should have seen them, they were black and had little straps, and they were shiny, very shiny. . .*

I had gotten to the corner where I usually jumped on a *por puesto* or hailed a cab, and I still hadn't shaken her. So I turned on her, embarrassed nearly to the point of tears now, and I shouted, "*Mira, coño,* what the hell do you want?"

Orchid stopped babbling; she stared up at me with wide eyes that reflected the streetlamps, and I noticed suddenly that people on the street all around me were staring now too. I felt blood go to my face.

But the woman was not at all bothered by the curious eyes that were focused on us; she kept looking at me as if I were the only other being in the universe. She appeared to be thinking, concentrating on something, trying to call forth a memory, and in a minute she said, "A man brought me to Caracas from Ciudad Bolívar. A man who was going to marry me. We lived for a month in a *pensión,* and he showed me how to drink *caña* and smoke *basuco.* Then he ran away and took all our money and everything else." She brought out a hand from beneath her garment and coughed into it delicately. Her voice was quiet now, a whisper rather than a song. "That is why I am here with you like this. You ask me what I want? I want no more than what anyone else has. I don't want very much at all."

She coughed again and looked up at me with expectation. The watchers on the street had gone back to their own business by then, and feeling only a little self-conscious, I grabbed Orchid's

arm and pulled her to the other side of the street and towed her in
the direction of the alien and naturalization office, the *Extranjería*,
which was the place that kept tabs on all the dangerous *extranjeros*
like me. I dragged her into a little dress shop near the Plaza
Miranda, and I shoved her doubled-over body in the direction of a
clerk, who backed rapidly away from us, eyes registering alarm.
The clerk had been waiting on a fat mother who was having her
willowy daughter fitted for a wedding dress. The mother looked
Orchid up and down, her mouth hanging so slack that her upper
plate nearly fell out onto her tongue, and then she grabbed the
daughter's hand and wordlessly headed for the door.

I coughed, feeling my face brighten, and I said, "This poor
woman lost all her luggage at the airport and she doesn't have a
thing to wear. Please fit her with a dress and a pair of shoes and
some stockings."

Then I opened my wallet, peeled out a handful of brown one-
hundred bolivar notes, and threw them onto a glass display case
that contained wigs of every color set atop featureless mannequin
heads.

I was almost out the door when the clerk called to me in a small
voice. *"Señor . . ."*

I turned, and she was clutching my money in her fingers. Orchid was giggling soundlessly behind a sooty hand, and the clerk's
eyes kept sliding rapidly between me and the near-naked woman I
had brought to her. "For this amount," the woman said, "you
could probably afford some other things that a . . . a lady would
need."

"Like . . ." I began.

"Interiores," she whispered, and looked away, her eyelashes
quivering.

I felt myself blush even more deeply. "Yes," I said, my voice
growing thick. "Of course. Whatever she needs."

I turned and bolted out the door.

After the Croaker's call, a familiar loneliness replaced the fear I
had been feeling and I decided to renew my attempts to make
friends with Mickey's children. I had not seen them since the appearance of Max the dog.

I launched a short but hard-fought campaign that began with

another period of cautious observation; for several days during my after-work hours, as the boys paced their special section of the Plaza Altamira, I sat on the low wall surrounding the stagnant concrete fountain and watched them. Of course they pretended to ignore me, but I continued studying them, always mindful of my own days of unspeakable solitude, and I became determined to work on them until I got them to talk to me.

Finally one Saturday I bought a couple of sophisticated Styrofoam gliders from a toy store near the center of the city. The gliders had adjustable ailerons, elevators, and rudders, with little lead clips on the noses to give them weight. Then I caught a *por puesto* to Plaza Altamira, where, from a distance, I spotted the brothers doing their ruminative dance across the concrete paving stones. Holding myself low, I wove my way through the thin throng of strollers until I reached the backside of a hot-dog wagon that stood close enough to allow me to eavesdrop on them while remaining hidden.

Floyd and Nestor were discussing a man with a gun; the man was somewhere out there on the shimmering horizon, and he was holding Bobby Oakes prisoner. The two boys were trying to decide how to rescue their friend. All around me, as I listened to them, I heard the murmur of Spanish conversation and the scrape of shoe leather on cement.

With trembling fingers I adjusted the control surfaces of one of the airplanes according to the directions on the package, and when I sensed the moment was right, I took aim and let it fly. It shot toward them at knee level, and then, as I had hoped it would do, it pulled sharply upward, the tip of one wing almost clipping Nestor on the nose. Dancing on its tail, the plane soared high into the air before looping and stalling, then settling quietly to the ground between the boys' nearly identical sets of dirty sneakers.

The boys stared at the little airplane; they seemed as surprised as if they had actually seen a toy drop from the empty desert sky. After a moment they turned suspicious eyes toward my customary spot on the edge of the fountain, but I remained hidden behind the hot-dog wagon. Nestor looked up at Floyd in a wordless appeal for an explanation, the crescent-shaped birthmark quivering on the side of his jaw, and Floyd began to turn his agitated head from side to side until I stepped into view and ended the mystery.

There was a fresh, startled openness in their wide eyes as they stood blinking at me, but something warned me to proceed slowly just the same.

"Sorry," I told them. "It got away from me." Floyd looked away; two emotions struggled on his face, and he avoided his brother's gaze. I walked over and recovered my airplane. After pretending to examine it for damages in a way that displayed it in all its sleekness and beauty, I turned and left the plaza without another word.

That Sunday they played with the airplanes while I watched from a respectful distance. And the following day after work, I bought a magic book that had been printed in Mexico and began pulling coins from their ears and passing a rope through my own neck. I got them laughing so hard that they had to run together to the bathroom, and when they returned, they asked if I would let them fly the gliders again.

In a week or so, the Styrofoam airplanes became battered and torn. But by then Floyd and Nestor and I had graduated to an ant farm that a departing German diplomat had given me. One afternoon after Mickey and Beatrix had left home on separate errands, as they so often did, we filled the narrow glass case with dirt from the small courtyard of their apartment building. Then the three of us crept around on hands and knees, scooping red ants into kitchen spoons and shaking them into their new prison. After enough captives had been taken, the boys carried the ant farm to their apartment to watch the construction of the first tunnels.

Late one night while I was trying to sleep, I heard the horns and engines of motorcycles as well as drunken shouts. I was used to disturbances by then, and I did not investigate.

When I got up the next morning, the whole neighborhood was gathered in front of the white gate. The neighbors were muttering among themselves as they stared up at a huge photograph of a shaggy head that had been pasted across the twin steel doors. It was an early promotional poster for the Prowlers, and around the blond singer's head orbited three tiny figures playing guitars and drums. The singer, the rock star himself, was scowling.

"Who put that there, Mama?" said a child in a frightened voice. No one answered him.

Beneath the rock star's face were the English words, RONNIE

60

NEUMON AND THE PROWLERS. And below that, in Spanish: *Coming soon. The last big party in Venezuela.*

I was fairly certain the Spanish line was an allusion to the looming economic problems. I don't know if my neighbors saw it the same way. But when the child asked again who had put the poster there, someone shushed him.

And then, suddenly, the eyes began to turn in my direction. Quickly I stepped back into my house and closed the door.

On my way to work that morning, I noticed quite a few Prowlers posters on buildings all over the city. And by the time I left work to return home, there seemed to be nowhere in Caracas where you could escape the apocalyptic stare of the rock star.

I had just finished feeding Max that evening when Adolfo climbed my stairs and began pounding on my door. I opened it; he was drunk, and he made an unsuccessful swipe at my face with his sharp thumbnail.

"*Extranjero,*" he said, breathing cane liquor all over me. "*Coño de tu madre.* That poster scared my boys this morning. I blame you for it."

"*Me?*" I said, pointing a finger at my heart. "*Estás loco de bolas.* How do you figure that?"

"It's foreign, isn't it?" he snarled. "Just like you. A foreign, gringo thing."

"That's it," I said. My voice was shaking with anger. "Get off my stairs, before I . . ."

"Before you *what*, you faggot?"

I had been about to say "before I call the cops," but I felt a strange heat rushing through me, and a moment later I found myself down on the street, preparing to fight Adolfo.

Adolfo said he was going to kill me. I told him I didn't care if he killed me or not, just as long as I maimed him as badly as I could before I died. We readied ourselves for the battle.

All the neighbors came out. They formed a shouting circle around us just the way schoolchildren ring a pair of combatants. Adolfo slashed with his thumbnail and missed; my old friend Tony came into my head and told me to circle away from his power, and I began stepping to his right, away from that thumbnail.

Suddenly a deep rumble filled the air. The neighbors cried out in alarm and backed away from the gate in the white wall, leaving

Adolfo and me standing by ourselves. Adolfo dropped his hands and looked up. His apprehension was contagious, and I let my own hands settle to my sides.

Then the picture of Ronnie Neumon, the rock star, split right down the middle and the two halves of the gate began to slide slowly apart. But the rumbling and movement stopped before the gate was fully open; there was a second of mysterious silence, then a man walked out through the narrow breach. He was a very thin man with long hair and sparse black stubble on his face. Next to his eyebrow he carried a heart-shaped scar. He looked at Adolfo and me and seemed not to notice the crowd standing behind us.

"*Pana*," he said, addressing Adolfo. "Buddy. We heard you could buy beer out here someplace."

Then he looked at me, studied me with his slanted dark eyes. His eyes widened after a moment, and he said, "*Coño*. I know you. You're the gringo from that party in Los Chorros."

I recognized him then, and I took a couple of steps backward, away from him. I was afraid both he and Adolfo would start beating up on me at once. "The Chileno," I said. "The guitar player."

"Packy, they call me. *Coño*, but I was drunk that night. Drunk on my ass. Sorry about the trouble, *pana*." Adolfo was looking from one to the other of us, his eyes bulging.

"That's all right. You and that big guy..."

"*Oye*. Let me buy twelve beers, if I can, and then you come back to the house with me. El Camión will get a kick out of seeing you again."

Packy found Lola and gave her some money, and she dropped twelve cans of Polar and some ice into a couple of plastic bags for him. Then he put his thin hand on the small of my back and guided me through the gate. I turned around as the gate was closing to look back at Adolfo and the rest of the neighbors. They watched me silently, with a mixture of expressions both sullen and astounded. Then the gate banged closed.

The estate beyond the white wall belonged to El Camión's parents. When Packy took me onto the estate, El Camión came out of a cottage on the grounds and hugged me like a lost friend.

"*Pana*," he said, "how good to see you."

As he showed me around, he told me about his parents.

El Camión's father was a Spaniard, and his mother was Venezuelan; both of them had come from wealthy families. They had bought the house and the guest cottage and the ten acres of land when El Camión was a tiny child; they had bought it from a good friend of the last dictator. The friend, who also happened to be a friend of Camión's father, had packed his family and his things and had followed the dictator to Spain about a year after the Venezuelan people rose up and chased the dictator out of the country.

Very recently Camión's parents had themselves gone to Spain to live. The silver limousine my neighbors and I had seen that time had been carrying them to the airport. Unlike the dictator's friend, they did not go to Spain for political reasons. They went because El Camión's mother was upset about how overcrowded and dirty and dangerous Caracas had become, and because Camión's father was homesick. El Camión had stayed behind. And now he reigned by himself over a ten-acre kingdom of rotting fruit and lawns that were rapidly reverting to tropical forest.

Camión told me that the large, two-story house where he had lived with his parents was empty now except for a few sticks of furniture and some worthless items left behind by his mother. He also told me that he did not much care for the house. He lived by himself in the guest cottage, which was a stone's throw from the main building. He had moved into the cottage several years before, when he was seventeen, and since then had rarely set foot in the larger dwelling.

Whenever a breeze blew, I could hear the music of wind chimes coming from that main house. Camión said that before she left, his mother had strung wind chimes of glass, metal, bone, and clay all around the outside of the second floor.

The cottage where Camión lived was surrounded by flower gardens; except for one small patch, they all were overgrown. The single clear area was a little mound on which two rosebushes grew. El Camión was conscientious to the point of obsession about keeping those rosebushes clipped, and he kept them scrupulously free from the entangling weeds that flourished everywhere else.

There was a second mechanical gate in the section of white steel wall that ran directly behind the main house and the cottage. This was the main gate; it was because of this other gate that the gate at the end of my cul-de-sac was opened so seldom.

63

Camión did not own a car; he claimed not to own a motorized vehicle of any sort, although the earthen driveway running between the vacant house and the main gate was deeply rutted with the tracks of motorcycles. I never really thought about the strangeness of this until much later.

The cottage was a comfortable place with a living room, a kitchen, and three small bedrooms. One of the bedrooms was full of wires and musical instruments and sound equipment. Another was done up as a gymnasium, with barbells and dumbbells and weight-lifting benches. The third was where El Camión slept.

We sat around the living room, talking and drinking the beer Packy had bought. Packy and I did most of the talking; El Camión, after giving me the grand tour, had fallen silent. He stared at the floor as if preoccupied with something. After a time he produced a marijuana cigarette from somewhere and lit it up. He drew deeply on the joint, then handed it to me. I took a polite hit, passed it along to Packy, and tried to bring El Camión into the conversation. I was feeling so elated now that I had found some good, accepting company that I was not as tactful as I should have been.

"So, why is it that you don't like to go into the main house?"

"¿Cómo?"

I repeated the question. But El Camión only stared down at the floor and pretended not to understand my Spanish. Packy made a motion, and I looked up at him.

"Camión has some things he doesn't like to talk about."

I nodded. "Well, I guess we all do," I said. "Don't we?" El Camión lifted his huge head and smiled at me then.

"I like you," he said. "You're all right. And not just for a gringo."

Later, as I was leaving, he pressed my face to his huge chest once again. "Anything I can do for you, you let me know," he told me.

But it was Packy I grew close to, rather than El Camión. Camión was too moody; he would be friendly and talkative one minute, and silent and glowering the next. Packy had been evicted from his apartment a week before I first stepped onto the grounds of the estate; El Camión was letting him sleep on the couch in the cottage. But the large Venezuelan refused to rent Packy a room, claiming he needed his privacy. Both Camión and Packy seemed relieved when I agreed to rent Packy my spare bedroom.

After Packy moved in, I discovered that he and I shared an unusual habit; he also enjoyed sitting on the balcony, watching the wasted mangoes and avocados falling from the trees on the property of El Camión's parents. And then I learned that Camión did this as well. The big man would ease his large form into a beach chair in the middle of one of his gardens, and he would smoke a joint and stare out into the orchards. Both of them could do this for hours, and I had trouble deciding whether they were brooding over the fallen fruit or meditating on it, but I was fairly certain that, between the two of them, this manner of brooding or form of meditation had started with El Camión. Why he wouldn't eat the fruit, or give it away, I couldn't fathom. At the time I didn't have the nerve to ask.

Aside from the money, which I welcomed, perhaps my greatest reason for renting to Packy was that I hated being by myself in the evenings. Packy was not as constant a housemate as I had expected, however. Although he quickly filled my spare room with his clothes and his musical equipment and his other possessions, he usually slept there only one night out of every three. The rest of the time I could not be certain where he was, but I assumed he was camped out on Camión's couch, and I eventually got the idea that he had wanted my apartment solely as a refuge during those times when the moody Camión could not bear human company.

Yet Packy sometimes seemed to prefer my company over that of Camión, and even when he was not planning to spend the night in his room, he was in the habit of turning up at unexpected times to talk to me. He told me stories about his life in a tone that was both urgent and strangely confessional, and he seemed to expect me to listen to them without interrupting and not to make any judgments once he was finished talking.

I would often come home from work to find Packy sitting on my stairs as if waiting for permission to enter his own home. He would follow me inside and sit down on the couch, and with few preliminaries he would light a cigarette and begin talking. Afterward he would smoke another cigarette, drink a beer or a glass of rum, and then he would rise and walk out into the night and disappear for another entire day or two.

Most of his stories were set in Chile, and the first one he told me had to do with his grandmother and her blue dog.

65

"My grandmother was a strange one," Packy told me. "A good woman, but a little touched by solitude, I think. She was always seeing my uncle's ghost. He would appear to her as a naked infant with a long white beard. And she had this bush, you know, a coca shrub, that grew by her back door. If she woke up with a headache, she'd pick a leaf, paste it onto her forehead, and walk around like that all day. My father *hated* that."

Telling this story, Packy laughed, his eyes narrowing to dark slits. "He always wanted her to pull it up and get rid of it, telling her she'd go to jail if the police found out. But she'd only hold her tiny fist in the air"—Packy, at this point, held up his own fist, which was not large—"and she'd say, 'For everything there are uses and there are abuses, and the government will not decide which is which for me.'"

Packy had lived in Santiago with his father, who was a serious but timid professor of Old and Middle English at the University of Chile, and with his mother. But he spent his summers in the country with his grandmother. The old woman lived near a small village in the high, cool beech forests in the shining lake country of southern Chile. Surrounding villages had been settled by light-skinned people who were the descendants of immigrants that had come from Germany and Switzerland. But nearly everyone in the village of Packy's *abuela* was dark and bore the stamp of the Indians who had once reigned unchallenged in the cloud-washed purity of the hills. Packy's *abuela* would often aim a crooked finger at the patient, snow-peaked volcanos that looked down upon the village, and she would swear to him that the exiled and brooding Mapuche gods lived up there still.

The low spire of the village church pricked a mountain sky so blue Packy could see it even with eyes squeezed tightly shut. The church was surrounded by neat white cottages with wood-shingled roofs, and in the square in front of it, at the very heart of the village, a tall fountain sent water sparkling down into the clean air. In the center of the fountain stood a winged creature made of stone. This creature had a flared beak that pointed at the sky, and as a small child, Packy had been afraid of it.

Packy told me, "I later learned it was an angel, blowing a horn."

Packy's grandmother lived in a house that was set off by itself, a little distance from the village. The *abuela* had lost her husband,

Packy's grandfather, years before Packy was born; she sometimes reminded him of a dry and twisted vine that had fallen away from a supporting tree, but still managed to hold itself upright. She owned two fine apple trees, a few black and white pigs, some chickens, a milking goat, and a mean, yellow-eyed bitch who was always hiding someplace, never to be seen, unless Packy was on his way out of the yard. This dog had a bluish cast to her smooth hide under certain conditions of light, a quality that put Packy in awe of her. Never in Santiago had he seen a blue dog.

If Packy were headed out of the yard, his grandmother would stand in the back doorway, her thin red hands wringing an apron as she whistled for the dog.

"She could whistle just like a man," Packy said. "It was strange, because she was so frail."

At his grandmother's mannish whistle, the blue bitch would appear from nowhere; would appear as if from the searing blue sky itself. Silently the dog would pad along behind Packy, following him wherever he went, always vigilant. If village boys tried to bully him, the bitch, with her yellow eyes that seemed to glow even in the daylight, would growl and charge forward and drive them away. If hungry pigs began to follow him, the dog scattered them.

And once, in a field, a bull with wide horns and huge, swinging balls went after the boy. The bull was black and shiny as volcanic glass, and the drumming of its hooves vibrated through the soles of his feet as he ran. Packy had been dimly aware of the angry barking of the dog before he tripped and the ground rose up to knock the light from his eyes.

When he came to, he was bleeding from a cut alongside his eyebrow. The cut was wide, and it later formed the white, heart-shaped scar that he forever after carried. The bull was gone, and the bitch was sitting nearby, tongue lolling and blood oozing from a wound in her side.

"I was so grateful, I was ready to cry," Packy said. And as he thought about it years later, he looked as if he were about to cry yet again.

"But when I put out my hand to pet her, all that blue hair stood up on her shoulders. She growled and acted ready to bite my arm off."

Packy had stood and headed for his grandmother's house with that surly, powerful dog limping along at his side.

My experience with Max, my dog, was nowhere near as inspiring as Packy's. Max had always been an aloof dog. When I petted him, he never shivered with delight the way other dogs did; never raked at me with raised paw to entreat me to continue. In fact I had to reach for him if I wanted to scratch his head or flip him over and rub his belly. He seemed willing to do without any of that. And any time I tried to roughhouse with him, slapping at him or rolling his new ball across the floor, he would squeeze in behind the couch and stay there, brooding, until I left the room. He possessed few qualities to recommend him as a friend or a companion.

Still, for some reason, as I traveled home on the crowded *por puesto* night after night, I found myself looking forward to the sight of him lying in the middle of my living room, head resting on forepaws. There was something in the slow, upward roll of his brown eyes that I took for gratitude or sympathy, and it delighted me to see him eating food that I had bought with my money and scraped into a bowl with my own hands. It made me feel important in a way that sending bad or boring news to New York could not.

As I had predicted, his looks did improve as he ate good food and rested from the rigors of the street. The oil stains on his fur, which had soaked through and dyed his skin a darker hue in some places, faded entirely, and the fur itself took on a density and a shine that bespoke nutrition and indoor sleeping. He began to carry his ears at an upright, rakish angle, and when he rolled his eyes now, there was an alertness at the back of them, like the hot points of needles, that had not been there before. He would still crawl behind the couch if I tried to get too friendly with him, but he was now eager to go outside whenever I would let him, and he developed a jaunty walk that drew smiles from people in the street and made me think he was showing off.

Even Lola paid him a compliment one day. She came out of her establishment, leaving a customer waiting, for no other reason than to scratch Max on the head with the gaudy nails of her ring-laden fingers and say, "*¡Qué bonito! ¡Qué simpático!*" Then Max licked her hand, something he had never done to me. But when Lola smiled at me, the *extranjero,* and walked away without leaving a withering comment to pucker the air behind her, I was too pleased and proud to be jealous.

Then, shortly after Packy moved in, the dog ran away.

I had just fed him, doling out the special horsemeat-and-liver mixture that had been recommended by his Argentine veterinarian, and was preparing to snap on his leash to take him for a walk, when he bolted through the half-open door. I went after him; I reached the door and found him standing unmoving at the foot of my stairs, staring up at me with wide eyes. When I started down the stairs, he snarled, drawing back his lips to expose teeth made clean and white by daily offerings of imported dog biscuits. He snarled a second time, leaving a clear warning trembling in the air, and then he was gone.

I got drunk that night. I took a taxi to an area of fine restaurants called La Candelaria and treated myself to a dinner of shrimp in garlic sauce and a bottle of Spanish wine. By the time the wine was finished, I had made up my mind that Max had been right to run away. He was, in fact, a wild animal, had grown up fending for himself, and had done me an honor by allowing me to nurse him back to health so that he could jump back into the brawling adventure of life on the street. It was wrong to try to make a house pet of such a Wild Thing. I drank a silent toast to all the Wild Things of the world and felt a glow of peace spread through me.

Later I found myself at the bar, arguing politics with a couple of middle-aged Spaniards of fascist persuasion. The Spaniards were lamenting the death of Franco and advocating the return of the Venezuelan dictatorship. Under the dictator, who had fled in 1958, there had been law and order, by God. Law and order and good manners. It still wasn't too late to bring the General back from Spanish exile and impose some sanity on the country.

Despite the rhetoric, I grew uncomfortable enough to leave only after the older of the gentlemen squeezed my knee with a thin, aristocratic hand and suggested that we all take his Mercedes to Avenida Libertador and track down a pair of willing transvestites.

The next morning I awoke with a wine hangover that was like a cleaver buried in the back of my skull. It was early, too early even for Adolfo to be revving his car below my window, but shouting

69

and laughter from my neighbor and his two children down in the street dragged me from my troubled sleep. I went first to the bathroom to press a hot washcloth against my eyes, then I stalked out onto the balcony; I was miserable enough to risk the long-term consequences of cursing out Adolfo and his brats. But the shock of what I saw scattered my anger like ashes.

Max, my dog, was dancing clownishly on his two hind feet, trying to snatch a stick from Adolfo's manicured fingers. The two boys, both of them miniature Adolfos down to the pot belly and the obscene smirk, were laughing so hard they looked as if they would be rolling in the gutter if they did not have the high white wall to lean against. Adolfo was laughing, too, his huge stomach riding up and down beneath his white T-shirt.

Adolfo made some signal with his hand, and the dog dropped to the ground as if shot, rolled onto his back, thin legs kicking at the air, then righted himself and looked up at my neighbor with shining eyes full of adoration.

"Good dog," Adolfo said, and he bent, groaning, to give Max a pat on the head.

"What a dog, Papa," said one of the boys. "Can we keep him?"

"*Qué simpático,*" the other fat child agreed.

"Hey!" I called. When they turned their faces up to me, squinting into the rising sun, I did not know what else to say.

Adolfo seemed undisturbed that I had been watching them without having announced myself. "Oh, hello, *extranjero,*" he said.

"My dog," I said.

"We found him roaming in the street this morning," Adolfo said. "He was very happy to see us. We are thinking of keeping him."

When I opened my mouth to protest, he cut me off.

"After all," Adolfo reminded me as a triumphant smirk pulled at his lips, "he is a Venezuelan dog."

I thought that stealing the affections of my dog might satisfy Adolfo's need to cause me pain and that perhaps he would let up on me after the theft had been carried out. But I was wrong.

One Saturday evening the neighbors threw a huge party in the street. They brought several boom boxes and a pair of live drummers, who pounded on hollowed logs. People came from other neighborhoods to participate.

Later in the night they began throwing beer bottles at the side of my house. I was in bed, and I heard the breaking of glass. I also heard Adolfo, who was drunk, standing beneath my bedroom window and shouting, *"Gringo, coño de tu madre."* He shouted it over and over. And then a beer bottle crashed through one of the living room windows.

Packy had not been around; he and El Camión were off playing in one of their bands. When he came by the next day, he looked at the broken window and said nothing. But his hand lifted dreamily until his fingers were touching the heart-shaped scar on the side of his head.

Very early on the following moonlit morning, the gate in the white wall opened partway, and El Camión passed through it carrying a huge speaker. He set the speaker at the bottom of my stairs, and then went back for another. Packy, meanwhile, ran a couple of electric cables from the house, and he used them to set up some other equipment, including his guitar and a microphone and a bass guitar I had not seen before.

Then Packy and El Camión began to play.

They sounded even worse than they had at the party in Los Chorros; the amplifiers were turned up so loud that Camión's voice, Packy's guitar, and Camión's bass guitar blended into an ongoing explosion of noise that shook all the windows in the neighborhood. As he played, Packy kept stepping close to one of the amplifiers so that it screeched with feedback. They played "Satisfaction" and "Requiem for the Devil," and "Honkytonk Woman," and a handful of Jim Morrison songs.

One by one, lights went on in the houses around us; heads appeared in the lighted windows, and then one by one, the lights went off again. Before I finally surrendered to my reflexes and slid my hands over my ears, I heard Max howling in pain somewhere, and I smiled.

Little Séptimo crawled from beneath his piece of corrugated metal to dance in the street. He was laughing and his eyes were shining with delight as he twirled and jumped around and did somersaults on the pavement. When the music was finally over, he surprised me by coming up and hugging me before he disappeared once more into his lean-to.

• • •

Of course Packy had another name aside from the one he was known by; this was a story in itself.

His real name was Beowulf; Beowulf Seco Dávila. The first name had been the idea of his father, the English professor. But although staid Professor Seco enjoyed the heroic ring of "Beowulf," he had used it to tag his tiny son for a much less frivolous reason than mere aesthetics.

"When you were born, there was another family of Secos living in Santiago," Professor Seco explained one day after Packy had come home crying from school. "Thoroughly disreputable people; always drinking and fighting, making enemies and drawing the attention of the police. In order to distinguish you from them, I needed to give you a name that the other Secos in a million drunken years would never place on one of their own children.

"Your name," Professor Seco assured him, "will keep you out of harm's way."

But it hadn't. And not long after he arrived in Venezuela, Beowulf began to answer to the nickname of Packy, which was short for *paquete*, the Spanish word for "package" or "bundle."

Packy had come to Venezuela at a time when thousands of Chilean refugees were arriving in search of a haven; many of these Chileans were broke and desperate and would do anything for money. A favorite scam involved planting an impressive-looking, but padded and nearly worthless, package of currency on the sidewalk in front of a bank. The trick was to hook a passerby on his own greed, fooling him into handing over his wallet in exchange for the privilege of holding onto the phony bundle until a meeting to count the money and divvy it up could be arranged. After a time the notorious flimflam became known as the *paquete Chileno*.

Packy had never resorted to dishonesty to make a living, but he did not object when Venezuelan friends began to call him *Paquete*. Beowulf had never fit him, and it was easy for him to see himself as a small neat packet; mysterious, tightly wrapped, containing the possibility of danger.

CHAPTER 3

One day a message came whining over the electronic teletype from New York. It read:

MSG CARACAS:
ATTN CALDERON

U.S. ROCK BAND "PROWLERS" KICKING OFF S.A. TOUR YR TOWN END OF NXT MONTH. GROUP RCNTLY FRONTED TIME, NEWSWEEK. PLS CONFRM U WILL GIVE SPOT CVRGE AND GD FEATURE. PLS ACK MSG.

CHEERS
NEW YORK

The message first surprised and then annoyed me. I had been extremely busy lately; as Mickey predicted, the finance ministry and the Central Bank were beginning to snipe at one another. The Central Bank president was saying devalue, and the finance minister was saying never. Also, I was waiting for the next development in the guerrilla situation, and the strain of the wait was exhausting.

Then, of course, there was the fact that my interest in the Prowlers had never gone much beyond their potential to provide me with emergency employment. Before learning that all the interpreting jobs had been taken, I had actually done enough research on them to convince myself that they were not my kind of entertainers. They were not the Beatles. They were not the Doors. They were not the Rolling Stones. Despite their large following in the States, they were not serious music makers. Artistically *I'm a night crawler, baby, gonna crawl on yooou, oh yeah* was about as deep as they got.

Ballesteros, the promoter, had been accurate when he described Ronnie Neumon as a six-foot-five golden boy who often wore pants that had no seat so he could jiggle his golden ass at the audience. He did not do this to break new ground in society or to make a point; he did it because he could get away with it, and because it made the girls scream and wet themselves. The other members of the band were just riders on Ronnie's train.

I did not immediately acknowledge the msg. Instead I tore it from the teletype and stuck it in my pocket, hoping to pull off a pocket veto. Sometimes if I ignored an assignment long enough, New York forgot all about it.

By the time that message arrived, the original posters of Ronnie Neumon and the Prowlers had begun to wear off walls all over the city. The poster on the wall across from my house was in tatters from the rain. But as I rode home that night, I looked out the side window of my crowded *por puesto* and began to notice new posters going up. The new posters showed only Ronnie; they did not depict the other band members. Ronnie's face was larger in the new poster, his scowl more threatening. The legend beneath the picture said simply, THE PROWLERS. COMING SOON.

After supper one evening that same week, Mickey called me at my house and asked me to come to his apartment. His voice sounded almost cheerful, and I thought that perhaps he had some good news to tell me about the personal problems that had been keeping him from the office. I dressed and went to see him immediately, but with no feeling of alarm.

I knocked, and Mickey came to the door and spoke in a whiskey-scented whisper, despite the fact that Beatrix was away from the house and the boys were playing in the plaza.

"I need to talk to you." His collar was open and his tie hung, loose and lopsided, down either side of his wrinkled white shirt. Lines of tiredness angled down from the corners of his eyes.

"What is it?" I said, finally feeling a twinge of apprehension. He jerked his head toward the stairs, then led me up them to the open door of his office.

"In there." He walked over and collapsed into the leather chair in front of his desk. I took a seat on the one uncluttered corner of the yellow desk and looked down at him. Mickey kept his own gaze on his hands, which were twining and twitching in his lap. To give him time, I looked around the room at the pictures of Nestor and Floyd decorating all the walls. But after several minutes I ran out of patience.

"So what is it, Mickey?" He cleared his throat and tried to smile.

"Just got back from the club. A couple of the girls were asking about you."

"Is that right?" I was immediately suspicious.

"Sure. Of course. Big mistake, you know, your not doing any of the women at the club." Anger flashed through me.

"We've talked about this," I said. "Haven't we already discussed this same thing several hundred times?"

Mickey sighed. He opened the bottom drawer of the desk a crack and stuck his hand in. He began to play with something inside that I couldn't see. "We did," he admitted. "We did. And I remember that you expressed certain sentimental reservations about paying for love.

"But as your boss and more experienced friend, I feel obligated to advise you that the only way for a man such as yourself to get any at all is simply to make up his mind to start getting some *now.* See, when a guy hasn't had it in a while, he begins to produce a certain odor." Mickey looked up at me to see if I was following him. "And women *hate* that odor, Jimmy boy, because it smells to them like failure, and as soon as they get a whiff of it, they turn around and run in the other direction." I felt like breaking something over his head.

"Hey, cut the shit, will you, Mick?" I managed to say.

Mickey shrugged as if it didn't make much difference to him. He rolled his eyes back down and continued playing with the unseen thing in the drawer.

"What is that in there?" I asked him. "Did you call me over here to talk to me about screwing whores? What's going on with you, anyway?"

"No, Jimmy. I didn't." He pulled open the drawer and carefully

75

drew out a square pane of glass on which rested a crumbling, powdery white lump the size of a pea. His hand returned to the drawer and came back out with a razor blade pinched carefully between his thumb and forefinger and a piece of plastic straw riding between his middle two fingers. He dropped the straw onto the desk and held the razor blade above the white chunk as if preparing to slice it. Then he looked up at me.

"You know what this is?"

"Jesus, you are pissing me off right now. What are you doing with that, anyway?"

"*Perico*, they call it here. Makes you chatter like a parrot, so they say. A recent discovery of mine." He crushed the white pebble with the flat edge of the razor blade and then began chopping at it, his big fingers moving daintily.

"Useful," added Mickey, "under even the most desperate of circumstances for recapturing the idiot glee of childhood for up to twenty minutes at a time." He continued mincing the cocaine and said, "I certainly do need a little idiot glee right now. How about you?"

I shook my head, a movement that he did not see because he was looking down. "No," I said. "I'm doing all right. Listen, you know that if New York gets any kind of hint of this . . ."

Mickey laughed, still working. "*New York,*" he echoed, as if it were the punchline of a joke.

Then, suddenly, he dropped the blade and fixed me for a second with lonely, almost vacant eyes. He looked away, at the pictures on the wall, fingers tapping tentatively at his lips as if assessing an injury there, and he spoke with a brittle voice.

"She cheats. Why do you think she's never in the goddamn house?"

"Beatrix?" I whispered. I was embarrassed, a little frightened, too, and I looked down.

"I don't know what the fuck to do about it," Mickey said in a fierce whisper.

A thick silence stood between us for a minute. I had no clue about what to say. Mickey stared off into space as if I wasn't there.

Finally he said, "Different men. She goes out on the town with them. Flaunts it. I'm wearing horns, for Chrissake."

"I'm really sorry, Mickey . . ."

"You want to know what I'm doing when I'm not in the office? Sure, you have a right to know. Well, I'm following my wife around, watching where she goes and how long she stays there. I'm keeping her scorecard."

I cleared my throat a couple of times, desperate to tell him something. "Well you have . . . Lulu."

Mickey gave me a sharp, startled look. "I don't *want* Lulu. Lulu is just to keep things even. I want Beatrix."

"Jesus, Mickey."

"But I fuck and I fuck, and I still can't get even. You know why?"

"No. I don't," I said. I couldn't look at him.

"Because I care. She doesn't. That makes all the difference."

Mickey looked wildly around the room as if searching for something, then he picked up the plastic straw, thrust it into one of his wide nostrils, and sniffed up some of the cocaine on the glass. He filled his other nostril, and then he looked at me for a second, eyes wide, white powder clinging to his trembling nose hairs, before he bent over the glass again.

Later Mickey left the apartment. Beatrix was still not home. I took a walk to the plaza to bring Nestor and Floyd back to the apartment and put them to bed. Then, because I didn't think it was a good idea to leave the two sleeping boys in the apartment by themselves, I drank a whiskey over ice and climbed into my one-time bed in the spare bedroom.

I wasn't quite asleep when Floyd and Nestor opened the door to my room and walked up to the foot of my bed. Floyd wore nothing on his feet, and he moved almost silently. Nestor had little slippers attached to his pajamas, and the slippers made him walk with a scraping sound. They stood looking at me, and finally Floyd asked, "Where are our parents?"

I shook my head. "I don't know," I told them.

They kept blinking at me, not speaking. There was something in their faces that was hard to look at. Finally I said, "Well, get in then," and without hesitation, they climbed into bed on either side of me. I fell asleep with a child under each arm.

Several of the *La Nación* reporters were hanging around the entrance to the newspaper building when I arrived the next morning. The one I knew best was Humberto Sanabria, a police reporter.

Sanabria and I drank together occasionally, and he sometimes gave me good tips about exceptional crime stories. Sanabria was incredibly ugly, with a round *criollo* face pocked with more ancient acne scars than all the moons of Jupiter. He was always shy with women; he was even shy with other men, when he spoke privately with them, until he got to know them well. But cops and groups of men brought something out in him; with cops, or as part of a group, he was usually witty, even a little vicious.

As soon as I had crossed the threshold of the building, the little group of reporters burst into laughter, brown fingers raised rudely to point at me.

"Gringo . . ." Sanabria said, and then he began choking because he was laughing so hard.

Guillermo Santos, a slick, affable Venezuelan who was Sanabria's understudy on the death patrol, flashed white teeth at me in a knowing smile. "Gringo," he said. "Don Jimmy. She is beautiful. Just gorgeous."

There was another round of laughter; the *La Nación* boys simultaneously drew index fingers across their throats and then shook them, snapped them briskly in the air, indicating that I was finished, screwed, *jodido*. My stomach sank as it dawned on me that all this had something to do with Orchid.

"What's going on?" I said, trying to force a feeble smile onto my face.

"You tell," Sanabria said, forming a snout with his lips and poking it in Santos's direction.

"No," said Santos, falling against a mirrored wall to keep himself from sliding to the floor. "*Tú.*"

So Sanabria began, and I could tell right away that it was bad, because his face was puckered with embarrassment.

"Well," he said, "earlier this morning a woman, a . . . a *señorita*" —at this there was a burst of laughter—"she came into the building with two boxes in her arms. She was dressed in . . . in a most unusual manner." He looked around at the others for confirmation and then continued.

"She was wearing a mechanic's jumpsuit draped over her shoulders like a cape, and beneath the jumpsuit she was . . ." Sanabria dropped his head to his chest, his modesty preventing him from going on.

"*¡En bola!*" "Naked!" the others screamed in chorus.

"*Sí,*" Sanabria admitted. "*Desnuda.* But anyway, she pulls a dress out of one of these boxes, it was a very pretty dress, too, and she said, she told everyone that her boyfriend, the handsome North American, had given it to her." The wavering smile I was trying to maintain collapsed on me then in a sudden spasm of facial muscles.

"She still *had* the dress," I said in a strained voice, "and she wasn't *wearing* it?"

"Wearing it?" echoed Sanabria. "Why, no. That dress looked like it had never been worn even once. A *pristine* dress, if I have ever seen one." The other reporters all bobbed their heads enthusiastically.

"And then," Sanabria continued, warming to his subject now, "she opened the other box, and she took out a pair of shoes and some nylons and some . . . some . . ."

"Panties!" came the rejoinder.

"*Sí,*" Sanabria said, and a little smile creased his face. "Very pretty *pantaletas,* I might add." The reporters screamed in appreciation.

"And she said, she told everyone, that these *pantaletas* had been given to her by . . ."

I could stand it no longer. I pushed my way between Santos and one of the other men and sprinted to the elevator, which was just beginning to close.

As soon as I reached the sanctuary of my office, the secretary ducked into the bathroom, and Carlos came up to me and looked me up and down as if I were a pickled insect in a specimen jar.

"Jimmy," he said. "The strangest woman was asking for you this morning."

That night I found Packy waiting for me on the stairs that led to my apartment. He came inside with me, then fixed us each a rum and Coke with a bright wedge of lime: a ritual that always marked the beginning of one of our late nights together. On those nights when he slept at my house, we would sometimes sit talking in the living room till six in the morning. We would drink rum, and Packy would smoke cigarettes and snort cocaine, if he had any to snort—I had learned that Packy, too, was strongly attracted to *perico.* He kept the loose white powder on a metal backgammon board, and as the night wore on, he would periodically take a rolled-up ten-bolivar note and use it to suck a thin line into his dark head.

Once, after he had bought a lot of *perico,* Packy spent the better part of an evening shaping snowy pictures against the silver and black of the backgammon board. He made cocaine houses with cocaine smoke curling from the chimneys. With the razor blade squealing against metal, he made cocaine hounds that bolted after cocaine rabbits. Finally he pushed all the powder into the center of the board and divided it into a large pile and a smaller pile. Both piles soon became powdery hearts of cocaine.

"Here," he said, jabbing the razor blade at the smaller of the two hearts, "we have the size of the average gringo heart."

He moved the sharp corner of the razor so that it hovered over the larger shape. "And here, the average Latino heart."

"Good," I told him. "That's accurate. Now pass that board and let me show you the average Latino brain."

We had both had a lot of rum to drink, and we laughed then till tears sprang to our eyes.

Once or twice during our time together at the Sebucán house, I touched a dampened fingertip to the cocaine and rubbed it against my gums. A snowy numbness would fill my mouth then; if the cocaine was of exceptional quality, I would even find myself drooling a little.

On many nights Packy's eyes would deepen, and he would settle back and tell his tales of life in a faraway land that had long since disappeared.

On other nights, even if it were very late, he would carry his amplifier and speaker onto the balcony and plug in his Fender guitar. Then he would pound the steel strings to make ugly, growling noises that echoed out over the sleeping neighborhood.

Tonight he began telling me about his early days in Caracas and his opinions concerning the city's various police organizations.

Apart from the Disip, which, along with the National Guard, had done the dirty work during the jungle fight against the guerrillas, Caracas had a couple of other police agencies. Most of the officers you saw on the street were blue-uniformed Metropolitanos. The Metropolitanos were the poorest-paid, lowest in status of all the Caracas cops; they also rode fast motorcycles, carried little Brazilian-made nine-millimeter submachine pistols, and were always hungry for any loose *plata* you might have loafing in your pocket. So unless you were tight with someone influential, or could at least manage to make yourself look connected, it was best to treat them with respect if you had to deal with them at all.

Next up on the rungs of law enforcement were the Technical Judicial Police, affectionately known as the PeTeJotas. These gentlemen were in charge of criminal investigations; the uniformed PTJ officers carried the same Brazilian weaponry as the Metropolitanos, while many of the plainclothesmen were armed with authentic Uzis. During their frequent downtown firefights with armed bank robbers, the PeTeJotas took no prisoners, and in their enthusiasm, they could generally be counted on to cut down an innocent passerby or two along with the bad guys.

Packy had special reason to dislike the PeTeJotas. His narrow Andean eyes, so like the eyes of an Arizona coyote, went wide and round as he talked about them.

"When I first got to Venezuela, I had no papers and no money," he told me. "I was an illegal immigrant. I was also in shock."

Packy then studied me sideways, in that guilt-inducing way he had. "I mean, when your government is overthrown by gringo-backed *militares* and you end up in such a *strange* country with no papers and no money, shock is a natural reaction. Ask any psychologist.

"Well, in this state of shock, I did nothing but ride buses and the *por puesto* cars. All day long I'd ride from Petare to Plaza O'Leary and then back again, stopping only to change buses. And the PeTeJotas, when I came, were in charge of looking for illegal immigrants. They'd come on the buses all the time with their machine guns, and they'd walk up and down the aisles, not caring where the stupid barrels pointed, staring into people's faces. At random they'd ask people for their *cédulas*. Funny thing, but they had a sense about it. Every time you saw them ask, the person more often than not wouldn't have one. They'd take him away and stick him in a cage in the back of a pickup truck."

"But they never got you," I said, making a rare interruption.

"No," he said, his eyes taking on a faraway look. He took a drag from his cigarette and absently touched the raised, heart-shaped scar on his temple. "The *coño de madres* never got me."

"Maybe because you don't look like a Colombian," I offered. "It's always the Colombians they're looking for."

Packy shook his dark, shaggy head and blasted emphatic smoke from his thin nose. "The Colombian looks just like your poorer class of Venezuelan. They're cousins, you know. No way for even PeTeJotas to tell that way. Could be a smell, though. A certain smell that some people have."

"Maybe fear? Would fear be the smell?"

Packy's eyes grew wide again, almost startled-looking. "I doubt it," he said, without a trace of a smile. "Because if it was, they would have gotten me before they got anybody."

Although he disliked the PeTeJotas, Packy was even more afraid of the Disip, which had been a secret, many thought sinister, arm of the government in the days of the military dictatorship. Now most of them wore uniforms and drove marked cars.

"Even so," Packy noted, "if the Disip is after you, you can be sure it's not for a driving infraction."

Along with the Metropolitanos, the PeTeJotas, the Disip, and the young, skin-headed legions of the *Guardia Nacional*, there was the shadowy DIM, the Department of Military Intelligence. They worked far behind the scenes most of the time, much as the Disip had once done. Packy dreaded running into anyone from DIM.

"They keep telling us this is a democracy," he complained. "Then why all the cops? Why is there a *paco* with an automatic weapon on every corner?" I sensed that this particular story was at an end and decided it would be safe to needle him a bit.

"To keep the order," I said.

"Order," Packy muttered. The faraway look returned to his eyes, and he nodded to himself, drew from his cigarette, touched his heart-shaped scar. *"Order.* Where have I heard *that* before?"

For the longest time Beatrix appeared not to notice my rapport with her children. Whenever I visited, she seemed to be constantly breezing in and out of the apartment, changing her clothes and speaking to no one before leaving again, and she would only glance at the boys and me as we played dominos on the dining room table or ran motorized cars through the living room.

But then, early one evening, while Mickey was at his club and I thought Beatrix was closed away in her room and out of earshot, I convinced the boys to sit and listen as I read a story aloud to them in Spanish. It was a simple story about a schoolteacher who kept a pet parrot in the classroom. I had found it in a Uruguayan children's magazine. The boys listened without fidgeting, and from time to time Nestor encouraged me by asking the meaning of some word or phrase.

When the story was over and the two of them had gone upstairs, I felt Beatrix standing behind me in the hallway entrance that led to the kitchen. Not daring to turn around, I wondered how long she had been poised there. She watched me silently for many minutes, her silence and her intensity making my scalp prickle. Then I heard a sound, heard the faint singing of ice against the side of a glass, and a moment later she spoke.

"Jimmy." Relieved, I allowed myself to turn now. She was wearing a thin bathrobe, her blond hair spilling down around her shoulders. She held a tall glass in her long fingers, and in the pale electric light of the living room there was something unrelenting about the sharp angles of her cheeks and chin. I managed a weak smile; she came over and sat next to me, the side of her leg touching mine. Her breath smelled of rum.

"Jimmy," she repeated. "I understand that you're seeing someone now. Seeing a woman."

Her words and the way she spoke them affected me like cold water dripping down the back of my neck. I was speechless as I tried to figure out what she was talking about and why she had opened the conversation. Had Mickey, for some reason all his own, lied to her and told her I was getting it on with one of his whores? Or was she teasing me because someone at *La Nación* had told her about Orchid? Then I thought that perhaps she only wanted to shame me for my involuntary habit of sleeping alone. Finally I shivered and cleared my throat.

"Well," I said. "That's not quite true. I wouldn't put it that way at all, no." My arms crossed my chest and tightened against me like cables. Beatrix went on as if she hadn't heard me.

"And I suppose that means we won't be seeing much of you from now on." I immediately assumed she was trying to tell me not to come over so often, and I began to sputter as I searched for a dignified response.

"Well, yes, I guess I do come over a lot, but, you know, I suppose that—"

"And that will be a shame, I think." She said "vill" instead of "will." "And quite unfair of you, as well." "Ass" instead of "as."

"*Unfair?*"

"To the boys. It is not fair to build a friendship with a child and then suddenly abandon him when something more fun comes along. Children don't understand these things." I felt my mouth grow wide.

"I don't have any *intention* of abandoning the boys. I don't even know what you're talking about, Beatrix."

Beatrix smiled an unfathomable smile, and then she said, "Well, good. Good. I was in need of your reassurance." Her bright eyes seemed to forbid me the relief of looking anywhere else.

"I was wondering," she said as the tip of her middle finger circled the rim of her glass. "Could you continue to teach them Spanish? They do need to learn, and I myself can't get them to speak a word of it."

"Sure. Sure. If they want to learn. I'd be happy to, you know—" She cut me off with another cool white smile, and she bent closer and stared into my eyes as if searching for something. I looked away.

"How is it going, anyway, Jimmy? With this woman friend?"

"Oh," I said. "It's nothing serious at all," I found myself saying.

Beatrix studied me for a long moment before saying, "Confidence, Jimmy."

"What?"

"Confidence. It's what a woman most wants to see in a man. You can't hold her without it." Then she laughed, her laughter shaking her arm and making the ice tinkle like jewelry against the side of her glass. After that she stood and floated gracefully across the room and up the stairs to the second floor.

The next day, as I was heading down the street toward the entrance to the *La Nación* building, I spotted Orchid standing on the sidewalk outside. She was wearing her filthy mechanic's jumpsuit, and she held a pair of tattered cardboard boxes in her arms. Before she saw me, I managed to duck into the yawning truck bays of *La*

Nación's circulation department. Then I climbed a flight of stairs to the newspaper's production floor and made my way between rows of tilted pasteup tables to the elevator.

At lunchtime I went down to those same truck bays and stuck my head out to search for her before hitting the sidewalk. I was relieved to find that she was not around and, congratulating myself for my cleverness, I headed up to Plaza Miranda to look for a kid to shine my shoes.

That was where she found me a short time later. I was sitting on a bench, enjoying the tickle of the brisk shoeshine rag as it slid around and around my feet, when I spotted her crossing the road that ran in front of the *Extranjería* and heading for me across the stone tiles of the plaza. There were cops all over the plaza; they were grabbing people left and right and asking them for their *cédulas,* sniffing out illegal immigrants. They were also snatching young men they suspected of trying to avoid military service. The police had already filled the caged-in beds of two white Metropolitano pickup trucks with hapless ones.

But no cops bothered Orchid as she came crouching between the palm trees of the Plaza Miranda, dress-shop boxes clutched beneath one arm. The clothing I had bought her peeked through tears in the weathered cardboard.

She sat down next to me, and the shoeshine kid, who was about six or seven, gave her a long, unblinking stare, his lips dropping apart a little. Orchid smiled at him and said, *"¿Colombiano, tú?"* breaking her spell of strangeness over him.

He went back to his work and said, "Yes, I'm Colombian. But my mother has a card."

Orchid and I did not speak for several minutes. Then I said, "You embarrassed me badly with some people I have to see every day. Is that how you pay me back for buying you clothes?"

At that she twisted violently away from me; she huddled so tightly into herself that she was tucked almost into a ball. Sitting like that, with her back to me, she presented such a perfect picture of feminine anger despite her horrible garment and her complete sootiness that I felt an irrational urge to put my hand on her back and apologize. Then the boxes flew out from her arms and landed on the stone; she sniffled loudly and turned her head just enough for me to see a crooked line of tears washing a channel through the dirt on her face.

"Clothes!" she said, her voice entirely lacking in melody now, full of hurt and scorn. "Americano, you must be a virgin, because you know nothing about women. What woman would not rather die than put a beautiful new dress on such a filthy body, a body that has months of grime and road tar on it?"

She turned away again and wept bitterly. The little Colombian studied us with wide eyes as I fished into my pocket for his money, then he snatched up his wooden box and went sprinting away. Orchid went on crying for a long time, and little by little my anger at the humiliation I had suffered began to melt and to be replaced by a measure of the guilt that I imagined a thoughtless and negligent husband was made to feel.

"Listen," I said finally. "I'll put you up in a *pensión* for a couple of days. I'll buy you soap and shampoo and anything else that you need. After that you could look for a job."

When she did not immediately respond to this idea, I got a feeling in my stomach like that of a downward elevator ride, and when at last she looked up at me and wiped her face with the back of her hand and spoke to me, the elevator kept dropping and dropping.

"Not even a *pensión* would take me in looking like this." She stared at me with eyes grown suddenly bright and hard, and I closed my own eyes and let myself slump against the wooden bench. Then I surrendered.

As Orchid and I stepped off the *por puesto* and headed down the little cul-de-sac toward my house, my insides tightened with dread at the sight of all the neighborhood's women, children, and men, including Adolfo and his brats, as well as my traitorous dog, Max, gathered before the high white wall of the hidden estate. It was another informal street party, and the adults were all holding bottles of Polar beer in their hands. A couple of the men were kicking a soccer ball back and forth, and the whole neighborhood vibrated with American music coming from a shiny silver boom box near the bottom of my stairs. My neighbors had been listening to a lot of rock, particularly the music of the Prowlers, ever since the posters had appeared.

"Oh, God," I muttered in English. I wanted to hide my eyes. I hoped desperately that Packy was home, yet I was certain, somehow, that he wasn't.

"What?" said Orchid, her voice calm and mellow and flutelike once more. She looked at me with questioning eyes. "Friends of yours?"

"No," I told her. "Neighbors. Not friends."

Orchid was wearing her new dress and shoes; one of my conditions for taking her to my house was that she had to put on clothes like a human being. She and I had folded her jumpsuit and hidden it under a pile of bricks at the end of an alley; she insisted that she might want it again and would not let me throw it in the garbage. But even though she was now dressed, she still looked as if she had been dipped in tar and dusted with ashes. Her hair was the worst part; it looked like the fur of some black animal that had been killed on the road and then left for a week or two to ripen beneath rainy skies.

I felt a sickening acceleration of my heart and my lungs as we walked down toward the house. Orchid picked up some of my apprehension, and she stuck close to my side, glancing up at me from time to time but saying nothing.

Then they noticed us. Above the noise of the tape player and the anarchy of voices rose an urgent voice that gasped a single imperative and then fell silent: "*¡Miren!*" Look!

Heads turned in our direction. We stopped, our feet glued to the street, and I felt a tremble working its way up my body.

Lola stepped over to the boom box and shut it off; she stood smiling at us. We all lived a long frozen moment during which there was no sound but the sweet trilling of birds in the mango trees on the mysterious other side of the wall.

Finally someone, some man, said "*¡Coño!*" drawing out the ñ for as long as he could, and the silence broke then as laughter rippled through the little crowd. I put my hand on Orchid's elbow and we began moving again, both of us looking at the ground.

Just as we reached the foot of my stairs, the vacant stairs on which I had hoped to see Packy, little Max came charging at us, barking and snarling. I turned and stamped my foot at him; he lunged at me, snapping, but missed my leg by an inch and then ran back to hide behind the crowd. There was more laughter at this, and Lola, who was still standing next to the boom box, said, "How nice. The *extranjero* has a wife. Such a lovely wife she is, too, *extranjero. ¡Qué bonita!*"

We ignored her and started up the stairs. But then Adolfo

stepped out from the group and hissed loudly and threateningly between his teeth in the disgusting manner some Venezuelan men adopt when they want to attract a woman's attention. He followed this with a series of juicy kissing and smacking noises and I could take it no longer. I turned on him, my fingers curled into fists, a voice in my head reminding me to look out for that wicked left thumbnail. We would finally have our fight.

But Orchid grabbed me by the arm. "No," she said. "Don't." I stopped.

Adolfo had moved to the bottom of my steps, and he was smiling up at us. His eyes were locked onto Orchid, but when he spoke, he spoke to me: "*Marico.* Faggot. Let's go."

To my surprise, Orchid held his eyes for a long minute. Her hand on my arm had an almost magic power over me; it kept me from leaping off those stairs at the man who had tormented me from the moment I arrived in the neighborhood. Finally Orchid smiled. She flashed those white teeth at Adolfo, stood smiling and waiting until his own smile wavered and began to slide off his face, until he became insecure enough to turn his head and silently search for support from those behind him. Then she led me up the stairs and into my house.

Once we were inside and had closed the door, the party down in the street erupted again. I showed Orchid where the bathroom was, and I self-consciously gathered shampoo, soap, a towel, a razor, a manicure set, and a pair of scissors for her, all the things she would need to bring herself back into civilized standards of hygiene.

After a few minutes I heard water begin to thunder into the tub behind the closed bathroom door. I tried to relax and watch television, but I couldn't. I tried to fix myself something to eat, but I found that I had no appetite, and I wound up shoving everything back into the refrigerator. I started to pace back and forth, back and forth across the ratty living room rug, pivoting and grinding my heel into the floor at the spot where little Max had always lain.

And then she started to hum. She made a soft noise at first; I had to strain to hear it over her splashing, but after a time she got louder and more sure of herself, opening her mouth to sing something operatic, and the sound filled the entire house. She had talent, there was no denying it. Her priest down on the southern plains had been right, she had the voice of an *angelito*. The sound that came from her throat was sweet and clear, with an indefinable, heartbreaking purity to it.

I went to the window and looked down. The cassette in the boom box had run to its end and stopped; there was silence in the street, and the entire crowd, including Lola and Adolfo and Adolfo's kids, were staring with open mouths toward the side of the house that held the open bathroom window as Orchid's song poured out and soared up and over the high white wall.

Then she called me.

"Americano," she said, "would you come here and wash my back for me, please?"

I pulled my head in quickly, because I was almost certain her words had carried into the street. I had suffered enough ridicule for one day. I went to the bathroom door and pressed my cheek against it. I felt hot moisture coming out all around it.

"Listen," I said, careful to keep my voice low. "I can't wash your back. You'll have to do it yourself."

She giggled then and resumed her humming. But in a minute she said, "I *need* somebody to wash my back. It hasn't been washed in a year, and without a good scrubbing the dirt will never come off."

"No." I was surprised, though, at her sudden eloquence; no more did she talk like a dazed child of poverty. Her craziness seemed to have evaporated with mystifying quickness. And someone, somewhere, had taught this girl to speak proper *castellano*. Then, of course, there was that singing. An uneasy feeling worked its way through me as I began to realize that Orchid was not as simple a being as she had at first appeared.

"Americano," she said, startling me. "I'm not getting into that dress again until you wash my back."

"No. You don't put that dress on, I'll toss you back out on the street."

She giggled again, hummed deliciously for a minute; I was becoming addicted to that soothing sound, and then she said, "*Please*. If you're too shy, I'll turn away and face the wall and you won't have to look at me."

My life sometimes appeared to be made up of nothing but a series of small surrenders. I opened the bathroom door and stepped inside. Orchid had turned to face the soap dish, and her naked back was shining wetly. Her back was marbled with grime and mottled with tiny, healing wounds as well as crusty black patches that looked like embedded pieces of pavement. But the shape of it was fine; she was slender, and long above the waist.

I swallowed, and she said, "Close the door, won't you. And please start scrubbing before the water gets too cool."

So I went down on my knees beside the bathtub, picked up a sponge and a brush, and went to work. Orchid had cut off most of her hair, and what was left stood up in uneven patches all over her head. But her hair was almost clean now, and there was a hint of a pleasing softness in one or two of the wet tufts that stuck into the air like horns. My mind drifted as I scrubbed, and in a minute I was thinking of Maria, the peasant girl in *For Whom the Bell Tolls*, whose head had been shorn by fascists. I was unable to control my runaway romantic mind after that. *Little rabbit*, I thought. *Little rabbit*, said my inner voice.

Orchid started giggling.

"What?" I said. "Does the brush tickle?"

"No, it doesn't tickle."

"Then what are you laughing at?"

"Yes, it does. The brush tickles."

After the bath Orchid looked much better, although she still had a long way to go before the gutter would entirely wear off her body and her face. Her face had actually been quite attractive at one time, I decided. I gave her an old shirt to use for a bathrobe, and she reached into the little pile of clothes I had bought her and pulled out a worn toothbrush.

"It's the only thing I ever carried," she said. "No matter how far I fell, I always took care of my teeth."

"Why was that?"

"My mother..." she began, but fell suddenly silent, shot a critical glance at her image in the steamy bathroom mirror, and reached for the toothpaste on the edge of the sink.

Later I told her to take the bed, that I would sleep on the couch. But she said, "No, keep your bed, *mi amor*. I wouldn't be able to stand such softness just yet. As it is, you may find me sleeping on the floor in the morning."

• • •

After work on the following evening I walked down into the Sebucán cul-de-sac and spotted Packy sitting near the bottom of my wrought-iron stairs. He was smoking a cigarette and staring up into the sky. Before he noticed me, I felt a touch of the same dread that had shaken me when I arrived home the day before.

Then he turned his head and gave me a wry, half-amused smile.

"Gringo," he said.

"Chile," I answered, and sat down next to him. After that he was silent, seemingly waiting for me to explain myself.

"So," I said after a time. "You've been in the house, then?" He cut his eyes at me.

"*Sí, pana.*"

"And, so, you met Orchid."

"Yes."

"Hmm. Well, that's a sad story, let me tell you. She was just hanging out by herself in El Silencio. Broke. Nowhere to go. No clothes, even. So, little by little, over a period of weeks, you know, I kind of made friends with her. And finally I realized that the poor thing stood no chance of finding a job of any kind looking the way she did, and I decided, I made up my mind, to bring her home for a few days to let her get cleaned up."

Packy turned and stared hard into my eyes, and I found myself looking away.

"After that, of course," I continued, "she could go out and find a job and get an apartment and whatever else she needed."

By then Packy had come to the end of his cigarette, and he suddenly flicked it down into the street with a practiced snap of his fingers.

"*Pana*, you are a rare one," he said. I waited for him to comment further, but to my relief he said nothing more. He just stared hard at the white wall as if he were able to see through it to the falling fruit on the other side.

"So," I said. "What do you feel like doing? Do you want to come into the house?" He lit another cigarette.

"No. I'd like to sit out here and enjoy the fresh air. Maybe you'd sit with me; I've got a story to tell. It's one of my best."

So I sat outside and watched the darkening sky with him, and he began to tell me about his early career as a rock musician.

Packy had bought his first guitar the year he entered secondary

91

school in Santiago. After that he studied hard at his music and cultivated an image, which he patterned loosely on Keith Richards of the Rolling Stones. He learned to smoke, and thereafter always dangled a cigarette from his lips. He starved himself so that his body would look as if it had been nourished on nothing but heroin, and he spent ten minutes before a full-length mirror each day practicing the poses of sinuous dissipation.

"The first song I learned was 'Jumpin' Jack Flash,'" he told me. "*Coño*, but my father hated that guitar more than he hated the *abuela*'s coca bush. But he let it go. We had just elected a new president in the country. There was a feeling of newness, like electricity in the air."

After a time, though, trouble began. While the new Marxist president had captured the imaginations of many of the people, particularly the younger people, his economic reforms were turning out badly. Some Chileans packed up and left the country to await saner times from abroad. Food shortages sprang up.

"In Santiago, in my neighborhood, there were marches," Packy said. "The housewives went through the streets banging on pots and screaming 'There is no meat, you fool. There is no chicken, you fool. What shit is this that's going on, you fool?'"

Political elements from the middle and the right and the far right began to consider not waiting until the next elections to put the president out of office. These elements were encouraged by the United States, which was brooding over the nationalization of the copper industry and other slights, both real and imagined.

But Packy kept rocking and rolling, despite the social turbulence. He formed a group with a like-minded singer, a bass player, and a drummer. The drummer had little talent, but his faults as a musician were more than compensated for by the fact that his parents were both deaf-mutes, who did not mind having a rock band rehearsing all night in their cellar.

"They only complained," said Packy, "if we made the floor shake so hard they thought another earthquake had started."

Then Packy's grandmother died. Packy and his father and his mother went to the mountain village to bury her and to sort through her things. The professor made a pile of old furniture in the backyard and he set it afire. Then, with great effort, he pulled up the stubborn roots of the coca bush and threw it on top of the blaze; he made Packy and Packy's mother walk with him to the center of the village, telling them they would go mad if they smelled the fumes from the burning shrub. While they stood near the village fountain watching the gray plume of smoke rising into the overcast sky from behind the *abuela's* house, the professor talked in low tones about the president. He said that the Marxist government had been an interesting experiment but that it had turned out badly and that a coup to restore economic sanity might not be a bad idea.

"But I hardly listened," said Packy. "I was too busy watching all my grandmother's things turning to dark smoke. Later, after my *viejo* said it was safe, I went back to the house to look for that blue bitch. I looked and I called and I whistled, but I couldn't find her anywhere."

When the story was finished, Packy stood up immediately, and without looking at me he said, "Well, Camión and I have some work we have to do. I'll see you tomorrow, gringo." A moment later I was sitting by myself.

The next night when I got home, I found Orchid sitting on the couch watching television. She was wearing a new blouse and a pair of pants I had given her the money to buy, and a red kerchief was tied around her head to conceal her unevenly shorn hair. She gave me a big smile, but there was an unaccustomed hardness in her eyes, and then she handed me a slip of paper.

"The Chileno left it," she told me. I could tell by the way she said it that she did not care for the Chileno at all. I read the note.

Gringo, it said.

> *Come to dinner at El Camión's. Bring beer. 12 if you can. Bring Séptimo si tú quieres. Main gate will be open.*
>
> > *Un Abrazo,*
> > *Paquete El Magnífico*

I thought it was rude of them to have invited Séptimo and not Orchid, and I decided to invite her myself.

"Listen," I said. "Packy and another *pana* are fixing dinner. Would you like to join us?"

"Why, no," she said. "I'd only be in the way."

"Are you sure? You're welcome to come."

"No, no, *mi amor.*" She was still giving me the wide smile and hard eyes. "You go ahead. Have fun with your friends. I'll fix myself some dinner here."

So I went out and knocked on the side of Séptimo's lean-to. The metal boomed like thunder beneath my fist. Séptimo crawled out and stood blinking at me; he had been asleep.

"Christ, look at you," I said in English. His face was so black with dirt, I could barely see the white blister spots. His nostrils were encrusted with dried snot. His little hands were filthy as well.

"*¿Cómo?*" Séptimo asked.

"Camión has invited us to his house. He and Packy are making dinner for us."

"Camión's house?" said Séptimo. His eyes grew round as half-dollars. "On the other side?" Then he looked nervously around us to make sure no one else had been close enough to hear him.

"Yes. But you have to wash up a little first."

"No." His face grew serious and he backed away from me. He readied himself to run.

"You have to, *pana.* It's either that or you stay here."

He thought hard. But then he turned and his eyes began to climb the wall until they were fixed on the forbidden treetops on the other side.

"Just my hands," he said finally. "No bath."

"Your face too."

Séptimo frowned, but finally he shrugged his shoulders and followed me into the house, where he spent twenty minutes cursing in pain as I scrubbed the dirt out of his pores.

El Camión had spread a linen cloth over the kitchen table. Candles were burning, and four places had been set with good china and monogrammed silverware. Camión explained that the engraved initials were those of the former owner of the estate, the dictator's friend.

Packy had done the cooking. He had made a salad and boiled potatoes and seviche, a cold dish of fish and onions marinated in lemon juice.

We opened beers and sat down. But Séptimo wrinkled his nose and refused to eat the seviche. He soon got up and ran outside. After dinner Packy and Camión and I stepped out into the tangled garden, and we spotted Séptimo running around in one of the orchards, peeling and eating mango after mango.

"The *carajito* is going to get sick," Packy warned. So I called to Séptimo, but he pretended not to hear me and kept on eating. I shrugged.

"Well," I said. "I'm not his father."

When we had gone back into the cottage, I drank beer and watched as Packy and Camión broke out the backgammon board and snorted a few lines of cocaine. Then I said, "So what is it, *chamos?* Why are we gathered here today?"

El Camión smiled a nervous smile and said nothing. Packy said, "We got a good job today, Jimmy. Temporary, but good. And interesting. We think we have it, anyway."

"Good. What is it?"

"Interpreters. You know, for those gringo *roqueros* coming in next month. The Prowlers." I was astonished.

"*What!*" I said. "That's funny, I was looking into that job myself. But you say you got those jobs *today?*"

"*Sí, pana.* Just this morning in fact."

"Well, that's so strange, because I talked to the promoter a while ago, and he said all the jobs were filled." Packy coughed and looked away from me.

"Yes, well, that promoter has had some bad luck. He had a crew all lined up, and then suddenly they all quit, and then he hired another three people, and they quit too. Last night they quit. This morning, I mean." I nodded as I absorbed it all.

"Wow. Well, hell, that's great. That's just the kind of job for you guys." But something was bothering me, and after a minute I figured out what it was. "*Coño.* But Camión doesn't speak English."

Packy smiled a sly smile. "I'm teaching him as fast as I can. I figure that in a month he'll at least be able to nod and grin at the right times."

The three of us laughed. Then I said, "That's funny. Just a few days ago I got a message from New York about that band. They want coverage. I wasn't going to do it, but if you two *chamos* are involved, I might change my mind."

Packy and Camión exchanged a look. Then Camión stood and went to the window and peered out. Packy said, "So, you said you were thinking about taking one of those jobs yourself. You must be a little jealous of us."

"Well, no, not really. At the time I thought I might have to quit my wire-service job in a hurry, and I was just looking around for alternatives. But things are a little better now, I guess." Packy sat blinking at me.

"Because, you know, we only *think* we have the jobs. The hitch is that we need another interpreter. Not only to cover Camión when he gets stuck but because they want three. The promoter says we have it if we come up with somebody else."

"*Coño,*" I said. I shook my head. "You know I have to work. I'm almost doing the job of two people now."

Packy leaned forward in his seat. His dark eyes were afire with cocaine urgency. "*Pana.* But you said you have to cover it anyway. You work with us, you get double pay. And think of the story." He smiled at me. "From de *een*side," he said in English.

The idea suddenly seemed possible, as well as attractive. But I knew it would mean having little time to rest for the duration of the band's stay in Caracas.

"Let me think about it. There might be something I can do." Packy's expression was serious.

"Think quickly, Jimmy. This means a lot to us." His eyes sought the floor. "We'd be grateful, *verdad*, Camión?" But Camión did not answer. Darkness was falling quickly, and El Camión was still at the window, staring off in the direction of the well-kept mound of rosebushes that stood out so noticeably from the anarchy of his gardens.

"Camión," I said. He looked at me. "I was thinking. All that fruit going to waste out there. Why not open the gate once in a while and let the people come in to pick it?"

He turned back to the window and was silent for a long minute. But then in a quiet voice he said, "I don't think you have any idea how much I would really like to do that." There was another pause before he said, "But I can't, Jimmy. It's something wrong with me. Something rotten inside me. I was raised here, and now I just can't make myself let it go."

He turned and walked out of the kitchen. A moment later I heard the door to his bedroom quietly close. I looked to Packy for an explanation, but Packy was looking down at his backgammon board, avoiding my eyes.

• • •

96

A couple of days later I received a phone call from the Croaker. "Mr. Angel," he said, "the fun is about to start."

I was sure he had gotten the line from some old American gangster movie, and I almost laughed. But then, after he hung up, I began to tremble.

A rapid series of Caracas bank robberies began immediately after that. The robberies were all the same: At rush hour six or seven men with black knitted masks over their faces ride up the concrete front steps of a bank on bouncing little motorcycles with knobby tires. Two men run inside to cover the bank guards while the others drag their bikes right into the bank with them. Guns are pulled on the bank officers; money is gathered. Then the robbers take their machines out either the front or the back of the bank, depending on which side the cops are likely to approach from. Sometimes they use both doors. Then, *phut-phut*, off they go on those little bikes, braiding a path through the creeping streams of cars, buses, and microbus *por puestos*. They wave at bystanders and punch their fists in the air as they head for the Ávila, the high green ridge that separates Caracas from the shore. Police cars with frantic sirens pursue, but lose them, because they cannot get through the tangled traffic.

I paid little attention to the first robbery committed by this gang; bank heists were fairly common in Caracas. The second time they struck, I took casual notice, and after the third heist, I finally picked up on the connection and I wrote a piece in which I rehashed all my conversations with the Croaker and quoted a couple of unnamed diplomatic sources as saying that the crimes might possibly be an organized retaliation for the guerrilla massacre and the murder of Victor Rojas. I called the gang by the English name that the local press had given them; the afternoon newspapers quickly began calling them Los Cowboys because of their mounted attack. New York sent that short and sweet piece over the Triple-A wire.

And then Los Cowboys killed somebody.

The fourth robbery did not go as smoothly as the other three. A bank guard spots them as they ride up to the front of his bank, and he charges out into the street, trying to jam a shell into his bolt-action rifle as he moves. Just as he gets the bolt closed, one of the Cowboys pulls out a revolver and shoots him through the heart.

97

Immediately after the shooting, a pair of Metropolitanos on a motorcycle happen to turn a corner to materialize in front of the bank. The cop on the back of the bike carries a Brazilian machine pistol; he jumps off and pulls the clip out of his pocket and starts to load the weapon. The same Cowboy who shot the guard shoots the cop; the cop falls wounded into the gutter. The other Metropolitano dumps the bike and takes cover behind a car and stays there.

All the Cowboys except for the shooter seem anxious to leave then. But the shooter growls something at them, and three of them run into the bank and come out a few minutes later with a bag full of money. Then they mount their machines and escape.

I heard about it while I was standing in one of the front offices of the *La Nación* building, watching the afternoon line forming at the pornographic movie house. An editor burst in looking for a couple of reporters to help with the story, and he shouted enough of the details to let me know that I should get myself to the scene. I went searching for Carlos the Jackal, who was not in the darkroom, and fifteen minutes later I found him sleeping in a bin of old newspapers in *La Nación's* production department. I dusted him off, stuck a camera around his neck, and pushed him behind the wheel of the company car, a Chevrolet. He scraped the fender on the wall of the parking garage trying to back out.

By the time we arrived, there were news people from all over, scores of cops, and half a dozen *guardias*. The place bristled with TV cameras and machine pistols.

Most of the cops were Metropolitanos, brothers of the man wounded during the robbery. The Metropolitanos looked shaken; they rubbed their chins and said little, even to each other. But there were also quite a few PeTeJotas and a handful of Disip men.

The wounded Metropolitano had already been taken away; the only sign that he had ever been there was a patch of wetness in the gutter. Even his motorcycle had disappeared; the cops had a thing about letting people see that they were vulnerable.

The dead security guard was a different story, however. He remained lying on the sidewalk with a plastic sheet spread over him, and just as Carlos and I showed up, a wolf pack from the afternoon rape-and-murder ragsheets was trying to talk a couple of Metropolitanos into lifting the sheet so they could get his picture.

The cops didn't want to do it, but finally one of the wolves whispered something to one of the cops, and the sheet came up for a moment.

Carlos woke up then and began to lift his camera; he got it to eye level before I said his name and shook my head. He looked relieved.

A Disip man I was slightly acquainted with walked up and poked me gently in the stomach. "¡Epa! gordo," he said. "Hey, chubby." Everyone in Venezuela was either a gordo or a flaco, a skinny guy. There was no in-between. By then I fell more into the gordo category.

The Disip man made a snout with his mouth in the Venezuelan manner and pointed it at a PTJ press officer around whom reporters and photographers were beginning to gather. "Get to the sow before all the tits are taken," he said.

I pulled out a notepad and a pen and walked over. The PeTeJota was explaining the very basic facts of the robbery, telling the gathered reporters how much money was taken, how many bad guys there were, and in which direction they had escaped. I gave the press officer my full attention for about a minute before I became distracted with worry. I was worried because I did not see Humberto Sanabria in the gathered crowd, and I knew that he would be there if the briefing had any real value. I knew he had to be somewhere else, digging out facts of genuine importance; I began to look around for him.

Then someone asked a question, and I heard the jovial PTJ press officer say, "Not guerrillas, no. The foreign news agency that is reporting this must have amnesia, because we eliminated our guerrilla problem several months ago." I felt people turning to stare at me, but I paid them no attention. I wanted to find Sanabria.

"Colombia has guerrillas," the press officer continued. "Venezuela has only thieves; Colombian thieves for the most part." The journalists laughed appreciatively. Before the laughter had died completely, I spotted Sanabria. He stood across the street, leaning against a car and talking to a man I at first did not recognize. I began to walk toward them, and as I walked, I realized the man Sanabria was talking to was Nelson Lugo Alvarado, the Disip official who had taken over my office during the hostage negotiations.

Lugo Alvarado was wearing dark glasses and a wide-brimmed hat; apparently none of the other reporters had recognized him, which seemed to be the way he wanted it. My feet slowed when I saw it was him, but I turned to warn Carlos away with a flap of my hand and kept moving.

"Jimmy Angel," said Sanabria when he saw me. "The *chamo* who translates all my best work into English and then puts his own name on it. My *pana.*" A friendly smile spread across his ugly face.

Lugo Alvarado was not happy I had spotted him. He greeted me with a *coño de tu madre*, and it was then that I noticed the three plainclothes Disip henchmen loitering nearby. When Lugo Alvarado cursed me, they stared at me and stirred like watchdogs testing their leashes.

I decided to try to break the tension by teasing Sanabria. I could usually coax a laugh from him and whomever we were with by teasing him about women. Women were even more of a problem for Sanabria than they were for me; given half a chance, I could at least bring myself to *talk* to them.

"Sanabria," I said. "*Pana.* You owe me a few beers. For introducing you to that girl, Maria Paz. Remember?"

But it didn't work. Completely deadpan, Sanabria said, "I don't know anyone named Maria Paz."

Then Lugo Alvarado glared at him and said, "You're not going to tell this gringo anything, are you?"

Shy Sanabria was not at all shy with cops. "I probably will," he said. "He's been *pana* enough to let me know whenever this Croaker *coño de madre* calls him so I get a jump on the competition. I owe him."

Lugo Alvarado turned to me, startling me with those sky-colored eyes set in that black, machete-shaped face. Lugo Alvarado was a definite *flaco*, in the Venezuelan scheme of things. He studied me for a moment, then frowned.

"What I told you was not for publication, Sanabria," he said, without taking his eyes from me.

"Then let it be not for publication for him too," Sanabria said. Then in English, he said, "*Off de record,*" and he smiled. "Okay, Jimmy?"

I hesitated, but curiosity got the better of me, and I nodded.

"All right," Lugo Alvarado said. "But, Angel, you better not let this out until we catch these *malandros*. When we have them, you can shoot off your fat gringo mouth as much as you want."

I turned to Sanabria. "What is it?"

"They got a fingerprint from the second robbery. Enrique Mosca."

"Wow." I became lightheaded for a moment. It was a thrill to have guessed correctly about the guerrillas, and I grinned. "How did he slip up like that?"

"Well, you know, Jimmy, those wool masks must be awfully itchy in this climate. In the bank Mosca took off his glove for a second and stuck his hand inside the mask so he could scratch. Then just before he put the glove back on, he touched the side of a marble pillar."

"And somebody in the bank saw him? Pretty sharp." Sanabria shook his head.

"They probably wouldn't even have noticed, but Mosca himself realized what he had done, and he pulled out a handkerchief and wiped the pillar. He drew attention by doing that. Kind of like waving a flag and saying, 'Look, people, I fucked up and touched this thing.' And he was in a hurry, so he missed a spot; they found a single perfect fingerprint that belonged to him."

"The near-perfect print of a middle finger," said Lugo Alvarado, and he lifted his own middle finger and nearly touched my nose with it. I stepped backward, away from him.

"So it is the guerrillas," I said. "Red guerrillas. Looking for revenge."

"Angel, listen to me," Lugo Alvarado said. He suddenly seemed as close to pleading as he could get. "We'll catch these bastards. Soon. But until then we prefer to say that they are common bank robbers. There are so many things you don't understand."

"What don't I understand?" He eyes turned hard then; he was pleading no longer.

"You don't understand how much other countries look up to us for being the leading democracy in the region. You don't understand how much it *means* to us to be respected as the leading democracy and as the birthplace of the Liberator. You don't understand how much it hurts our pride and our prestige when the world hears that we have Marxist guerrillas shooting police officers and running around loose in our capital."

I held up my hands. "Look, the fingerprint information, I won't mention it. It only confirms what I already knew. But if you expect me to pretend that these guys are some common *malandros* from the slums of Petare . . ." Lugo Alvarado made a sort of twitch with his head, and one of the Disip men stepped forward suddenly and hit me with an uppercut to the stomach. His knuckles seemed almost to touch my spine, and I deflated slowly to my knees. Then Lugo Alvarado's dark face was down at my level, and when he spoke, spit from his lips flew into my tearing eyes.

"Be careful what you write, Angel," he said. "I'm still very curious about why these people called you in the first place."

"You hit me," I gasped, "in front of another journalist. Sanabria . . ."

But Sanabria was not looking at me. He was carefully studying his fingernails. "No," Sanabria said after a moment. "I've thought about it, Jimmy, and I don't think I know *anyone* named Maria Paz."

CHAPTER 4

My original plan had been to allow Orchid to stay at my house for a week or so, long enough for her to get cleaned up and rested and ready to go out looking for a job. But the night after Séptimo and I had gone to Camión's house together, I came home to find dinner, a sweet red seafood stew, waiting for me on the stove and fresh flowers filling two vases that had stood empty since I bought them on impulse shortly after moving into the place. The following evening there was broiled steak with fried bananas, and all my clothes were cleaned and pressed and fresh-smelling and hanging in the closet instead of lying wadded beneath my bed. And the night after that cold rain was dancing in the streets, and she had a glass of warm Chilean wine waiting for me as soon as I walked in the door. It was then that I decided that I should be generous and let her stay long enough for her hair and nails to grow out and the stain of filth to fade completely from her skin.

Séptimo came to my door on one of those evenings. I was eating, and Orchid got up from the table and rushed out to see who it was. A minute later I heard her shooing him away. I made a resolution then to explain to her that Séptimo was a special friend of mine and that he rated special treatment, but it somehow slipped my mind to mention it, and Séptimo went away that evening and did not come back for many days.

Orchid began to fill out almost immediately. The hollows in her face disappeared, erasing the sharp angles of destitution, and the lines of her body softened and became feminine and pleasing. Orchid was not beautiful in the classical sense, but she was quite pretty, and her life on the streets had given her features a stamp of complexity, of melancholy and character, that was fascinating. I was not the only one to notice this, either.

One evening as we returned from the supermarket with sacks of groceries in our arms and were walking down into our cul-de-sac, we ran into Adolfo and two of his friends heading in the opposite direction. The three of them blocked our way for a minute; they began to look Orchid up and down, open contempt on their faces. But then, as they registered the changes she had undergone in my protection, I was certain that I saw shock and then respect fill their eyes. Adolfo's two friends stepped out of our way; I thought I heard one of them whisper an awe-filled *coño* before they left Adolfo to face us by himself.

Adolfo was drinking from a long-necked bottle of Polar beer, which bore the familiar polar bear on the painted label. He tipped the bottle back and drained the last of the beer, and then it seemed as if he were going to follow his friends' lead by stepping out of our way. Instead he forced a smile onto his face, his eyes holding Orchid's, and he fished into his pocket and drew out one of the little quarter-bolivar coins known as a medio. He held the coin and the bottle toward her and said, *"Mira,* do you know how you tell whether the bear is a male or a female?"

Adolfo let heavy lids fall halfway over his eyes, making bedroom eyes at Orchid, and I felt like taking a swing at him, killer thumbnail or not.

But Orchid just smiled and said, "No, I don't know. Let's see it."

"Well," Adolfo said, his voice husky, "you take a medio and you put it over the hole." His fingers with their gleaming nails carried the coin to the mouth of the bottle. "If the coin does not fall in, the bear is a *macho.* If it does fall in"—he spread his fingers, and the coin clinked into the wet foam at the bottom of the bottle—"then you have an *hembra.* A female."

He rattled the coin back and forth, studying Orchid, and he let his eyelids drop a fraction of an inch more. "You would be surprised," he said, "how few real *machos* you find these days."

With that, he said *ciao* and slid to one side, letting us pass.

Later, as we were putting the groceries away, I said, "That Adolfo is some kind of brute, isn't he?"

Orchid was humming softly to herself, not paying attention, and she didn't answer me. This annoyed me much more than it should have, and I nearly shouted, "Isn't he?"

"What?" she said, startled.

"A brute. Adolfo. A *coño de madre.*"

"Oh," she said, and smiled. Her eyes got a dreamy, far-off look that made me want to slap her. "Maybe he is. I guess he is. Depending on the perspective."

"The *perspective?*" I was holding a box of crackers, and I dropped it into a sink that was half full of dirty water. "You can't tell me that you *like* anything about him or the way he acts?"

Orchid sighed, and the smile left her face. Her chin trembled, and she said, "You have to understand, *mi amor,* that he is like many Venezuelan men. Not all, but many. And many little Venezuelan girls are raised to become women who like a man who acts that way."

She pulled my dripping box of crackers from the sink, set it on the counter, and took a tissue from her pocket to dab her eyes.

After we had finished dinner that night, Orchid set down her fork and asked me if I thought it was time for her to leave my house.

"No!" I said immediately, the panicked tone of my voice betraying and embarrassing me. I looked down at the table, feeling like an idiot. A suddenly vulnerable idiot.

Orchid reached and set thin fingers on top of my hand. Her nails had grown in nicely by this time; they were a little long, and she had shaped them, and they were painted pink. I swallowed and closed my eyes.

"You want me to stay, then?"

My cover of cool was already blown. "Yes," I said. "I want you to stay. I want very much for you to stay." It was a strain to force those words out; it was as if I were uprooting them from hard, parched soil deep within my chest.

She slipped her hand into mine, pulled me from my seat. "Come on," she whispered. "Come on." Like a dream-walker, I let her lead me toward my bedroom.

105

I had some difficulty, as I often did the first time I was with somebody, but she told me to never mind, it wasn't important, and we went on and did other things. And in the end it went just the way we wanted.

When we were almost ready to fall asleep, I said, "But you've been with men like Adolfo before, haven't you? You know they're no good?" I thought I did a pretty good job at keeping the desperation out of my voice.

Orchid sighed. "Men," she said. "I had a great future, down in Ciudad Bolívar, until I became attracted to men. I suppose I'm a lot like my mother that way."

"Your mother . . ." I began, but she cut me off.

"Told me my father was an American. But she couldn't say which American."

"An American," I echoed.

"But maybe he was really an Italian," she said. "There were Italians around too. Most Americans are blond, are *catires.* I am not a *catira.*"

"An Italian," I said.

"Men were my greatest vice, too," said Orchid. "And they all pushed me down. The last one pushed me down so hard, I almost didn't want to get up again." Orchid yawned. "I want to stay up this time. To do that, I'm going to have to keep men in their place. Far away. Far, far away."

She fell asleep then, leaving me to a feeling of apprehension that was growing and prickling in the pit of my stomach, and to the sound of my heart, whose slow, steady thumping seemed to fill the entire room.

I never doubted Mickey's unhappy assertion that Beatrix was sharing herself with other men; the amount of time she spent away from home combined with those lupine looks she always gave me served to make his claims more than credible. But late one afternoon I did get the idea that her infidelity had entirely unhinged him and brought him to the pathetic point where he was hallucinating reflections of her naked body in every masculine pair of eyes that met his own.

We were crossing the Plaza Altamira on our way to his apartment after a hard day of reporting on the governmental waffling and infighting concerning the true size of the external debt.

106

Mickey had surprised me that morning by turning up for a few hours of real work in the office, and as we walked, we carried on a friendly debate about which official we thought had done the most lying over the course of the day. Suddenly Mickey froze and stared off across the plaza, an action that I immediately misinterpreted.

"Really?" I said. "I didn't know you were that fond of the old weasel. All right, I take it back."

"*There*," he said from between gritted teeth. "The *coño de madre*." I followed his eyes, half-expecting to discover the official we had been talking about, but all I saw was a well-dressed, Nordic-looking gentleman standing at a flimsy metal news kiosk and dropping coins into the news seller's hand.

"You know him?" A shiver of apprehension went up my back.

"Know him? I should get a gun and blow his goddamn head off." He began moving forward, not taking his eyes from the newsstand, but I made a quick couple of hopping sidesteps and got in front of him.

"Whoa," I said. "Hold it. What's going on, Mickey?" He seemed almost relieved that I had stopped him, and he looked at me with eyes gone suddenly soft with sadness.

"He's fucking my wife. He's fucking Beatrix, Jimmy."

"Oh, Jesus." I put a hand on his arm and turned to study the man with a new appreciation. He had looked like a Scandinavian-embassy type to me. But he had already paid for his paper and vanished.

"Well, he's gone now, anyway," I said. "Do you know who he is?"

"*Gone?*" He pressed against me, seemingly ready to shove me out of the way. "Are you blind? He's still there." I looked again, and there was no one but the news seller. He was a short, dark, dirty-looking little man with a receding thatch of curly black hair. Another plume of dark hair grew from a large mole on his cheek. He had not noticed us, and as I watched him, he thrust his middle finger into his mouth and began gnawing hungrily on the nail.

"Not *him*? You're not talking about the news guy?"

"Who the fuck did you think I was talking about? While I'm at work the little bastard is busy leaving snail tracks on my sheets." Mickey was breathing hard, and I felt hot dampness coming through his clothes where I was touching him.

"Oh, no. You have to be . . . Are you sure about this one, Mickey.

I mean, Beatrix has more taste than that." The news seller, oblivious, was now meditatively scrubbing his thin nose with the back of his wrist. Mickey's hands rose suddenly and clamped my shoulders. He was not looking at me.

"I mean, the guy sells comic books and month-old magazines. You mean to tell me..." Mickey shook me; it was not a hard shake, but it was enough to get my attention.

"What do you know about Beatrix?" he asked.

"Well, I know..." He shook me again.

"What do you know about Beatrix, Jimmy?"

"Nothing, I guess. I don't know anything, Mickey." The news seller was now yawning, showing a wide, dark space in front where teeth should have been.

"You're damn right, you don't know anything. So if I tell you that she'll fuck the plumber or the delivery boy or the guy that sleeps under the mango tree every night, you ought to believe me, don't you think."

"Mickey, what I think is that these problems have been getting you upset lately. Maybe you and Beatrix ought to..." But he wasn't listening to me. He was concentrating on breathing, on sweating, on staring at the newsman. I was afraid he would tear himself away from me and do something to get himself thrown in jail. But finally I felt him relax.

"Fuck," he said in a croaking, defeated voice. "I need to do a couple of lines."

Beatrix was not at the apartment, and Mickey and I sat talking in his upstairs office for a long while. I arrived home that night exhausted by Mickey's problems and looking forward to a quiet meal with Orchid. But Packy was sitting on the stairs waiting for me, and without a word he rose and followed me into the house.

Orchid heard us come in, and she appeared at the kitchen doorway with a sweet smile on her face. When she saw Packy, her smile grew brighter, and at the same time cooler, and then she excused herself and walked into my bedroom, closing the door behind her.

After staring at the closed door of my bedroom for a moment, Packy looked at me with a surprised expression on his face. Then he turned back to the bedroom door. Finally he shrugged and walked into his own room to hunt for his backgammon board.

While he was gone, I searched my mind for a gentle way of getting rid of him so that I could lure Orchid back out. I quickly decided, however, that not only was it impossible to ask him to leave a house on which he was paying rent, but that on this night the need to talk that I sensed in him seemed even more urgent than my own desire to be with Orchid.

When Packy returned, he sat next to me on the couch and snorted a couple of lines of *perico*. Then he lit a cigarette and began his story.

In the Chile of Packy's youth the military finally staged their coup. The soldiers acted with the blessing of politicians from the middle and the right and the far right; those in the middle were convinced that the country would experience no more than a temporary suspension of democracy, after which would follow a return to democratic rule by elected moderate politicians.

But the general who had been placed in charge of the rebel forces had other ideas. He decided that if the constitution was so little thought of by the politicians that it could be suspended for a period of weeks or months in order to deal efficiently with a national problem or two, then it was his right, his patriotic duty, in fact, to hold the constitution in suspension for an even longer period so that he could, with great efficiency, go about eliminating all the woes of Chile and all the troubles, yet unthought of, that would inevitably plague it in the future.

The coup, which cost the life of the president, turned deadlier still as the general sought to discourage with finality the supporters of the dead president as well as the people who had not been his supporters but who were calling for a premature return to the inefficiency of democracy. As the general went about consolidating his power, his troops swept up leftists, and leftist sympathizers, and people suspected of having leftist thoughts and of plotting to destroy the country with the contamination of their ideas. Many moderates were shocked to find themselves caught in bloody bristles of the general's broom.

The cleansing of Chile was difficult work, and it took many days, and when it seemed finally to be finished, the general could not shake the nagging suspicion that dirt still lay hidden somewhere; perhaps it lay hidden in a lot of places. After a time the general concluded that the Chilean people were making dirt; they were actually quite a treacherous lot, the Chileans, and they would always continue making dirt from cleanliness, so that the purification could never really end.

Almost everything had been in the open at first, with the filth being hauled away in broad daylight, but because of the mendacity of the Chilean people, the national ablution had to be continued indefinitely, and it had to be carried on at night when the people were asleep and did not expect anyone to be looking for the dirt they had made and were hiding.

One day a squad of soldiers materialized as if by magic in the cellar where Packy and his friends were rehearsing.

"We still had hope," said Packy, "which is why we continued to play. But suddenly we were surrounded by all these gorillas with guns; the drummer's parents were out, and I guess we were making so much noise we hadn't heard their boots on the floor above our heads."

The soldiers put the four of them on the floor and held the cold barrels of rifles against their necks and ran ungentle hands up and down their bodies. The lieutenant in charge was young and had a harelip that he tried to conceal with a mustache; his was the only face that Packy later remembered. The soldiers kicked in the drums and smashed the guitars, saying that only anarchists played such instruments. Then they dragged Packy and the other three boys out to a bus, where several other people were already being held. The bus bore the markings of the military school.

"They made us lie on the floor," Packy said, "because it was broad daylight, and they didn't want the people in the streets to see that the bus was carrying prisoners. They put us facedown and told us to keep our hands clasped behind our backs. Then the bus started to move."

There were about seven soldiers, not including the bus driver, and during the journey the soldiers smoked and walked up and down the aisle of the bus over the backs of the prisoners. The soldiers flicked ashes indiscriminately as they walked and smoked, and Packy saw gray, burned tobacco shower down on his three friends.

The trip ended in a field outside the city, about half an hour after it had begun. Packy had started out frightened, had wet his pants even, but during the bus ride he had mercifully become numb to the danger. He felt very far away inside his own head as the soldiers unloaded everyone from the bus.

There were perhaps a dozen prisoners altogether; most of the others were men in their twenties. Everyone was made to line up against the side of the bus.

"One guy was sick; I don't know whether it was fright or something else," Packy said. "But he leaned back against the bus, and two soldiers grabbed him by the arms and took him away."

Other soldiers moved about in formation on the opposite side of the field, and two miniature whippet tanks of the type the people called *tanquetas* were grumbling around the perimeter without purpose or direction, like ungainly water creatures that had lost their way to the sea. The entire field was grown over with golden hay. The hay waved and hissed in a mild breeze, calling to mind the open pastures around the village of Packy's *abuela*.

"You! Put your hand down," a soldier shouted. Packy realized he was touching the heart-shaped scar he had gotten when the black bull had chased him and he had fallen. He lowered his hand.

Another officer came, a captain; Packy remembered him as being tall and blond, but could recall little else about him. The captain asked about the four young musicians first; the harelipped lieutenant saluted and told him how it was that they happened to be arrested. The captain then ordered the other men taken away to some other part of the field. He asked a few questions of the boys in a voice that was almost kind, and afterward he took a folding knife from his pocket and handed it to one of the privates and instructed him to use it to give haircuts to Packy and the drummer and the singer and the bass player. The knife sawing through Packy's hair made a sound like that of a horse cropping dried grass.

Following the haircut, the captain and two soldiers marched Packy and the other band members partway across the golden field. They were made to lie down in the golden hay; the standing hay was warm and it seemed to feel quite pleasant to stretch out on it, although that might have been a hallucination of Packy's memory. The captain signaled one of the *tanquetas*: The machine pivoted and clattered toward them, treads crushing down the proud grass and pressing it into the earth. It came to a stop when the upward curve of one tread was only inches from Packy's head. The tank rumbled and gave off heat like an iron stove; Packy closed his eyes.

The untalented drummer lay on the other side of Packy, farther from danger, but he was crying softly into the grass. Packy was not crying or feeling much of anything; he was dreaming a pleasant waking dream in which he wandered through an orchard with his grandmother's yellow-eyed bitch at his heels.

The captain started speaking, saying that they were bad boys and asking if there was any reason that he shouldn't order the tank to roll over them and press them into *empanadas*. The bass player, lying beyond the singer, who lay next to the drummer, said, "My mother." He said it calmly, then he said it again, and after a moment again and again and again, calmly still, but with more frequency. He kept at it, saying, *"Mi mamá, mi mamá, mi mamá,"* until a soldier went to him and prodded him gently in the ribs with the toe of his boot. Then he stopped.

In the end the captain let them go. He told them that they had been warned and that they were now to stay out of trouble. Then he pointed them in the direction of the road and told them to start walking back to the city.

Packy's memory gave out almost completely after that. He could recall almost nothing of the following three days; he remembered only that he got a bottle of *pisco* from somewhere and that he started walking south, hitchhiking and hiding from military traffic during the day, and hiding from all traffic at night. He remembered neither his arrival at his grandmother's empty house in the mountains nor what he did in the house for the entire day he spent there before his father came to get him. He remembered only coming back from somewhere dark, coming back slowly after his father had come and made him tea and fixed him something to eat, and he remembered telling his father that he had been looking for his grandmother's blue dog. The dog was the only thing he would talk about until they were back in Santiago.

When he was finished with the story, Packy sat blinking at the wall. He still trembled slightly from the lines of *perico*, and after a minute he moved his jaw from side to side, grinding his teeth loudly enough for me to hear. Finally he gave me a sharp look.

"So," he said. "The Prowlers are here in three weeks. Are you with us or not?" I shrugged.

"I don't know yet. I haven't been able to decide if I'll have the time."

"*Coño de la madre, chico.* But you've had more than enough time. I don't think you realize how important this is."

"Hey, I'm tired. Could you ask me later?"

"I need to know now, *pana.* I already told that whore of a promoter that I had two other people." I showed him the palms of my hands. Exhaustion endowed me with the selfishness I should have had much earlier in the evening.

"Packy. Ask me later."

During the time Orchid stayed with me, I achieved something akin to true happiness for the first time since the days when my friend Tony would tell me stories through the picket fence in the backyard of my grandmother's house. Orchid and I dined by candlelight in the evenings; we did dishes together and made love while tropical frogs sang to us from their sanctuary on the other side of Camión's white wall. We awoke together to the angry growl of Adolfo's car engine beneath the bedroom window; my jovial neighbor was getting up earlier than ever these days, and he was warming his car, revving it, each day for about twice as long as before. Adolfo was the neighborhood lion, roaring at dawn and pissing on rocks and bushes because an interloper was scoring in his territory.

Contentment at home gave my work a flavor, a spice, that it had lacked before. I began to enjoy the rounds of meetings and press conferences; I wrote what I thought were brilliant reports on the oil minister's calm demeanor beneath hot TV lights as he explained yet another slip in the price of crude, a slip that would cost millions. I wrote incisive, cynical pieces on the hollowness of claims by the president and the Central Bank that all was well, that the mighty bolivar would never lose its value, and that the Good Life was a permanent condition. Venezuelans continued buying cars and stereos and imported apples at a dollar each; continued buying Bolivian cocaine and Scotch whiskey and flying to Miami for weekends. But the city of Caracas was even then vibrating with the realization that a wave of bad times was on the horizon, that Saudi Venezuela was going be knocked back into reality, back into Latin America. I sent up a feature in which I compared the atmosphere to that in the United States of aibi just before the crash.

113

The story ran on three continents, and New York telexed a rare compliment.

I even enjoyed writing about Los Cowboys and their continuing string of bank robberies; my previous predominant feelings of fear and dread concerning the urban guerrillas had been changed to excitement by the alchemy of love.

Orchid gave me a confidence that I had not had before. I bought her some evening gowns, spending more than I could afford, and took her to a couple of receptions at foreign consulates, receptions that I had avoided before because I did not know anybody and because I was afraid of being snubbed. She and I drank fine whiskey with writers and poets and diplomats from all over the world. To my pleasant surprise, Orchid knew how to act; she was witty and poised, and not too forward. She smiled, and did not eat or drink too much, or laugh too loudly. Her mother, who had been a teacher, had taught her those manners, she told me during one of her rare and fleeting moments of self-revelation.

During a party at the Peruvian consulate for a prominent writer of that nation, she even sang a song. She had told the writer's wife that she was familiar with a certain Peruvian folk song that came up in conversation. The writer's wife suggested she sing it, and although I did not think it was a good idea—tried to stop her, in fact—she defied me and went ahead with it anyway. And she was beautiful; they bathed her in applause, those wealthy and well-dressed people. I was nearly lifted off my feet with pride that night.

Things were not perfect, however. Orchid insisted on talking to the neighbors, whose contamination I had wanted her to avoid. She would go over and sit with Lola, who had taken a liking to her, and she would return home hours later smelling of Polar and filled with information about the filthy doings of everyone along our cul-de-sac. And sometimes when I got home at night, I would find her on the street, standing close to Adolfo, talking to him. She would smile at me and continue her conversation; Adolfo would not even glance in my direction.

One afternoon I was struck by a headache during work. I took a taxi home, carrying with me the pleasant anticipation of a neck rub from Orchid, and when I arrived, she was not there. I forgot my headache then; I went out looking for her at every store within easy walking distance, but she was not to be found. I was so desperate, I even visited Lola. Lola was full of smirks and giggles but no answers.

Orchid finally showed up about two hours later. Falling into the tired role of jealous husband, I demanded to know where she had been. She wouldn't tell me. I yelled, calling her an ungrateful bitch. She yelled back with the cliché about me not owning her. Doors were slammed. Neighbors gathered in the street below our windows. In the end, of course, it was I who apologized.

A day or so after this argument took place, Mickey called me at the office and asked if I would meet him for dinner at a restaurant in La Candelaria later that afternoon. He sounded extremely depressed, and I agreed immediately.

After I hung up, however, I realized I had no money; payday had come and gone the day before, and I had neglected to cash my check. I scanned the incoming wire to see if there were any urgent messages, and I checked the official government wire copy for breaking stories of importance. All was quiet on the southern front. I took my check and headed out to the agency's bank, which stood on the Avenida Urdaneta, about a quarter-mile east of the presidential palace.

Outside the front door of *La Nación* I was nearly run down by the strange motorcycle messenger that one of the afternoon papers sent to the agency each day to collect a selection of sports photos. The paper was too poor to afford its own photo machine and a full subscription.

"*Perdón*," said the *motorizado*, as he put down the kickstand on his machine. He was at least six-four; he always looked extremely awkward riding a scooter that seemed made for a child. He had a face that appeared to have been hammered out of dark granite and left unfinished.

Amedio saw the near miss from behind the counter of his coffee shop, and he came out on the sidewalk to upbraid the *motorizado*. Amedio twisted his apron in his huge red hands as he spoke.

"*¡Coño!*" he shouted as I tried to signal him that I was all right, that he didn't need to say anything. "What do you think you're doing, you *criminal*? You wouldn't drive that way if there was a police force in this town!"

The *motorizado* slowly drew his head out of his helmet and fixed Amedio with a brief, uncomprehending stare. Then he turned to me and said, "Señor, is there someone in the office to give me pictures?"

"There is," I said. "Carlos will give them to you. But you should drive a little more carefully, you know."

He gave me granite eyes until I turned away and headed up the street.

Motorizados were a class unto themselves. As a group they were arrogant and mannerless. They zoomed in and out of traffic, swerving dangerously close to pedestrians, and they parked everywhere. Often they formed packs and went down the road in a slow-moving block that no car could penetrate. Then there was the noise; nothing is quite so maddening as the sustained monotone shriek of straining Suzuki engines passing below your window all day long. So many *motorizados* acted like hooligans that you couldn't keep your heart from giving a little leap when you saw seven or eight of them standing around on a street corner, frantically searching their pockets for important papers while a couple of Metropolitanos with Brazilian machine pistols clasped in one hand pawed through the luggage boxes of their machines with the other.

On the other hand, you occasionally had to feel sorry for them when you saw the Metropolitanos giving them a hard time. Because *motorizados* were almost universally disliked and held in low esteem, and because they were mostly poor, working-class boys from the teeming hills of Petare, the cops were always pulling them over to ask for papers, to search them for drugs and weapons, and to show the citizens of Caracas that they were doing their job.

It seemed to be my day for run-ins with motorcycles. As I was crossing the Avenida Baralt, two cops on a bike shot past and brushed me. I could have sworn that the Metropolitano riding on the back turned his foot on the peg a little just so he could run the toe of his boot along the leg of the gringo's dress pants.

And when I had almost reached the Plaza Bolívar, three *motorizados*, messengers from different stores in Prados del Este, started a race. They came around a corner by the Congress, all of them with helmeted heads low to the handlebars, and they throttled up, their machines screaming, bouncing over the cobblestones of the little side street, and flew at me three abreast. I caught my breath and did a twist like a bullfighter, arms in the air, and closed my eyes. I was sure they would hit me.

But they got around me somehow. I felt hot exhaust on my legs and heard the receding scream of their Japanese engines, and I opened my eyes. I stood in shock until a car horn from close behind me brought me around. I turned and saw an angry matron in a Volkswagen making emphatic gestures for me to step out of the road.

Cursing the mothers of all *motorizados*, I entered the Plaza Bolívar in search of a little tranquility before I finished my trip to the bank. The Liberator himself looked down upon the plaza from his pedestal and his rearing horse. His feet were planted firmly in the stirrups, pigeons sitting on his shoulders like living epaulets, and his hat was off to his admiring public, or perhaps to one of the many lovers he had known during the romantic days when he struck at the Spaniards up and down the cordillera, traveling from the snowfields to the jungle and then back to the snowfields.

"Buenas tardes, Don Simón," I found myself whispering.

Bolívar had been born in a house that stood near the plaza. The plaza was the emotional heart of Caracas; of all of Venezuela itself, in fact. The Venezuelans even claimed that it was the spiritual center of all Latin America, a notion in which some of the other nations humored them.

I always felt that Bolívar had to be lonely up there all by himself. He had been a small man; as Orchid once said, the leather boots on display at his natal home were almost child-sized. But he was deified to such an extent that it seemed as if the Venezuelans had elevated him beyond all warmth of the human race. Now he hovered coldly above Caracas, worshiped with a passion reserved for Christ in other Catholic countries and with a frenzy that would be unthinkable in connection with Washington, or even Gandhi. During the daylight, if you ran past this statue or carried a package by it, you risked arrest for lack of respect for the Liberator.

Mickey's theory, during the days when he thought about other things besides Beatrix and *perico*, was that the deification was the result of Venezuelan guilt. After independence was won from Spain, Bolívar had wanted Venezuela, Colombia, and Ecuador to remain one country under the name of La Gran Colombia. But other Venezuelan leaders did not want to remain forever in the shadow of other nations, and they exiled Bolívar; they sent him to Colombia to die. Later, after he was safely dead, the Venezuelans brought back his bones and had a statue built for him and began the cult of Bolívar.

At night the plaza held a certain shadow-shrouded mystery. On one or two drunken evenings I could have sworn I heard a whispering of phantoms around the base of the statue and among the trees. More than once I was startled by a spectral sloth crossing my path in the lonely nighttime plaza; the solitary sloths, looking like fetal bears, hid in the trees during the day.

But there was little mystery by daylight. Old Venezuelan men sat on folding chairs and talked. The little gentlemen were always dressed well; they were the last generation to follow the old custom of not visiting the Liberator in anything but the finest clothing. The plaza was also full of squealing children who first fed, and then stampeded, the fluttering clouds of pigeons. There were milling families of ice-cream eaters, and just outside the borders of the plaza, there were vendors who sold snacks and newspapers. When the sun was shining, the park was always patrolled by one or two unsmiling government officials in safari suits whose job it was to halt, and sometimes to punish, any disrespect toward the statue. I had seen one of them actually hit a young man in the stomach for continuing to walk across the plaza one morning during the playing of the national anthem.

After the close call with the motorcycles, I sat for a minute on a concrete bench to catch my breath and to scan the trees for sleeping sloths. Then I stood and headed up toward Avenida Urdaneta.

The bank stood on the other side of the wide, busy avenue, and as I was crossing, I heard the whine of a motorcycle coming from the direction of the presidential palace. I turned my head to look for it, but there was not a motorcycle to be seen. I got across the street and started up the stairs toward the big tinted windows of the bank and the air-conditioned coolness they promised; broad, steep stairs on three sides rose from street level to the level of the bank lobby. At the top of the stairs stood a fat uniformed bank guard who wore a single-shot shotgun slung so that it pointed forward and turned when he did. As I went up the steps, he twisted his body to watch me, and the yawning barrel of the gun tracked me the entire way. The guard kept his hands clasped behind his back.

Just as I was about to pull open the door of the bank, I heard another motorcycle. This one was in an alley someplace, because the sound was diffuse and seemed to come from all directions at once. I turned to hunt for it, faintly hoping to see a cop pulling over one of the racers who had nearly run me down. But I saw nothing.

I opened the heavy door and headed across the marble floor between thick marble columns toward the tellers. My transaction took but a minute. I cashed the paycheck and stuffed both my front pockets with wads of coffee-colored hundred-bolivar notes, the notes that are called *tablas*, or "slabs." I glanced nervously around me while I did this; if you were filthy, you always had to be on the lookout for some *malandro* who would stick a knife through the space between two buttons on your shirt and ask you if you wanted your blood pressure lowered. There seemed to be no one dangerous as I walked back toward the door. Just a huge old woman with legs like tree trunks who was towing a small boy in overalls who was towing a red helium balloon. Behind them was a businessman, his head down, sorting through a handful of envelopes, and behind him a thin young man who was tugging a ski mask over his head. It didn't dawn on me until I was past him what he had actually been doing, and I turned to glance at him over my shoulder, feeling no fear yet, only puzzlement. He was wearing the ski mask now and he went up and began talking to the lone armed guard inside the bank, a *criollo* who wore a .38 on his hip like a potbellied cowboy.

Then I was jolted at the shoulder; I half-expected it to be a motorcycle striking me from behind. But it was a man who had struck me and then stepped around me as if I were an inanimate thing, a tree perhaps. He was wearing a black wool ski helmet. His partner and the armed guard turned and headed toward the locked back doors of the bank; the guard's face was wry with distress, but no one else had noticed yet. The man who had bumped me strolled up to the closed-off section of the bank beyond the tellers' windows, where the lower-level bank officers worked. He placed his hand on the thick wooden wall that separated this section from the lobby and then, lightly as a cat, he kicked his heels into the air and over the partition. I heard a muted scream then and I burst out the front door.

The idiot guard outside was still standing on the uppermost step, making sucking noises at a woman passing in the street, the barrel of his shotgun pointing at people walking below. I ran down onto a step just below him, stuttering at him about the robbery in progress. He just looked at me with a seemingly permanent leer frozen on his face while I screamed *robo* and *atraco* at him. He only began to move after I called him a name. He unslung his shotgun then and cracked the breech and slowly began to dig a shell out of his pocket. I don't know if he had finally figured out what I was talking about or if he was planning to shoot me for insulting him.

In any case he never got the chance to fire that shell. There was a collective roar that seemed to come from a hundred motorcycles, an inferno of motorcycles, and then a dozen Cowboys riding little knobby-tired bikes came out along the side streets that ran on either side of the bank building. They all wore street clothes and ski helmets and little knapsacks on their backs that made them look like schoolchildren from some cooler climate.

While the guard and I looked on like a pair of statues, they simultaneously slung the knapsacks forward, opened them, and began drawing out weapons. Most of the Cowboys drew out pistols; there was a mixture of revolvers and automatics. But two of them had Brazilian guns just like the police carried. There was a Brazilian gunner on either side of the bank building.

Then the scream of sirens began to reach us from all directions; it was noon, and the streets were full, and I knew the law would have a hard time making it to the bank through the traffic. The Cowboys seemed to know this as well, and they were almost leisurely in their movements. The guard standing on the steps with me awakened now; it seemed to be the sirens rather than the sight of armed men that drew him from his trance of amazement, and with slothlike languor he finished pulling the red twelve-gauge shell from his pocket and moved it toward the gaping breech of his weapon. It was as if he thought that by moving slowly, he could avoid attracting the attention of the Cowboys.

I blinked, and even though it was a blindingly sunlit day with hardly a cloud hanging, a shadow fell across the face and body of

120

the guard. I took a step down from him, away from him, moving slowly in the hopes of avoiding attention myself now.

The Cowboys raised their weapons, and I winced, not sure whether any of them were pointed at me.

"*Pana,*" said a slender Cowboy with a black revolver. I looked at him and saw gray eyes peering out through the narrow slit in the ski mask. The eyes were focused on the guard. "Don't be an idiot."

I looked up at the guard, and the shadow was still on him. "*Pana,*" I whispered, echoing the words of the Cowboy, "don't be an idiot."

But he did not even glance at me.

Beneath the inexplicable shadow on the guard's face, I saw an unrelenting, fatal pride surfacing. There was a turmoil of shifting facial muscles; within a second or two I saw fear, anger, shame, and many other things I couldn't identify appear briefly and then submerge, then his features settled into a mask of calmness and acceptance, giving him the appearance of dignity for perhaps the first time in his life. I took another step down from him.

The guard faced the man who had spoken to him and finished sliding in the shell. Then he snapped the breech shut. The Cowboy nodded slightly; I sensed a current of intimacy between them as they stood on those steps in the hot sun that was as strong as the intimacy between lovers under cover of darkness. There was that nod, then flame spat from the dark bore of the revolver and there was a clap of thunder and the guard was toppling off his step, toppling toward me.

The heavy guard hit me like a domino falling. He knocked me over and we rode down several steps together before we stopped in a tangle. The loaded shotgun went past me like a sled down an icy hill.

In death the guard was heavy and soft and hot, his body still damp with sweat. I expected to be covered with his blood; I was prepared to feel blood and then to begin screaming as loudly as I could. Blood would have been too much to take and it would have broken through my comfortable state of shock. But there was no blood; it was there somewhere, running, but it did not touch me, and I remained quiet and almost calm.

Then motorcycle engines screamed, drowning out all other

sounds but the approaching sounds of sirens, and the Cowboys were climbing the steps with their machines. The motorcycles bounced on the concrete steps, jarring their riders.

When they had all gone up, I pulled myself away from the sprawling limbs of the guard and began crawling, crablike, for the bottom of the steps. When I reached the last step, I rolled myself across the sidewalk and into the gutter between the curb and an unmoving pickup truck, and there I stayed.

I looked up. All of the Cowboys had dismounted; two of them had entered the bank, and the rest took up defensive positions behind the heavy cement columns that supported the roof of the building. It was then that I finally saw the blood of the guard. The blood was moving slowly, creeping out from under him like a shapeless, living thing, darkening the concrete steps.

Out on the street, traffic had come to a standstill as people stopped their cars to get out and watch the robbery or to dive beneath the seats. From out of the frozen river of traffic, two white police motorcycles emerged onto the sidewalk on the opposite side of the street about fifty yards east of the bank and roared along until they were directly across from me. There were two men on each motorcycle, the passenger on each of the machines carrying a Brazilian machine gun, and the machine-gunners began firing even before they dismounted. They continued to fire as they sought cover behind stalled automobiles. They fired in long, un-disciplined bursts that emptied the clips in seconds.

Between the prolonged stutter of machine pistols, there came the popping of revolvers and semiautomatics. I looked up to the top of the bank steps and saw a bright winking of muzzle flashes so prodigious they looked like fireworks; I covered my head with my arms.

Out in the street I heard the repeated shattering of car windows punctuated by human screams. The noise itself now seemed like enough to flay a person; when the big bank windows finally exploded inward with a sound like the end of the world, I began to rock myself back and forth in the gutter, irrationally trying to work myself deeper into the pavement. A numbness had spread all through me; I had scarcely a thought but the desire to somehow dig myself a hole through the concrete. A scrap of an old hymn I must have heard somewhere as a child kept running over and over through my mind:

Father, lead me day by day
Even in thy stormy way . . .

After a minute, the firing from the Metropolitanos' side of the street diminished. Fire kept coming from the top of the steps, but then one by one each motorcycle roared to life for a second before the sound of it quickly faded; they were taking them inside the bank. Finally the only firing came in short bursts from a single Brazilian gun sheltered behind a stone column in front of the bank.

Then I heard a motorcycle bouncing down the steps, and I looked up to see a Cowboy coming at me, revolver aimed at my face. Time froze. I did not blink, and my head held no thought; my consciousness was taken up completely with the image of the man in the ski mask who was aiming a weapon at me. He was a thin man, and when he got closer, I saw that he had gray eyes; he was the same man who had shot the guard. He kept that gun trained on me, and when he reached the bottom of the steps, he set his foot on the curb next to my head.

"Angel," he said. Somehow it did not surprise me that he knew who I was.

"Mosca," I said, my throat nearly too dry to talk.

The Cowboy nodded. Then he pulled back the hammer of his pistol. I squeezed my eyes shut. Hot colors exploded behind my eyelids.

But someone shouted at him; it must have been the Brazilian gunner who had stayed behind to cover him. The man shouted again, and then again, an edge of desperate rage to his voice, and I heard Mosca gently release the deadly hammer. He throttled up on his bike; exhaust scorched my face, and then he was gone. I opened my eyes in time to see the Brazilian gunner sling his weapon, kick his bike to life, and follow Mosca around the side of the building.

It was over then. The other bikers escaped out the back door of the bank, and I heard the receding whine of motorcycles climbing toward the ridge of the Ávila, as well as sobbing and cursing out in the street.

The police finally arrived in force to seal off the bank and take up positions in the street. Rescue vehicles came, and workers spread white sheets over the bank guard and another man, a civilian who had been accidentally shot to death by the motorcycle policemen as he crept between the jammed cars, trying to escape. No one else had been killed, although several people in cars had been wounded by flying glass. The bleeding injured were helped into rescue vehicles and taken away.

My watch drifted into my field of vision; the whole robbery, from the time I had gotten my money to the finish of it, had only swallowed ten minutes. After checking to make sure the watch was still working, I began to feel extremely disoriented.

While the cops were still busy with other things, I wandered past a pair of Metropolitanos and into the bank, where a PTJ official was interviewing several people, including the bank president. I was there long enough to overhear them saying that about thirty thousand dollars in Venezuelan and American currency had been taken. Then two or three more PeTeJota officials showed up and began shooting suspicious glances at me, and I started to understand the jeopardy I was placing myself in by stumbling around inside the bank like that. I left to avoid being questioned and possibly detained.

Outside, traffic was beginning to move again, horns blowing and glass crunching beneath tires, and a pack of reporters had gathered at the bottom of the steps; they were trying to talk their way past a combined line of Metropolitanos and PeTeJota foot soldiers. None of the reporters noticed me except for Sanabria. He had watched me come out, and instead of howling in outrage as some of the others would have done, he slipped quietly away from the group and intercepted me at the bottom of the steps.

"*Coño*, look at you," he whispered. "You've been rolling in the street. Were you here during everything?" He placed a hand on my arm to detain me; I let him keep it there.

I opened my mouth to tell him something, but nothing came out save for a dry squeak. Finally there it was. Shell shock. I nodded.

"And you saw inside?"

"Yes," I said, my voice returning to me a little now.

"Well, you're going to give me something, aren't you?" His eyes brimmed with a greedy, not-to-be-put-off quality that seemed almost obscene after what I had been through.

"Later," I told him. Then I shook his hand off and wobbled around him and into the street.

124

"I'll come by your office," he shouted from behind me. I lifted a hand to let him know it would be all right.

Across the street, right at the spot where the four Metropolitanos had conducted their part of the battle, a black Buick drew up to the curb. The passenger door opened, and Nelson Lugo Alvarado, with sunglasses wrapped around his face, stepped out onto the pavement. I cut back quickly to cross behind the car, holding my breath and hoping he would not spot me. I had just entered one of the brick pedestrian walkways that led down to the Plaza Bolívar when he called.

"Angel," he said.

I kept moving as if I hadn't heard, my heart climbing inside me.

"Angel, come back here."

Luckily there was a large throng standing on the walkway watching the goings-on at the bank, and I was able to plunge into it and lose myself.

By the time I got back to the office, I was floating, caught up in a surprising euphoria. For a few minutes I even felt like laughing, but I was afraid to give in to the laughter, because it seemed to be the kind of thing that could get out of control. Instead I went into the bathroom and splashed water on my face with trembling hands, and then I sat down at the telex and punched out a quick, four-paragraph lead about the robbery, as well as a message telling New York that more was coming up. Then I sat down at the typewriter to commit the full story to paper.

Sanabria came up about an hour later, and we talked for a time. I was still shaking, but I was able to speak in sentences. He went away with a promise to take me to dinner after we had both finished our work.

We ate dinner in a Mexican place close by. It was a good place when you had company, and we drank several beers. Before we were finished, he had me laughing with a good, controlled, healing laughter, and I left for home quite late. I had forgotten all about my date with Mickey.

As soon as I reached the top of the hill above my little cul-de-sac, I saw the fire. The neighbors had built a bonfire in front of the white gate in the steel wall, so that if anyone had wanted to leave Camión's property through that gate, they would not have been

125

able to do so. Someone was drumming loudly and frantically, drumming probably on a hollow log to create the bewitching, disquieting, African rhythm that the fisherfolk in isolated villages on the hot shore to the west of Caracas loved to dance to. The drumming was as much a nighttime sound as the trilling of crickets, the keening of a woman's passion, or the cries of a child in the throes of a nightmare.

Human figures danced before the fire, silhouetted against the flames. I saw a female figure dance briefly by; it was hard to tell for sure, but she appeared to be naked. I asked God not to let it be Orchid.

The bonfire and the dancing had the appearance of some kind of *brujería*, some witchcraft; it occurred to me that Adolfo and Lola were conducting a ritual to exorcise Packy and me from our house and their neighborhood.

Hesitantly, with sweat springing out all over and soaking my already soiled clothes, I started down. It was a sultry night as it was, and from a surprising distance, I began to feel the heat of the fire; it washed over me in sickening waves. The sound of the drum reverberated uncomfortably inside my ribcage, making me feel hollow inside. As I drew closer, I began to recognize faces; I saw Adolfo's face, glowing red with reflected flame, and I saw the faces of several of the men he played dominos with. They were laughing faces, faces that flashed teeth and gold or else exposed the gaping void where teeth should have been. Adolfo was holding a bottle of *caña* in his hand. The clear cane liquor absorbed the color of the fire so that it seemed to glow from within. Adolfo tilted his head back; for a moment he looked as though he were about to bay at the dark sky, and then he lifted his bottle and began to pour *caña* into the shapeless dark wound of his mouth. *Caña* filled his mouth and then ran out of it and down the sides of his face, darkening the light-colored material of his T-shirt. Adolfo threw his head forward, grimaced, coughed, and burst into laughter. Then he began staggering in a tight circle near the fire.

I was relieved to discover that the woman I had seen from farther up the hill was Lola; Orchid was not in sight. Lola was dancing before the fire with her eyes squeezed tightly shut. She swayed through the little crowd of men with her arms raised, hands buried in her dark hair. She was barefoot, wearing a tight pair of shorts and nothing over her breasts. Lola was the high priestess of the festivities; she moved from man to man with little mincing steps, making her small breasts jiggle in time with the frenzied drumming, and each man in turn fondled her briefly, without passion, almost ceremoniously, and then guided her toward the next.

The drumming itself came from a long, dried, hollow log that had been placed across a makeshift stand right in front of my house. I had not seen it from farther up the hill because my house blocked the view. There were two drummers: a young, sweating black man from the neighborhood and a young, sweating *criollo* I had never seen before. Both of them were stripped to the waist. They were sitting behind the drum, working it with heavy sticks. So fierce was their concentration that they never looked up.

Near the wrought-iron front steps of my house stood Adolfo's two little boys and my ex-dog, Max. The boys' eyes were wide, reflecting the flames, and they stood together, their shoulders touching. The younger boy look frightened; the face of the older boy contained a little fright as well, but also hunger.

Max finally spotted me, and he scrambled forward, his head held low, black lips drawn back in a snarl. My fear and weariness gave way to anger then. I kicked at Max, swearing at him in English. But instead of backing off the way he usually did, he advanced on me, then suddenly dove low and snapped at my shin. He almost got me; I jumped away just in time. I heard laughter and I looked up and saw that Adolfo's fat little boys were watching me rather than the dance now. In excited voices that I could barely hear over the thunder of the big drum, they encouraged Max to attack me again.

I backed away, planning to escape around the corner of my house, since Max was cutting me off from the stairs. But he pursued me, whining eagerly, and was readying himself for another lunge, when suddenly a small rock streaked in from somewhere, fast as a bullet, and ricocheted off his head. He yelped, whipped his head back and forth in pain and confusion, and then slunk away into the shadows.

It was then that little Séptimo stepped out from the shadows beneath my stairs. I had no idea how long he had been crouched there, watching the flaming spectacle beneath the white wall and observing my battle with Max.

Séptimo smiled brightly at me and gave me the American "okay" sign. He moved toward me, seemingly eager to speak. But Adolfo's two boys had spotted him, too, had seen what he had done to their dog. They wheeled away from the stairs and advanced on him with bunched fists.

The smile closed down abruptly on little Séptimo's face. His grubby hand went to his pocket, and then he was holding another stone. He cocked the hand with the stone and glared steadily at the fat little boys until they turned and shuffled back to their positions by my stairs.

I would have thanked Séptimo, except that the drumming slowed raggedly to a halt, and then all at once the dancing stopped and everyone around the bonfire was looking at me. They had discovered me at last. Adolfo was the first to speak.

"¡Extranjero!" he said, his face full of drunken glee. He tried to move toward me, but his legs carried him two steps to the side for every step forward he took. Finally he gave up and stood pointing at me, his body weaving in a tight circle.

"¡Extranjero!" said Lola. She opened her eyes and walked in my direction, her breasts riding up and down. "Let's screw. I want to see how a gringo screws." She used the verb *tirar*, which means to shoot, or throw, an expression that always made me imagine a vicious, bucking ride rather than the gentler throes of lovemaking. Then her body turned suddenly liquid; she fainted and melted to the ground in a puddle of overheated flesh.

"¡Extranjero!" barked the drummers between their raw gasps for breath. "¡Extranjero!" said the rest of the people around the fire. "¡Extranjero! ¡Extranjero!" they all said, hissing the word, making it sound like a curse, making my flesh crawl. I saw gritted teeth and flashing eyes.

Adolfo took another abortive step in my direction. "¡Extranjero!" he said. "You are all finished. Your run of luck is at an end!" He made a chopping motion across his throat with one finger. His lacquered fingernails, especially the long thumbnail, gleamed wickedly in the firelight. "The police are aware of your criminal activities."

He was pompous with alcohol, slurring his words. I was not about to put up with him. I turned to climb my stairs; it was only then that I saw that the door to my house was wide open and that no lights were on inside.

I ran up and into the darkened house, tripping over an out-of-place chair near the doorway. I turned on the light near the doorway and almost shouted aloud at the shambles I found. Someone had trashed my house with great thoroughness. The stuffing from the couch lay spread across the floor; mixed in with it were papers that included my tax records and shredded bits of Packy's sheet music. The television was smashed and overturned, and when I went into the kitchen, I saw dishes broken against the linoleum and Packy's ivory dominos scattered about like broken teeth.

"Orchid!" I screamed. But there was no answer.

In my bedroom and in Packy's bedroom it was apparent that someone had taken something long and sharp, something like a bayonet, maybe, and slashed the beds. There were clothes all over; some of my white shirts bore the imprints of sooty feet. In the bathroom the porcelain cover to the toilet tank lay cracked in several pieces. The metal rod that held the toilet float had been bent so that the float stuck out of the tank, pointing toward the ceiling. A jagged round hole had been hacked into the hollow float.

Orchid was nowhere to be found.

I felt helpless, and so tired I wanted to cry. Instead I went out onto the top of the stairs and confronted the smiling faces of my neighbors. "Where's Orchid, and who the hell did this?"

"*¡Policía!*" came the chorus.

"*¡Policía!*" shouted Adolfo, who was frozen in the spot where I had left him standing. Then he started laughing. He laughed so hard he fell to his knees and began to vomit into the street.

"Police?" I said. Like a sleepwalker, I descended to the bottom of the stairs. "What police? PeTeJotas?"

"PeTeJotas!" came the chorus. There was laughter.

I felt a tug on my pants leg and I looked down. Little Séptimo was there, and he looked grave. He was shaking his head. "Not PeTeJotas, Jimmy," he said. "Disip."

"Disip?"

"They took Packy away. There was a man, *un negro*, who looked like . . ." He made a V of his hands with the open part toward him, and brought the hands up until they covered his face. I understood then. Sickness and fear moved in me.

"They took Packy? But where's Orchid?"

"She ran. She was helping Adolfo wash his car, and when the police came, she ran away." I stood glaring at the sinister assembly

129

in front of the white wall as I caught my breath. I was thankful that at least Orchid had escaped.

After a minute I made up my mind what I was going to do.

"Good boy, Séptimo," I said. I fished a cinco from my pocket and pressed it into his hand. He held the coin as if he were not quite sure what it was, and he looked from it to me. He was not smiling.

"When Orchid comes back, tell her I'll be home later."

I touched Séptimo on the top of the head and headed up the street. I did not find a taxi until I had walked all the way down the hill to the main avenue.

CHAPTER 5

I had the taxi driver take me to the Disip offices. There was a small park across the street from the offices, and when he dropped me off, it was about one in the morning; crickets were singing out in the park, and beneath the streetlights in the children's play area I could see a lady derelict rocking herself to sleep on the swing set. The swing made a forlorn creaking sound. I was reminded of Orchid, and I shivered in the chill, damp air of early morning.

The first floor of the blocklike Disip headquarters was well lighted, but the windows in the floors above it were all dark except for one on the uppermost level that I knew was the window from which Nelson Lugo Alvarado looked out over Caracas. That window was brightly lit, and as I stared up at it, I saw the swift-moving shadow of a man pass across it and vanish.

A uniformed Disip officer sat behind bullet proof glass at the reception desk in the entrance hall; three or four plain clothes piranhas were cruising the lobby with cigarettes in their jaws.

"Angel?" said the cop behind the glass. He had his own cigarette, and he took a short drag off of it and spat a burst of smoke at me out the little hole that was there for him to talk through. "Yes, he said you would probably drop by." He smirked wordlessly for a moment, smug in his apparent conviction that it had been the force of Lugo Alvarado's superior will that had brought me here, rather than the fact that he was holding my friend hostage. He made me surrender my *cédula*, then he issued me a plastic clip-on visitor's badge.

My hands were sweating as I rode up in the elevator. I wiped them against my pants, which I had not changed since rolling in the gutter that afternoon, but they were damp again immediately.

Both Packy and Lugo Alvarado were sitting in Lugo Alvarado's office. Lugo Alvarado was behind his desk, facing in my direction, and Packy sat on the other side of the desk, with his back to me. Lugo Alvarado was smoking a cigarette; his eyes focused hotly on me as I stepped through his door, and he did not smile. A separate stream of smoke rose from in front of Packy, and for a moment it looked as though they were having a relaxed chat. But then I saw the *pucho* of marijuana and the *tubo* of cocaine sitting between them on the desk, and at that same moment Packy turned and gave me a sad, dark smile, showing me bloodied teeth. He held me with frightened eyes for a minute, then a fat fly came whining slowly through the still air of the office and tried to settle onto his swollen mouth. Packy waved the fly away and looked down.

"Jesus," I said, as fear and shame spread through me. I was sure all this had happened because of me. I felt weak and loose inside, but I tried to put on a show of outrage. "Jesus. Lugo Alvarado. *Gorila del coño*. You—"

He held up his hand to stop me. *"Por favor.* Don Jimmy," he said, narrowing arrogant eyes at me. "We found drugs in the house."

"That doesn't excuse—"

Lugo Alvarado sighed. "I wouldn't have hit him if he hadn't given me a lot of shit. But that was hours ago now, and it's practically forgotten. *Verdad*, Beowulf?"

Packy wiped blood off his mouth, then stared down into his reddened palm. He said nothing.

"Look," I said, raising my voice in a desperate bluff. I knew the *perico* could get Packy some jail time in Catia if Lugo Alvarado wanted to push it. "You found a *miseria* of some stuff that every kid in this city has, and you tore up my house. Now look, I've got friends in the press here. You—" I had planned a filibuster, but the fly was buzzing around my head now, and in the two seconds it took me to wave him off, the fatigue finally caught up with me and I forgot what I had been about to say. I was left sputtering.

Lugo Alvarado watched me patiently, smoking, his eyes half-lidded in a feline way and a little smile twitching on his lips. The bothersome fly zigzagged past his dark head and settled on the closed metal blinds over the window. Lugo Alvarado lifted a rolled-up newspaper from his desktop, and in a single fluid motion, he pivoted in his swivel chair and crashed his paper club into the blinds; Packy rose three inches from his seat at this sudden and unexpected violence. Lugo Alvarado lifted away the paper, and the crushed fly dropped to the floor, leaving a faint smudge on the white metal.

"We've got a problem," said Lugo Alvarado.

I nodded and said nothing.

"First, we have a group that's trying to destabilize our government. This group, after staying pretty much in the countryside and out of sight for two decades, has now come into the city and is causing trouble, making us look helpless at a time when we have other problems that need all our attention. Problems such as an economy that is turning to shit."

"I think I'll quote you," I said, trying to build myself the leverage of a little humor. But Lugo Alvarado only stared humorlessly at me, making me regret the words.

"Secondly," he continued, "we have some misguided people who are sympathetic to this group, mostly college students who have not lived under a dictatorship and do not appreciate this imperfect democracy, but also some foreigners who come from soft countries and have lost their appreciation for democracy..."

"¡Mira!" I said, becoming genuinely angry now. "I hope you're not talking about me. I'm a journalist, that's all I am; a foreigner, true, but I know more about democracy..."

Lugo Alvarado rose from his chair, his face twisted with anger, and he planted his knuckles on the desktop like a true gorilla. He began to shout at me over the top of Packy's head; Packy cringed and settled deeper into his seat.

"You take phone calls from them," he said. "They call you when they want to get a message across to the world." His face had taken on an enraged purple hue. Spittle flew from his lips and peppered my face, but I was furious myself and I only shoved my own face closer to his. "You just happen to be there when there's a bank robbery, and then you get into the bank afterward, I don't know how, and start wandering around..."

"It's true. I was cashing a check." I was shouting.

"Do you think I'm a cretin?"

"Sometimes I do, yes."

"You know something about all this, Angel, that you're not telling me."

"I don't know anything about it."

"I have ways of finding out."

"I don't know anything about it."

"I'm going to have you followed, night and day."

"*I don't know anything about it. I don't know anything about it. I don't know anything about it.*" I shouted this over and over until I was hoarse and shaking and could shout no more.

Lugo Alvarado settled back into his seat. He let his face rest in the palms of his hands for a moment, then he looked up at me. "It's been a tough day," he confided. There was a sudden tiredness in his ice-colored eyes.

I stood panting, my hands resting on the back of Packy's chair. "You're fucking right about that," I said. We were joined for a minute in a camaraderie of weariness.

Lugo Alvarado leaned back in his swivel chair and let his arms drift behind his head. "I'm still going to have you followed. You watch me."

"You go ahead. I don't have anything to hide."

He sat blinking at me and then, with an almost childish tone invading his voice, he said, "You would tell us, wouldn't you, Jimmy? If you knew anything?"

"I might. I'm a journalist. My telling you would depend on a lot of things."

"Listen," Lugo Alvarado said, leaning forward with sudden eagerness. "You're an American. What do you think of our democracy here?"

I was caught off guard by the question. I was also suspicious.

"Well, I don't know," I said, speaking with great caution. The phrase that I plugged into at least half the stories that I sent to New York sprang into my mind: *Venezuela comma Latin America's strongest democracy comma . . .*

"Did you know," said Lugo Alvarado, "that I hold a master's degree in political science from the Central University?"

"No. No, I didn't." The revelation of Lugo Alvarado's intellectual inclinations would have been interesting under other circumstances, but I was so tired now that I felt my body starting to sway.

"Yes!" Lugo Alvarado hissed eagerly. "I studied with leftists, some Marxists even. I know how they think. I know how you think."

"I really don't—"

"For instance, I bet that you look at our society sometimes, the way it runs, particularly the way the law enforcement system works, and you think to yourself that we are not a true democracy."

"Well . . ."

"Americans think like that, I know. But what you don't understand is that our democracy is very young. It is in peril, like a tiny spark that has to be nurtured. So many problems we have. The economy, these damn guerrillas, the fucking Colombians pouring over the border like it was their country, the fact that the entire population has not been educated yet . . . don't you see, a little crudeness, a little brutality if you will, is sometimes necessary to save the society as a whole when things have not stabilized yet . . ."

"I could argue this," I said. "I really could. But the thing is, I'm so damn tired now."

Lugo Alvarado thumped his fist on the desk, startling Packy out of his seat once again. He jabbed an index finger at me. "You don't understand this, of course, coming from as secure a place as you do. Such a fat and happy place. Consider the alternatives!" he commanded. "Angel, consider the alternatives to our democracy."

"It's the crudeness, the brutality I'd like to consider alternatives to," I said, rallying myself finally. "Here and in my own country." I nodded down at Packy. "And in his country, and in Cuba, and in every country where there is crudeness and brutality. It's all the same to me, no matter who does it."

Lugo Alvarado seemed not to hear me, however. "And then, of course, there's the military," he said. His voice was quiet now, reflective. "Does the military scare you, Angel? Because it certainly scares me. I can name quite a few countries where they've used a little annoyance like this Cowboy shit as an excuse to take over and break heads for years on end. It's a rich tradition in this part of the world. But they won't get the chance to do it here; not if I can prevent it, anyway."

"Yes?" I said. Lugo Alvarado had made a point; I now felt less sure of myself. Less smug. But I pushed on anyway. "And how are

135

you going to stop them? By doing all the head breaking yourself? What sense does that make?"

But Lugo Alvarado considered the conversation to be over. He rubbed his face with his hands and looked up at the ceiling. "You can go now," he said. "Take the fucking Chileno with you."

Packy rose slowly and stood looking down at Lugo Alvarado with a thoughtful expression on his face. He stood looking for a long minute, fingers touching the heart-shaped scar, and at first, when I tried to tow him toward the door, he jerked his arm away from me. Then, when he was finally satisfied, he came quietly. Lugo Alvarado did not glance at him the entire time.

As we were heading out the door, we heard a loud *sniff* behind us, and we both looked over our shoulders at Lugo Alvarado, official of internal security police and political philosopher. He had dumped Packy's half tube of *perico* onto a sheet of paper, and he sat hunched over it, a coffee stirrer screwed into his nose. He sucked up another line, and then he looked at us, a smile lifting one corner of his mouth.

"I've got another couple of hours to work tonight," he explained. Then he bent over the paper once again.

In the taxi on the way home I was overcome with guilt. "Packy," I said. *"Pana.* I think they dragged you in and beat up on you because of me."

Packy said nothing; he just stared out his window at the street.

"I'm sorry, *pana,* I really am."

He kept staring, saying nothing.

"I think they broke up the house because of me. See, I went to the bank today. . ." He turned and pressed a hand over my mouth. There was an intensity in his eyes that I could not read.

"Pana," he said. "Relax. It's all right." Then he pulled his hand away; his fingers left a feeling of dampness over my lips. "I'm just happy to be out of there." He turned and went back to staring out the window.

He did want to speak to me later on, however.

When we got home, Orchid was back, waiting amid the wreckage with a worried look on her face. Packy muttered a greeting to her and disappeared into his room, and I sat down on the couch and started to sob as quietly as I could. Orchid seated herself next to me and put her arm around me; after a moment she began to push her fingers through my hair. Soon she took me by the hand and guided me to my room.

I was lying in what was left of my bed, drifting along beneath a thin gray skin of sleep, when I sensed him standing in the darkness among the scattered and trampled clothing I had not bothered to take from the floor. He waited for me to open my eyes, then he turned and walked out into the living room. I rose as quietly as I could so as not to wake Orchid and I followed him.

"I just need to know one thing," he said when we both stood in the living room.

"Yes, *chamo*, what is it?" I answered as the guilt returned to my waking mind.

"Two weeks. The Prowlers are coming in a little over two weeks now. Will you *please* take the job so that Camión and I don't get fired?"

"Sure, yes, I'll do it," I said without even thinking. "Why not? It might even be . . ." But before I could finish, Packy had turned and walked out the front door of the apartment.

I slept badly the rest of the night. When I did manage to doze, I was chased through my dreams by shapeless dark things that had no name.

And it wasn't until morning that I remembered Mickey and Mickey's problems, which would undoubtedly make my promise to Packy a hard one to keep. And then I recalled, with a sour, sinking feeling, that I had forgotten my date with Mickey the day before. I tried calling his apartment, but the phone rang and rang and nobody answered.

Following the bank raid by the Cowboys in which I was almost killed, the president finally called out the *Guardia Nacional*. Two brown-faced *guardias* with white helmets and white spats and automatic rifles took positions in front of every bank in Caracas.

A couple of days after the posting of the *guardias*, the Disip, acting on a tip, surrounded a *rancho* in the hills of Petare and called out for the occupants to give themselves up. The occupants answered with automatic-weapons fire, and the Disip argued back by shooting in a tear-gas canister and, when that failed to work, a rocket-propelled grenade.

The grenade killed the four men in the *rancho*. Along with the bodies, the authorities found a machine pistol and several other weapons, three thousand dollars in cash, four *tubos* of cocaine, and the wreckages of six motorcycles. Two of the dead were identified as residents of Cumaná, an old city on the eastern coast. The other two were Caracas natives; one was a Central University student, and the other had been studying at the Simón Bolívar University. None of them was Enrique Mosca.

The government finally admitted then that it was fighting a tiny war with Marxist guerrillas. But it said it was winning the war; the successful battle in Petare had proved that.

I wondered whether one of the two university students killed had been the Croaker. I did not wonder for very long, however, because he called me the next day.

"Meester Angel," he said. "Baby, you just ain't seen notheen' yet." Then he hung up.

At this same time the government was in the midst of a series of public events that were supposed to culminate in the celebration of Bolívar's two-hundredth birthday the following year. On the Sunday after my close call at the bank and Packy's seizure by the Disip, a ceremony was scheduled to take place at the National Pantheon, the shrine where the Liberator's bones had been laid to rest. The usual speeches were planned, as well as a special treat: a performance by Venezuela's favorite daughter, Victoria de Córdoba, an opera singer who had made it big in Europe. Victoria was flying in from France specifically to sing the national anthem.

Orchid wanted to go; she had always wanted to hear Victoria, the Venezuelan coloratura, in person. This might be the last chance of her life, she said.

Despite the fact that I hated those things, I would gladly have taken a break from repairing my apartment to escort her there, but an unexpected crisis came up. The son of an American couple living in San Cristóbal, near the Colombian border, was kidnapped early that day by Colombian M-19 guerrillas. Even though it was a weekend and most of the usual sources of information were closed, either Mickey or I had to serve some office time to show New York we were making an effort. I said good-bye to Orchid, who was disappointed nearly to the point of tears, tried one last time to get Mickey on the telephone, and went out to hail a taxi.

Once I reached the office, I turned on the television to glean any recent details, then I called the local police in San Cristóbal; I also contacted the Disip and the PeTeJotas. Nobody could tell me much. After that, though I felt like a vulture, I called the home of the kidnapped child. Someone picked up; when I announced who I was and what I wanted, they disconnected without a word. The next time I called, the line was busy.

The TV news ran a short clip on the kidnapping, then they cut to the Pantheon, where the president was making his speech. Thousands of people were gathered in the circular concrete amphitheater outside the Church of the Holy Trinity. The outer circles of the throng contained ordinary people with brown *criollo* faces. The innermost ranks, nearest to the platform and podium where the president was making his speech, were filled with fairer faces and military uniforms. Colonels and generals and admirals were watching the president through dark glasses, their expressions stern. Among them stood a sprinkling of news photographers and plainclothes cops with wires coming out of their ears.

The speech droned on for a time, then the setting shifted abruptly to the airport, where local journalists were awaiting the arrival of Victoria de Córdoba, whose plane had apparently been delayed. The cameras showed me Sanabria's pockmarked face for an instant while the president continued to speak, unseen. There was also a shot of a waiting army helicopter that apparently would whisk Victoria to the Pantheon as soon as she arrived.

Back, suddenly, to the Pantheon, where the president, wearing a broad red, blue, and yellow sash, was finally winding it up. It was getting near time for the anthem. Then a panicky announcer broke in over the applause for the president, saying that word had just arrived that Victoria de Córdoba's plane had run into mechanical problems and had been forced to make an emergency landing in San Juan. La Victoria was unhurt, but she would definitely not make it to Caracas in time to sing the hymn. Another announcer started speaking, as well, and the two of them began to argue about the consequences this unexpected turn of events would bring.

At the Pantheon all was chaos. They could not possibly close the ceremony without *"Gloria al Bravo Pueblo."* The crowd was murmuring now, and the camera focused for a minute on the American ambassador, who looked extremely uncomfortable in the hot sun. Generals made emphatic gestures with their hands; members of an army band began to hastily assemble next to the now-empty reviewing platform and podium.

Then I saw her. Orchid, in one of the new gowns I had bought her, was heading through the crowd toward the podium. In all the confusion no one noticed her; had she been an assassin, she could have easily reached the president, who was back standing among his family now within the innermost circle of the crowd, and gunned him down at point-blank range. But she walked right past the president, not even looking at him, actually brushing the shoulder of the president's eldest son with her own, and she walked out onto the platform.

A hush swept through the crowd as people took notice of her; a TV microphone picked up the voice of a child asking someone, "Is that her? Is that Victoria?"

About twenty cops surged toward her then. I recognized some of the cops. They were all tugging guns out of their jackets. I was too stunned to feel anything yet; all I could do was stare at the TV screen.

Orchid paid no attention to the cops. She closed her eyes, and her face took on an expression of sweet concentration. Then she began to sing. She sang right into the microphone that the president had used only minutes before, and her voice was strong and true, bell-like in its clarity and resonance, and the magic of it froze those cops right in their tracks.

> *Gloria al Bravo Pueblo que el yugo lanzó*
> *La Ley respetando la virtud y honor . . .*

Glory to a valiant people that threw off the yoke. She sang every verse. When she was done, there was a long moment of silence, and then the Pantheon erupted with shouting and applause. A crowd rushed forward to surround Orchid as a flustered announcer gasped and stuttered, unable to say anything but *"Incredible. It's just . . . incredible."*

The last thing I saw before I squeezed my eyes shut and dropped my head to my chest was the president gathering little Orchid into his big arms.

• • •

She did not come home that night or the following night. But after the initial shock, I was only mildly concerned; the TV news informed me that she had been invited to the president's residence, where she sang once more. After spending the night with the president's family, she became caught up in a furious round of media interviews. She looked right into the TV cameras, and with an unwavering smile on her face she told the nation that she was the daughter of a rancher who had been murdered by Victor Rojas and that her father's martyrdom had increased her appreciation of her country and its democratic institutions. She now wanted to dedicate the rest of her life to singing out against the enemies of Venezuela.

I was convinced that Orchid, who had been catapulted into the public eye, had become an instant celebrity, a heroine, a *patriota*, thanks to the wonders of Japanese and gringo technology, would fade just as quickly as she had risen when the cameras finally found a fresher, more exciting subject. I guessed that in a few days, as soon as the Prowlers hit town, Orchid would once again find herself facing the prospect of life under a torn mechanic's jumpsuit, and I would have her back.

It was while I was waiting for Orchid to return to my house that things began to fall on me.

Caracas was full of highrise apartment buildings, and overnight I seemed to become a magnet for objects that tumbled from windows, dropped from balcony railings, or blew off clotheslines. Once, when I was walking along thinking of Orchid, I was taunted by a black brassiere that came fluttering out of nowhere to drape itself across my shoulders like some kind of obscene stole. Another time I was pondering the problem of Séptimo, wondering whether I should contact the child-welfare authorities about him, when a perfect scoop of strawberry ice cream struck the top of my head and exploded into pink droplets that went streaking down my clothes to the pavement.

Shortly thereafter I was worrying about Mickey when something flashed through the air a few feet ahead of me and shattered on the sidewalk. I winced as I felt water splash up into my face, and then I saw the broken glass and the tiny goldfish that lay unmoving against a shining wet patch of concrete.

141

After the first two incidents I frequently lifted my eyes to the sky whenever I walked the streets beneath high buildings. But of course, nothing ever fell on me when I was ready for it. And nothing ever seemed to happen during those rare moments when I was strolling along in a regular, empty-headed mood, humming a dumb song or thinking of food. I seemed to draw objects from the air only when I moved through the streets with my head lowered and my lips forming silent words; the undergarments and ice cream and airborne housepets found their way to me only when I was frustrated, worried, or trying to solve a problem.

Overnight the third and newest wave of Prowler posters appeared.

These posters were huge, billboard-sized, and they depicted all four members of the Prowlers in grainy black-and-white. The Prowlers stood with folded arms, and they looked out over the struggling city with stern expressions that suggested they had judged Caracas and found it lacking. The legend on the poster read simply, VIENEN LOS PROWLERS in letters large enough to make you think it had some religious significance.

The publicity people and other advance men for the Prowlers began to arrive; Packy and El Camión and I went to work. We had several meetings with the advance men and with Ballesteros, the promoter, who wanted to have a look at Camión and me to make sure we were up to snuff. Packy and I kept Ballesteros so busy using his limited English that he never did discover that Camión could not speak the language at all.

Tickets for the three performances went on sale, and they sold out in half a day. When the last tickets were gone, there occurred several near riots that had to be broken up by Metropolitanos.

The daily papers reported many thefts of tickets; among the worst of them was a robbery and murder by bludgeoning in which the assailants left three hundred bolivars behind while making off with four concert tickets.

The words VIENEN LOS PROWLERS showed up in spray paint on buildings and on the walls of highway underpasses all over the city. In a couple of spots where the graffiti had always been dedicated to radical and Marxist messages, I saw the Prowler legend painted over the older announcements in darker, more forceful colors. That sight gave me a vague feeling of dread.

And the TV stations, with that mind-altering, reality-bending power that only television possesses, provided a fertile yeast for the brew of hype and hysteria with their constant reminders to the people that times were changing and that this could be the last Great Cultural Event that Venezuela would see. Now that debate over a devaluation had become public, such sly warnings were easier to get away with.

Of course there were girls. Somehow word leaked out that the band and their roadies would stay at the Caracas Hilton, and women ranging from the early teens up to forty began to gather on the sidewalk in front of the hotel, gazing upward with glassy eyes toward its highest floors. I felt a stab of jealousy whenever I went by and saw that.

I wrote a couple of stories about the Prowler frenzy for the New York office; they loved them and sent them worldwide. Even though I was suddenly so busy that I had time to write about little else, and had recently seen nothing at all of Mickey in the office or anywhere, the company told me to use as much of my time as I wanted on the Prowler developments. This go-ahead from New York allowed me to breathe easier, but only for a very brief time.

On the sixth evening following Orchid's public performance, I arrived home from the office to find Packy sitting in his accustomed spot at the bottom of my stairs. He smiled as soon as he saw me and waved an unopened two-liter bottle of *caña* in the air above his head.

"Sit," he said, "and have a little drink with Packy."

I returned his smile and said, "I don't usually drink it straight. Let me go up and get a couple of Cokes." But when I tried to get around him on the stairs, he put a gentle hand on my knee and stopped me.

"Sit," he insisted. So I sat, and he immediately opened the bottle. "The first sip for my friend, Jimmy Angel." I drank and passed the bottle to him.

Packy took a drink then, and said, "*Coño*, such a beautiful evening sky. I think we should drink to the sky, gringo." We drank first to the sky, then to the setting sun, and then to the first star we saw. And when the silver sliver of the moon appeared, we drank yet again.

After a time Packy settled his thin forearm atop my shoulder, and I thought he would begin another one of his stories. But instead he said, "You know, you're a lucky man, Jimmy."

"*¿Sí?* How is it that I'm lucky, then?"

"You have people who care about you. That's a very important thing."

"Lucky," I mumbled, mulling it over.

"Me, for instance," continued Packy. "I consider you to be my brother. I'd do anything for you, *pana.*"

"Well, that's good—"

"Camión, *la misma vaina.*"

"I don't know if I would—"

"And Séptimo. More than anybody, probably. When he looks at you, he sees a father." This last comment made me uncomfortable, and I squirmed. Packy suddenly grabbed the bottle from me, drank deeply from it, and sucked in his breath.

In a moment he said, "She was here this afternoon."

"Orchid?" Packy nodded, then slid his arm all the way across my back so that he was gripping my opposite shoulder.

"She picked up all her things. Said to tell you good-bye."

"*Good-bye?*" The cane liquor stroked sickening fingers across the lining of my stomach.

"Someone gave her a TV ad to do, singing about dish soap."

"*Dish soap?*"

"*Sí, pana.* There's big money in bubbles, I guess." Packy named a sum equal to four months of my wire-service salary, and I was impressed in spite of my despair.

"She said the dish soap was only the beginning. She said she was going to find a way to become a real star." He gave my shoulder a little shake. "Fat chance, if you ask me."

I began turning my head from side to side to side. The night became a Ferris wheel of gray, swirling lights.

"Anything else?" I finally managed to croak.

"Yes. She said she'll never forget you and that she wants you to be happy." My head began to go the other way then, nodding. After a time, still bobbing my head, I tried to open my mouth to thank Packy for breaking it to me so gently. But there seemed to be something in my throat that I could not swallow and that would not let me breathe, or speak.

• • •

I found myself in a deep, blue fog after that. During the remaining few days before the scheduled arrival of the Prowlers' road crew, which was when the real interpreting work was supposed to begin, I made a habit of going directly to Mickey's apartment whenever I had a spare hour or so. I never found Mickey at home, and Beatrix was gone most of the time as well; Floyd and Nestor and I were usually alone in the elegant emptiness of the Altamira apartment, and the three of us tried to console one another without speaking of the things that were hurting us.

Early one evening I traveled by foot to Altamira from my home in Sebucán. School had apparently just let out, because as I toiled slowly up an Altamira street toward Mickey's building, small knots of children wearing blazers and carrying books kept passing me. I felt like an old sea turtle among quicksilver minnows.

Suddenly, as I was walking beneath one of the highest apartment buildings, metallic raindrops came streaking down all around me to dance on the sidewalk. They rang brightly as they struck the concrete, then they bounced two or three feet into the air, fell again, and sang a flatter note. I reached and caught one on the rebound; before I could examine it, I was surrounded by laughing children who snatched all the others from the pavement and then continued up the street in a shrieking swarm.

I opened my fist and was disturbed to discover that the thing I held was the empty casing to a nine-millimeter bullet. I rolled my head back as far as it would go in order to see to the top of that apartment building. But I spotted no one at all, much less anyone I could accuse.

Feeling a worm of dread, I lowered my head to find a child standing before me on the sidewalk. He wore the same blue blazer as those in the throng that had just gone by, but he was much smaller, with ears that stuck out like handles; he was also much thinner than the others and, it was an easy guess, not as quick as they to grab up an unexpected treasure from the sky.

He neither spoke nor met my gaze, but of course I knew what he wanted. And it was with gratitude that I gave it to him; seeing it through his eyes helped me to shake off my feeling of horror. I laughed and pressed the harmless bullet shell into his small, moist palm and continued along to Mickey's building.

Neither Mickey nor Beatrix came home before the boys' bedtime that night, so I put them both to bed and then climbed into the bed in the guest room, which was right next door to them.

Much later Beatrix stole into my darkened room. I pretended to sleep as she undulated out of her sweater and let her skirt fall to the floor. Through the open door I could hear the soft, even breathing of Floyd and Nestor as well as the unexpected sound of Mickey's booming snore from farther down the hallway. I held my breath as she peeled back the covers and slid into bed with me. When she began to rub her hand on my bare stomach, I opened my eyes.

"Poor Jimmy," she said in a voice that was not quite a whisper. "The boys tell me you've had a heartbreak." For some reason she sounded very German in the darkness.

I coughed loudly into my fist and kept on coughing, hoping that somehow the coughing fit would make her nervous enough to leave. But she only waited until I had coughed myself dizzy and had to stop.

"But you're a man," Beatrix said. "And I'm very good at helping men get over their heartbreaks."

I wanted to shout, but I knew that Floyd and Nestor and Mickey would all come running if I did. I thought of threatening to tell Mickey, but I had a feeling that was what she wanted me to do. I was trapped.

In the end, though, I was rescued by my body's own wisdom.

"Jimmy. You are not much good to a woman," she said as she tugged her sweater back on. She left the room without a further word.

I waited until I could no longer hear her rustling about the apartment, then I grabbed my clothes and sneaked out as quickly as I could.

When the full entourage of technicians and mechanics and roustabouts for the Prowlers finally arrived, the atmosphere in Caracas turned to that of a small town in the old days when the circus train pulled in. Were they the retinue of a circus, however, it would have been a circus with a black side to its childish amusements; a circus where the town homecoming queen was found hiding, bruised and hysterical, in the lion tamer's quarters, a circus where the sideshow freaks injected themselves with morphine between performances, a circus where little boys went home crying after speaking in the shadows to the happy-faced clown.

And the city loved it.

The road crew arrived by charter plane at the Simón Bolívar International Airport two nights before the group itself was scheduled to come in. The Venezuelan promoter hired seven stretch limos to carry them from the airport; the cars assembled in front of the Hilton and then traveled in convoy like a long black python over the high hills and down to the shore.

Packy, El Camión, and I rode in the front car. Packy and I talked excitedly, and from time to time, whenever he thought the driver was not looking, he would bend over and sniff a little *perico* from the tiny hollow in the back of his hand. El Camión was quiet; he stared somberly out the window.

The parking lot of the airport was full of milling people. They were mostly young people, and many wore the Prowler T-shirts that some enterprising bandit had begun silk-screening in recent weeks. The T-shirts were poorly done, the portraits on them looking as though they had been drawn in crayon by a child. The crowd seemed full of a dangerous energy that had no ready outlet.

A line of uniformed *guardias* stood before the main doors to the terminal; they held the crowd at bay while other *guardias* checked the identification of everyone trying to go through those entrances. People who were older and well dressed were passed through more quickly than anyone who might be a Prowlers fan.

Apart from this large throng, there were two smaller groups standing nearby. One group was protesting the arrival of the Prowlers in Venezuela with signs that said DOWN WITH COMMUNIST CULTURE. The other group was also anti-Prowler, and their signs said, DOWN WITH IMPERIALIST CULTURE. As we rolled past in our limousines, the two groups appeared to be having an argument.

Our caravan of limousines swept regally through the crowd; the people parted for us and then stood on either side of the vehicles with mouths open, as if witnessing a miracle. Hands were stretched to touch the cars that would carry the men who would set the stage for the legendary band.

We went around the terminal through a guarded gate to a side entrance that was reserved for VIPs, and then the drivers pulled up in a line and parked. An airport official met Packy and El Camión and me and escorted us to a VIP lounge. An attendant there served us coffee.

The chartered gjg carrying light and sound equipment, musical instruments, and the people who would put them all together touched lightly down, did a pivot at the end of the runway, then drew up beside the terminal with a steady jet-engine sigh. It was nearly dark by then. We went out onto the cooling tarmac to wait as airport workers in orange jumpsuits rolled a movable stairway into place.

Reporters, photographers, and television people stood about twenty yards from the plane, cordoned off and watched over by young *guardias*. A few of the newspapermen recognized me; outraged, they shouted my name, which made me gleeful. I waved at them and they hissed angrily back at me.

A well-built gringo with long dark hair and a pointed beard came down the stairs and introduced himself as John Stewart, road manager for the Prowlers. He carried a worn leather jacket that he cradled as carefully as if it were a child. Then the rest of the roadies came out and followed Stewart into the VIP lounge to wait for the passports and luggage to be pushed through customs.

The lounge filled immediately with cigarette smoke. Porters in red jackets wheeled in several carts bearing bottles of Polar; the carts nearly caused a riot as the roadies tripped over each other to get to them. There were almost sixty of them, most of the men in their twenties and thirties, with a few women who could have been wives or girlfriends or technicians in their own right scattered among them. Among the men and the women there were young fresh faces that you might at first glance have called innocent, and there were faces that were portraits of hard living. A man named George introduced himself to me; he was English, with a crudely tattooed syringe on his left forearm and a pasty face marred by ridges of red blemishes. He was, he told me, a specialist in visual effects.

The technicians found Packy interesting, and they crowded around to talk to him. Since I lacked an Andean face and an exotic accent, I was quickly shunted to one side following the initial whirlwind of introductions, and I was soon joined there by El Camión, who could not compete in the free-for-all English conversation. I drew a measure of comfort from El Camión's brooding company. But after a few minutes he went out to help load trucks with equipment from the airplane, and I was alone again.

It did not take long for Packy to lose his allure, however; the technicians began to hunger for satisfactions beyond mere cultural exchange. They turned to me then, seeming to guess that I was the best equipped to point them toward the earthly pleasures. The competent, worldly American.

In small groups, with heads craning warily over their shoulders in search of John Stewart, they asked me about the possibilities of obtaining things.

"They got cocaine in this country, man?"

"Any pot? Got any on you?"

"What about cunt, man? Can you get some cunt for us? Tonight, do you think?"

They acted like men and women recently released from prison, or who had undergone some other terrible ordeal of denial. I steered them back to Packy, and soon I was standing by myself again, unwanted.

Packy was more than ready for them. He soothed them with a glowing, impossible fantasy of Caracas as a giant bordello and opium den, ripe for plundering. I felt in awe of him as his promises of upcoming delights grew like a magical castle rising from the earth in an old fairy tale. He told them of Andean snow purer than any that ever fell from the sky. He told them of women who at a blue-eyed glance would burst into flame. Packy seemed to invest his promises with a great importance; he acted as if fulfilling their wishes were his one purpose, his solitary mission on earth. Yet as he spoke, his eyes had a strange light to them, and his face bore a taunting, almost cruel expression that I found disturbing. It was the same look he wore during those early-morning occasions when he serenaded my neighborhood with his electric guitar.

The wait for the passports was a long one. After a time all the questions about drugs and women and the acceptable level of hell-raising in Venezuela had been asked; the technicians began to speak longingly of hotel rooms and beds and food and hot showers. They became sullen as a scolded classroom; they smoked, sulked, and swore at one another, rubbing their eyes and spreading their bodies across the plush upholstery of the VIP room in that sprawling manner that only Americans have.

One dwarfish little man whose name was Charlie and who wore earrings in both lobes brought out a thick stack of Polaroid photographs that depicted members of the band and their technicians engaging in numerous sexual acts with women. Charlie, who was the personal guitar-squire to the Prowlers' wizard electric six-string player, shuffled lazily through these photographs, a cigarette dangling from the corner of his mouth. Few of his friends joined him in this perusal; it seemed that most of them had ʒeen the photos many times before.

I hesitated, but finally my journalistic curiosity got the best of me and I approached him and peered over his shoulder; Charlie grinned a conspiratorial grin and turned himself to give me a better view. The pictures were of poor quality, tending toward the shadowy side, and no one in them seemed to be having fun. If it were not for the fact that I recognized most of the male subjects, none of the photos would have rated a second glance. I was disappointed, as well, that the collection included no photograph of Ronnie Neumon doing anything to anybody.

Eventually the equipment cleared customs, the passports came back, and Packy, El Camión, and I crowded into limos with the sixty technicians and headed back over the hills into Caracas.

A small problem occurred as soon as the caravan pulled up and stopped in front of the Hilton. As the Hilton porters, officious in their red jackets, stepped in to open the many doors of the limousines, a few of the women who had been gathered outside day and night for nearly a week managed to rush by them and throw themselves into the vehicles, their hands clawing frantically, their mouths open in mindless squeals of devotion and frustration.

One girl, whose nails were dangerously long and painted a psychotic shade of red, flew into my limo and landed in my lap, her fist bunched painfully in my groin. I shifted quickly, and she lost her balance and fell sprawling across me and the two technicians on either side of me while screaming as loudly as she could for Ronnie Neumon.

"Ronnie!" she cried. "*¿Dónde está? Yo lo quiero mucho.*"

The technicians were reaching, filling their hands with her and giggling, as I explained that the rock star would not arrive in Caracas for another two days. Her tone shifted then to one of outrage; she drew herself back toward the door, swiping with her dangerous nails at the faces of the roadies. Still giggling, they each grabbed one last feel, and then she was gone.

"What'd she want? She wanted Ronnie, right?" asked George, the visual-effects specialist, who was sitting next to me.

"Sure," I told him. "You think she's been waiting here for you?"

As we climbed out of the cars, the porters and two Metropolitanos who had been standing there were herding the last of the women away from the caravan. The girl who had jumped into my lap was screaming that she had been raped, but the police were paying no attention. The two Metropolitanos and the porters were all smiling, enjoying their work.

Once we all stood clustered on the sidewalk, George came up next to me and draped an unwelcome arm across my shoulder. I turned my head and saw that it was the arm with the syringe tattoo.

"See, Billy," he said to me. "At first these broads *all* want to squeeze the band. They're all star-fuckers for the first day or two. But let 'em hang around for a while, they'll settle for any hot rock 'n' roll meat that's around."

I nodded and looked away, then slid diplomatically out from under his arm. "Jimmy," I muttered. "My name's Jimmy."

"Say," said George, "you did say this Vennie-Wailin' pussy is pretty good, right?"

I didn't get the chance to answer, because someone shouted, "Hey, George, what'd that broad want? Squeeze the band?"

"Squeeze the band. Squeeze the main man," said George. There was laughter.

We got the roadies inside, moved them past the gawkers in the lobby to get them registered, and then took them up to their rooms. There was a flurry of unpacking and filling of drawers and showering; they came close to being ordinary, innocent travelers during that brief time. But the lull did not last. They soon renewed their demands for women and liquor and cocaine. They were to be frustrated in most of these desires; it was after nine and the liquor stores had already closed, and the hotel management would not allow unregistered women up to the fourth-floor rooms. Some of the horniest technicians decided to go down to the street and talk to the girls to see if an arrangement could be made. They tried to enlist me as an interpreter for this adventure, but I told them I had

other things to do. Packy went with them willingly, that unfathomable smirk still lighting his face.

Another faction convinced Camión to take a stack of money and
go out in search of *perico*, and still another group, including Charlie, the guitar man, finally talked me into going with them to a bar
to buy a few under-the-table cases of Polar. Charlie and the others
were oddly reluctant to walk the streets unescorted, even as a
group, although I assured them it was fairly safe.

We went to several places before I found a Spanish bartender
who was willing to sell me four cases of beer. People stared at us
on both legs of the trip; girls waved timidly and smiled, and men
gave us hard, Venezuelan looks as if searching for evidence of
manhood in us. My technicians either ignored or did not see the
silent hostility. They waved and grinned and mugged like the rock
stars they were not.

There was a scramble for beer as soon as we had bootlegged it
back to the fourth floor. It disappeared quickly, and even the people who had managed to grab a can or two were left looking
thirsty. There was talk then of breaking down and going to the
hotel bar for drinks, but a counterargument by Charlie, who cited
the high prices of bar beer and well drinks, won out.

After a time Camión returned with a quarter-ounce of Peru's finest tucked into his underwear. Packy rode up in the elevator with
him, and we three watched the seven people who had invested in
the cocaine as they opened the foil parcel beneath a desk lamp in
George's room, divided the rock and white powder into seven
roughly equal parts with a Swiss army knife, and then squirreled
away to their separate quarters with their separate stashes, leaving
behind three pairs of lines as a tip for Packy, Camión, and me.

"*Coño*," said Packy when they had gone. "I thought there was
going to be a party." He looked at me. "These gringos certainly are
strange." I could only shrug.

Packy gave me an incandescent smile and sucked up his two
lines using a rolled-up *tabla* in place of a straw.

I told Packy and Camión that they could each snort one of the
lines that had been laid out for me, which they did without hesitation.

Packy stayed overnight at the hotel. One of us had to be there at
all times in case someone was in need of an interpreter. Camión

152

and I took a taxi back to Sebucán. When we arrived, he invited me to his cottage. I had been thinking about Orchid and was not yet ready to face my empty apartment, so I gladly accepted his invitation. He led me through the main gate onto the grounds of the estate; we pulled chairs out of the cottage and set them in the garden.

Before he sat, Camión disappeared into his house for a minute more and came out with a single Polar and a bottle of *caña*. He handed the beer to me, then he opened the bottle and sat down and began to drink.

Camión was in one of his moods. I said a few things to him, but he did not respond. He just kept sucking away at that raw cane liquor. I gave up on talking to him and settled back in my chair to listen to the night frogs and insects and the formless music of the wind chimes that had been strung by Camión's mother. Camión seemed to be listening to the wind chimes as well; his ear was cocked in the direction of the main house.

Finally he spoke, his voice startling me in the darkness.

"Gringo. Did I never tell you about the unknown soldier?" The *caña* made his words swirl together like water.

"Unknown soldier?" I said. "Does Venezuela have one?"

He jumped to his feet and stood swaying above me, the bottle hanging from his hand. "Sebucán has one," he said. Then he reached down and wrapped his free hand around mine and he pulled me from my seat as easily as if I were a child.

"*Epa,*" I told him. "Easy does it."

He towed me across the garden until we were standing before the little mound with the rosebushes that he always tended so carefully. The red roses looked gray in the darkness. Camión bowed his head. His grip on my hand tightened. Suddenly it was he who was the child.

"*El soldado desconocido,*" he said.

"What do you mean? Camión? You mean there's somebody buried there?" When he didn't answer right away, I grew frightened. I wondered whether the unknown soldier had been a friend of his. I knew that if I tried to pull my hand away from his, I would not be able to. I imagined him killing me and burying me in the garden and planting roses on me. I shivered.

"Camión..."

"He broke into the house," Camión said. There were tears in his

153

voice. "Black. *Un negro del coño*. My parents were out, and he must have thought no one was home." Camión rubbed his nose on his sleeve, and then he continued. "It was dark. I went downstairs and I saw him. I was scared, and I thought I saw him pointing a gun at me, so I lifted the pistol and I shot."

Camión looked down at me. I felt something wet fall from his face and hit my wrist.

"Camión," I said. "It wasn't your fault."

"I turned on the light," Camión said. "Blood all over the tiles of the living room. He was breathing strangely, and then he stopped. No gun."

"*Pana*. You can't blame—"

"My parents came home. My father checked him for identification and didn't even find a *cédula*. He had thirteen *bolos* in his pocket. Thirteen." Camión sniffed loudly and looked up at the stars. "My father said, what the hell, he's only a *negro del coño*. Let's bury him in the garden." He looked back down at me. "I was fifteen years old."

I managed to free my hand. I placed it on his back. "Camión. It's not right to blame yourself."

Suddenly he lurched away and fell to his knees in another part of the overgrown garden. He began to throw up. I wanted to go home. I was beginning to feel sick myself. Instead, I went over and knelt by him; I began to hum.

"Jimmy," he said after a while. He wiped his mouth on his sleeve. "I want to open the gates. For the people. So they pick the fruit. But I can't. Something rotten inside of me."

"It's okay," I said. "You don't have to."

"No. It's not. It's not okay."

I helped him to bed after that. Just before he passed out, he looked up at me and said, "You're all right, Jimmy. And not just for a gringo. Anything I can do for you, you just let me know."

I let myself out of his cottage and found my way through the darkness to the main gate by walking in the hardened wheel rut of a motorcycle. The lonely sound of wind chimes followed me home.

The next morning I went over and woke Camión and gave him coffee. He would not look me in the eye as he dressed and drank his coffee. He seemed to regret having confided his secret to me. I regretted it, too; I did not know what to say to him.

Afterward we caught a cab together. But on a sudden impulse I had the driver let me off in Altamira and sent Camión by himself to the Hilton. All night long, memories of Orchid had settled like stones against my chest, and I now felt the need to see Nestor and Floyd before they went off to school that day. I wanted to touch them and to reassure myself that some goodness remained in the world. The Prowlers and my own fear of Beatrix had kept me from them for the past three days.

I was about to cross the mouth of the parking garage beneath Mickey's building when the scream of metal against concrete from deep within the cavelike garage conscripted my attention and froze me where I stood. In a moment a blue Chevrolet bearing rental plates came screeching in reverse up the entrance tunnel, the fenders and doors on the passenger side crumpled and torn and the tires smoking. In the front on the passenger side sat a chaotic mound of women's clothes; this would have been all I saw, except that the driver, apparently mistaking me for someone else, slammed on the brakes as the car was passing. Then Beatrix craned her head around the mountain of clothing, her lips forming a dark, ambiguous letter O. There was an oval bruise on her cheek that she had apparently tried to powder over with little success. She rehid herself as soon as she saw I was not the man she was looking for, and the car fired out into the street, plowing unrepentantly into the fender of a passing taxi and starting forward for the first time.

As Beatrix sped away, the resigned faces of Floyd and Nestor stared out at me through the rear windshield. They barely had time to raise white hands in farewell before they were gone.

At the building entrance a large dark woman with drying tears and a look of satisfaction on her upturned face brushed by me and headed for the street. In the lobby the doorman looked on with an amused smile as a stocky *criollo* wearing a fireman's uniform walked past me with a steel battering ram under his arm. I ran for the elevator, rode it to Mickey's floor, and stepped out into the hallway in time to see the news seller that Mickey had pointed out in the plaza coming out the open door of the apartment with a thoughtful, almost sorrowful expression on his ugly face. I wanted

155

to ask him something, but before I could stir myself to speak, he had moved around me and disappeared behind the closing doors of the elevator.

I went through the apartment calling for Mickey. Finally, when I got to the second floor, I heard him moaning and found him lying on the bed behind the shattered door of his bedroom. Both his eyes were bruised and rapidly swelling shut; thick blood ran from his nostrils and both corners of his mouth. One side of his face was so puffed it looked as if he were holding a peach pit in the pouch of his cheek.

"*Oh*," I said.

I stood looking down at him, wanting to go for a wet washrag, but unwilling to leave him alone. After a moment he spoke, easing some of my fear.

"'Immy," he said.

"What happened? Wait. Don't talk."

"Help me up."

"Can you?"

"Help me."

I slid my arm behind him and helped him raise his shoulders from the mattress. He grimaced and convulsively pressed an arm against his side.

"*Ahhh*! 'Atch my ribs, huh?"

"They kick you, Mickey? You look bad, buddy." His eyes shone at me through narrow slits in the lids.

"You see 'em? Fucker with the battering ram?"

"Yeah. Who was he?" Mickey moaned and gingerly kneaded his damaged ribs.

"Brother-in-law of the bastard in the plaza. Wasn't even any of his business."

"Brother-in-law."

"The fucker. Got Johnnie Walker downstairs, Jimmy. Okay?" I brought him a glass of the whiskey; he drank, and yelled from the burn in his torn mouth, and drank some more. It seemed to revive him.

"*Perico's* what I really need. Hell with it." He drank again and turned his ruined eyes to me. "Thought I was lying, didn't you?"

"I don't know what I thought." He looked down and nodded.

"Two days ago I finally got fed up. You know, I been patient, but after a while, it gets ridiculous. So I hit her. I shouldn't've, but I did."

"Ah, Mickey." I did not know what else to say; I felt helpless.

"Twice, I think, before Nestor came up and whacked me across the ass with that long truck you gave him, and Floyd punched me in the balls. That brought me to my senses, and I took off; went down to see Lulu." He massaged his crotch with his fingertips and laughed sadly.

"Mickey, Mickey."

"So when I come back, she's locked in here with the fucking plaza clown himself. I beat on the door at first, but that gets me nowhere, so I cry and apologize and say that maybe now that things have come to a head, we can make a new beginning and be a family again. But she only tells me to get my tears and my horns the hell away from her." Mickey swallowed and sent a slow, swollen tongue to sweep his lips before continuing.

"This goes on for about a day; I send the kids next door and keep pleading, and then the telephone rings. It's the clown's *wife*, of all people, and she wants to know where her old man is. So I tell her, and she says can she speak to him, and I go to the door and I say, '*Huevón*, your wife wants to speak to you.' But he just tells me, '*El huevón eres tú*,' and he won't come out."

"Sort of heavy, the wife? Dark?" I asked, because I felt the need to say something.

"Heavy? She's a fucking sow. No wonder he..." He started to rub a hand over his torn face, then gave a gasp of surprise at the pain his own fingers caused him.

"The fat bitch starts calling me every two hours, then every hour, then every half hour; finally every fifteen minutes. Wants to talk to the father of her uncountable children and can't understand why I refuse to put him on. I'm so *unreasonable*, right?" Mickey was talking excitedly now, waving his arms in his usual manner, and he sent flecks of spit mixed with blood flying in my direction.

"Then, about an hour ago, she calls from down in the lobby and says can she come up. A minute later she shows up at the door with her brother the *bombero*, who's wearing his *bombero* uniform and carrying a battering ram. So I tell them, right this way, folks, can I maybe get you something to drink, and I take them upstairs, and the fucker of a brother-in-law proceeds to smash down the door to the bedroom, definitively ending, or so I think, the entire situation of the past two days.

"And at first, Jimmy, it *does* go according to my expectations. Exit Beatrix, who locks her indignant bruised face, by herself this time, behind the door to the spare bedroom. Enter fat wife, who gives her man a sharp *take that* across the face and then sobs, hugs him, and leaves the nest of shame as fast as she can.

"But then, the fireman and the clown, they put their heads together, and in a matter of less than a minute they have decided that I, because of the irresponsibly loose reins that I keep on my wife, am to blame for having jeopardized the integrity of their upstanding Venezuelan family. They pounce on me and beat the living shit out of me, and that, Jimmy boy, is where you found me. Too bad you didn't get here earlier; you could have gotten in on the action." Suddenly Mickey's eyes opened to near-normal width.

"My boys," he said. "Did you see them, Jimmy?" I studied my trembling hands.

"Beatrix has them, Mick."

"You're sure?"

"I saw them." He stood suddenly, and although his face twisted with pain, he made no sound.

After a moment he said, "I'll fix her. I'll get her."

"You need to see a doctor." He flapped an impatient hand at me.

"Later. I'll shut off all the bank accounts and the credit cards. She won't get a fucking cent. I'll tell the PeTeJotas to grab her ass. They'll get her for kidnapping."

"That's it," I said. "Call the cops. The other stuff can wait. Let me take you to the doctor, Mickey." He glared at me.

"You go to work, Jimmy. *Somebody* has to." He held his side and followed me down the stairs. He was on the telephone before I had even gotten through the front door.

I did not know what else to do, so I went to the hotel. Packy immediately grabbed me and began telling me about how John Stewart had come in at three in the morning after unloading equipment at the Poliedro, the indoor arena where the concerts would take place, and that he had counted heads and found two men missing. The two dragged back at about six o'clock, but the road manager was waiting for them, and he gave them a lecture and told them he would put them on the next Los Angeles-bound airplane if they stayed out again without permission. Packy pointed out the pair; they seemed duly chastened.

After listening to Packy's account of the previous night, I found a chair and sat down to try to think things over. I was shaking all over and I felt sick. Useful thought eluded me.

Limousines came after breakfast. We all got into them and rode out to the Poliedro.

It was good to see the crew work; watching them took my mind off my own problems as well as those of Camión and the Calderón family. Despite their unruly ways when they were on their own time, they knew their jobs well and they went about them seriously. The Poliedro was a polyhedral building with a wide-open floor stretching away from the stage as well as several tiers of seats that rose up and away from the floor around the side walls.

Two carpenters who had come with the team went to work near the back of the floor area, banging together a platform for the sound mixers and their equipment. Two Venezuelan carpenters worked with them; the Americans nearly provoked a fight by ordering the Venezuelans around as if they were apprentices. I had to wade in and soothe the Venezuelans and explain to the roadies that they couldn't get away with insulting their local help.

George went up on a high scaffolding to fix several sophisticated braces of lights against the ceiling. Despite his awkward appearance, he was as unconcerned and graceful as a monkey up there.

Speakers in huge cases lay toppled like dominos all over the concrete floor. Venezuelans who worked at the Poliedro as well as some of the lower-level help from the States unpacked the speakers and lifted them onto the stage with a forklift, then stacked them one on top of the other. They worked quickly, sweating, speaking little, and on either side of the stage they built two high black walls of cabinets that looked as if they would soon touch the ceiling.

Five or six gringos struggled with ropes and pulleys and wires to get a rolled-up canvas backdrop in place. Among them I recognized the two men who had stayed out all night.

Other men were laying thick electrical cables across the stage. Camión was working with them. He said little as the gringos alternately joked and swore bitterly about the difficulty of their jobs.

John Stewart wandered from place to place with a clipboard in his hand. Packy followed him like a smiling dog, interpreting for him and trying to engage him in conversation. Stewart snarled more than he smiled, giving Packy curt answers, but I could see that Packy was slowly wearing him down. I went up to them and tried to speak to Stewart myself, but he only stared at me. I wandered away, muttering under my breath.

Backstage there were several small dressing rooms and a larger room where an act could get together before going out before the audience. In one of the rooms I found little Charlie testing a cordless guitar amplifier that picked up signals through an antenna. He was smoking a joint, and he offered me a hit, which I accepted. He was in a good mood, and after a minute he produced a tiny bit of cocaine in a glass vial. This I declined; I watched him snort up, and then I listened to his explanation of how the amplifier worked. He seemed quite proud of it.

At about one in the afternoon Camión and I went out to buy hamburgers and drinks for everyone. Lunch was quick, then the growl of the forklift, the grunting and swearing of men, and the banging of hammers resumed.

Teen-aged children started gathering in the parking lot of the Poliedro. They listened to the vague sounds coming from within as if the racket itself carried some message of salvation. The outer doors were guarded by three Metropolitanos and a handful of American security men, failed football players all, who kept the starstruck children from wandering in.

Still later in the day I got a nervous tickling in the pit of my stomach. I dialed Mickey's number, let his phone ring fifteen or twenty times, then called my office. Carlos answered in a groggy voice.

"Carlos. Anything going on?"

"No, Jimmy. Nothing." The certainty in his tone annoyed me.

"Are you sure? Are you keeping an eye on the government wire for me, like I asked you to?"

"*Por supuesto*, Jimmy. Just like you asked me to."

"And the radio?"

"*Claro*. It's on every minute." He was beginning to sound indignant.

"Okay. All right. No phone calls, then?"

"Not one, Jimmy."

160

"What? Not a phone call all day?" Carlos gave an uncertain chuckle.

"You're not still worried about the guerrillas, are you?"

"Sure. Yeah. With good reason, Carlos. And while I'm doing this rock 'n' roll thing—"

"Well, you shouldn't worry. The police gave them a lesson they won't forget for years. All the *periodistas* are saying it now. All except for Humberto Sanabria, whom I personally always thought was a little strange anyway."

"Thanks, Carlos. That makes me feel much better." He did not catch my sarcasm.

"Bet your life on it," he said. Then he hung up, presumably to resume his siesta.

That night, after the limos had disgorged the sweaty pack of roadies onto the sidewalk in front of the Hilton, John Stewart turned to Packy and said, "Tell the drivers to come back in an hour. We'll all be going out someplace."

Then he began herding his men into the hotel; he followed them, keeping an eye on them to make sure that none wandered away to accost women in the lobby, and he stood by the elevators to watch them go up in small groups. Packy, El Camión, and I stayed behind with him, and then the four of us ascended together. On the way up, Stewart backed himself into a corner of the elevator, his suspicious eyes leaping from one to the other of us. He seemed to have sought the corner either to protect his back or because it was the best place from which to scald us with his eyes, which were a hot, dark color that changed shades under different lights.

"This is going to be a tough night," he said, almost seeming to confide in us. But then we knew he wasn't confiding because he said, "Any one of them gets in trouble, you all are getting the blame. Understand?"

I felt sure that Packy would stand up to him finally and tell him to screw off. I was prepared to back him up.

But Packy only said, "Understand," and gave Stewart one of his meekest looks, probably the same look, in fact, that he had given the army captain that time in Chile when they were considering squashing his head with a tank.

Camión looked at Packy and tried to mirror his expression of meekness. His version was a trifle too sharp around the eyes, but if Stewart noticed, he didn't let on. "Understand," Camión said, making the *u* sound like a double *o*.

I said nothing, and for a minute I thought I would get away with it. But when the elevator stopped at our floor, Stewart reached and pressed the Close Door button and glared at me. "What about you, pal?" he said. "You understand too?"

My blood cooled. "Yeah," I said after a moment.

"Yeah *what?*" Suddenly I was in a childhood flashback, trying to face down a bully without getting my face rubbed in the dirt.

"Yeah, I heard you." I had to struggle to put force into my voice.

Stewart, a man used to giving orders to unruly men, apparently took my reluctance to submit as outright defiance, and he took a step toward me and began to raise an open hand toward my face. I had a split second to decide whether to brush his hand aside, take a swing at him, or say something stupid and pompous like "Look here, I'm really a journalist, not an interpreter. How do you think this will look in print?" All those possibilities ran through my mind as his fingers moved closer to my face.

I was saved from having to choose between unsatisfactory courses of action, however, because the elevator door, no longer paralyzed by Stewart's finger over the button, roared suddenly open. From the corner of my eye I saw that a woman stood waiting to board. An artificial smile spread across Stewart's face and his hand settled to his side. He turned his smiling face toward the woman.

"*Ola,* Jimmy," said the woman in a musical voice. It sounded like Orchid's voice; I looked and it was Orchid.

"*Orchid!*" I said. I immediately forgot John Stewart.

"*Coño,*" I heard Packy mutter, but I paid him no mind.

Orchid was smiling, and she carried a cardboard folder containing the Prowlers press kit under one arm. I was ready to lift my hand and touch her face until I remembered that I no longer had the right.

Stewart, still smiling, stepped out next to her and turned, his mouth nearly touching her ear. "Well, hello," he said. But she ignored him and continued to smile at me, and in a moment his face and neck turned pink with sudden shyness or insecurity. He looked away, and Packy and El Camión stepped out around him and went down the hallway.

"Well, how are you?" I asked. I tried to remember whether I had combed my hair recently. The shock of seeing her had worn off, and sickness began to trickle through me. "What are you doing here, anyway? You know, when you didn't come back, I—"

"I'm a journalist now, just like you, Jimmy."

"What?"

"*Sí.* A free-lance one, anyway. After I did the dish-soap ad, I kept going back to the offices of the people who set it up for me. You know, I'd wait for them outside their door, and finally they told me that if I could arrange an exclusive interview with Ronnie Neumon and get something good out of him, they might be able to come up with some more work for me." She seemed quite pleased with herself; quite excited about her prospects. I had to clear my throat to speak.

"That's a big goddamn *if.* Maybe you should think about why they said that to you. People like that—"

"I'll get it, Jimmy. I'm working on it." I would have laughed then, but the determined look on her face reminded me of the first time she had stepped up to me in her street rags; that memory chilled the impulse. I looked away and nodded.

"Well, good luck. But don't let them use you. Those TV types can be pretty scummy." She gave me an indulgent smile and was about to say something else when Stewart, who until then had been standing by frowning at our incomprehensible Spanish, decided to interrupt. He had apparently caught Ronnie Neumon's name.

"The Prowlers?" he said, his voice a husky whisper. "You're looking for the band? El bando, baby? I'm with el bando."

Orchid shot him a puzzled sideways glance and then looked at me, wrinkling her nose like a rabbit. "Who is this man?"

My chest filled with a sudden and malicious glee. "*Un obrero,*" I told her. "A worker."

"Well, he's very forward. Are you going down to the lobby?"

"No," I said, feeling a shameful blush. "I'm staying." As if to demonstrate, I stumbled out of the elevator; Orchid intercepted me, stood on her tiptoes, and gave me a dry little kiss on the cheek.

"Well, then, *ciao, mi amor.*" Then she boarded the elevator again and the door closed. I felt tears gathering somewhere deep inside me for a moment, but the feeling passed quickly.

Stewart suddenly wanted to be my pal. "Hey, you know that chick?"

"Sure do," I said, and I stepped around him, heading down the hall. I felt a sweet burn of satisfaction; the next best thing to having Orchid was seeing someone else not have her. Stewart chased me, matching my stride. It was a pleasure to see infatuation robbing him of his dignity the way love had robbed me of mine.

"I think she liked me," Stewart said. "Don't you think so? Did she say anything? Do you think she'll be around here again?"

"She said something," I said.

"What? What did she say?"

I smiled at him. "You don't want to hear." I looked down at the carpet, which was so thick it felt strange beneath my feet; I felt as if I were sinking into it.

"I want to," he said. Then his voice took on a commanding tone once again, and he took my arm and spun me gently around. "What was it?"

I looked into his eyes. They were eager eyes, and I knew I had him good. "I can't. You'll just get mad." Then I walked away.

After crushing Stewart's self-esteem into the thick hotel carpet, I decided to visit Charlie's room, since he was the friendliest toward me of all the roadies. The room was crowded and noisy; there were two or three arguments going on, and Packy seemed to be trying to mollify someone's flaring temper. I needed to listen for only a few seconds to understand what the problem was. The cocaine had run out, and the boys were being chastised for not having more at hand. Two of the men were accusing Packy and Camión of holding out on them in order to drive up the price. Packy was trying to explain that they couldn't get any more until that evening, when the "poosher" would be home.

Finally an agreement was reached under which more *perico* would be delivered later that night at the same price. The angry roadies had to be satisfied with this, and they wandered away grumbling. El Camión left to track down the cocaine, his rage at the roadies' accusations barely disguised.

Then Stewart came in looking unhappy. He avoided my eyes. George was on him at once.

"Hey, John," George said. "There was a chick here just a few minutes ago. Some TV bitch. She was out-fucking-rageous. What's her story, man?"

"Oh, her?" Stewart said. "Forget about it. She wants to squeeze the band."

Anger flashed through me at that; I wanted to call him a liar and a poor loser. Instead I said nothing.

George laughed loudly. "They all want that at first. Give her a little time to face reality, though, and bam..." He made a gesture with a fist and an extended forearm. I turned away from him.

"Well," said Stewart, cheering instantly, "by the looks of that one, she might just make it. But if she doesn't..." He let the sentence go unfinished and stretched an arm to give George a hopeful squeeze across the shoulders. I walked out into the hallway and stood by myself for a time.

While the roadies were showering and getting dressed, the Caracas representative of the Prowlers' American record label came to the hotel. He was round and soft, with a collection of gaudy rings that looked as though they were permanently embedded in the white flesh of his fingers. As soon as he walked into the room, he began caressing the better-built roadies with liquid-brown eyes.

The roadies, who were arguing and laughing and making deals with one another, all turned to inspect him for a minute, apparently found nothing either interesting or threatening about him, and went back to their business. The man waddled over to me and surrounded my hand with his own. The feel of his handshake was similar to the sensation of plunging all five fingers into a bowl of warm dough. He said his name was Roberto something or other, whispered his name close to my ear, and then he shook Stewart's hand and went around the room like that, shaking hands and whispering Roberto something or other. A few of the technicians stared at his hand for a second or two before taking it.

Roberto then announced that he had arrived to take the roadies on a tour of Caracas nightlife. There was cheering then, and a general tossing of clothing and towels into the air, followed by frantic rushing from room to room as the crew struggled to ready themselves.

A bad night followed.

Roberto took everyone to the outdoor cafés of Sabana Grande for the first stop. It was an impressive thing to see the caravan of limousines pull up near the Gran Café; Roberto of the dough-hand was in the lead car, and he stepped out smiling, grinning at all the people seated at the outdoor tables who had turned to stare at us.

You would have thought that he himself was a rock star. He had produced a pair of wrap-around sunglasses from somewhere and he was now wearing them; the reflected light of the streetlamps made bright starbursts on the dark plastic lenses.

Packy and I stepped from the second car, and we began collecting the roadies into a tight group that could be easily supervised. The technicians started smiling when they saw all the people; it was their experience that where there were people, there was possibility.

But as usual, Sabana Grande held a fairly sophisticated crowd. After they had gawked as long as they needed to ascertain that the band members themselves were not with us, the people went back to their drinking and nibbling and conversation. A few of our men made remarks in the direction of tables where attractive women were seated, but drew only blank stares or polite smiles. We got them settled at a group of round metal tables and bribed a waiter to bring us forty beers, *rápido*.

By the time the second round had arrived, it became clear that Sabana Grande was a bust. The roadies began grumbling and shooting dangerous glances in Roberto's direction. He acted surprised and hurt, but then he promised to take them someplace where there was plenty of action.

I did not get to accompany them, however. As I was getting ready to climb into one of the limos, John Stewart, who must have been brooding about Orchid, came up to me and poked a finger into my chest.

"You," he said. "We don't need you. Take a cab back to the hotel and wait there."

I was disappointed, of course. But in light of what happened, I was lucky.

The entire war party returned to the Hilton less than two hours later; all the roadies were oddly silent, and there was something murderous in their silence. Packy lured me into a corner, a will-o'-the-wisp smile on his face.

"That Roberto? He took everyone to a gay bar."

"*No!*"

"*Sí*. He wanted to show them off."

"Holy shit. They didn't hurt anybody, did they?"

"No. They just carried Roberto out on their shoulders and

dropped him in a fountain. They were quite gentle with him, actually. Considering the circumstances, anyway."

"They're not planning to blame us, are they?" Packy shrugged.

"Who can tell what they'll do. Fucking gringos are unpredictable."

Camión returned. He had scored the *perico*, and he carried it to the room George shared with two other men in order to cut his bulk purchase into grams beneath a lamp on the writing table. The roadies who had contributed to the cocaine kitty gathered around him like hungry animals; they snatched the grams as soon as they were ready and took them away to consume in privacy.

Within fifteen minutes many of the roadies were crazed with *perico*. They wandered from room to room, grinding their teeth and shouting. Several of them worked themselves into a fine, violent rage at having been taken to a gay bar on a night when they had wanted to look for a good time. They got on a couple of telephones and made loud, incoherent calls back to the States.

A riot soon threatened, and Stewart seemed reluctant to do anything about it. He was nearly as outraged as the others.

But Packy telephoned Ballesteros, and at two in the morning the promoter showed up and spread oil on the waters. He brought with him two ounces of coke that he said was for everyone to enjoy, free of charge, and he promised the roadies a party after all the setting-up at the Poliedro had been completed.

"A good party," he said, winking. "With everything you could want."

Thus pacified, the roadies hoovered up the free *perico*, then they laughed and screamed nonsense at each other until dawn.

When gray light crept through the hotel windows and most of the members of the road crew lay collapsed across their beds, I decided to take a long walk to try to clear my head. I went out and strolled with my face to the ground and my hands in my pockets, paying little attention to where I went.

Suddenly, as I was passing beneath a tall apartment building, I felt a couple of warm splashes on the back of my neck. I had not expected rain, and I lifted eyes to the sky. I spotted him then; a man in a light-colored bathrobe was peering down at me from a high balcony. At first I thought he had spilled something on me, spilled a few drops of coffee or warm beer, and I was ready to allow him to apologize and call it an accident. But then I saw him fumbling below his waist with his dark hands.

"Hey!" I shouted. His hands stopped fumbling then; he lifted them against his shoulders, showing me his palms, a gesture that meant the problem was mine alone. Then he laughed.

"*Pana*," he called. "It's Angel Falls. I've saved you the expense of flying there." Laughing, he turned and disappeared into his apartment. A minute later I was uncertain which anonymous balcony he had been standing on.

CHAPTER 6

Two days later I met the rock star, Ronnie Neumon. Packy and El Camión had met him first, had met him the evening after the disastrous night out with Roberto, the Venezuelan record representative. They had gone to the airport to greet the Prowlers as they came in from Los Angeles. I was unable to make that airport trip because I had to fill a rush order for some foreign debt figures that someone in the San Juan bureau needed to flesh out a wrap-up on the Latin financial picture. Mickey, of course, had been unavailable to do the job; I thought the work might be good for him and had tried calling him many times, but he was either not in or not answering his telephone.

Despite the fact that Ronnie and the band had been retrieved and brought to Caracas by Packy and Camión, the promoter decided that I should act as the rock star's personal interpreter. Ballesteros said he thought that of the three of us, I would be the one most likely to understand the gringo vices and perversions Ronnie was noted for. He assigned Packy to follow the three less troublesome band members, and he kept Camión in the Poliedro, where his strong back had proven useful time after time.

I met Ronnie in his private suite, a floor above the rooms occupied by his roadies. The meeting took place during the heat of day, long after all the roadies and the other Prowlers had gone off to the Poliedro to do their work.

Magazines that paid attention to rock music were always calling

Ronnie a rock 'n' roll hero. And he did look like a hero; he resembled a strictly physical hero of the ancient mold, a hero of the tall, strong, head-bashing type. A Viking, a warrior hero who is born rather than developed and cultivated with education and character-building challenges. He was the kind of specimen who makes you feel a little hollow inside with the realization that no matter how hard you strive, you will never achieve that kind of magnetism and force, who seems almost to stand on a slightly higher evolutionary level than anyone around him.

And he did, when I shook hands with him, give me that hollow feeling. In spite of his appearance and the things magazines said about him, however, Ronnie seemed at first to possess an ego still trim enough to fit into a hotel suite with a little room to spare.

At my knock he opened the door and spread his mouth in a smile. He shook my hand; his own hand was large and strong and hot, and his wide blue eyes turned flat and hard for a moment as he tested the strength of my hand and looked me over head to foot. But that initial look of appraisal was a fleeting one, and then his eyes were shining with humor and goodwill. All the while he held my hand, the smile on his face never changed, never flickered. His teeth were perfect, movie-star teeth. He had blond hair that reached his shoulders, and high cheekbones that made his eyes seem even larger than they were. He stood about six-five, and he was slender and arrow-straight.

"You're Jimmy?" he asked. "C'mon in." I followed him into the room and closed the door. I had expected him to be decked out in all his gaudy, intimidating rock-star trappings, and the fact that he wasn't was a relief. He was wearing faded jeans, sneakers, and a short-sleeved Hawaiian shirt. He did wear an earring, though, a large gold hoop that flashed whenever he turned his head.

"You want a drink?" asked Ronnie Neumon, rock star. "A beer, something like that? Smoke a joint?"

"Beer'd be okay," I said. I was looking hard for something to immediately dislike about him, but I was not having an easy time. He even had open suitcases scattered all over his suite, just like any rumpled bachelor recently arrived in a hotel room.

Ronnie smiled at me as if reading my mind. Then he disappeared into the kitchen of his suite and returned a moment later with two bottles of Heineken.

170

"I always bring my own brew wherever I go," Ronnie Neumon said, handing me a bottle. "You never know how you'll like the local stuff."

"S'right," I told him. "Cheers." We tilted our heads back and drank. The cold beer ran right to all the hottest and darkest places inside of me, and I shuddered.

"I'm from California," he said after a minute. "L.A. How 'bout you?"

"Connecticut, originally."

"Connecticut? No shit. My wife's from there."

There was a piano in the room; it had been one of the prerequisites in his contract with the Venezuelan promoter, and a photographic portrait of a woman decorated a picture frame standing atop the instrument. Ronnie Neumon snatched up the picture and handed it to me. "That's her. Right there." His eyes glowed with the pride of possession.

I held the photograph carefully as I looked down at it. She was his physical match, there were no two ways about it. Unlike Ronnie, she had black hair, but her eyes were as blue as his, and her skin was the color of milk and her face was a perfect, heartbreaking oval that hinted at sweetness and reasonableness and intelligence. There was something extremely familiar about her, and I wondered whether I had seen or met her somewhere else before. She was from Connecticut, probably from near my grandmother's rich little town, so it was not impossible.

I almost gushed out with a stupid exclamation, awed as I was that any man, even Ronnie Neumon, could have a woman that looked like that for a wife. I had to curl my tongue to keep myself from speaking.

"What do you think?" he asked. He seemed genuinely interested in my reaction. He was grinning at me now, and it pleased me that I had finally spotted a flaw in him: He was a gloater. It was just a small thing, but enough to help even us out in my mind.

"Very nice." I tried to keep my voice neutral.

"She's an actress." His eyes no longer focused directly on me, engaging me, but looked upward, over my head someplace, and they shone with glee at his good fortune. "She goes by her maiden name, which is Hart. Loren Hart."

"Really?" I said, taking a sip of my beer and adopting a journalist's cynical frown. I made a point of seeing all the major American pictures that came down to Venezuela, and I didn't remember Ronnie's wife as having been in anything important. "Stage, or film?"

His eyes dropped then; they met mine for a second, then slid away and sought the carpet. "Well, just a made-for-TV movie or two," he said. "I don't guess you would have seen them down here."

"No." I was beginning to enjoy myself.

Then he looked me in the eyes again. "But she's been on a television show for the past five years."

I took the risk of gently taunting him. "A soap opera?"

Ronnie Neumon made an angry face. But his expression quickly became good-natured again; so quickly in fact that it made me uneasy. No one could shift emotions that fast; it was possible only to *pretend* to shift them with great speed.

"Not a *soap* opera," he said. He made his mouth look as if he had just tasted detergent. "You think I don't have any class, or what?" I shook my head and displayed the palms of my hands to show that I meant no harm. But inside I was laughing.

"No. It's one of those sitcoms, called *Sisters*. Maybe you—"

"Oh, wait," I said, overcome by a flood of recognition now. In spite of myself, I was suddenly fired with excitement. "I've seen her. Loren Hart." I rolled the name in my mouth as if it were an incantation. "*Sisters*. It's the one where the two college girls, two sisters, get an apartment together, and then their divorced mother moves in with them."

Ronnie was pleased to see that I was finally, suitably impressed. "That's it," he said happily, and took a long suck from his beer. I was unable to stop myself.

"Yeah, I used to watch it sometimes. The mother, that redhead, what's her name, becomes just like another sister and starts taking classes . . ."

"That's it. That's it," said Ronnie, his huge eyes shining.

". . . and she starts going out with younger guys." It was a mindless show, as I recalled, with recorded laughter poured on thick as syrup. But I also remembered that the program was redeemed to a certain extent by the physical attractiveness of the three women.

"Yeah," I said. "That blond sister, she was a Miss America, wasn't she. What a knockout."

Ronnie was serious all over again. "Listen," he said, worry pulling at his face now. "Who would you say was better looking, that blonde, or Loren?" He was staring at me with intensity. His tongue came out and swept hungrily around the outside of his mouth.

Then, in a suddenly hoarse voice, he added, "Not that it really matters, you know. I'm just curious."

I was tempted to say the blonde, even though I could remember nothing about her except her hair color and the fact that she had large breasts. But then I thought the better of it.

"Loren," I told him. "Definitely Loren."

Reassured, the rock star smiled. Then he said, "That's good, that's good. She's coming down, you know. To Venezuela. She'll be here tomorrow or the day after. I'd like very much for you to meet her." Once again he was a great, warm, magnetic pal. I couldn't help but like him.

"Yeah," I said. "I'd like that a lot."

He nodded, and smiled and changed the subject. He asked me how well I spoke Spanish and where I had learned it. My job with the agency and my student days in Mexico seemed to impress him. Then, after we had opened another beer, he reached into a nearly empty hotel-room dresser drawer and produced that inevitable still life, cocaine on mirror with razor blade and hundred-dollar bill.

He scored out four lines and reddened his own nose on both sides before he offered me the rolled-up bill.

"Blow?" he asked.

"No."

"You don't do it?"

I hesitated. "Hardly ever." I didn't have the courage to give him the absolute truth; the absolute truth about anything is almost always shameful.

Ronnie's face took on the superior, yet concerned expression you saw on the faces of religious proselytizers, the look that is supposed to show worry for your soul but that actually reveals only the fear of standing alone in weakness and insanity. I recognized that look and braced myself.

"Why not, Jimmy?" Ronnie asked. His eyebrows were lifted in my direction like the doors to a pair of baited box traps.

"I just don't," I answered, my hands tightening into fists. My eyes settled to the carpeted floor and blood began moving to my face. I prepared myself for a long siege on the issue of cocaine; I was ready for him to tell me how good it really was for me and how it would make me feel like Superman. But to my surprise, Ronnie relented; his box-trap eyebrows settled gently, without springing, and he smiled. His hand came up, and he began circling the inside of his earring with his index finger.

"Well, shit," Ronnie the rock star said. "I read someplace it was bad for your heart. You may outlive us all." He gave me a friendly sock in the shoulder. "Even if you don't have as good a time."

Ronnie laughed, lifting his eyebrows just enough to prod me into laughing, too, and I did laugh. I laughed for show at first, but then the two of us got going on it, letting it roll up and out of us, and then I felt the genuine laughter tickling me from inside. I couldn't help but feel a little grateful that he had not persecuted me about the *perico*.

When the laughter died, Ronnie turned his attention to the remaining two lines on the mirror and he hoovered them up. Then he smiled and said, "I think you're pretty cool, Jimbo. I like you."

I never liked to be called Jimbo, but the fact that Ronnie said he liked me made me glow a little.

"I mean it, pal," he said, as if I had protested. "You've got kind of a . . ." He let a slow hand roll through the air as he searched for the words. ". . . kind of a *Bogart* quality to you, you know, tough and vulnerable at the same time." Blood burned my face. I was pleased in spite of myself.

"Yeah?" I muttered. I looked at the floor.

"So," Ronnie said. He had been leaning toward me, but then he backed off, as if giving me room to breathe. "Foreign correspondent. Pretty cool. Pretty *goddamn* cool."

I forced myself to meet his gaze. Felt a crooked smile pulling at one side of my face. "So," I managed to croak. "Rock star."

He laughed, and he got me laughing again. Then he reached and gave me a slap on my shoulder; I felt warmth and comradeship flow from him to me. He left his hand on my shoulder for a minute, and after he finally took it away he began speaking to me in a low, conspiratorial voice.

"Listen, Jimbo," he said. "When I come into a strange town like this, they usually set up a lot of shit for me, you know, like dinners at restaurants and dates with expensive whores and TV shit and meet this important asshole and smoke a joint with that important asshole and have their fat wives grab my cock under the table, you understand me?"

I nodded.

"Well, shit, man, I hardly ever get to see what's really going on in the town. I want you to *show* me things; I want you to take me out, incog-fucking-nito and show me around."

I smiled. It seemed as if he might be a regular, misunderstood guy after all. "Sure," I said. "We could do it."

"Great, Jimbo, great." He had dropped his eyes by then, and was toying with the razor blade as if thinking of laying out another pair of lines.

"One thing, though," I said, feeling embarrassed and even a little unreasonable to be bringing it up.

"What's that, Jimbo?" He had begun grinding a particularly stubborn pebble of *perico* with the side of the blade.

"Don't call me Jimbo. Okay?"

He looked up, startled, and I thought I saw anger in his face. But the anger, if it had been there at all, was fleeting. He smiled warmly at me. "Sure," he said. "Jim."

"Can call me Jimmy if you want. Friends do that."

His smile widened. "Jimmy," he agreed. Then he was back to work on that obstinate little piece of white pleasure.

Ronnie and I had another beer together and talked about books. He surprised me with his knowledge of books, surprised me and made me envious of the way he knew his own interests and one of my stronger ones as well. He was familiar with most of the contemporary writers I had read.

"I like a writer who makes you feel something in your gut," Ronnie said. "Makes you care about something. Know what I mean?"

"Yeah," I said. "I think I do."

"I mean, I can't stand a writer who cares about nothing but how words hold hands on a page. That kind of writer is like one of those guys who traps you in a corner at a party and won't shut up. He may speak well, but what he's saying is boring and contains nothing you can relate to, and on top of it, the guy is such a pompous jackass that he thinks you should be fascinated by this rap just because it's coming from his mouth."

"Yes," I said. I was trying to picture Ronnie trapped in a corner by anybody. "But if it's all gut, as you say..."

"Then it's even worse," Ronnie said. "Then it's like listening to some blubbering drunk in a bar talk about how he wishes he could make himself stop beating his wife and kids. It's shocking at first, and you want to listen, but it goes on and on and the guy repeats himself a hundred times and pretty soon you figure out that he doesn't really want to stop at all, he just wants a little cheap pity for himself, and then you stop caring about him, and you don't really care about his wife and kids because he hasn't told you enough about them to make them seem like real people to you, and pretty soon you're throwing five bucks on the bar and running out the door."

I laughed, and then Ronnie smiled and began laughing too. I had a good feeling about him then; I was beginning to see him as the ideal friend.

Then Ronnie said he had to get ready for some things that were going on that afternoon. He told me he would just be a minute and to make myself at home, take a drink from the bar, eat something from the refrigerator. Anything I wanted.

"Or," he said, emerging half naked from his bedroom a minute after I'd already settled into the sofa with *Playboy* magazine, "you could go ahead and score out a couple of lines for yourself."

I looked at his sincere face and saw that he wasn't joking. It bothered me a little that he seemed to have forgotten that I didn't snort coke, but I nodded at him anyway, and he disappeared. A few minutes later I heard the distant roar of his shower.

I didn't get to read for very long. A minute or two after I heard the shower stop, Ronnie Neumon poked his head out of the bedroom door and said, "Hey, Jim, can you get me my shaving cream, man? It's in the suitcase under the window. And my razor too, please."

I rose reluctantly from the couch and went to stand above the expensive piece of luggage that lay opened on the carpet. I didn't see his shaving cream and razor right away, so I had to stir things around a bit; I had to move aside a brilliant collection of silk ties and a book that looked like a photo album and stick my hand beneath a pile of bright bikini underwear-briefs before I found the items. Then, before I knew what I was doing, I had lifted the cover of the photo album; the first photo was in color and showed a naked Ronnie squatting between the knees of a grossly fat, reclining woman who was not his wife. The rock star was smiling at the camera.

I closed the book and began to feel guilty. I knocked on the bedroom door and handed Ronnie his toilet things, and then I sat back down on the couch and picked up the magazine. I was trembling a little because of the photo album. Before I could open the magazine, he was asking for something else.

"Jimmy," he said, calling through the now closed bedroom door. "My damn leather pants, man. Get them out of the closet by the door, okay?"

With some distaste, I got to my feet and went to the closet. I expected to find the disgusting pants that were wide open in back, but all I came across was a shiny black garment with a crimson seat. I carried the pants to the door of the bedroom and knocked. He kept me waiting for nearly a minute before he opened and took them.

"Thanks," he said, smiling. He draped the pants over his muscular forearm and stroked the red seat affectionately. "Fuckers made me cover my ass," he said. "Can't let it hang out in this country apparently."

The rock star retreated and closed the door, and I went back to the couch. I was studying the centerfold and wondering about the fat woman in the photograph when he called me again. "Jimbo! That same closet? I need my snakeskin vest."

I sighed and got up and picked the vest off its hanger. I marveled at how quickly I had slid down the ladder from intellectual buddy to valet. The vest was real snakeskin; it had come from some poor endangered species with huge hollow diamonds all over its body. The vest still felt like a living cold-blooded thing. I took it to Ronnie's door, and in a minute he stuck out an arm and snatched it away from me.

He didn't need me for a while after that. He just stayed behind his closed door and began to tune his voice. He sang nonsense syllables over and over for a time, and then he began to warble like a bird. I decided then that he possessed nowhere near the natural talent that Orchid had. When he was finished with the warbling, he started on a series of high, rough sounds that were like some jungle cat in pain or a blues singer with his foreskin caught in a zipper.

The photo album began to tempt me. I sat on the couch thinking about the fat woman and trying to imagine what the rest of the book contained. Dwarfs? Animals? Finally I resolved to take the risk and I stood, but just at that moment, there came a knock at the door. With a heavy feeling of lost opportunity, I walked over and cautiously opened it.

A thin woman who was obviously American shoved past me as if I weren't there and then stood in the middle of the suite, rolling her head from side to side, seemingly getting her bearings. I guessed that she was in her late thirties, but the deeply seamed skin of her face made her look even older than that. Her hair was dyed a tired shade of rust-brown, and in her mouth a piece of chewing gum tumbled like a dirty shirt in a washing machine. She held what looked like a large attaché case in one hand.

"Ron," she shouted after a moment. "Ronnie?"

Ronnie Neumon stopped singing then and stuck his head out the door. He was wearing the snakeskin vest, and it did not quite meet in the middle to cover his chest and stomach. "Oh, hi, love," he said. "Be right out. How much time do we have?"

"'Bout forty-five minutes," she said with a petulant New York accent. Ronnie started to close the door, but the woman shouted, "Hey!" and he opened it again and looked out at her with wide eyes.

She jerked her head in my direction, the first indication she had given that she knew I was in the room. "Who's he?"

"I don't know," said Ronnie. Then he closed the door.

The woman and I glared at each other until I finally looked away. Then she sat down on the couch and opened her case and took out aerosol cans and combs and brushes and other hairdressing items and set them on the glass-topped coffee table. When she had finished laying out her wares, she knelt on the carpet and scraped the razor blade against Ronnie's mirror and then sucked up a couple of lines of *perico*.

After Ronnie finally came out, she worked on him for over half an hour. She spread a purple silk cape over the front of him, and then she fluffed his hair and sprayed it and spiked it out. When she was done, he looked like a blond-maned lion on an LSD trip.

Then she did something to his eyebrows to make them sharper and darker and more dramatic. She also patted something on his cheeks and gave him a tube of something to rub on his lips, and then she closed everything back up in her dark case and rewarded herself with another pair of *pases*.

Ronnie studied himself for two minutes or so in the mother-of-pearl hand mirror the hairdresser had given him before he finally swept aside the cape and jumped to his feet. He was wearing what looked like ballet slippers, but were probably some kind of martial arts shoe, and for a minute he stood in the middle of the suite, leaping and throwing a series of high, twirling roundhouse karate kicks into the air. The kicks looked impressive to me, but then, I knew nothing about the martial arts. When he was done, he looked over at me for the first time since he had sat down to get his hair done. He smiled.

"What do you think?" he asked. He was touching his earring again; it was a curiously feminine gesture that I began to find annoying.

"Yeah," I said. I looked back down at the magazine.

"Hey, uh . . ." He seemed to forget my name for a moment, but then he recovered. "Jimbo," he said finally. "We've got a press conference right fucking now, *amigo*. Let's go!"

Up to that time I had been under TV lights many times, but never as the focus of the cameras. Whenever I'd found myself in that hellish glare whose penetrating heat always made me imagine myself to be a small, bloody roast sitting in a microwave oven, it was as a working newsman, and if I appeared in the broadcast footage at all, the people watching their TVs saw me standing off to the side, a pad and pencil or a tape recorder in my busy hands. But after the Prowlers came to Caracas, the cameras began to aim directly at me.

When Ronnie and I left his suite, we found a couple of husky gringo boys pacing the carpet-muffled hallway outside. They said hi to Ronnie, and then one of them fell in behind us as we walked to the elevator. The three of us waited for the elevator, saying nothing, until finally it stopped at our floor and opened, revealing a small pack of Venezuelan girls.

"Ronnie!" the group cried as one. Two girls, both of whom wore thick swaths of makeup beneath their eyes, tried to step out into the hallway, but the security man behind us moved up and pushed them back inside.

"No you don't," the security man said. I could see he was being as gentle as he could, but one of the girls he pushed went all the way to the back of the elevator and bumped against the wall. Her teeth clacked together and a sudden film of water covered her dark eyes. But the mindless, Barbie-doll smile remained on her face.

Ronnie, the security man, and I stepped in, and the door closed. The security man touched a button and we started to drop. Immediately the girls began to touch Ronnie. They reached tentatively at first and then, when they saw that they were not scorched or turned into pillars of salt, they reached with more self-assurance. They touched Ronnie's skin and clothes as if they were starving and he was something edible and delicious but forbidden, taboo.

Ronnie said, "Hello, girls," and he was smiling, but I saw that his smile was also the plastic, faraway smile of a doll. I looked away, feeling inexplicably sorry for him.

The elevator opened onto the lobby, and there were more girls waiting there. They surged forward screaming, "Ronnie! Ronnie!" I saw that there were a few young boys mixed in with the girls now.

Ronnie Neumon peered out over the tops of their heads, found the little circle of press people and unlit TV lights that were waiting for him, and he pushed his way through the throng toward them. The lights came to life then, so strong that they were like something physical pressing on me. Phallic microphones poked at him from everywhere. The guard and I followed Ronnie into the center of this media bullring. Before anyone could ask him anything, Ronnie stuck a fist in the air and said, "¡Me gusta Venezuela! ¡Me gusta mucho!"

There was applause and laughter, and then the reporters began firing their questions. The phrase that Ronnie had parroted had nearly exhausted his Spanish, so he reached and grabbed me by the arm and pulled me close. He was still showing his teeth, but he seemed suddenly unnerved by the crossfire of unintelligible words. His face was sweating.

I nodded in the direction of a newspaperwoman who was staring at Ronnie with adoring eyes. "She wants to know how you think your music will affect Venezuela," I said.

180

Ronnie's smile died then; he struck a dramatic pose with one foot forward and his hands on his hips, a pout where the smile had been a moment before. "I think," said Ronnie, and paused— giving me a chance to say, *"Yo creo"*—"I think that after the Prowlers leave Venezuela, the country will never be the same again. There will be earthquakes and floods and your oil wells will run dry..." There was a gasp from all around, a sudden mass intake of breath, and the faces surrounding us became serious. If the TV lights had been hot before, they were now unbearable, nauseating. Ronnie had unwittingly struck the apocalyptic economic note that had been vibrating in the warm Venezuelan air for months; he did not know what he had done wrong, and he gave me a worried look.

"Hey," he said, and nudged me with an elbow. "It was a joke. Tell them it was a fucking joke, will you, Jim?"

"Fue una broma," I said. "He didn't mean it." There was some uncertain laughter, and then the smiles returned one by one like streetlamps going on. These representatives of the Venezuelan people were anxious to forgive, were eager to resume their diversion.

Ronnie began breathing again when it became clear that his confusing mistake had not been a fatal one. He said, *"Shit,"* very softly so that only I could hear him.

Another woman reporter spoke; most of the men were smiling crookedly, obviously captured by the excitement, but seemingly embarrassed to be a part of it.

"What do you plan to do in the days before the first show?"

Ronnie cackled. "What do I plan to do?" he asked, his voice rising so that the people twenty yards away behind the registration desk turned their heads. "What *don't* I plan to do?" He began to elaborate, but just then I saw Orchid emerge from one of the hotel's side lobbies and head toward the front doors. She was by herself, and when she looked over and saw me in the crowd, she smiled and wiggled two fingers at me before heading out of the building. I stared after her and wondered how far she had gotten with the Prowlers' publicity people in her quixotic quest for an exclusive interview.

"Hey," said Ronnie.

"What? I didn't hear." The members of the local press were staring hard at Ronnie and me.

"I *said*, I plan to rehearse hard, party my ass off, and make love to as many Venezuelan girls as possible."

I interpreted, and there was laughter. Then, in bad Spanish, Ronnie shouted, "Venezuelan *muchachas, mucha bonita. Adiós*." He tugged on my shirtsleeve and headed through the crowd toward the front doors.

"Come on, man," he said, and both the bodyguard and I struggled along behind him. There was a gray limousine waiting for us right outside the door, and we dove into it and sat catching our breaths while a red-jacketed doorman closed us in. The air conditioning in the limo was as intense in its own way as the TV lights had been in theirs.

"Shit," Ronnie said again. "Man, I thought they were going to lynch me for a minute there." He cradled his chin thoughtfully in his hands for a moment, then he turned to the bodyguard. "Listen, we won't need you for a while."

"Sure?" said the man. He sounded doubtful. A discussion began between them then, but I saw Orchid step off the sidewalk in front of the Hilton and head toward a taxi, and I tuned them out. I don't think she saw me sitting in that car and watching her, but she walked as gracefully and as deliberately as if she knew she had an audience. The taxi swallowed her and rolled down toward the highway.

"Okay," I heard the bodyguard say. The door opened and closed and he was gone.

The rock star turned to me and winked. "Alone at last, sweetheart," he said. He was touching his earring; I gave him an uneasy smile.

"Hey," said Ronnie Neumon. "That chick." He paused to lift a silver tube to his nose, some kind of fancy cocaine inhalator, and suck up a blast. "I saw you looking at her. You know her?"

Jealousy rose in me instantly. "Yeah, I know her." He sat nodding at me until the silence became embarrassing. Then I said, "She's a singer. A journalist. Something like that." It suddenly occurred to me that it was not really possible to put a tag on Orchid's occupation.

Ronnie filled his other nostril. "Well, shit," he said. "We go on TV with her tomorrow for an interview, did you know that?"

"*Really? Is that right?*" Orchid's success touched my heart like a needle.

"Yeah. Bitch has balls, too, I guess. They tell me she wouldn't take no for an answer." Ronnie gave a low chuckle and fixed me with a bright look of appraisal. "You know, if I could use, you know, my influence to fix you up or anything, just let me know."

I forced myself to smile. "Thanks," I said. "I really don't need any help, though." He was grinning, and it was very hard not to like him.

"It often works, you know," he persisted. "I say, 'Now honey, go with this guy,' and she goes. I mean, she probably does it because she figures she's kinda fucking me in a way, or else she thinks the other guy will tell me how great she is, and I'll want her." He hid his little tube and rubbed the back of his wrist across his nostrils. His nose had become red as a cranberry, and jagged veins were creeping down from it toward his upper lip. "But reasons," he said. "Why are reasons important? The fact that she puts out is important, not why she does it, am I right?"

I shook my head. "No. No, you're not." The idea of using Ronnie to get close to Orchid was tempting, though. It suddenly seemed possible, if not probable, that Orchid might want me again if she spent some time with me.

Ronnie was looking at me, and I tried to strike his eyes with my own, but my gaze slid greasily away. Unreasonable hope and shame churned bitterly inside of me. "Not with this girl anyway." But Ronnie misunderstood me.

"Bet?" His hand came toward me and hovered rock-steady in front of me. Startled, I looked up at him.

"*Bet?*" I echoed in a voice that seemed ridiculously tiny.

"Say five bucks, partner?" His voice was low and raspy and seductive. I felt ill. I shook my head, tried to tell him that he had misunderstood me, and that I would never accept Orchid if she came to me as a favor from another man.

But then, before I knew what I was doing, I had lifted my hand a little, and the rock star reached and brushed my fingers with his own.

"Okay," Ronnie said. "Let's roll. Show me this frigging city, what do you say?"

I told the driver to roll, and he rolled.

We drove aimlessly for a while. There seemed to be billboards everywhere. Bain de Soleil, General Motors. European underwear. We saw several for the Prowlers; the apocalyptic poster where

Ronnie and the other musicians stared down at the city they plan to sack and pillage. Ronnie was a product, another bit of heaven from overseas the Venezuelans were afraid they weren't going to be able to have anymore. And in case they couldn't have him in the future, they were going to get as much of him as they could right now.

Ronnie was in a good mood. He was all pumped up on *perico*. For a time the coke seemed to have anesthetized the part of his brain that filtered out the unimportant and the inconsequential, and he gave me a long stream-of-consciousness rap about how if he weren't a rock star, he most probably would be a writer. But he was glad he was a musician, because he figured that it would take him longer to transform the world with the written word than it would with music.

"I mean, like, everybody listens to music," he said.

"Everybody," I agreed. I was only half-listening. I was still in shock from the touch of Ronnie's fingers and from the realization that my feelings for Orchid had turned me into a moral hyena.

"And, at least at some level, those lyrics have to be sinking in, don't you think." I thought, *I'm a night crawler, baby, gonna crawl on yooou, oh yeah.*

"Sure, Ron. I think . . ."

"But I mean, writers. Who the fuck reads anymore? I mean, good stuff, of the type I would write. You know, I think I'd be quite a bit like Hemingway. I've always felt a spiritual connection with him."

"Well," I said, somewhat reflexively, "of that generation, probably the best is Faulkner . . ."

"Faulkner," he said, flapping a hand at me dismissingly. "He could've never been a rock star. Not in a million fucking years."

He let that relevant thought hang heavily between us for a minute before he said, "Hey, you know what I really want to see? I want to see the slums."

"You can't really take this car into—"

He cut me off quickly. He seemed to have something against letting me finish sentences. "Sure we can," he said. Then he giggled and rubbed his hands briskly together. "Take this buggy into the slums. Won't they shit? That's just the thing. Let's do it, Jimbo."

I tried to talk him out of it, but he was determined to visit a poor neighborhood in the limo. So I told the driver to head for Petare; as I recalled, the roads between the *ranchitos* were wider there than in some other places. We would be able to get the car in easily and, more importantly, to get out in a hurry if we had to. The driver studied me in the rearview, holding my eyes for a long time before pushing the big Cadillac up onto the highway they called the Cota Mil and heading along the slope of the Ávila toward Petare. The sun was just beginning to go down.

There were little pullouts along the Cota Mil for people who wanted to drive in and look down upon the lights of the city. The lights were strung along the valley like diamonds and emeralds and rubies in an impossibly elaborate necklace; it was a beautiful view. Ronnie had the driver stop for a moment, and we got out and looked down. The early-evening air was heavy and sweet, and we heard the mingled sounds of traffic from the streets below and insects and frogs from the mountain forest above us.

"Caracas, Venezuela," Ronnie said, and smacked his lips. We did not stay there long, because he was fidgety with cocaine and wanted to move on.

We left the highway, wound our way along a couple of secondary roads, and started our descent through Petare. There were *ranchos* everywhere now; they were jammed into gorges below the level of the street, and they stood above us on embankments that were sure to crumble during the next rain. They were all made of the same tired-looking brick, topped with the same rusting, corrugated steel, and surrounded by the same sterile yellow dust. It was dusk now, and one or two lights shone from each of the tiny houses. At first I thought Ronnie might be content to cruise through on the main descending street and gawk from the car, but I was wrong.

"Let's go up a side street," he said, his face excited as a child's.

"Not a good idea," I said.

"Hey," he said, his face becoming stern. "Jimbo. All right?"

I sighed and told the driver that we wanted to turn onto the next large side street, either to the left or the right. I thought the driver would balk right then, but all he said was *coño*, and in a minute he made the turn.

The road we entered was fairly wide, but any pavement that

may have ever covered it had all been washed away during rain-storms, and there were huge holes and ruts. The driver had to slow the car to about five miles an hour to get us through. There were *ranchitos* tight on either side of us now, and people were coming out of them to stare. They were dark people, Venezuelans who had migrated from the countryside and Colombians who were either unemployed or who worked in the sweatshops closer to the center of Petare. We were not far from the house where the Disip had blown up the four guerrillas. I chewed my lip and hoped the people would not form a crowd that would keep us from passing.

We saw mostly children and young men, but we went bumping past an occasional old man pushing a wheelbarrow or old woman standing out on her stoop. One of the young men we passed carried a machete, and he made a lazy swipe at the antenna of the limo with it.

"Stop the car!" Ronnie suddenly shouted. "Tell him to stop! This is the spot, Jimbo, right here!"

Fear sat in me like a tumor. "Hey, Ronnie, we can't—"

"Right *fucking* here," the rock star cried joyously, as if he hadn't even heard me.

"Ronnie, I don't think—" He turned on me then, so quickly I didn't have time to react, and he gathered the front of my shirt in one of his big hands and jerked me close.

"You tell the driver to stop," he said, foam flying from his lips into my face. I was mad enough to swing at him then, but I knew that he was all coked up and would probably go crazy and we'd end up struggling in the middle of the street while the local barracudas circled in for the kill. Plus, I'd undoubtedly get hurt and end up with loose teeth and blood all over, and then he'd steal the limousine and I'd have to walk home through Petare.

"Okay," I told Ronnie. "Let me go." He released my shirt and sat glaring at me, breathing heavily, his nostrils flaring. My chest stung where his knuckles had dug into me.

"*Pana*," I said, calling to the driver over the front seat, "*párate aquí*." The driver gave me big, moon-shaped eyes in the rearview.

"In this shit? Cut the crap, *chico*. I'm not stopping in this *vaina*," he answered.

Ronnie the rock star jumped on that immediately. "What's he saying? He's not going to stop?"

"That's what he says."

"You tell him if he doesn't stop right here, I'll make sure he never works again." I hesitated, so he reached once more for the front of my shirt. "Tell him," he said.

I relayed the message, and the *criollo* found me in the mirror again. He held my eyes for a moment before wiping his hands together in the air above his head, indicating that he would not take responsibility. Then he pulled over and immediately reached inside his jacket to produce a small semiautomatic pistol, which he set in his lap. After that he dug into his top pocket for a cigarette. He lit the cigarette and threw his arm across the back of the seat as Ronnie and I slid from the car. I was grateful that he left the motor running.

Ronnie's mood changed as soon as his feet hit the ground. It was as if the memory of the last few violent minutes had slipped from his mind. "Great!" he shouted, and threw his arms wide. "South America!"

It was almost dark now. The road around the car was deeply pitted, and we stumbled into potholes as we wandered around the vehicle. Ronnie seemed to be collecting his bearings in order to plunge off in one direction or another. I promised myself that no matter where he went, I would follow him only for as long as I could see the car.

People were sticking heads out of their houses. There were no doors on most of the *ranchitos*, only a species of sooty curtain that hung down across the doorway to create a little privacy; the people who stood in the doorways wore these curtains like cloaks as they stared at us. The people had wide eyes that seemed slightly luminescent in the falling darkness. Not a smile flashed anywhere.

In a minute young boys began squeezing out from around the bodies of their mothers and wandering toward us on bare feet that made no sound against the packed dirt. The cry of a young child came to me from somewhere: hunger unsatisfied. From another direction came the sound of a violent argument, a man shouting drunkenly and a woman shrilly remonstrating. From still another direction, a loud blaring of salsa music.

On a stool in front of the *rancho* closest to us sat an old woman. She was thin and she wore a black rag wrapped around her head and a long, dark dress. The toes of her bare feet peeked out from beneath the hem of the dress. She was smoking a cigarette and silently watching us. Every time she puffed on the cigarette, the hot end brightened and made her face glow yellow and cast shadows into the deep seams of her cheeks. It had gotten so dark that the burning tip of her cigarette and that of the driver were like twin fireflies now.

From the clusters of houses above us and below us, I saw lines of shadowy bodies moving up and down the paths and steep wooden stairways that connected one level of the tiered hillside with the next. The lines were all moving in our direction.

"Ronnie," I said. "This could get really..." But he laughed and banged his hands together.

"Out-fucking-rageous," he said. Then he turned and lurched away, heading directly toward the old woman on the stool. "Ever see the inside of one of these places?" he asked me. Before I could even try to stop him, he sidestepped the old woman, who rolled her head back slowly to look at him, and he shoved aside the dirty curtain that separated her house from the street. Then he was gone, leaving only a rippling wake in the fabric over the door.

I stopped before the old woman. "*Señora*," I said, my voice quavering, "excuse the gentleman. He's very drunk." She stared at me with an unfathomable expression on her face and took a draw from her cigarette. Smoke twisted off into the dark air.

Then a child's excited squeal came from somewhere unseen. "*¡La bruja!*" the little girl said. "The witch! They went into the witch's house."

I studied the old woman, who did not return my gaze. She did not look like a *bruja*. She just looked like a worn-out crone waiting for death. Still, when the invisible child squealed "*¡La bruja!*" again, I began to shake badly.

The shadows moving up and down stairways and paths were getting closer. A few had already arrived and were admiring the limo. The driver was showing them his pistol, smiling at them and pointing the gun toward the roof of the car. I turned and stepped hesitantly over to the hovel into which Ronnie had disappeared. After drawing a deep, ragged breath, I pushed aside the still-moving curtain and stepped inside.

The main room of the tiny house was lit by a single bare bulb hanging by a cord from the ceiling. The floor was hard-packed dirt except where loose planks had been laid down, and for furniture there was a beat-up old sofa with holes in the cover and a few wooden chairs.

In one corner of the main room lay a deep pile of old blankets. Against one wall stood two small chests of drawers decorated on top with photographs of smiling children. The photos were not held by frames, and most of them were curling in on themselves. Nothing witchlike at all.

At first I did not see Ronnie; I only heard his feet scuffling against packed earth in some other part of the house. I noticed two curtains that covered what were probably smaller side rooms. One of the curtains was a tattered and oil-stained American flag that had been patched in spots with odd pieces of material so that the red and white stripes were broken by islands of black and green and purple.

I stood in the center of the main room for half a minute before the curtain that was not the flag lifted aside and Ronnie poked his head out. Light from another bare bulb spilled out around him. "Hey, Jimbo, come on in here." Then he disappeared again.

I was about to refuse, but I decided that I might more easily get him out of the house if I humored him. So I pushed aside the curtain and stepped into a tiny room that was taken up almost entirely by a table covered with a soiled white cloth. The tabletop held the remains of a meal for two people. They had eaten *arepas* and black beans, and there was still a half-eaten *arepa* on one of the plates. Above the table hung a picture of a sad, upward-looking Christ with a bloody thatch of briers wound around his head like black barbed wire. The room also contained an ancient electric stove as well as a row of splintering cupboards hung low enough on the wall for a frail old woman to reach.

Ronnie had his arm in one of the cupboards and was shoving things around inside. He came out with a child's plastic drinking cup. The cup bore a flaking cartoon I recognized as the magic whale that was always carrying the little boy to see Jesus on Venezuelan television. Ronnie squinted in puzzlement at the cup before putting it back. Then he brought out two more cups and held them in his large hands; there were American cartoons on these cups.

"The Jetsons!" he shouted. "George Jetson. And what the fuck was his wife's name?"

"Ronnie," I said, glancing over my shoulder at the dirty curtain. I heard voices close to the front of the house.

"God," he said, looking at me with glowing eyes. "What a trained anthropologist could do with this place. This is a cultural treasure house. Look at these fucking cups!" He reached back into the cupboard.

"Flintstones!" he cried a moment later.

"Ronnie," I said, "leave the people's things alone. What's the matter with you?"

He looked at me with eyes full of mock injury. "I'm an American scientist, for Christ's sake. You can't tell a scientist to leave things alone."

But in a moment he put everything back and shoved past me to reenter the main room. I followed him and watched him cross the room and pull aside the American flag to expose a slop bucket covered by a board. The rock star sniffed loudly, probably for my benefit, then he laughed and let the flag fall back into place.

"This is great," Ronnie said. "A flag. To us, it's a flag, right? Symbol of a fucking nation. To her it's a convenient rag to cover the shit pot with. Humbling, isn't it?"

Before I could answer him, he had gone out through the curtain over the front doorway. Out in the street I heard many Spanish voices. In a moment I heard Ronnie begin to address the small crowd, telling them in English who he was. They grew silent as they listened.

I was about to go stumbling after him yet again when I was startled by a stirring in the pile of blankets I had seen earlier. Suddenly a young girl sat up from among the blankets, appearing out of them as if by magic. The shadows cast by the single light bulb must have hidden her before, but even as I told myself this, I was unable to keep myself from drawing away. My heart shook me from within.

"Papa?" the girl said, staring right at me. Something about the backward tilt of her pretty little head let me know she was not seeing me. I stepped forward then and looked at her more closely, bending toward her and placing my hands on my knees. Her irises were the dead color of pale moonlight on water. I tried to speak, but nothing came out of me save a sad hiss of air that was not quite a sigh.

"Papa?" she said again.

"No," I told her. "Not your papa." My voice sounded ungentle to my own ears. I expected her to be frightened, but her expression did not change.

"I heard strange voices," she said. "Who are you?"

By then I was already reaching into my pocket for my wallet. I had a few hundred bolivars, and I drew out one coffee-colored *tabla* and folded it. Food for a couple of days.

"I came into your house by mistake," I told the little girl. "But I'm a friend." I pressed the bill into her tiny hand, and her fingers closed around it. Her face remained expressionless.

"I've been waiting for my papa," she said. "If you see him, would you please send him?"

"Yes," I told her. "I will." I went out through the curtain then. I was no longer afraid to step back into the street; my fear was gone, replaced by a terrible sadness. My throat was thick, and I felt pressure behind my eyes.

Ronnie was still talking. He was out in the middle of the street, surrounded by *rancho* people, but I could detect no fear in his voice. He was laughing and singing little snatches of his songs for them. His voice sounded nothing like it did when it was purified and brightened by electronics; he just sounded like a man with a head full of coke-laden snot. Many, though not all, of the people in the street were laughing.

"Jimbo!" he said when he saw me. "They were going to fucking rob me, man! But then they saw who I was." I could tell he was delighted.

"¡Epa!" I looked down and saw the woman. I had almost bumped her as she sat on her little stool. Before I could apologize, she said, "Why did you go into my house?" She had a hoarse, querulous voice like that of a magpie.

"My friend," I said. "He—"

"He has no respect," she said. "He doesn't think we're people like he is."

"He doesn't think anyone is a person like he is." I started to laugh, but then stopped when the woman failed to join me.

"No," she said. "But he thinks we're even less like he is than most people, because we have no *plata*, no money. He thinks that our blood and our insides are different even than yours. That's why he walked into my house without asking."

I felt a thread of guilt tighten in me when she said that. At some

191

level I was sure that I, too, thought my blood and insides were different, better, than the blood and insides of those who swarmed on the hillsides. I bent over to look into her withered face. "Where is the little girl's father?"

"At the prison in Catia," rasped the old woman. Her thin arm came up with a lighted cigarette that burned close to her fingers, and she drew off it. "He killed her mother."

Her words turned me to ice. When I finally could speak, I blurted, "I gave her some money. A hundred bolivars. Is she your granddaughter?"

The woman dropped her cigarette stub on the ground and thumped it with a bare foot. Part of it kept glowing.

"No," she said. "She has no more family. Do you expect me to say thank you?" She had been looking down until then, but now she tilted her head back to look directly at me. I expected to see piercing, unbearable eyes, but her eyes were lost in the folds of flesh around them. Her head shook ever so slightly from side to side.

I averted my own guilty eyes from her unseeable ones. "No," I said. "I don't." I turned to leave then.

But her voice rose and arrested me. "Your friend," she said. "He's in terrible trouble. Some he deserves, and some he doesn't." I looked back at her, and her voice fell. She lowered her face. "I see things," she muttered.

"What kind of trouble?"

"I don't know."

"That's helpful," I said, trying to make light of it even though the back of my neck was full of needles. Then, drawn by a horrible fascination, I asked, "What about me? What do you see for me?" I regretted my words as soon as they were out.

"You?" she said in a derisive bark. "For you I see . . . *la soledad.* Loneliness."

Stunned, I stood staring at her until she turned her face back up at me. Her "*la soledad*" vibrated like pigeon wings in the night air. "There," she said, her voice almost masculine in its harshness. "That's a hundred *bolos* worth. Now go, and don't come back here again."

"*La soledad*" affected me deeply. It affected me so much that when we got back into the limo, I was no longer angry at Ronnie, although I should have been. I began to think wistfully of Orchid, and accompanying that wistfulness was the unreasonable, wicked hope that perhaps Ronnie would win our bet after all. As we rolled back down toward the paved streets of Caracas, I dreamed a hopeless dream in which Orchid, after spending a night with me on Ronnie's suggestion, discovered that she loved me.

I was so relieved to be back on civilized streets that I almost forgot that I had ever been angry.

The driver, without being told, rolled west from Petare. We went through El Marques and Altamira and Chacao. Ronnie had apparently bought a *tubo* from someone in the hillside throng, and he knocked a couple of *pases* onto the back of his hand and vacuumed them up. After that he talked happily, meaninglessly for a while, before he finally began talking about what he wanted to do next.

"Every new city I go to, I look for the poverty first," he explained. "First the poverty, then the corruption. You'd be surprised how the qualities of poverty and corruption vary from place to place, Jimbo."

I decided I would correct him about my name once again while he was pretending to be both reasonable and philosophical. I turned to him. "Look," I said. "You think you could remember to call me Jim, Ronnie? Jim or Jimmy, okay? Not Jimbo."

He lifted his box-trap eyebrows at me. I thought he might pick a fight, but instead he raised his hands and showed me his palms. "Sure, Jim. I'm sorry. I get forgetful sometimes."

Still, his eyebrows remained lifted, and when I faced forward again, I watched him warily out of the corner of my eye. He resumed talking with a slight edge on his voice that betrayed his annoyance at having been corrected.

"Anyway, Jim, I'd like to see a little corruption now, if that's all right."

"Sure," I told him. "What kind of corruption are we after tonight? Spiritual? Political? Moral?" I knew I was taking a risk by needling him like that, but I was getting tired; I was getting to the point where it was hard for me to care anymore. What I really wanted was to settle in somewhere and drink some beer and then go home.

Those box traps stayed baited and set. "I'll take the moral corruption, Jim. The seamy, sexy stuff."

I laughed. "Well, the spiritual has always been my forte. I guess we'll leave the political for tomorrow, what do you say?"

I went too far with that one, and he closed a hand around my arm; the strong fingers sank in a little. "Hey, Jim, you *are* being paid pretty well for this." It was my turn now to show him open palms.

"Sorry," I said. "I'm a sarcastic bastard when I'm tired." He gave me a cool smile and raised a hand as if to pat me on the cheek. But then he seemed to think the better of it and let that hand drift up to his hair.

I took him to the section of Avenida Libertador where the *transformistas* hung out. It was a warm, dry night, so there were plenty of *transfos* patrolling the sidewalks and the bridges that crossed the broad, divided avenue. Slow Mercedes and powerful American cars filled with young men were doing the circuit; they cruised one side of the avenue, crossed the bridge to the other side to travel in the opposite direction, and then went across yet another bridge to start all over again. There were some men who did this for the better part of a night; they were gawkers or window shoppers rather than buyers. Our driver seemed to know this game, and he rolled the big Cadillac along with tantalizing slowness; Ronnie glued himself to the window.

We had no light on in the vehicle; the *bichos* could not see us very well, but they knew the big car meant money and excitement. They called to us, smiling and waving arms that were almost thin enough to pass for female, and one *transfo*, standing at the edge of the highway bridge, pulled his pink sweater over his head to show us the miracles wrought by silicone and estrogen. He bounced his tits at us and flapped his sweater in the air.

On our second pass we went by a blond in red shoes and a red dress who stood on the sidewalk. He looked like Marilyn Monroe.

"Shit," Ronnie said. "That's not a guy!" He turned to me for confirmation; I shook my head.

"It's a man, Ronnie."

"Come on. I can tell, and it's not." He seemed angry as well as disillusioned. But there was some other disturbing quality in his voice that I couldn't quite figure out, and he kept running his finger around and around the inside of his big hoop earring.

"Sure it is," I said. "This is the *bicho* section, the transvestite and

194

transsexual section. The authentic whores don't come here because they don't want to be mistaken for men, and if these guys go where the whores hang out, the whores cut them up."

"Shit!" he said. Then he said, "Can we go around again?"

We did the circuit for about fifteen minutes. Ronnie stared at everything, but he seemed most interested in Marilyn Monroe. Marilyn waved at us and called out encouragement every time we drove by.

After a while I told the driver to head away. I was afraid that the cops would spot the big limo and would pull us over and try to shake us down. So that Ronnie would not be too disappointed, I took him to a sleazy little nightclub that I knew of in Chacaito. This place had none of the class of Mickey's club. It was one of those grade-B establishments where the whores masquerade as entertainers; they wear miniskirts and bowler derbies and take turns standing in a spotlight, mouthing the words to "New York, New York." And after they finish their numbers, they circulate beneath the vigilant eyes of the management and encourage the patrons to buy them expensive drinks.

The men in the tuxedos recognized Ronnie right away. They swarmed around our table and shook our hands and would not allow us to pay for drinks. But the girls began ignoring me as soon as I told them I was not a member of the band. They concentrated on Ronnie, who threw bad, phrase-book Spanish at them. The girls responded by simpering and running their fingers through his hair, by opening his reptilian vest to pass hands over his chest.

I didn't care that the whores ignored me, though. Not even when the whore who had eyes a little like Orchid's came up and started trying to speak English to Ronnie did I care. The snotty-looking bartender kept sending us free drinks, and I ordered Chivas Regal on the rocks. Because I had just survived a dangerous roll through the slums and was now surrounded on all sides by idiot whores, I thought I deserved to get good and lit. It was a rare, perfect opportunity anyway, with free drinks and a limousine to take me home afterward.

After a time I was able to tune everything out and enter an inner world guided by my fantasies and governed by my rules. I was enjoying this vacation until Ronnie poked me in the side with his finger. I looked up from my glass and saw that all the women but

195

one had left our table. The remaining woman was sitting on Ronnie's lap. She was less pretty than many of the others, and she had
a wide, pink scar running all the way down one side of her face. It
was disturbing to think he might have chosen her for that feature
alone.

"Jim," he said, "have you got a spare rubber on you?"

"A *what?*"

"My wife, you know? I can't take the chance of taking something
home. I left mine at the hotel."

I smiled. I was tired, or I would have laughed. The irrepressible
rock star worried about catching something. My head felt all foggy
inside; I knew I would have trouble walking a straight line. "No," I
said. "No rubber. Be hard to get now, too, this time of night."
Then something occurred to me. "Might have something here. I
could ask."

He appeared to think about it. Then he said, "No, I guess not.
Not a good idea right now anyway." He did not seem very disappointed. He was touching his earring in that annoying way he
had. He thought for a minute more; his eyebrows were lifted, but I
was too tired to be suspicious, and then he said, "Listen, is there
someplace we can go to get away from here and have a drink?
Someplace where we'd be visible but not vulnerable?"

I felt my mouth stretch into a smile. "All done with the corruption for tonight, then?"

He looked away and didn't answer. Instead, he pushed the girl
off his lap and stood, digging into his pocket to get her a tip, and
then he gave me a solid thump on the shoulder. "Let's go," he
said. He was still fondling his earring.

I told the driver to take us to Sabana Grande. Ronnie had him
park the car and then asked him to come with us for a drink. I
thought that was democratic of him, and the driver liked it too; he
gave us a smile for the first time that night.

We sat at a metal table beneath the bright lights in front of the
Gran Café and drank Polar. People recognized Ronnie and they
came to adore him. Americans and Venezuelans and Europeans.
Starstruck. Soon the waiters had to fight their way through a four-
deep crowd to get to our table. Still, when they got to us, they
were smiling, which was not like them at all. Ronnie was smiling
too. He was enjoying everything.

The beer here was not free, but Ronnie paid for it and I drank it. I went into my own world and now it took me a while to come out of it, even when I wanted to. I got up to go to the bathroom one time, and when I returned, the driver was gone. His absence did not bother me, and I did not ask about him. Ronnie had the driver's hat, and he was wearing it atop his elaborate hairdo. I called the waiter and asked for another beer. The waiter had been carrying a tray loaded with open bottles of Polar to another table, and he gave me one of those beers as soon as I spoke. In a minute I heard him telling someone that he had miscounted his order and that he would be right back with the missing bottle.

After a time Ronnie was standing behind me, pulling me to my feet. I heard him saying good-bye to people, and then we were walking in the direction of the car. I stopped to throw up once, and after that I closed my eyes and let Ronnie guide me to the limo. He laid me gently across the backseat, and then he got into the driver's seat and started the engine. I don't remember thinking that this was strange. I remember feeling a strong wave of gratitude toward Ronnie for taking care of me.

I came to sometime later, and we were parked. Someone else was in the car, and she and Ronnie were conducting a halting bilingual conversation. I struggled into a sitting position and looked out the window; we were parked on a turnout from the Cota Mil, with the city sparkling below us. I looked over into the front seat and saw Marilyn Monroe. "Jesus!" I said. The strangeness finally struck me then, but I had a hard time holding onto it, drunk as I was.

Ronnie turned around. He looked worried, but he tried to laugh. "Hey, look, man, it's just a weird thing, you know? I just wanted to talk to him and see how the other half lives."

A wave of nausea rolled over me. "God," I said, and I settled back into the seat, my eyes squeezed shut. My stomach contracted and hot vomit rose to my throat, but I choked it back down. Better to suffer pain than embarrass myself in front of Marilyn.

Ronnie seemed anxious that I not think ill of him. "You know what I mean, Jim?" he said. I don't remember whether I answered him or not.

After a time I floated back to consciousness. I heard crying and the sound of slaps, and I sat up quickly. My stomach sloshed with sickness. Ronnie and Marilyn were out of the car, standing at the edge of the steep drop-off where the level pullout ended. Marilyn's wig was off, ghostly white as it lay in the weeds, and Ronnie had him by the short brown natural hair beneath it. He was slapping him hard, over and over, and Marilyn was crying and begging him to stop in a voice that was just a touch too low for a woman's.

"Stop!" I shouted, but he seemed not to hear me. I opened the car door and rolled out onto the ground. I climbed shakily to my feet and moved toward them even as the vomit splashed from my mouth. "Ronnie, you're killing him," I said, but my words all ran together, and he did not pay any attention. Onward I stumbled.

Then I saw Ronnie pull back his hand yet again, this time with his fingers drawn together in a fist. I leaped with all the energy that was left in me, catching his arm just as he was sending it forward and slowing it enough so that it only grazed Marilyn. Marilyn fell sobbing into the grass.

Ronnie turned to me with a face filled with horror. His heavy eyebrows were snapped down low, and I noticed that his earring was gone. There was a spot of blood on the earlobe where it had hung. He reached and gathered the front of my shirt in his hands and shook me; I was spent, too feeble even to try fighting.

"You didn't *hear*," Ronnie said, his voice high and raw as a hysterical guitar. He shook me again. "You didn't hear what that faggot said to me."

Then he threw me down, or rather he let go of me, and I fell of my own accord and he walked away.

Marilyn lay crying in the weeds. I rested a minute and then on hands and knees I crept over and gathered up his wig. I crawled to him and set the wig on the ground where he could see it and I pulled out my handkerchief and started wiping his face. There was a lot of blood, but it didn't look like there was an open wound or anything broken.

At first he let me wipe off the blood. I couldn't help but think how pretty he was. As pretty as he was pathetic. And none of it, really, was his fault. "Poor," I whispered in English. "Poor thing."

After a minute he said, "*Déjame sola.* Leave me alone," and sat up. But there was still a trickle of blood creeping down from one nostril, so I reached again with the handkerchief. "*¡Déjame!*" he said again, and doubling his fingers into a loose fist, he hit me in the face and knocked me into the weeds.

Then Marilyn was standing over me, cursing softly and examining the broken nails on his punching hand. In his other hand he held the wig. *"¡Coño de tu madre!"* he hissed at me. Then he walked off into the night.

I rested in the weeds until Ronnie came back and helped me up. I think he apologized, but I am not sure. Then he put me in the car and started the engine.

CHAPTER 7

I came to again at the foot of the stairs that led up to my apartment. I lay sprawled between the broken pavement of the street and the flattened grass at the bottom of the stairs. I sensed someone breathing nearby, and I turned my head to find him. I was relieved to see that it was Séptimo, and I was about to greet him when a pain like a spike drove through the middle of my skull. I shuddered and squeezed my eyes shut.

"Timo," I said when I was able. My teeth felt like chalk, and they ground together strangely when I spoke.

Séptimo was hunkered next to me with a grubby hand on my shoulder. "Jimmy," he said. *"Estás muy borracho."* It was a statement of fact; there was nothing at all judgmental in his tone, and I was grateful for that.

"Yes, drunk," I told him. "Good and farted. *Bien pedo."* The slang was Mexican, but I was sure he would understand it.

I didn't feel like getting up just yet, and Séptimo squatted quietly beside me for a while. He was a patient and good boy; I decided then that if ever I had a son, I'd want one just like Timo. Closer to my own coloring, perhaps, but just like him otherwise.

After a time he said, "Adolfo saw you lying here. He came over while you were asleep and stood looking down at you." I shuddered again as I imagined Adolfo weaving like a ruby-eyed cobra above my unconscious body.

"Is Packy home?" I asked, and knew right away it was a stupid question. I would not have been lying on the street if he were.

"No," said Séptimo. *"No está."*

After that there was a long silence during which I eased myself into a sitting position. My stomach crawled, but there was nothing left to throw up anymore. The stars of early morning whirled around my head like fireflies. Séptimo duck-waddled farther into the street so that he could look into my face. His own scarred little face was serious; when I smiled at him, he did not mirror my expression.

"He took out his *huevo*," Séptimo said in a low, secret-telling voice.

"Adolfo?" I was startled.

"Sí. He was going to piss on you."

"Jesus!" I ran a hand through my hair, searching for dampness. I found none.

Séptimo's eyes were always bright and penetrating; they held a mixture of hope and hardness that seemed to vary in ratio from day to day. You could practically see the hope and innocence being crowded out by other qualities more useful to a street child. He dropped those eyes from me now, as if he had something shameful to tell.

"I made him stop," Séptimo said. "I told him that if he did that to you, I would beat up both his boys. Good *coñazos* to make them bloody, not just a little push and shove."

He kept his eyes lowered, and I said nothing for a minute as my awe at his bravery worked its way through me. Adolfo, if he had been drunk, could very well have killed Timo and stuck him in a ditch somewhere, and nothing would ever have been done about it.

"Jesus," I said. "Timo. You're a hero, *pana."* I felt a combination of gratitude and admiration. Of course there was also the inevitable prick of resentment at owing him.

"There was nothing else to do," he demurred, his eyes still averted.

"A damn hero," I repeated in English. I made a move to grab him and hug him, but he jumped away and stood staring down at me, his spotted pixie face squirming with conflicting emotions. If I'd had more energy, I might have gone after him.

"You don't have to do that," he said finally. "You want to go in the house now? I'll help you."

I stood shakily and started up the steps. I felt like an old man with a terminal illness. Séptimo followed, both hands on the backs of my legs, pushing. I really did not need his help, but I didn't tell him to stop. Once inside, I gulped three glasses of water from the kitchen sink, then sipped a sour glass of passion-fruit juice. I asked Séptimo if he was hungry, and he said he wasn't. But I knew better, and I fixed him a sandwich, which he devoured in half a minute. Then I told the boy to sleep on the couch if he wanted, and I stumbled off to my room.

When the sun was up, I found Séptimo asleep and curled in a ball on the floor in the exact spot where Max the dog used to lie. I was still sick, of course, but I felt no worse than I had expected to feel. Nothing hurt, although my skin was numb and my head had that vacant feeling I always imagined was similar to the aftermath of electroshock therapy. As quietly as I could, so as not to wake Séptimo, I put coffee on to perk and jolted my nervous system with a belt of cold passion-fruit juice.

Then I sat at the kitchen table with my head in my hands, thinking. It was soothingly dark in the kitchen, and I found it pleasant to sit there, waiting for all my normal avenues of thought to become unblocked.

I knew that I probably should quit the Prowler gig. Ronnie Neumon, the rock star, was just too strange and dangerous and unpredictable. If he hurt someone or destroyed something or got arrested for cocaine, there was a good chance that I would get caught up in it. And if that happened, it was a sure thing Ronnie's money and power would get him off, while I would be left for cockroach food in Catia.

But there were some other sides to this coin. I still had to send Prowler stories to New York; if I quit the circus, I would be giving up a serious journalistic advantage. I might be blowing a good chance to impress New York and perhaps to get them to consider making me a named correspondent.

I would also be breaking my promise to Packy, whom I considered to have suffered in my place at the hands of the police.

And then there was a part of me that actually liked the danger and the risk. Craved it, even. Perhaps putting myself in a little danger for the chance of some excitement and the opportunity to explore something new was a reasonable thing to do. What, after all, was a life for if not to explore?

Of course there was also the five-dollar bet with Ronnie Neumon, which I did not want to think about because of what it told me about myself.

I wasn't certain how I should handle things, and I made it a rule never to decide anything important when drunk or hung over or severely depressed. I finally resolved to play the entire day by ear; I would check in at the office, get a feel for the status of things there, and then, if I felt sure that my job and Mickey's job were both secure for another day or two, I'd go dip a cautious foot into the dirty rock 'n' roll waters at the Hilton. If I couldn't work out a deal where I did not have to spend too much time with Ronnie, maybe I would take the option of dropping out.

I took a long shower and dressed and tried calling Mickey; he did not answer his phone. Little Séptimo was still sleeping on the floor when I left the house.

At the office I hit immediate complications in the form of a couple of mixed reviews delivered through the morning messages from New York. The first, and most positive, one was directed to me.

MSG. CARACAS:
ATTN ANGEL

TOKYO REPRTING YR FEATURE "PROWLER FEVER" SPLASHING MAJOR DAILIES THERE. KUDOS, AND CAN WE EXPCT FRQNT UPDATERS? MUCH THANX. PLS ACK MSG.

SALUDOS
NEW YORK

Before I read the second message, I sat down at the telex in order to ack the first msg. I wrote:

PROWLER UPDATERS UPCMING.

CHEERS
CARACAS

Then I tore the tape off the encoder, ran it through the transmitter and picked up the message directed at Mickey.

MSG CARACAS:
ATTN CALDERON

UNHAVE MNTHLY BDGET FRM U. UNSITE UPDATED LIST OF SUBS.
WHERE ARE U? PLS STND BY FOR PHONER 2 P.M. TODAY. PLS ACK MSG.

CHEERS
NEW YORK

As I read this demand for Mickey to be on the receiving end of a telephone call later that day, my hangover suddenly got worse. It was one thing for Mickey not to write any news stories; he could get away with that for quite a while, if not forever. But neglecting to handle the routine paper shuffling for the office was another matter. There was nothing that could draw New York's evil eye more quickly than failing to make the monthly offering of numbers to the gods of accounting.

I walked into the bathroom, flirted with sickness for a couple of minutes, then came out and dialed Mickey's number. Of course he did not pick up, and I knew then I would have to visit his apartment and convince him to speak to the masters and give them a believable excuse for not having sent either an office budget or the most recent list of the agency's Venezuelan subscribers. His job now depended on it.

In fact I would have left for Altamira immediately, but the first message we had received made it necessary for me to get to the Hilton before I did anything else. I was already running late; if I lost the interpreting job, Mickey would not be the only journalist in jeopardy of sudden unemployment.

And even before I left for the Hilton, I needed to check on one more matter that had me worried. I quickly went through the morning papers looking for news of the Cowboys. After seeing, to my relief, that there was nothing, I dialed Humberto Sanabria's newsroom number.

"Humbo," I said when he answered. "I need just one thing."

"Gringo," he said. "You need so much more than that. But you're wise not to take on too much at once."

"*Oye*, what I need is your assessment of the Cowboys thing. They won't do anything in the next couple of days, will they?"

"*You*, the Croaker's lover, are asking *me* what the fuck is going on?"

"Hey, I've been out of the office a lot lately. So has Mickey. Now, come on, I don't have time for any *huevonada*."

"*¿En serio?*"

"*Serio. Muy serio.*"

"Okay," Sanabria said, all humor leaving his voice. "My personal feeling is we'll see something soon."

"Soon? How soon? Not in the next day or so? Will they?"

"Soon," said Sanabria.

"Yes, but how soon *exactly*? Any idea?"

"When you get worried," said Sanabria, "you sound just like my grandmother." Then he hung up.

I found Packy in the lobby of the Hilton. There were also a few roadies standing listlessly about; they had just eaten breakfast and were waiting for a ride to the Poliedro. The roadies' eyes were sleepy, half-lidded, and they widened not a bit as I approached. They mumbled greetings and then went back to talking and waiting for the limos to come.

Packy's clothes were damp-looking and wrinkled; it was a sure bet he had slept in them, and his eyes, although alert, were full of angry blood. At the very tip of his nose was a telltale smudge of white powder, fine as butterfly dust. He did not see me at first; he was looking around with a sparrowlike nervousness that was unusual even for him, and his eyes swept past me once without registering me, and then continued their sweep of the lobby. I walked up to him and as I touched him on the shoulder, he did a ballet hop into the air, twisting and coming down with hands in front of his face. "*¡Coño!*" he said. "Don't do that!"

"Packy! What the hell is the matter with you?"

"*Coño, pana.* My nerves," he told me. "These people are driving me crazy. They stick *perico* into their faces, and it makes them crazy, and the crazier they get, the more *perico* they want."

I was going to say something about the evidence of his own cocaine consumption being right under his nose, but he was quicker on the draw than I with the personal observations.

"You look dead," he said. "The fucking *roquero* killed you, didn't he? He came back without you last night, and he kept on partying. I don't think he slept. He says he never sleeps when he's on tour.

He stuck some girl in his room and they howled like cats all night. Crazier than a shot in the air."

"He's a challenge," I agreed after thinking for a moment. "I had too much to drink last night. That's why I look like this. Things were so weird that I kept drinking." Packy narrowed his eyes at me.

"They weren't so weird that you're thinking of quitting on me, are you?"

"I'll tell you, Packy, this morning I was thinking very hard . . ."

"Because if you quit, both Camión and I are through, too, you know. The promoter would be mad that we didn't hold our team together, and he'd replace us in a minute and a half. Now that the Prowlers are finally here, he's got interpreters knocking his door down. You can't do that to us, Jimmy. You can't let us down."

"I'll try not to. I don't think I could if I wanted to, now, because—"

"Trying is not enough, Jimmy."

"Jesus, Packy. Relax."

"You owe it to me, *pana*. You owe it to me not to let me down."

"I won't," I said finally. "I've been trying to tell you. I've got some problems right now, but I won't let you down."

Packy nodded then and appeared satisfied. After a minute he said, "Things *must* have been weird." He stared hard at my face, seemingly worried, suddenly, for some reason I couldn't grasp.

"They were unbelievable." He stepped closer to me.

"Tell me. *¿Qué pasó?*" Just then, I became conscious of the fact that more roadies had come down from the rooms and that they were milling about all around us. Even though Packy and I were speaking Spanish, I was wary of talking about Ronnie the rock star while they were within earshot.

So we wandered across the lobby and found a pair of blue plush lounge chairs to drop into. My chair was so comfortable that I was tempted to slide back into it and close my eyes for a long time. But Packy gave me a tap with his foot, and I sat up and recounted the tale of the night before.

"*Coño,*" he said when I was finished. "That's strange about the *transformista*. You think Ronnie is a little bit . . . ?" Packy flopped his wrist at me.

"I don't know, Packy," I said. "I think he has something wrong with him, but I couldn't tell you what it is. All I know is I'd rather not have to take any more long periods of time with the guy. Could we arrange that, do you think?"

Packy settled back into his chair. He looked sleepy as well. "That's not so bad," he said, as if to himself. "None of that is so bad. It's not what I expected." His eyes were closed, his lids fluttering lazily.

"What?" My voice went high with annoyance. "What the hell did you *expect?* What are you talking about?"

"Nothing." His head shook slowly. "I'm wrung out. I could sleep for two days, gringo."

I was still mad. "Listen, tell me . . ."

Packy's eyes shot suddenly open. I thought I saw fear in them, and something else, something unreadable and unsettling. But perhaps it was only that the coke had finally melted the remaining insulation from his nerves. He closed his eyes again, but I could see his eyeballs tracking restlessly beneath the lids.

"We hear that he likes weapons sometimes," he said. There was no hint of humor on his face; his serious expression caused me to lean forward and listen carefully.

"He's into all that martial arts stuff," Packy continued. "And sometimes he'll get a gun and keep it on him."

"Christ," I said. I was certain now that I didn't want to work with Ronnie anymore.

"You didn't see a gun, did you?" Packy's eyes were open and fixed on me. Fear. I definitely saw fear. And the other thing I couldn't identify.

"No."

"¿Seguro?" He was stretching a hand toward me. "You'd tell me, wouldn't you? If you saw a gun?"

"Packy, what's wrong with you? Did he threaten you or something?" He collapsed back into his seat.

"No," he said. Then he said, *"Pana,* this shit is killing me."

I didn't know whether he meant the work or the coke or something else, but I was almost afraid to ask, and I let it go.

In a minute he said, "I don't think you'll have to screw too much with Ronnie anymore. At least not for a whole night. His wife just got in this morning, and the promoter wants you to look out for her. Ronnie's coming to the Poliedro to rehearse today, and we can take care of him there." I nodded, and Packy added, "You meet her here at eleven o'clock."

I nodded again, grateful that I was safe from Ronnie for at least the rest of the day. I was also relieved that I would have a little time to try to see Mickey. Then I thought of something worrisome. I thought of my rotten wager with the rock star.

"But what about the TV interview with Orchid? I can still do that, can't I?" Packy gave me a crooked smile.

"That TV interview is with *Orchid? Coño,* but the little bitch works fast." I thought I heard admiration as well as surprise in his voice.

"Yeah, well, what about it? Do I get it, or not?"

"I think," he said. "I haven't heard that you couldn't."

"Okay," I said. "All right." No guarantees, but better than nothing. After a minute I thought of something else. "How will I know her? The wife?" Packy grinned broadly now.

"You'll know her. She's the type that's hard to miss, even when you haven't seen her before."

Then I recalled her picture in Ronnie's room. And the other pictures, the ones in the photo album that I had not seen but that my imagination created for me. The son of a bitch. Crazy or not, if there were a button I could have pushed to become Ronnie the rock star for a day or two, I think I would have pushed it. And I might not have come back.

I was in too much of a hurry to bother with the *por puestos,* and I sprang for a cab to take me to Mickey's building. I went armed with a well-packed *tubo* of cocaine that I had gotten from Packy; I suspected that if he had not succeeded in finding Beatrix and the boys, a pinch of idiot glee might be one of the few things that would induce Mickey to cooperate in saving his own skin.

As I walked into the foyer of Mickey's building, where I fell beneath the watchful, disapproving gaze of the doorman, it suddenly struck me how incongruous and startling Beatrix's affair with the news peddler must have been, set against this subdued and dignified background. Dirt in dirty settings does not stand out half as much. The doorman was an aging but solid-looking *criollo* well over six feet tall. I thought I saw a sneer tug one corner of his upper lip when I told him whom I had come to see. Then he directed me to the elevator with an exaggerated flourish of a white-gloved hand.

No light issued from beneath Mickey's door or through the transom above the door. I stood in front of the door and touched my pants pocket to reassure myself of the tube of *perico* that I carried there. I tried to ring, but the bell wasn't working; I knocked, waited, and knocked again. After that I was almost ready to leave, but something made me press my ear against the door.

I heard him then. Mickey, obviously in much worse shape than I had even imagined, was breathing in the darkness on the other side of the door. He was breathing rapidly and shallowly in the way that excitement or panic or insanity or cocaine can cause you to breathe. I wondered which combination of factors was controlling Mickey's breathing now.

"Mickey?" I pictured maddened eyes shot through with red veins like lightning bolts.

"Mickey? I hear you in there, boss. Let me in, would you? I want to see how you're doing. I need to know what you've found out about Nestor and Floyd. I'm worried about them too, you know." When he continued to listen without answering, I pulled the crumpled message from New York out of my pocket, smoothed it against the door, and began to read it. It was then, to my great relief, that he took the bait.

"Go away, damn it. I mean it, Jimmy. Let me alone."

"I can't, Mickey. I can't let you lose your job. You won't have anything then."

There was an ill-disguised sob in his voice as he broke into a spate of cursing. He mixed all the worst of Venezuelan and Mexican and Cuban and English profanity, and he spat it through the door at me, the words punctuated with dry croaks of despair.

I waited for this little storm to abate before I said, "Is that it now? Do you feel better now? Open the fucking door, would you; I'm very hung over, and I'm about ready to lose my lunch here." Even as I spoke, the lining of my stomach seemed to sprout a growth of fur.

"Jimmy. I'm sorry, boy. I can't make it to work. I'm all fucked up. Come back tomorrow, would you?"

I thought of Beatrix and of the scarred, leering face of the cuckolding news seller and of the sneering superiority of the doorman/prison guard. I also thought of the New York office, full of seamed, humorless faces, and I pressed my cheek against the door.

"Just a glass of water. *Please*, Mickey. Nobody's going to make you work until you're ready. I've been covering for you pretty well on the news side. I only want to see how you are and to talk to you about being on the end of the one little phone call that will save your job." There was a long pause as he thought it over.

"You didn't meet me that day." I could tell he was running out of reasons not to let me in.

"The day of the bank robbery? I was almost killed that day, otherwise I would have met you, and we would have had a good talk just like the one we're going to have now. And I couldn't apologize because I didn't see you until that day you got beaten up, and you haven't been answering your phone."

In a minute the locks began to click open one by one. Finally a crack appeared at the edge of the door and I waited for the door to swing inward, but it didn't, and finally when I pushed it open and stepped into the apartment, Mickey was not within reach. It was as dark in there as the inside of a cave; I stepped gingerly, leaving the door open so that the feeble illumination from the hallway would light part of my way.

"Mickey?" After fumbling on the wall for a minute I found a light switch, but when I flicked it, nothing happened. I made my way from the entrance hall into the living room with my hands stretched before me like a blind man. Moving in darkness, I was afraid I would run into something at face level, something sharp that would maybe fall at me and put my eyes out and render me permanently blinded.

"Mickey, for Chrissake." My voice was desperate now, and it echoed through the large rooms of that apartment on whispering bird's wings. There was no answer, and things, perhaps they were pieces of dried food and maybe they were living cockroaches, kept crunching beneath my feet. I ran my shin into a table, swore at it, and miraculously caught a lamp that I had caused to tumble from the table toward the floor. I yanked its little chain, but the bulb stayed dead.

"Over here," said Mickey. "I kept forgetting to pay it, and they finally shut it off two days ago."

"God, Mickey," I said.

"I kind of like it, though. The dark, I mean. It suits my mood right now."

If I squinted, I could just make out his silhouette and the silhouettes of the two couches that dominated his living room. He was sitting on one of the couches. I felt my way around the furniture to him; I reached and grabbed his arm. He was wearing a bathrobe, and feeling him through the bathrobe, I was startled to find that he seemed to have lost weight over the past few days. The dark air of the apartment was heavy with the odor of decay.

"What the hell are you doing in here, pal?" I asked. "You've got to quit this."

Mickey sighed; I felt his hot breath on my face, and he drew his arm from beneath my fingertips. "I don't know that it's much use," he said. "They may have given me the knockout blow. Do you know I haven't been able to change the sheets on that bed? I've been sleeping down here on the couch."

Feeling a rush of sadness for Mickey and for his boys, I reached for his arm again. But he somehow sensed that I was about to touch him and he said, "Jimmy, sit on that other couch, all right? I need a little space here."

His tone was uncompromising, almost paternal, and I moved quickly. We sat across from one another in silence for a few minutes. He kept rubbing his face, the whiskers making a dry sandpaper sound. Then he said, "Sorry. It's just that I'm feeling so inhuman. It brings out all my inferiority to have someone on top of me like that."

"Hey, Mick, as long as you're breathing, there's hope." But in that dark and stinking atmosphere, with my stomach crawling like a snail, it was difficult to convince even myself. Mickey sighed; it was the only appropriate response.

Then he said, "Just so you know, I'm not moping about nothing here, Jimmy. Beatrix and the boys have left the country." His words settled inside me like a cold weight.

"Oh," I said. "Oh, no. Are you sure about that, Mickey, because . . ."

"Hey, I had the PTJ out looking for them. The trail ended at the airport, and they're gone, and there's nothing I can do about it."

"Oh, Jesus, Mickey." I thought of Floyd and of Nestor, and I felt like crying. Until then I had assumed that things would be resolved in some manner and that I would see them again shortly.

"Argentina they went to. That is, unless they only changed

planes there and headed somewhere else. I'm still waiting to hear; she'll be needing money, so I'm sure she'll get in touch with me."

"Floyd," I said. "Nestor."

"Beatrix," said Mickey. We mourned in silence for a time.

Finally Mickey said, "So you think talking to those bastards on the phone this afternoon might do it?"

"If you tell them what they need to hear, I think it will."

"Because I can't make a big effort right now. It'll take me another while yet to get on my feet."

"Listen." I was growing hopeful. "Talk to them. Give them the numbers they want. Tell them everything's great. I'll do the rest. All the news. I'll keep doing it for a while anyway, until you feel better and have some information about your family." His hot breath seemed to reach me from the other couch.

"I'll be counting on you," he warned. "I'll be counting on you more than ever to be my crutch, Jimmy boy."

"I won't let you down," I said for the second time that day. "Just let me know what I can do to help you get ready to go into the office." As soon as I said this, I knew it was a mistake.

"Well, Jimmy, you know, there is something," he said, pouncing on my words. His voice took on an oily tone. "As you know, I've got a fondness for the *perico*. You wouldn't happen to know where I could get some right now, would you?"

My hand instinctively went to my pocket. I felt the truncated, powder-packed plastic straw through the material of my jeans. He sensed my movement in the darkness.

"Why, you thoughtful guy. You brought some with you, didn't you?"

"I shouldn't have, I guess. It was a bad idea."

"Oh, *please*," Mickey said. I could see his once-stout arms reaching out into the darkness for me. "Just one *pase*." He was speaking Spanish now, which he hardly ever did with me. It annoyed me, because I knew how easy it was to hide feelings within the convolutions of a foreign language; I did it all the time. "Make that two," he said. "Two little ones if you want. One for each side. Tiny."

"I don't know, Mickey."

"It's what I need. To help me sweet-talk the New York bastards. And for my ribs. Beatrix's friends cracked two of them on me, and they still hurt like hell. Come on, now, and let's see what you

212

have." The stench in the place had gotten worse as it mingled with my own sweat and Mickey's sweat and unwashed emanations.

"So you're guaranteeing me . . ."

"Yes. No problem, Jimmy. Score a couple out, would you? The mirror is right there, on the coffee table."

I dug into my pocket and pulled out the tube and held it in a closed fist. I felt Mickey's eyes on me. Then I stuck two fingers into the top pocket of my shirt and found a box of matches; I struck one so I could see his eyes.

"So if I score out a couple for you now, you'll take a shower and eat something if I fix it for you?" His eyes narrowed, pained-looking in the sudden flare of light. It was hard to tell much from them. His face was still badly bruised from the beating he had taken. Then the match burned my fingers, and swearing, I dropped it onto the coffee table. The returned darkness was filled with phantom illuminations.

"Shower, *sí*," said Mickey, eager to please. "And eat. *Por supuesto*. But first . . ."

"Well, I can't see a damn thing, you know, Mickey . . ." I said, his Spanish setting me on edge.

"*Momento*," Mickey breathed. He rose and went away, and in a minute he came back with a lit candle. The flame of the candle streamed backward as he walked. The candle was in a dish, and he set it down on the coffee table. On the table lay a litter of newspapers and partly eaten things that looked like pieces of doughnuts or dried-out teabags, as well as an expensive mirror with several razor blades scattered around on the glass.

"Been doing much of this?"

"No. Not much at all." His tongue gleamed wetly in the candlelight.

I pinched open the top of the tube, poured out a modest amount of cocaine, chopped it up with one of the razor blades, and scored it into lines. When I was done, I leaned back into the couch; it was soft, the pillows almost without shape, and it seemed to want to draw me inside of it like a big upholstered womb. I looked across the coffee table at Mickey, whose features flickered with the light from the candle. One battered cheek was a bit swollen, giving him a lopsided, almost comical appearance.

Mickey reached with both hands and lifted aside some of the

newspapers that were on the table. He did not find what he was searching for right away, and he became frantic, lifting papers and food wrappers and pieces of food that were stuck to wrappers and throwing them to the shadowy floor until he found it: a bit of plastic straw a little longer than the straw the cocaine had come packaged in, a piece about the length of what they gave you to stir your coffee in a Caracas café. Mickey had been as panicked over it as a miser who discovers he is missing a coin.

"Damn, things are hard to find around here," Mickey said. "Beatrix used to tidy up once in a while. No more."

A minute later, and he was smiling. "Damn that bitch anyway. I'll track her down. I'll find her."

"Yeah? Then what?"

"I'll get the kids. That'll fix her. Listen, I think there's beer in the refrigerator. It'll be a little warm, though. Bring me one, too, would you?"

I felt my way into the kitchen and opened the refrigerator; swept the nearly empty shelves with my hands. No beer. I went back out and sat across from Mickey. "No beer, Mickey. Not a one."

But Mickey was no longer thinking about beer. He was staring at something that appeared to be hanging just above the crown of my head; I looked up and there was nothing.

"Don't you think that's a good idea?" he asked. "Taking the kids?" His face was thoughtful now, troubled even.

"Maybe," I said with caution. "If it's really the kids you want." But the mere idea made my stomach twist.

Abruptly Mickey changed the subject.

"Why not score out another couple of lines, Jimmy?" he asked, his voice becoming a childish wheedle once more.

"I think we'll wait a little bit."

"Why don't you do a couple? It's no fun doing it by myself."

"Listen," I said. "Take a shower. Put on some fresh clothes and eat something. Then we'll see about doing more lines."

"But I'm not hungry, Jimmy."

He put up a long argument, but in the end I got him to take off the horrible bathrobe and get into the shower. There was plenty of hot water for him; the water came from a common source in the building. While he bathed, I explored his refrigerator once again. I saw nothing at all but open cans and slimy piles of mold that had once been vegetables. I took the candle and went through his cup-boards and found an intact can of spaghetti and another of beans as well as some peach halves in heavy syrup. I mixed the spaghetti and the beans together over a low flame on the gas stove. I added a little pepper, both red and black, that I found on top of the refrig-erator.

While he was still in the shower, Mickey called me into the bathroom and asked me if I would take the scrub brush and wash his back. He said his wife had always done this for him, and it would make him feel better if I did it now.

I overcame my natural reluctance and picked up the well-worn brush. Mickey's wet back in the candlelight was broad and hairy almost to the point of abnormality. He handed me the slippery soap and I got the brush all foamy with it, spattering myself a little with soap, and then I set to work. Despite my initial revulsion, I soon lost myself in the work; perhaps it was the humid darkness and the sputtering candle that brought on the reverie. After a time I became caught up in remembrance; a lump rose to my throat and my hand paused in midstroke. Mickey must have thought I had finished because he turned away and began rinsing his back be-neath the showerhead.

I returned to the kitchen after that to stir the food and to escape the warm dampness of the bathroom. When Mickey got out of the shower and began to shave, I went in once again and held the candle for him, pointing out the places he had missed.

Later, after he put on a pair of jeans that had been left on the living room floor but did not smell too bad, as well as a clean shirt that I was forced to find for him in one of his bedroom drawers because he refused to go up to the bedroom himself, I sat him down at the cluttered kitchen table and set a bowl of spaghetti and baked beans in front of him. He tucked a napkin into the open collar of his shirt and went to work on his meal with a soup spoon, slurping loudly. Once, he lifted his head to smile at me, and his chin was red with spaghetti sauce.

When he was finished, I sent him into the bathroom to wipe his face, and I washed the dishes. Then, looking at my watch and realizing I was already late for my appointment with Ronnie Neu-mon's wife, I started for the door.

"Good-bye, Mickey," I said. I was without a candle now, so I picked my way carefully around the hidden furniture toward the entrance hall. Mickey followed me, not moving half so carefully as I despite his damaged ribs.

"Wait," he said. "Aren't you going to leave me some? The nose candy."

I was ready to give it to him, but then I stopped and turned to study his broad silhouette. "I'll call you at one-thirty to make sure you're in the office."

"Yes, yes. No problem."

"In fact," I said, as an idea struck me, "I'm going to take this *tubo* with me and put it in General Jorge's drawer. You can have a couple of lines and a chat with the general just before you talk to New York."

"Oh, Jimmy. Don't do this to me."

"I think it's the best thing. Listen, I'm worried. You *are* starting to recover a little, aren't you, now that the shock has had a couple of days to wear off?" His voice turned serious.

"I don't know how much I've recovered," he said. "I have learned something, though. I've learned that love is an impossibility. Once I can fully absorb that, I think I'll be better off."

I shook my head. "I don't believe that. I don't think I could live if it were true."

He gave a mean laugh as his hungry eyes settled on the hand in which I held the tube of cocaine. "What are you talking about, Jimmy? You've been burned so many times your heart is black." I couldn't have been more stunned if he had hit me from behind.

"My heart is *not* black," I said. I walked out and shut the door, but Mickey's angry shout pursued me to the elevator.

"Of course it's black," he said. "Look at how you treat *me.*"

Loren Hart was a pretty woman trying to hide her prettiness beneath round sunglasses and a wide-brimmed hat. It wasn't working. Immediately after I arrived on the main floor of the hotel and spotted her standing by herself as she waited for me, I sensed that there had been a shift in the usual conversational hum of the lobby; the tone was higher and thinner, the pulse of it more rapid. I imagined that the living vibration of a beehive shifted in a similar way when the young virgin queen was preparing for her mating flight.

People, men and women, were trying to act cool, sliding their eyes at her when they thought no one was watching. It wasn't that they recognized her; she had spent the majority of her career on a television show that had not yet made it to Venezuela. No. It was her appearance, her presence alone. Pretty, poised women generally had a glow to them; the longer you were with them, and studied them, and appreciated them, the brighter and warmer and more colorful that luminescence became. But Loren Hart was one of those unusual women whose lights and colors had none of that subtlety. They were all there to be seen in the first accidental glance. I looked at her long enough to take in the glasses and the hat as well as the tight-fitting jeans and Western blouse she wore, and then I had to look away.

After a few minutes the drone of the lobby went back to near normalcy as the shock abated. I blew my nose into a dirty handkerchief, and then I began to circle her slowly, stealthily. I observed her from the corners of my eyes, lest her eyes meet mine directly and turn me to stone. I needed to see her at all angles, to get used to her a little, before I could go up and smile and acknowledge her as a fellow human with quirks and qualities other than those of a blindingly beautiful freak.

Loren Hart stood still as a statue for several minutes, as if hoping not to be noticed. Then she began tapping one red shoe against the blue-carpeted floor, and she took a cigarette from a small white purse she wore on her arm and pressed it between her full, unpainted lips. A balding, light-skinned Venezuelan man left the side of the check-in desk when she did that, and he headed toward her with a box of matches in his hand. But she did not see him. She lit her own cigarette with a gold lighter, her red-painted thumbnail sticking up next to it like a companion flame, and he stepped past her, a self-consciously dignified expression on his face, and pretended to be heading to meet a friend on the other side of the lobby.

Aside from the movement of her mouth to accept and draw on the cigarette, her face remained an unmoving, unreadable mask. She made me think of one of my grandfather's rare songbirds standing rigid on a branch while waiting for an unwitting cat to pass beneath the tree. It was only the tightness across her high, fine cheekbones that betrayed her discomfort.

I felt bad for making her stand there on display as she waited, but I could not help it; she was affecting me the way strong light affects the nerves of an insect's wings. Finally, though, I gathered the courage to step up and introduce myself. In preparation I ran shaking fingers through my hair and ran my thumb around the waist of my pants to tuck my shirttail in, and I passed a hand over my zipper. My zipper was yawning halfway to the floor; fogged in as I had been that morning, I had apparently neglected to check it before I left the house. I jerked it to full mast, then belatedly looked around to assure myself that no one had been watching. After that I became frightened that something else was horribly awry with my dress or my appearance, and I turned and rushed off to one of the first-floor rest rooms.

I was sometimes pleased with the way I looked in a mirror. If I were in a good mood, I would usually find little things to admire about myself. I could become almost smug about the straightness of my nose or the strength of my chin or the rakish way my hair fell across my forehead. I would smile at myself, or even wink.

On most occasions, though, I saw myself as nice-looking, but bland. And when I was depressed or hung over, I invariably saw myself as bordering on deformed; I would imagine that people were staring at me because of my uncommon ugliness.

It was one of those days. In the mirror above one of the bathroom sinks, I saw dark circles like bruises under my eyes, and my cheeks seemed puffy, pumped full of poisonous fluid. I stretched my lips in a horrible smile and saw teeth yellower than a sewer rat's. In fact I became so upset at the sight of myself that I made some kind of noise and tore myself away from the mirror; I had to pace the full length of the bathroom seven or eight times before I could return to the sink, and then I carefully avoided my reflection while I finished washing my face and combing my hair. I undid my belt and smoothed my shirt down inside my pants and checked and rechecked my zipper before I went out to meet Loren Hart.

I walked straight up to her and stuck my hand out and ran my words together as I introduced myself. Relief briefly relaxed the muscles around her huge sunglasses as she pressed a cool hand into mine, and then her face grew taut once again.

"You're somewhat late, Mr. Angel, aren't you?" she asked, her voice frosty and her lips drawing back so slightly that I saw only the bright tips of her front teeth.

"I am, yes," I said. "Public transportation in this town, it's bad. I meant to be here fifteen minutes ago." I would have gone on out of sheer nervousness, but she glanced at her watch and then peered over the top of my head in a way that let me know it was useless to elaborate. There was a long, awkward silence during which I noticed that we were drawing surreptitious glances from nearly everyone in the lobby.

"Well," I said, and smoothed my damp palms down the front of my jacket, "what do you think you would like to do?"

Now she lowered her face until I could see myself in the dark lenses of her glasses. My face looked distorted and frightened. I watched my hand rise up and crawl over my faintly damp hair and flutter away again. The corner of Loren Hart's mouth twitched upward then; she looked as if she were about to smile. But she drew her mouth back into a tense line and said, "And just what is there to do here, Mr. Angel?"

"Jimmy," I said. "You don't have to call me Mr. Angel, Ms. Hart." I thought that maybe she would then ask me to call her Loren, but she only looked at me. The corner of her mouth began to lift again, an impulse which she quickly killed.

"Well," I said, "if you haven't eaten, we could go to brunch. Then we could go to an art museum, or shopping maybe . . ."

"I've had breakfast," she said.

"Oh. Well, Plaza Bolívar . . ."

"First I would like a drink. Is there a bar in the hotel? Just one, I think, for the fatigue of the flight and everything else. Then we'll decide what else to do."

It was not quite eleven-thirty, but I was grateful that she had elected to go for a drink. I didn't even bristle at her tone, which was more a mistress-to-servant tone than the appropriate helpless-gringa-to-knowledgeable-interpreter tone.

We sat at a small table in the hotel bar and ordered drinks. I ordered the old hangover remedy, a Bloody Mary, and she asked for a Scotch and soda. When the drinks arrived, Loren Hart lit another cigarette and stared wordlessly at the wall above my head. Once in a while she would lift her glass to her lips without lowering her eyes, and then she would take a drag from the cigarette and let smoke curl slowly out of her nostrils. She acted as if I weren't even there. Although the bar was no brighter than the inside of a tunnel, she did not take off her dark glasses.

When her drink was gone and she still had not looked down, I signaled the barman for another round. He brought the drinks quickly, his aging face grave with the importance of his job. Then he stepped away from us.

"Ms. Hart," I said. "Is something the matter?"

She looked at me then, seemed to study me, and she spread her mouth in a bright smile. It was impossible to tell whether the smile was genuine because of the glasses, but it was a beautiful smile, and I found myself grinning in return. The drink had washed some of the pain and shyness out of my system.

"Jimmy, is it?" she asked.

"Jimmy."

"Tell me about yourself, Jimmy. What do you do when you're not working as an interpreter? How long have you been here?"

So I found myself talking. I told her about the agency and the work that I did there, and I said that I was only working the Prowler gig to keep myself amused on my vacation. She nodded frequently as I spoke, and smiled encouragingly at me. But she said so little that I soon began to wonder whether she was really listening. Just at the point when wondering was about to turn to suspicion, however, she broke in with a few questions; she asked me how I liked Caracas and how I had come to learn Spanish. Soothed, I continued.

Finally, while I paused to take a sip from my drink, she looked down at a dainty silver watch on her thin wrist. Her smile faded then, and her glasses flashed darkly at me.

"My husband is rehearsing at the concert hall, isn't he?"

"Yes, he is."

"I would like to go there. Can you call for a car?"

I left to summon a limousine, then returned for Loren Hart. I killed the dregs of my second Bloody Mary as she was standing, preparing to leave. I noticed that her own second drink stood untouched, the ice cubes nearly melted.

The Poliedro parking lot was empty except for a few limousines, a couple of trucks, and a sprinkling of other cars. Four or five Metropolitanos were guarding the doors, and handfuls of young

Venezuelan rock fans were clustered at each entrance. The Cadillac dropped us off near the main entrance; we heard the deep but distant thrumming of the Prowlers' bass guitar as soon as we stepped out.

The young Venezuelans stared at us as we passed among them. Loren Hart walked by them quickly, rigidly, her head lifted to the sky, but they said nothing to her and did not try to touch her, and then we were inside the building. Husky American security men with little earphones plugged into their heads said hello to Loren Hart, and she nodded, unsmiling. She asked them how we could get backstage, and they pointed and spoke. Then we headed down a wide, dark hallway.

We could hear the band clearly now. The authoritative bass. The rapid drums. The laughing, insolent guitar. And Ronnie's voice. It was hard to make out the words, but he slid from a croon to a menacing rasp and then back again. Amplified and electronically altered, his voice sounded better than I had ever heard it. Loren Hart seemed not to hear; she kept walking straight down the empty hallway, her high heels clicking sharply against the floor. I followed her at a respectful distance.

The hallway curved to follow the rounded contour of the building; we followed the bending walls until we came to a wire-screen barrier and a narrow gate guarded by two ex-football players in polo shirts. Beyond the screen the hallway widened and we could see the back of the stage. It was crowded back there, with roadies working and roadies loafing about and publicity people and handlers in jackets and ties looking as if they'd been sucking on Tums all morning. The security men grinned self-consciously at Loren, their smooth, smiling faces like those of eunuchs in a harem, and they stepped aside for us, admitting us into the storm of confusion. People began to greet Loren Hart; roadies in torn jeans and shirts open to the waist waved almost shyly at her and mouthed her name, and other, better-dressed members of the entourage walked up to her and kissed her on the cheek. Loren accepted the greetings and the kisses with a chilly little smile on her perfect face.

Up on the stage, with their backs to us, Ronnie and the band continued playing. The whole concert hall vibrated and echoed with their noise. Seen from behind, surrounded as they were by dark curtains and colored lights, as well as by men pulling ropes and passing hands over consoles filled with mysterious buttons and switches, the Prowlers looked like magicians in the midst of an elaborate trick.

One of the dressing room doors was open, and roadies and other crew members passed freely in and out of it. Frequently one of them would walk in empty-handed and come out smoking a joint or drinking a beer. The rest of the backstage doors were closed, and after a brief conversation with a young, long-haired publicity man, Loren went to one of the closed doors, pulled it open, and disappeared inside.

Enthralled by the noise and motion and excitement, I was slow to follow. When I finally went in after her, I found myself standing alone in a room that was a greatly shrunken version of an airport VIP waiting room; there were padded plastic chairs, a worn leather couch, and a table spread with cold cuts, bread, and liquor bottles.

At the far end of the room was another door, and that door was open a crack. Through the crack I could see someone moving about. I knew it had to be Loren Hart. I stepped across the brown carpet and pulled the door open.

Beyond that door lay an inner room, a room containing nothing but a dressing table and a cot; Loren stood facing the dressing table with her back to me, and because of the music, she did not hear me open the door behind her. She stood very still, and something about her posture told me she was involved in some private act or ritual and did not want to be disturbed. I knew that I should leave, but the voyeur-journalist in me would not allow me to. Instead I lingered in the doorway, watching.

A huge, lighted mirror hung above the dressing table. Reflected in that mirror I saw a framed photograph of Loren that stood on the table's far corner, and I saw a silver tray containing a long, cometlike streak of white powder. I guessed that at least an ounce of *perico* lay spread across that tray. I also saw the inevitable razor blade and straw.

Loren Hart stood unmoving as a deer in the forest and in her hands she held something I could not see. I realized then that I had never before met a person who could remain as nervelessly quiet as she; Loren Hart had an awesome gift for stillness.

She stood for many minutes in frozen contemplation, and then

222

she turned a bit so that I glimpsed the object she was holding. I saw only a corner of it, but that corner was enough. What I saw was the photo album that had been in Ronnie Neumon's suitcase. The album was closed, but by the way Loren stared down at it, I could tell that she found the monotone cover to be at least as eloquent as the lurid documentation it concealed.

After a time Loren Hart moved again; holding the heavy book, she let her hands settle slowly to the top of the dressing table. There followed another long minute of stillness, which made me wish I could see her face to read whatever feelings she allowed it to betray, then she took a small step to the side and bent down over the silver tray and the cocaine. In the mirror I watched as one of her fine, white hands with its ruby nails carefully picked up the razor blade from the tray. Loren paused, and then she began shoving cocaine around with the razor; I heard the shrill, familiar complaint of sharp metal against metal. It did not take me long to realize that she was writing a message in the snowy powder.

I could not read her message in the mirror. By then, in any case, I was beginning to feel powerfully ashamed of myself. So I turned and stepped out into the middle of the larger room and waited for her while the air around me buzzed and shook with the Prowlers' noise.

I wondered as I waited, though. What sort of message would such a wife write to such a husband with a razor blade for her quill and a silver tray laden with white gold for her paper? Could it have been anything as obvious or improbable as *I love you?*

After a time she came out of the inner room and smiled at me, not at all surprised to see me standing there.

"My faithful translator," she said as she stepped past me on her way to the backstage area. She turned the lenses of her sunglasses to me briefly and then turned them away. "Let's go watch the show for a while, shall we?"

Loren wanted to see the band from the front, but she did not take the easiest and quickest route, which was to go out between the curtains and along the side of the stage. Instead she passed through the guarded gate and around the curving perimeter of the building. There were many numbered sets of double doors along the bending inside wall of the hallway, all of which led into the arena, but Loren did not push through any of these until we were on the opposite side of the building from the stage. Then she walked through without glancing back at me, and when I caught up with her, she was already sitting in a sea of empty wooden seats, her hands clasped primly in her lap.

Ronnie paced the stage, singing and strutting and wrapping himself in his microphone cord and then unwrapping himself, twirling and kicking his long legs high into the air. He was barefoot, wearing jeans, and naked from the waist up, his skin gleaming with sweat. Even though I had grown to dislike him, I could not help admiring his energy; he had the effortless control of a star, there was no denying it. For the second time that day I felt my envy of him rising in me strongly. At the same time that envy was pricking me, I found myself shifting my shoulders in time to the music and tapping my feet. I had a sudden desire to get up on the stage and laugh and scream and kick my feet into the air in exuberant lawlessness. I imagined myself singing, *I'm a night crawler, baby, gonna crawl on yooou, oh yeah.*

Loren and I were not the only audience. Out in front of us, with their backs to us on a platform that reminded me of the wheelhouse of a ship, the sound mixers, with earphones around their heads, manipulated complex batteries of controls. And here and there around the concert hall sat small groups of people, mostly young Venezuelan women. I guessed that these were special guests of the crew. But Loren Hart and I were the farthest of anyone from the stage.

I turned to look at her. Each dark lens of her glasses held a tiny, gyrating Ronnie Neumon; she did not return my gaze. The fact that she did not look at me caused unexpected anger to flash through me, and I kicked my feet onto the back of the seat in front of me and faced straight ahead. After that the music suddenly seemed loud and simple and tedious and joyless. I wished I were home sleeping, with Séptimo watching TV in my living room.

The band played two more songs and stopped. Ronnie put down the microphone and said something to the other Prowlers that I could not hear, and they all walked off stage. Before he vanished, Ronnie turned and peered out in our direction, his fingers gently touching the golden hoop in his ear. He appeared not to recognize us. A moment later he was gone.

My ears rang in the silence. The women seated in front of us got up and began climbing the stage, and the sound men stepped off their platform and began passing a joint between them. I forced myself to look over at Loren again. She had turned herself to stone, her lenses darkly blank where the bright image of Ronnie had rotated only a moment before. She stayed like that until I said, "You probably want to go backstage again now, don't you?"

Silence. Rigidity. I sighed and was about to stand and begin to walk away when finally she said, "No. I'd like to have lunch now, if that's all right."

She remained unmoving for a long minute while I studied her. Finally she turned to me and I could see the reflection of my angry and hung-over face in her glasses. She smiled then and startled me by placing a hand on my wrist.

"Can we do that, Jim?" she asked, her voice calm and soft. Her touch did something to me so that I could not trust my voice; I had to fight myself to keep from looking down at her hand. After a moment I nodded and looked away from her. Then we rose together and went out to the waiting limousine.

Loren Hart both pleased and impressed me by saying she did not want to go to a hotel to eat. She told me to take her to someplace interesting for lunch, someplace that was not necessarily expensive, but which I enjoyed myself. So I directed the driver to take us to La Candelaria.

The restaurant I chose was a Spanish place with cured hams hanging from the ceiling, bullfight posters on the walls, and a long bar of dark wood where men stood two deep arguing about politics. Most of the tables were full, and the place was hazy with smoke. I could tell right away that Loren liked it by the way she smiled as she looked around; it was an authentic smile with cheeks in it as well as lips and teeth. For a moment, before she became conscious of herself, she looked like the very young woman she really was.

A blue-eyed Spaniard in a red vest conducted us to our seats and held Loren's chair for her. While she was getting settled, I looked around and noted with relief that most of the customers were too involved in their own business to stare at us. The two or three men that I did catch looking slid their eyes away as soon as they saw I had noticed; their envy gave me a good feeling.

Loren took a sip of her water and then folded her pale hands on the white linen tablecloth. "This is a Venezuelan place, then?"

"Oh, no. It's Spanish. Venezuela is like the States in that the most interesting food is ethnic."

"So then I'm not getting a genuine taste of Venezuela?" A single dark eyebrow rose from behind her glasses.

"Have you ever eaten beef?" I asked. "Any of a dozen different cuts, but always well-done, with potatoes or rice? Or maybe black beans? A little avocado salad on the side?"

I was feeling happy all of a sudden. I was conscious of the beating of my heart and of the smile that strained my face.

Her smile broadened. "That's it?"

"For standard restaurant fare it is. Unless you want fish. Different cuts of beef. Steaks, mostly. Fried bananas are big, too. The varieties of Venezuelan bananas are more numerous than all the categories of snow recognized by the Eskimos. Feel like steak and some nice fried bananas?" She laughed, and I found it easy to laugh with her.

"I guess we should eat Spanish," Loren Hart said.

I was still feeling hung over, so I ordered a red soup made with squid and mussels and baby clams. I suggested the shrimp in garlic sauce for Loren, and she agreed. We also asked for white wine, and I was feeling pleasantly drunk even before it arrived.

Things went very well until about halfway through the meal, when I sensed a subtle change in the atmosphere of the restaurant. I looked up and saw heads turning, saw that Orchid had come in with a well-dressed man whom I recognized as a Venezuelan television executive.

I gave a little grunt of distress and tried to keep my eyes away from her, but I could not.

Orchid was wearing a low-cut European dress, and her dark hair was swept dramatically back in a bun. She was smiling, showing off the teeth she had taken such good care of for all those years.

Orchid and her escort stood in the middle of the floor for a minute and spoke to an important-looking man who had risen from his seat and gone to greet them. I watched her until she was seated, and then I forced a smile at Loren Hart and looked down at my wineglass.

After a while I felt Orchid's light touch on my shoulder, heard

226

her inevitable kiss beside my ear. She stood next to me, smiling, and she rested a hand on the back of an empty chair, signaling that she wanted to sit down.

So I stood and kissed her cheek, which was dry and hot against my lips, and introduced her to Loren. I introduced them twice; once in Spanish and the second time in English. Then I held her chair and she sat.

After that, as I sat between those two women, stammering at them in their separate languages, I was nearly overtaken by vertigo.

Although Orchid appeared almost plain when compared with Loren, she had a kind of attractiveness that Loren did not possess: a certain sunny quality, a warmth or heat that seemed connected to her smile and the sweetness of her voice as well as other, more mysterious elements of her. Loren and Orchid discussed the upcoming Prowler concerts, and I acted as uneasy interpreter. All the while there was a certain look in Orchid's dark eyes, a sharpness, that let me know she was sizing Loren up, evaluating her for poise and appearance.

Loren was friendly, yet cool, nothing about her suggesting that she was playing the same game. I imagined that she was far above matching herself against anyone.

Meanwhile, at Orchid's table, the TV executive was shooting us some sharp looks of his own from over the top of a beer glass. I was not worried about him, however; I knew he would put on his best smile for Orchid as soon as she left us and returned to him.

The conversation between Loren and Orchid went on and on, and time seemed to stand still. My shirt began to stick to my back. Then finally Orchid touched me on the arm and told me, "*Bueno, mi amor,* we've got to get together more often." She made little movements as she prepared to stand.

"What do you mean?" I said. "We'll be seeing each other later this afternoon. I'm going to be interpreting for Ronnie Neumon when you interview him."

Orchid's smile flickered. "Oh, no, *mi corazón,*" she said, her voice trilling brightly. "That was discussed, and it was decided that Ronnie should have a woman interpreter. A person was hired to do that."

"What?" I said, shaming myself with my obvious dismay. "They didn't tell me that."

I looked at Loren Hart and said, "Is that true? Did you hear that they've hired someone else to interpret for Ronnie on television?"

Loren nodded and pouted sympathetically. "I think they decided it would make better TV if they had an attractive woman doing it."

"Oh." I looked up at Orchid and pretended to smile. My eyes were burning.

"Well," Orchid said, standing and looking down at Loren. *"Mucho gusto."* I should have stood, but I didn't.

"Mucho gusto," said Loren, smiling and pronouncing carefully.

Orchid kissed me and went back to her friend.

We ordered coffee and didn't say anything for a time. Then Loren said, "You know her quite well, don't you?"

"Yes," I told her. My eyes would not lift to meet hers. I looked at her hands, which I decided were the most beautiful, flowerlike hands I had ever seen. "She is a good friend."

I felt Loren Hart's stare on me for a long minute, and then her hands fluttered up from the table like a pair of doves, and when they returned, they were holding the sunglasses.

I caught my breath and looked at her face. Her naked eyes were a pure, improbable Caribbean blue, the type of vulnerable blue that makes you worry that direct sunlight might strike them sightless. And they held an innocence that was surprising after you had met her husband and had imagined a little of the life she must lead with him. Without the glasses she looked a bit younger than her twenty-two years; her reasons for wearing them were no longer a mystery to me.

I was embarrassed by my staring, but I was unable to let my own eyes fall away from hers. Her eyes moved left and right, sweeping from one side of my face to the other; they were studying me, photographing me. Her gaze was as intimate as a kiss, and I felt myself growing red beneath it.

She said, "I would have guessed that she was more than just a good friend."

"Who?"

"What's her name? Orchid. That pretty girl."

"Oh." The spell broken, I looked away. "Well, yes, I guess." Of its own accord my hand rose from the table and the cool palm settled against my forehead.

"Was she a lover?"

"I really don't like to talk about it." She put one of her hands on the arm that I had left on the table.

"Jimmy. I'm quite a good listener."

How feminine a thing that is, thinking that a wound can be healed by talking about it. How young Loren Hart was suddenly beginning to seem. I looked up at her, but my eyes jumped quickly away.

"Listen," I said. "I really, really, hate to talk about it."

She didn't mention it again. But she kept her sunglasses off for me until we were back out in the Venezuelan sunshine.

When we arrived at the hotel, we found that the roadies had already begun to trickle back from the Poliedro, although none of the band members had yet returned. In the lobby Loren Hart gave me a faint smile and said she was going up to Ronnie's room to read for a while, then she vanished.

I took advantage of the lull to call my office.

"*¿Sí? Dígame.*" It was Mickey, and I felt a smile spread across my face.

"*Jefe.* How'd it go?"

"Ah, Jim. Okay. They weren't happy, but they were almost satisfied. I didn't have to beg or anything."

"You would have begged?" I was surprised to hear even the word come from him.

"Hey," said Mickey, "as you were kind enough to point out, I don't have anything else. Just this fucking job." He sounded bitter as well as tired.

"Go home," I said. "Find a park and take a walk." I myself longed desperately to walk and then nap for the rest of the day.

"I may. But make sure you remember your half of this deal. Now that I'm on the semishit list, I can't afford any screwups." It was my turn to sound bitter and tired.

"Leave it all to me, Mickey. I've got big shoulders."

"Lucky for both of us," he said. Then he hung up.

I stood by myself for a time until Packy and Camión drifted in. Camión was sullen, and Packy was still jumping with the nervous energy that had shaken him that morning.

"*Coño*, gringo," Packy said. "How good to see you!" He threw one of his thin arms across my back, and I could feel him trembling. El Camión gave me a quick smile and then began rubbing his eyes with his huge fists.

"What's wrong with you boys?" I asked. "Tired?"

"Yes! Tired!" they said in unison. Packy began laughing, and Camión looked startled for a moment before reburying his face in his hands.

I pulled myself out of Packy's embrace. Their strangeness was starting to annoy me. "Too much *perico* for you two? Is that why you're acting this way?"

Camión made wide eyes at Packy. "*¿Perico?*" he said, his voice an octave higher than normal. He seemed about to say something else, but Packy gave a high horse laugh that drew stares from around the lobby and then he hit me with a stinging slap between the shoulder blades.

"*¡Perico!*" he whispered. "Yes, *perico.* Too much *perico* for anyone to handle."

"Quit slapping me," I said, managing to put more anger into my voice than I really felt. "If the stuff makes you act like this much of a *huevón*, then quit doing it."

Packy made that high, grating laugh once again, and then he threw his arm around the back of my neck and gathered Camión's head in the crook of his other arm. He looked like a scarecrow hanging between us.

"Good, gringo. Funny. But, *oye,* more than anything else right now, Camión and I need a drink. To bring us down from this bad *perico.* What do you say? Just the thing for that hangover of yours, *¿qué no?*"

I had been seriously considering going home and going to sleep. But the thought of sitting in a comfortable place and having a laugh was a seductive one. I nodded and Packy laughed, and the three of us headed for the hotel bar.

The bar seemed different, more mysterious somehow, than when Loren Hart and I had sat there that morning. We sat in near darkness, long stripes of shadow across our eyes and mouths. The lone barman served us a round of *ron y Coca* and then retreated behind his counter, where he worked incessantly with unseen hands. We were his only customers, and our laughter and everything we said seemed to hang in the quiet air for a moment before fading away.

We joked about the members of the band and their roadies; Packy and Camión had come to know them all quite well. But neither of them mentioned Ronnie Neumon, and whenever I tried to talk about him, they would exchange a glance and change the subject. I decided that this was probably because they had spent less time with Ronnie than with the others.

After a while I stopped talking. I was tired, and both Packy and Camión seemed so anxious to fill the air around us with a soft cushion of meaningless words that I decided to let them. I settled deeper into my comfortable seat and listened, my eyes half-closed. And I swallowed drink after drink that Packy ordered for me. I did not really want all those drinks, but I knew he would give me a hard time if I didn't put them away, and I was in no mood to argue. So I just slid them down.

Finally, to keep myself from falling asleep, I broke through the drone made by their mingled voices. "So what about the gun?" I asked.

There was sudden silence. Then Camión said, "What gun?" His voice was sharp, and he leaned across the table toward me, his face drawn tight as a fist. Packy was staring at me as well.

"The *gun*," I said. "You know, the one you thought Ronnie Neumon had, that you wanted me to look out for?"

"Did you see a gun?" asked Packy. He was not smiling.

I had myself a good laugh, but I stopped laughing when I began to feel dizzy enough to fall to the floor.

"No, I didn't see a gun. What the *hell* is wrong with you today?" I made a cradle of my arms and let my head drop forward to rest in it. I think that I must have slept then because after a time I felt Packy shaking me. I lifted my head and folded my arms around my chest; I was cold suddenly.

"Jimmy," Packy said. "Go home, *pana*. You're drunk." His face was uncharacteristically severe.

"I'm tired," I said. "Did this drinking twice in a row." My Spanish tongue was thick with rum, and I had trouble getting the words out.

"Why don't you go home and sleep? You want us to get you a cab?" Packy and Camión exchanged a dark look, and I thought that it was because I had gotten so wasted. This was funny to me, and I laughed.

"Don't look like that, *huevones,*" I told them. "All I had was a few drinks. No two coke fiends have a right to be staring at me."

Another quick look passed between them, then Camión said, "How about it, then, gringo? You want to go home?"

I nestled my face in the hollow of my shoulder. My body felt like an unfamiliar vehicle. "Too tired," I said in English. "May crash in the lobby for a while."

I heard Packy's voice close to my ear. "Jimmy. There are a couple of empty suites on the floor where the band is staying. Why don't you go up there?"

I opened my eyes and looked at them. A soft bed, five minutes away. In a private suite. Free. I shivered and nodded.

The two of them saw me to the elevator. On the way, Camión looked at Packy and said, "I think there's a chance Jimmy may be asleep for a long time."

Packy nodded. Then suddenly he stepped forward and hugged me. It was a fierce hug, a hug such as a person gives another when one of them is about to leave on a long journey. I felt Camión slapping me on the shoulder. "See you later, gringo," Packy said. I hugged him back. Then the two of them were pushing me into the elevator.

"Remember," said Camión. "Suite six or seven. Those are the empty ones. Both of them are unlocked." I nodded, and the doors of the elevator closed.

My rooms stood three doors down from Ronnie's suite and were identical to his. Same kitchen, same leather couch, same rectangular glass table. Only, this suite was vacant, and every noise you made came back at you off the walls. I went right into the bedroom and closed the door. The bed was soft as snow, and it swallowed and smothered me.

I awoke disoriented in the darkness I don't know how many hours later. The glow of the city was like starlight coming through the window, and I heard the sound of traffic in the street far below. But it was another noise that had awakened me, some faint stirring in the living room of my suite. I was suddenly frightened, aware of my vulnerability, and I drew myself into a sitting position and rolled my eyes helplessly around the dark room in search of a weapon. I was close to being sick from drinking, and the room was spinning slowly on its axis.

Then the sound reached me again; it was an anguished moan that made my scalp tighten. I could think only of murder. The roadies were murdering somebody, or, more probably, Ronnie Neumon was choking someone to death in my suite. I stood, rubbing my eyes, ready to charge out and stop him, when I heard another moan, and then another, a woman's moans, and they came in a series like waves rolling in at high tide, each sharper and more urgent than the next, building one upon the other. Then I heard a second voice, and I knew it was Ronnie's, because he made a shrill, wordless exhalation similar to one of the sounds that he produced on stage.

I sat down on the edge of the bed and laughed silently. A killing of the good sort, apparently. Tears of laughter and relief squeezed themselves from the corners of my eyes. I heard gasps and sighs, a single wet sound that could have been a kiss or a more intimate coming apart, and the small, muffled noises that bodies make when they roll around on a carpeted floor. I rubbed my hands over the short stubble of my face, my fingers tracing the bowed lines of my laughing mouth, and I prepared to wait it out. After my laughter had died, I felt both sick and sober. I began to visualize Loren Hart's face without the sunglasses, and a thread of jealousy wove slowly through me.

A quiet minute passed, and then Ronnie haltingly whispered something in Spanish. I didn't catch it. The woman answered in Spanish, just a word or two, but it was enough to let me know she was a native speaker. I stood then and moved toward the door, wondering whether Ronnie had found Marilyn Monroe again and had somehow gotten him into the hotel.

For a long while I heard nothing but the noises of bodies shifting in the dark. But then the woman began to hum. The woman hummed like a perfect angel, and as soon as the first few notes were out of her throat, I knew who she was.

Slowly I settled to my knees. I let my hands creep up my face into my hair; beneath my brow my hands found wetness.

There was more humming, and then the humming gave way to talking, but I seemed to be somewhere else for a time and did not pay attention. Then, shaking with anger, I began to come back; I began to listen.

In English now, Ronnie was saying, "You want that? Is that what you want?"

And Orchid was saying, "*Sí, mi amor. Así.* This way."

I heard footsteps on the carpet, and Ronnie asked, "With the light?"

"*Con la luz,*" Orchid agreed. Sudden light spilled beneath the doorway.

More footsteps, then Ronnie said, "Okay, you little brown bitch. Here goes." Then there was silence except for a puzzling tapping sound like that of a leaky faucet.

I stood and pushed open the door and stepped into the other room.

Orchid lay beneath the glass table, her naked body at right angles to the tabletop. Her eyes were wide and unblinking and her head rolled slowly from side to side. Her mouth was parted slightly, and I saw gleaming teeth stained with lipstick. Rain pattered the glass above her, and her fingertips were making circular movements against the bottom of the table as if to touch it.

Ronnie, also naked, was standing over her. His back was to me, the muscles in his shoulders and back tight and well defined in the weak light of the small lamp he had turned on, but I could see where his hands were and I could see where that rain was coming from. It pooled at the center of the table and then ran off the edge to splash down onto Orchid's belly and breasts, making her skin gleam darkly.

Had it been any other kind of physical affection, I probably would have just slipped right out the door like a whipped dog and gone somewhere to brood. But this way, because I had confided in Ronnie about my feelings for Orchid, I felt that it was an outrage and an incredible insult. I stepped forward just as he was turning his head to look at me, and I grabbed his shoulder and spun him around to face me.

I don't know what I would have done then if he had looked frightened or concerned or even angry. Anger would have at least shown respect of a kind. But he only blinked at me, his blue eyes half-lidded in an insolent way, and then he smiled.

"Hi, Jimbo," he said.

I made a noise that sounded shrill and desperate to my own ears, and I threw a punch to his jaw that knocked him back away from the table and over the couch. I felt a wave of pride, even as the pain traveled from my knuckles into my shoulder. Then I shouted and leaped over the couch after him, landing on his naked body, and I got in one more good punch to his slippery face before he threw me off.

Ronnie Neumon rolled on top of me, hit me two, three, four times, making stars explode in front of my eyes, and then he sat straddling my chest the way you see a kid straddle another kid's chest. He was heavy.

"Get off," I told him. My voice was a tired, shameful wheeze. I didn't hurt yet, but I found that I could not lift my head from the carpet. I felt a sticky wetness like syrup or grape jelly around my mouth.

Ronnie just sat there for a minute, smiling, but with anger bunching the skin around his eyes. I felt sure he would spit on me or empty an ashtray on my face or perform some other act of childish humiliation. But then he just stood and walked away.

I was still struggling to rise from the carpet when he returned wearing a pair of baggy white trousers. He stared down at me while I tried to show him some defiance, tried to meet his eyes at least, and then he dug into the pocket of his pants and drew something out. I squinted, and saw it was an American five-dollar bill that he had.

"Here, Jimbo," Ronnie said. "I guess I lose the bet."

He crumpled the five and flicked it at my chest like a marble. As he was walking away, he cocked his head to look at me over his naked shoulder. "I would have paid you; you didn't have to go attacking me."

The door of the suite opened and closed. Then he was gone.

I was still groggy, still in too much shock to feel anything yet, and for that I was grateful. Just as I pulled myself into a sitting position, Orchid came and squatted by my side. She was wearing jeans now and a white blouse. She was barefoot.

"Jimmy," she chided in that beautiful voice. "What's the matter with you?" She had a damp washcloth in her hand, and she reached and began mopping my face with it. I did not resist. I could not look her in the eye.

"How could you do that?" I asked her. I was pleased that my voice was not shaking too badly; I knew that would come later, and when it did, I would not be able to talk at all or to show my face to anyone.

"Do what?" she said, and smiled. "Make love with a man? You didn't used to mind."

"Love?" I said, and shoved away the hand with the washcloth. The word came out in a thin quaver, and I knew I would have to speak fast. "That wasn't love. It was . . ."

"It was one of the forms of love," Orchid said, nearly singing to me now. She reached to push her fingers through my hair, but I twisted away from her. I felt tears straining to break free. I fought them back.

"Hell it was," I said, my voice beginning to squeak. "What do you know about love anyway?"

She looked down at me. There was an infuriating pity in her eyes, and her smile did not waver.

"I know a lot. I know it's like anything else that people want, and that only a fool gives it out without getting something in return."

There was at least some truth to this, I knew; I had been a fool more times than I could count. I had certainly been a fool with Orchid. The tears wouldn't be put off now, so I lowered my head and turned away to keep her from seeing.

"*Ciao, mi amor*," Orchid said. She bent forward and kissed me on the temple. Then she stood, picked a pair of shoes from the floor, and headed for the door.

"Orchid!"

She turned quickly. That pitying smile. Tears and snot were coming out of me now, and I was shaking, but I had to say what I had to say. "You really *don't* know anything about love."

Orchid's smile tightened, and she lifted her eyebrows at me. Her hand encircled the doorknob. "Well, tell me, Jimmy," she said. "Tell me who does."

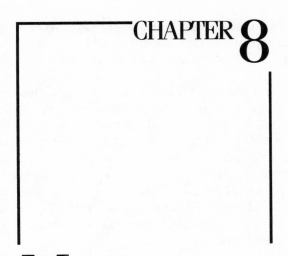

CHAPTER 8

My sorrow gave way to numbness in the taxi on the way home. I stopped crying and stared out the window at the cold lights of Caracas.

But by the time the taxi dropped me at the foot of my stairs, I had gone through another complete transformation; my feelings of humiliation had turned back to anger. I was so angry it was as if someone else were controlling my actions, and as I stood by myself on the dark, empty street, I ground my teeth and clenched and unclenched my fists, and I beat my hands against my sides. My head was filled with a heavy blackness that smothered all sane thoughts the moment they were born.

Finally I stomped up the metal stairs and opened the door to my apartment. The house was unlit, but the TV was going, and for a minute I thought Packy might be home. But I searched and did not find him, and then I realized it had probably been Séptimo who left the TV on when he let himself out that morning. A new wave of rage flashed through me; I wanted to hit Séptimo, and I went to the open door and bellowed his name down into the street. No answer.

Then, as I stood looking out the door, I noticed that there was a light on in Lola's house, and a dark idea settled over me, possessed me like a demon. I laughed because it was so good, and then I went into my bedroom and took from my dresser drawer the heaviest pair of socks I could find. They were white athletic socks with green stripes near the top, and I stuffed one sock inside the other and stuck them into my back pocket and walked out of the house.

I pounded on the front gate of Lola's *quinta*, making it rattle loudly, and then I took out Ronnie Neumon's five-dollar bill and I smoothed it against my palm and studied it, laughing, in the weak light of the nearby streetlamp. Lola's abused mother came to the upstairs window and stuck her head out through the drapes next to the parrot cage. Her hair was done up in gray braids that wound around her palsied old head. *"¿Qué quieres?"* she asked me.

"I want Lola," I said. "I need to speak with Lola. *Urgente.*"

"Lola is asleep," the old woman said in her quavering voice. "Come back tomorrow, *extranjero.*"

"I need to see her now," I said. I was shouting, dancing on the sidewalk with impatience.

"Mañana, por favor."

"Now. Now. Now! Now! Now!" She just stared at me, so I said, "I'll scream all night! All fucking night!"

She vanished then, and Lola appeared at the window. Lola was a wraith with drawn-back hair and a mask of white cream all over her face. She was wearing a white terrycloth bathrobe that she held closed at the breast. Under other circumstances, I might have laughed at this display of modesty.

"¿Qué quieres, extranjero?" Lola asked, her voice piercing as a needle.

"Change!" I shouted. *"¡Cambio!"* I held up Ronnie's five-dollar bill and stretched it tight between my hands. "And I need it right now. This minute. Open up the beer shop, would you?"

Just at that moment I saw little Séptimo come up the alleyway that ran along Camión's white wall. He came slinking along the wall in an uncharacteristic manner, as if trying to hide, but I paid him no attention. I was too busy with my sudden obsession.

Lola glared down at me through her death mask of cold cream until suddenly the green parrot in the cage by her head gave an evil squawk and thrust its bill through the wide bars and snapped at her ear. Then she thumped the cage with an open palm, knocking the parrot from its perch, and said, *"Extranjero,* you're crazy. *Loco de bolas."*

"Shut your snout, *puta!"* I shouted. "I am not crazy. But I do need change, and if you don't open the shop, I'll stay down here all night. Understand? Understand?"

She looked down at me for half a minute longer, then her head disappeared. Soon lights came on in the first floor of the *quinta*, and Lola was at the gate, undoing the lock. I followed her into the little concrete courtyard where she kept her refrigerator and the table that held her cash box.

"Coins," I told her. "Coins of one bolivar."

She did not look at me as she took out the key and opened the wooden box; she only pulled the five-dollar bill from between my fingers, smoothed it down on the table, and scooped out a clinking handful of bolivars. She counted out twenty of these and let them drop to the tabletop, then she flashed narrowed eyes at me, daring me to demand the official exchange of four-point-three rather than the even four she had given me. But I said nothing. Instead I yanked the socks from my back pocket and began pouring the coins into the innermost one. When I was finished, I was disappointed to find that five dollars' worth of bolivars barely filled the toe of my doubled stocking.

"Son of a bitch," I said in English. I snatched more money from my wallet, Venezuelan money now, and I made Lola sell me the rest of her bolivars. When I had finished stuffing them in, the sock was still not sufficiently full, so I wound up buying her remaining change, her cincos and reales and her medios. The tiny medios came to the top of the heel and finished the job. I tied a knot just above the coins to hold them tight, then I worked the sock into the front pocket of my pants. This was difficult to do, because the pocket was not large.

When I was done, I turned and rushed out into the street. Lola said the inevitable thing about my mother and slammed the gate behind me, but I paid her no mind. I was trying to decide where to go to get a taxi.

But then I saw Séptimo. He was beyond my house now, moving slowly along the darkest part of the wall, an area where a big palm tree grew close to the wall and cast large shadows against it. Timo was moving sideways, sliding his back against the white metal.

"Timo!" Séptimo stopped, but did not answer. This angered me, so I headed toward him, the stocking full of coins pressing against my thigh as I walked.

When I got close, though, the strange expression on his spotted face broke through my rage and touched a reasonable part of me. I saw that something had gone out of him; his mouth was slack and his eyes were sunken back. He looked as if he were in shock. I settled to my knees on the ground in front of him.

"What is it?" I said. "What's wrong with you?" He seemed to appraise me with his dark eyes, and then, slowly, he shook his head.

"Nothing? There's something, Timo. Tell me." He started to turn away, so I stood and grabbed him by the hand. "I bet you haven't eaten," I said. "I'll take you in and fix you something."

I began to tow him toward my house, and it was then I knew that the cause of Séptimo's alarming loss of spirit was neither hunger nor loneliness. With his rough little hand in mine, he walked as stiffly as a wooden soldier; his gait reminded me of the way I had once walked after suffering a bad sunburn at the beach.

I drew Séptimo beneath a streetlamp, and before he could protest, I knelt and untied the piece of rope that he used for a belt, and I jerked his pants to his ankles. At once I saw the grid of long thin welts that ran from the backs of his upper legs to the small of his back. Each welt was red and stood a quarter of an inch above his brown skin. I let go of him, so dizzy, suddenly, that I had to stick a hand behind me to keep from falling over.

"Adolfo?" I asked him. He looked down at the street and nodded.

"Because of me?" I asked. I don't think he would have answered that even if I had given him the time. No sooner were the words out of my mouth than I was rushing onward to my next question. "What did he use?"

Séptimo did not reply at first. But I lifted my hand and shook him gently by the shoulder, and finally he said, "*Un gancho.* A wire coat hanger."

"Jesus!"

Timo's voice sounded tiny and broken. He was a toy that had fallen from a window ledge. "He bent it to make a long rod." He demonstrated by lifting his hands and making a twisting motion in the air.

Then he looked at me. The way Timo looked at me was awful; by the utter hopelessness in his eyes, I could tell he was seeing me as a fellow victim rather than as an adult, an authority, who could

240

bring justice and sanity to his little world. And the horrifying thing was that he was right. In fact I was perhaps even more helpless than he; did I not need Packy and Camión to protect me from Adolfo and his friends? Had little Timo himself not had to place himself in danger to defend me?

I squatted there in the street for a long minute, stewing in the bitter cauldron of humiliation heaped upon insufferable humiliation while Séptimo stood before me, his pants lying limp at his ankles and his tiny, uncut manhood thrusting outward like an accusing finger. Then a roaring began somewhere, a rolling waterfall of sound, and my grandmother's hand came out of the night sky, her diamond glinting like a cold, sharp star, and she hit me again and again. I tasted blood.

I stood, the taste and the heat of my blood spreading through me until the air around me was the color of blood and the falling-water roar I heard kept me from hearing the cautious voices in my own head.

In a moment I was standing in front of Adolfo's house, pounding my fist into the metal door. My fist seemed made of stone, and I felt no pain. When he did not answer right away, I backed off and threw a kick; the door buckled inward. Just as I was getting set to throw another kick, I heard the lock turning and then the door opened, and Adolfo was standing there. He was naked except for a pair of stained white jockey shorts that clung beneath his smooth, rounded belly. His right hand rested at his side and held a black twenty-five-caliber pistol.

"Gringo," Adolfo said.

I did not examine his face for signs of fear or anger, and I only glanced at the gun. As soon as he opened his mouth, I had that sock out of my pocket, and I cocked my arm and swung the bundle of coins and cloth like a tennis player backhanding a serve. The rounded weight of my weapon met the tautness of Adolfo's stomach and made a nest for itself there before jumping away like a stone bouncing off a trampoline. Adolfo doubled forward, and the gun clattered to the broken pavement in front of his house.

Adolfo was making little noises that sounded like *ay, ay,* but I quickly wound up again and brought the piggy bank down across the back of his neck. He collapsed then, his body stretched out over the threshold. From somewhere back in the dark depths of the house, I heard Mrs. Adolfo, her voice only faintly alarmed, saying, "*¿Adolfo, quién es? ¿Adolfo, qué pasó?*"

I stood over Adolfo until I heard him begin to moan again, and then I jammed the sock into my pocket and got down on my hands and knees so that I could peer into his face. His eyes were open, although they were as dull as smoked glass and the lids were fluttering.

"You hear me, *huevón?*" I whispered. After a few seconds Adolfo swallowed and then nodded once, his unshaven face making a sandpaper sound on the pavement. His lips were parted, and a long thread of drool ran from the corner of his mouth to the ground.

I said, "If you ever touch Séptimo again, I will kill you. *¿Comprendes?*" There was a pause. I was still whispering, my mouth inches from his ear. There was a strange intimacy between us; I was sure he could feel my damp, hot breath on him, and I tried to imagine what my breath must feel like.

"I have money," I told him. "I'm a rich gringo; you know that. And if for some reason I can't kill you myself, if I'm in Catia or if I'm dead, I'll pay someone to come and kill you. I'll pay a Colombian to slit your throat and flap your tongue out like a necktie. *¿Comprendido?*" Adolfo scraped the side of his face against the ground once more and made a tiny hissing sound as if trying to pronounce the word "*sí.*"

I reached over and grabbed the little pistol, and after examining it for a moment I stuck it in my jacket pocket. I had never fired a gun and never intended to, but now that I was suddenly calmer, on a rolling boil rather than caught in an explosion of steam, I was beginning to think again, and one of the things I thought was that the gun might come in handy for scaring Ronnie Neumon. Scare him with the gun, then cave him in with my Venezuelan piggy bank. All accounts would be balanced after that. I stood and walked away, a little unsteady on my feet.

I found Séptimo standing in the street by the steel wall. He had pulled up his pants and retied his piece of rope, but his clothes still looked in disarray. I guessed that he had seen everything; there was a strange smile twisting his little pixie face.

"*Vamos,*" I said, and I put my hand on his shoulder and guided him up the stairs to my apartment. Once I had opened the door, I turned on a light and then I removed the key to the front door from my key chain. I knelt and pressed the key into Séptimo's hand.

"Timo," I said, "I think you ought to have a key so that you can come in and out, and don't have to sleep in the street anymore." His eyes and his smile both widened, and this gave me a warm feeling of satisfaction that I did not quite understand. I almost laughed aloud despite the anger that still gripped me. I had not meant to give him the run of the kitchen as well, but the offer came out seemingly on its own. "You can eat whatever you want. Just remember to wash your hands before you go in the refrigerator."

He came forward then and hugged me; he was laughing in my ear. This should have been another satisfaction, but it suddenly seemed to me that his aloofness and his independence were collapsing too fast; I did not have time to adjust.

"I have to go now," I told him.

"Where?" His voice took on an alarmed tone I had never heard before. It made me feel all the more eager to leave.

"I have to see someone," I said. I turned and started down the steps. When I reached the street, I looked back at him to remind him about washing his hands. He was staring down at me with his accustomed stony indifference, and after I had spoken, he did not answer me, and he did not wave. I found this somehow reassuring.

It was still a couple of hours before dawn, and I had to walk down to the foot of the big hill, to the closed news kiosk at the corner of Avenida Rómulo Gallegos, before I found a cab that was willing to stop. As I climbed into the backseat, I felt the weight of that sockful of coins in my pocket, and although the cabbie had no meter in his car, I did not even bother to fix the price with him before we set off. I told him to take me to the Caracas Hilton.

The lobby was nearly empty. Aside from the desk clerks, there were only five or six old Venezuelan men who stood in a drunken circle, gossiping and laughing about someone named Teresa. I walked past the clique of old men and stepped into the maw of a waiting elevator and I rode it past the floor that the roadies inhabited, up to the floor of suites that the Prowlers occupied. As the elevator stopped and opened, my mouth went quickly dry. My legs seemed rooted to the floor.

I had suddenly remembered that there would be security men. If I hit Ronnie, *when* I hit him, they would come running, and there was no doubt they would give me a good working over before they called the hotel security. For my bit of revenge I'd pay with a few bruises at the very least. Broken teeth were likely, and a flattened nose was a possibility. They might even break a few ribs on me—for a moment I had an awful vision of a snapped rib turning inward and punching through one of my pink lungs in a geyser of blood. The madness was wearing off, and I was beginning to come back into my everyday senses. And along with those senses, my normal cowardice was also returning. The hand I had used to batter Adolfo's door was starting to throb. I rubbed it and noticed that it was swelling and becoming discolored.

But my humiliation remained; it was unbearable, and I knew that if I did not move forward and punish Ronnie for what he had done to me, I would not be able to live with myself. I would end up like Mickey Calderón, shut away in my house, insulating and anesthetizing myself against the world. My poison would be alcohol rather than *perico*, and I would slowly kill myself with it. All these thoughts ran through my head as I stood in that empty elevator, and finally, as a cold act of self-preservation, without the aid or anesthetic of blind, red rage, I stepped out into the hallway on trembling legs.

I had by then made up a lie for the gringo security men about delivering a message to Ronnie. But the carpeted hallway was empty and eerily quiet. The only sound was a faint ghostly buzzing made by the fluorescent hallway lights. The doors to the suites were all closed except for the door that led to the rooms where I had fought with Ronnie earlier that night. That door yawned, and light came from within.

I had intended to go directly to Ronnie's suite, but when I started for it, my legs, seemingly of their own accord, turned me and carried me to the suite where I had slept and awakened to the sounds of Ronnie and Orchid making love. Perhaps there was some clue for me there, some message of absolution from someone or something that would allow me to turn around and go home and sleep peacefully and dreamlessly until long after the arrival of unambiguous daylight. But I crossed the threshold and stood in the middle of the suite, and there was no such comforting message.

Instead of a message, I saw the still-wet top of the glass coffee table and the darkened spots on the carpet below. This evidence of my shame was a silent reproof, and it brought back some of the welcome anger. I felt myself nod as if in answer to a question, and I pulled the sockful of Venezuelan coins from my pocket and then I withdrew from the room. My legs were solid beneath me now.

I walked down to Ronnie's door. As I turned and faced it, I wrapped the loose top of the sock once around the knuckles of my bruised right hand. Breathing was a conscious thing for me now, and I concentrated on it as I stared into the wood-grain finish of the door and formed my battle plan.

If Ronnie himself answered, the attack would be identical to the one I had made on Adolfo; I would wind up as he was getting the first word out, and I would give him the first shot right in the soft hollow at the bottom of the breastbone. Number two across the back of the neck. I imagined him twitching and drooling into the immaculate carpet, and I almost smiled. Of course, he knew some karate, and he might be quicker than Adolfo had been, but I could not let myself think about that. And if Loren Hart answered the door—I imagined her in a flowing white nightgown, without her dark glasses and with her hair hanging down past her shoulders —I would have to bluff. I would have to hide the piggy bank behind my back and tell her I needed to speak with Ronnie right away. Some little emergency at the Poliedro, it would have to be.

I raised my fist to knock, and it was then I noticed that the door was ajar by a hairline crack. I lowered my hand and considered barging directly in, swinging the sock ahead of me like a flail. But in the end I decided to stick to the original plan. I knocked once and then again, and when there was no answer, I knew, with a painful, sinking feeling, that no one was home.

I nearly wept at my own stupidity. Why had I assumed that Ronnie would be in his suite just because it was half past four in the morning? I should have at least suspected that he might be out on the town with Loren, or else catting around on his own. Asleep, in his own room, like a solid, middle-class citizen? What an idiot I was. And now I had lost the momentum; and I knew that I would never be able to gather myself to do this thing again.

I raised my bruised hand to my mouth and bit myself in punishment. I began to turn away, but then I heard a faint rustling from inside the suite; it could have been a breeze-blown curtain or it could have been a person moving, and hope fluttered into my chest on feeble wings. I reached and pushed open the door.

The first thing I saw was a pair of huge lumps on the carpet of the living room. For a moment they looked like twin mounds of clothes at a rummage sale, and the strangeness of them stopped me dead. I stood blinking until one of the piles shifted slightly, and then, as if a dark lens had suddenly lifted, I saw that I was looking at two large men lying on their sides. I stepped closer and saw that they were two of the Prowlers' security men, ex-football players grown heavy on the good life, and that they were bound with ropes, hand and foot, with coarse white tape sealing their mouths.

I moved into the room and glanced into the bedroom to make sure no one was there, and then I dropped the sockful of coins and went over to the men and knelt by them. The men were both of about the same size and shape, although one of them was young and blond, and the other was darker and older and bald. Both the security men had faces that were red and puffed from trying to make noise through their gags. I decided that the older-looking of the pair would be the one most worth talking to, so I reached and tore the tape from his mouth. He yelled in pain, which I had expected, but then he began to wail senselessly about Ronnie, his eyes grown suddenly wide and wild. Something to do with Ronnie, and not a clue about what it was.

The man was still yelling when I tore the tape from his friend's mouth. The blond security man snarled as the tape came off, and then he twisted his head to glare at the darker man.

"Shut up," he said, his voice calm. "You hear me, Al? Shut the fuck up." Al quieted then and began struggling with mute fury against his bonds. The blond rolled cold eyes back to me. "The ropes, pal," he said. "How about it?"

It was strange, to have come to hurt Ronnie only to end up aiding his distressed henchmen. I felt displaced in time, almost drugged.

"Ronnie did this to you?" I asked, crawling behind the blond's back to work at his wrists.

The blond growled with impatience. "What are you, stupid? Ronnie? The fucking kidnappers, asshole. Hurry up."

His words were like a blow to the back of my head. I left off untying him, and I bent over so that I could look into his face. "What do you mean?"

I saw now that he was crying, teeth clenched and tears running down his well-fed cheeks. He began to wail now too. "They came in here and tied us up, and they took Ronnie away. Now fucking untie me before I go crazy!"

Stunned, I went back to work. After a moment I said, "What about Loren?" My voice had begun to shake; strangely the first feelings to hit me were feelings of guilt, as if the kidnapping had somehow been my fault.

"I don't know," the guard shouted. "Hurry up, goddamn it!" He kept saying, "Hurry up, hurry up," until I had finished untying him. Then he jumped up and started helping Al out of his bonds.

"What kind of people did this?" I asked. The guilt and a vague dread I couldn't place were growing in me. While the blond security man was working on his friend's wrists, I edged over and kicked my Venezuelan piggy bank under the couch.

"Kind of people?" the guard yelled. "Motherfuckers, that's what kind."

"No, I mean—"

"Spicks. What the fuck do you think? Greaseballs wearing ski masks. I'd like to get hold of every fucking one of them..." But I was no longer listening. I was seeing Enrique Mosca sighting down the barrel of his weapon at me; I was hearing the voice of the Croaker telling me, *You just ain't seen nothin' yet.*

This had to be it. No more bank robberies. No assassinations of cops. No bombs. Just the nearly nonviolent kidnapping of a single man, a relatively easy job that would guarantee worldwide publicity for them and their hazy cause. It was frightening, and it was almost admirable, and something odd about it was bothering me very much.

The two big men elbowed me aside and lumbered out into the hallway. A minute later I heard the elevator door rumble open, and suddenly I needed to get down to the roadies' floor and talk to Packy and Camión. I thought about the two of them and I began to worry; a sudden, sharp image of the mysterious motorcycle ruts in the tainted dirt of Camión's property flashed through my mind.

Most of the doors along the roadies' hallway were open, and

there were people, male roadies mostly, but also a few Venezuelan women, drinking in the rooms and snorting cocaine, and laughing and necking. A few doors were closed, however, and I could only guess what was going on behind them. John Stewart's door was one of the closed ones, and while the two guards pounded on it with huge fists, I wandered up and down the hallway, looking for Packy and El Camión and growing more and more worried when I did not find them. Roadies squinted at me through eyes that were as narrow and red as cracks in a furnace door, and a couple of them smiled and offered me beer and shots of rum. I asked them if Packy was around, and they all shook their heads. Packy had not been seen since dinnertime, they said. Neither, in fact, had Camión.

Worry gnawed hard now.

John Stewart finally answered his door. He was naked except for a towel around his waist, and I could tell by the way he stood blocking the threshold that he had someone inside. The guards began their explanation, and I drew close and listened to them tell about how the guerrillas had knocked and then pushed their way into the room, waving pistols around, and had tied up Ronnie and the two guards. Then, after stuffing Ronnie into a huge trunk, they had wheeled him into the hallway and closed the door. Simple and fast and clean. In spite of myself, I once again felt something akin to admiration. I watched Stewart's face shift from anger to surprise to alarm, and then he retreated into his room and slammed his door and came out a minute later wearing a pair of jeans; he went up and down the hall, shouting. In a few minutes everyone in the hallway was shouting and waving arms and grabbing for telephones. Some of the Venezuelan girls came into the hallway and began to scream; I looked into their eyes and saw the blaze of excitement there, and I knew they were screaming for dramatic effect. They had wonderful, strong lungs, and they seemed to enjoy themselves.

I stood against the wall in the hallway and watched the commotion; part of me wanted to laugh, and another part thought of Packy. I felt the dread of a black hunch proving itself right.

I knew I needed to get out of there before the cops came; Lugo Alvarado's hatchet face bloomed in my mind's eye. John Stewart was passing me, running nervous hands through his hair, and I reached and touched him on the elbow. He whirled and drew back a fist as if to hit me, and when he recognized me, he did not throw the punch, but he kept his hand cocked. His bearded face twitched with confusion.

"Listen," I said. "Ronnie's wife. Loren. Has anybody seen her?"

"Oh," John Stewart said. His expression softened to worry. "Oh, Jesus Christ. You mean maybe . . ." His hands came together on his forehead, fingers kneading his brow as if to rub away the deep lines that had formed there. Then he looked up at me, and he almost smiled.

"No. Wait. Wait a minute. She took a plane someplace last night. Some city someplace, where she has an uncle. Some city that has oil."

"Maracaibo?" I asked.

"That's it. Ronnie took her to the airport earlier." I nodded, and he sighed. "So she's out of it. At least."

I turned away from him and walked to the elevator. The fact that Loren had not been grabbed should have been a big relief, but there was too much else that was wrong.

In the lobby I went to a pay phone and called Mickey at his apartment. I had to wait a long time for him to answer; when he finally picked up, he still had one foot in the world of sleep.

"Jimmy," he muttered. "What time is it? I was dreaming about my boys. Funny, isn't it? Never dreamed about them while they were here." Sadness rose in me, but I was in too much of a hurry to indulge in it.

"Better wake up," I said. "It's time to go to work." Leaving out my worst suspicions, I reeled off all the concrete details. He tried to interrupt me several times, but I did not allow him to.

"You've got a good jump, Mickey, if you roll out of bed now and start sending news. The other agencies won't know a thing until they turn on the radio this morning."

"Jimmy," he said, managing somehow to scold and whine at the same time. "It's your story. Remember what you promised me. You're even downtown, for Chrissakes. I'm not ready for anything like this."

"Well, you'll have to *get* ready, Mick. I'm sorry, but this is an emergency, and I've got things I have to do." I was picking my feet up and impatiently setting them down on the carpeted lobby floor.

249

"You lied," Mickey said. "You tricked me into taking that phone call."

"I didn't lie. How did I know this was going to happen? Now look, I'll try to help you as much as I can. But you have to start working right away, or else neither of us is going to have a job. Be a newsman, Mickey, will you?" He seemed to realize then that I was serious, and that I could not be shamed into doing the entire job for him.

In a chastened voice he said, "Okay, Jimmy, I'll do it. I'll try, anyway. But you'll come into the office later today, won't you?"

"I don't know. If I can, I will." He must have caught something in my voice.

"Is something wrong, boy? Are you okay?"

"I don't know," I told him. "Maybe I'm not." Then I hung up the phone.

I had a cab drop me off in front of my house. It was beginning to dawn by then, and birds were singing on the estate of Camión's parents. I went up the steps and through the front door, my heartbeat seeming to echo in my ears. The television was on, displaying a whining, vibrating test pattern, and little Séptimo was curled up on the floor in front of it. I stepped softly over and shut the TV off, and then I pulled a blanket from the couch and covered the boy with it. He stirred and muttered.

"Mama, no," Séptimo said.

I checked Packy's bedroom and saw that he was not there. Then, just to be sure, I looked for him in the kitchen and in my own bedroom; those rooms were empty. I went back outside.

The neighborhood was quiet. Not even Max the dog was roaming about. I stood watching for a time as the sun broke over the horizon, and then I went to the white wall and began to climb.

It certainly was not the difficulty of the ascent that had always kept my neighbors from scaling that wall, and in less than a minute, choosing my hand- and footholds carefully as I went, I was at the top. I straddled the top for a time, looking out over the acres of overgrown lawn and the untended mango and avocado trees, then I picked my way down and headed for Camión's cottage.

The cottage was dark and quiet. It was also empty, the front door yawning.

I walked through the rooms of the cottage, calling for Packy and El Camión, knowing they were not there. I was lonely. I hungered for some last word from them. But then I remembered how Packy had hugged me before the two of them pushed me onto the elevator the night before, and I realized that they at least had not abandoned me without saying good-bye.

It turned out that they did leave me a final message, however. On the kitchen table I found a small tape recorder. I pressed the Play button and, following a couple of seconds of static, I heard the Croaker. The Croaker spoke in Spanish for the first time.

"Gringo," he said. *"Cuídate bien.* Take care of yourself."

I rewound the tape and ran it through again. Then I knew. The voice of the Croaker was Camión's voice. I played that message once more just to hear it, then I erased it.

After that I stood for a minute in the overgrown garden surrounding the cottage. The sun was now up, and it felt warm on my face. Over at the main house the wind chimes were playing their forlorn music. Listening to that music, I walked over and picked a rose from the grave of Camión's unknown soldier. Something connected inside me as I held that rose; I had a vision of Camión planting the bushes and then I was imagining Camión's mother as she strung her wind chimes. And I knew suddenly that she had put the wind chimes up for the same reason that Camión had planted his roses and joined forces with Marxist guerrillas. Flowers had been planted, music played, and war made to appease the ghost of a thief.

I decided I would enter the main house. A path of gray flagstones led between the two houses, and I followed it. As I walked, I kicked at the long tufts of grass that had grown up between the flagstones, and I noticed that some of the stones themselves were being lifted from below by unseen roots. I knew that in five years or so, if no one tended the house and the grounds, the trees would revert to a junglelike tangle and the stones would end up as scattered as if someone had intentionally pulled them up and tossed them around. The house itself would develop leaks and become infested with bats.

But right now, as I followed the uneven flagstones, the sunny, two-story wood-and-stone dwelling still had a certain deserted charm to it. The unending musical conversation of the wind chimes grew louder as I approached; I heard the mournful babble of glass on glass, wood on wood, brass on brass. The front door was open. I paused just before I reached the veranda in order to mop my face with a handkerchief. Then I went through the open door.

The house of Camión's parents was in great disarray. The furniture seemed to be in its proper place, but clothes lay strewn all through the first floor, even into the kitchen; they were military clothes, mostly, and the kitchen floor was littered with boxes and cans of imported food that looked as if they had been hastily dumped out of the cupboards. From the kitchen I went back into the large living room and then down the hall toward the two first-floor bedrooms. In the hallway I found a wooden keg that was filled nearly to the top with the spent cartridges of a dozen different firearms. My heart froze when I saw that barrel, and I stopped and ran my fingers through the shells, letting them fall, clinking, through my fingers, a cascade of brass and copper and steel.

One of the downstairs bedrooms was empty except for dust and old furniture. But the other was a mess of oil-stained rags, empty motor-oil cans, and scattered motorcycle engine parts. The stripped frame of a light bike straddled a pair of cinder blocks.

When I went upstairs, I found myself in the room that must have belonged to Camión before he moved into the cottage. It looked like a teenager's room; the walls were covered with faded pictures of rock bands and cars. The unmade bed looked as if it had been slept in recently, and on the dresser, beneath a poster of a pouting blond model sitting on a Lamborghini, stood a stack of nine-millimeter cartridge clips for an Uzi or a Brazilian machine pistol.

I picked up one of the four clips and examined it and knew right away what it was. The clip was empty, all of them were, but I set it down as quickly as if it were radioactive. I looked around for a half minute more before I found the black ski cap lying beneath the bed.

That was it, then. There was enough evidence here to salt Packy and Camión away for life, if they got caught. And I was incriminated as well; it didn't take much imagination to see the overcrowded hell of Catia in my future. I dropped the hat and left the room.

I checked the other two upstairs bedrooms and found nothing of interest. But one of the bedrooms had a balcony that overlooked nearly the entire property, and I opened a sliding glass door and walked out onto it. I knew I should get out of the house and off the estate as quickly as possible, but first I wanted to assure myself that the grounds were as peaceful as when I had climbed the wall.

Everything seemed calm; the birds were singing and the warm sun was reaching the fluttering tops of the mango trees, and the wind chimes around me were carrying on their idiot song. But then I noticed a slinking animal movement that did not belong on the landscape. I squinted at it and then I shuddered as I made out the camouflaged shape of a man, rifle sticking like a dead branch from his printed pattern of leaves, sliding from behind an avocado tree to the distant side of a palm that was closer to the house. I continued scanning the terrain and picked out two more *guardias* creeping toward me. One of the men had a huge black antenna rising from a radio that was strapped to his back. The antenna was mounted on a spring, and it waved back and forth, back and forth, whenever he made the slightest move.

I was close to tears; there was no escape. If I was able to see these three men, that meant there were at least a dozen more I could not see crawling in from all directions. If I tried to run, they would shred my body in a storm of automatic fire; I would see the red winking of the rifle barrels, but by the time the sound reached my ears, I would be dead. And if I stayed in the house, they would probably kill me as well. The stony face of Victor Rojas floated before my eyes.

The soldier with the radio was staring toward the house. He spoke into his mouthpiece without taking his eyes from the house. No. I did not stand a chance.

Then, as I watched the *guardias* creeping even closer, I heard a noise that sounded like the distant clatter of construction machinery. I did not know where it was coming from, but after a minute I heard the high cry of metal on metal and the white gate that closed off my cul-de-sac bulged inward for a moment before crashing to the ground. An orange bulldozer rumbled onto the grounds over the fallen doors, then the driver ground gears until he found reverse, and he rolled his machine back into the street and out of sight.

A line of soldiers holding M-af's and wearing regular monotone *guardia* uniforms trotted through the breach and came toward the house. Someone barked an order, and four men broke out of the middle of the column and headed toward the cottage. I saw them step into the cottage and disappear. The others kept coming toward me. They followed the decaying flagstone path, the soles of their boots scuffing in cadence against the old stones.

I took myself off the vulnerable balcony and went down the stairs to the first floor, where I sat on the bottom step. I folded my arms in an attempt to stop them from shaking.

I thought of my friend Tony then; over and over I saw him opening his jacket and letting that beautiful red bird fly. I also saw little Séptimo asleep on the floor of my living room, and I felt a wave of almost unbearable tenderness. And I saw Loren Hart lift her sunglasses for me; I felt longing.

I heard boots on the veranda, and then the barrel of a rifle entered the house, followed by a *guardia*. He was a young boy, not even as old as twenty, and he was dark, as were all soldiers of low rank. He swept the house with worried eyes, and when he spotted me, he lifted his rifle and said, *"¡Alto! ¡Quédate allí!"*

I would have assured him that I planned to remain right where I was, but I was afraid a word from me would make his trigger finger jump. I stayed still as a stump as he pointed his wavering rifle at me and screamed, *"¡Quédate! ¡Quédate!"*

Then the other soldiers entered, the column splitting and fanning around the first floor, and two of them came over and grabbed me by the back of the collar and hurled me to the ground. The wind left me; as I struggled to fill that sudden terrible emptiness between my ribs, one of them dropped his knees onto my back and jerked my arms behind me painfully. I felt nervous, inquisitive hands going down my sides, reaching for a moment into one of my jacket pockets, pausing at my crotch for a second, and then continuing down my legs. I also felt a rifle barrel pressed into the soft space beneath my earlobe. I heard boots and shouts on the floor above.

In a minute there were fingers in my hair, and my head was drawn back so that I was staring, bug-eyed, into the face of a plump *guardia* captain. He had my hair in one hand and the ski mask in the other. He dropped the mask on the floor in front of me.

"Where's the gringo?" he asked. I knew he did not mean me. I tried to smile.

"I'm the gringo." Uncertainty flickered in his eyes for a moment. "*¿Tú eres norteamericano?*"

"*Yo, sí. Soy periodista.* I'm a journalist." Lines of worry twisted across his forehead. He released my hair and told two of the soldiers to pick me up and put me in a chair in the kitchen. They hauled me up by my armpits; I found that my wrists were tied behind my back.

I sat in the kitchen for many hours while two young *guardias* hovered in the doorway, staring at me unblinkingly. I had not eaten anything since my lunch with Loren the day before; my stomach was rumbling, but I knew it was useless to ask. I was tired and thirsty as well.

Finally, in the late afternoon, I heard an authoritative voice from outside, and a regular army officer entered the kitchen. He was so wide at the shoulders he almost had to turn his body to make it through the doorway. He had big, square, hairy hands, and the block of fruit salad he wore on his breast seemed as large as a dinner tray. The two *guardias* saluted him, and he told them to leave. They clicked their heels and stepped out of the room.

The officer was a major, and I guessed, from something about his face, that he was with the DIM, the Department of Military Intelligence. I looked at him, and he did not look away. I had to drop my own eyes. He *was* DIM. My stomach curled in on itself like a snail; I wanted to shrink and to lose myself through a crack in the floor.

The officer took a black, nine-millimeter semiautomatic pistol from his side holster and set it on the table in front of me. The gun made a solid, heavy sound against the wood. My heart began to gallop in my ears.

"I'm Major Gallardo," he said.

"I'm Jimmy Angel . . ."

"You're American?"

"Yes. A journalist . . ."

"You're a liar." That statement hung heavily between us for a minute while I struggled to make my eyes meet his.

Finally, I swallowed, and I said, "I am. I'm with the agency—"

"You're an American, true. But you're a terrorist. A red terrorist." He pulled a chair from beneath the table and placed one black-shod foot upon it, and he stared down at me. His gaze was like the hot focus of a magnifying glass on an insect.

There was another long pause. When I finally tried to speak, I had trouble getting the words out; it was as if my voice were trying to hide in my throat.

"I am not a guerrilla. I'm an American, and a foreign correspondent." I knew I was relying too heavily on the totem of my nationality, but I could not help myself. It was all I had. "I am not a communist. I have friends in the government—"

"And other friends, too, *gringito*," he said. "We know that you lived with one of the guerrillas who took the *roquero*. And that you were part of the gang that infiltrated the road crew of the music group. There is no way to deny that."

There was no denying it. I knew that. Panic was like a hand at my windpipe.

"Hey. I want to see the American consul. Right now, I want to see him." But Major Gallardo of the DIM went on, as if talking to himself.

"Then, to add to all the other evidence," he said, "we come here, to the headquarters of the communists, and we find you and your ski mask."

"Not my ski mask." My voice was shaking.

"Where is the rock musician?"

"I don't know."

"Better tell me, or it's going to get very difficult."

"*Yo no sé*, I told you." I was still fighting to meet his eyes.

"Where?" It was then that fear made me lose my grip on Spanish for a minute, and I gave him an unintentionally flip answer, an answer that would have been fine on the street, but was fatal when speaking to an army major.

"*Yo no sé, pana*," I said. I regretted it as soon as it was out.

"I'm not your *pana*," he told me. As if to provide further proof, he took his gun from the table and raised it into the air. I barely had time to wince before he brought it down on my skull.

When I awoke, there was no light. I wanted to raise my hands and touch my eyes to make sure they were open, but my wrists remained joined behind my back. I was lying on a mattress someplace, nearly smothering in stale bedclothes, and as I struggled to roll onto my back to breathe, I remembered the pistol butt coming down and striking me. My thinking was still scrambled by the blow, and by the time I had managed to turn so that I was facing the ceiling, my arms twisted painfully at the shoulders, I became convinced that DIM Major Gallardo had damaged something vital in my brain, had broken the connection between my eyes and my mind. I was blind.

I began to shriek, dry yelps bursting from my throat. I found comfort in these sounds of panic; they drowned all thought, and I began to thrash around on the bed as if in the throes of a nightmare. In my thrashing I found the edge of the bed, and I rolled off and struck the floor.

I heard a doorknob turn, and the darkness was split by a bar of light that fell across my face. Then, with the click of a switch, there suddenly was too much light, so much light that I had to narrow my eyes to a hair's width. Relief.

I gasped loudly and adjusted to the blessed light. Two pairs of feet entered the room, one right after the other, and they came to a stop six inches or so from my face. When I had finally gotten used to the abundance of light, I looked up into the machete face of Nelson Lugo Alvarado as well as the amused, well-fed, obviously American face of a man I had never seen before.

"Lugo." I felt strangely comforted to see him. Compared with Mr. DIM, he was almost a friend.

"Honestly, James. Such a lack of dignity. Aren't you ashamed?"

"I thought I was blind," I said. "That fucking gorilla hit me hard."

"Shh," said Lugo Alvarado. "He's still in the house. You don't want to anger him again."

"No," I said. "No, I don't." I looked around me for the first time. I was in Camión's bedroom; I had been lying on his bed. Even though the shades were pulled and the curtains drawn, I could tell it was nighttime. I wondered why they had kept me here all these hours rather than taking me away. I felt suddenly uneasy, even though the presence of the American was a good sign. I jerked my head in his direction.

"Who's he?"

The American smiled. He was a plump man with thinning sandy hair. "I'm from the consulate, Jimmy." He spoke in English.

257

"Thank God! What's your name, sir? Get me out of here, can you?"

The man's smile slid down on one side, and his eyes narrowed. He tugged at each cotton leg of his suit pants and then he squatted in front of me.

"My name is not important right now. You just need to know that I'm from the consulate. Why don't you call me Smith."

"*Smith?*" In spite of myself, my voice rose with fear. I had a sudden, desperate need to use the bathroom. "Who are you? What's going on here?"

I looked to Lugo Alvarado for some kind of reassurance, but he only shook his sharp head at me.

"Angel," Smith said. I turned wide eyes at him. "I am not here on official business. Not yet." It was impossible for him not to have been a diplomat, the way he measured every word as if it were a quantity of gold dust or *perico*.

He said, "We may be able to help you very soon, maybe even get you out of the country, although we can't promise anything. But we need your help first."

"I don't know—" He held up a hand to discourage me from interrupting. His face had turned somber.

"An American citizen has been kidnapped. A very important, very wealthy American citizen. The TV networks back home are going crazy, as is the entire State Department. There is pressure, Mr. Angel. Pressure on the ambassador, pressure on the Venezuelan authorities. Pressure on me. None of us likes pressure."

"But I don't—" His hand stopped me again. I let the air out of my lungs in a long, deflating sigh and dropped my head to the floor. I knew then that I was in a trap I would never get out of. The inside of my skull was beginning to throb badly from the blow Major DIM had given me.

"We know that you know at least two of the kidnappers. You *lived* with one of them, for God's sake. You worked with them as an interpreter for the rock entourage. Now how is any reasonable person supposed to believe you when you say that you know nothing about the kidnapping?"

"Maybe a reasonable person couldn't," I said. My voice was small, and he bent closer to hear me. I looked down at the floor rather than meet his eyes. "But it's true. They were friends; I knew them as musicians. They had a mysterious side to them, but I never..." I shook my throbbing head, which suddenly seemed to weigh as much as a cannonball, and I stopped talking.

Smith sighed. Then I saw his hand come down and place a small pistol on the floor so that the end of the barrel nearly touched the tip of my nose. It was the pistol I had taken from Adolfo earlier that night.

"Oh, God," I said. "Listen, I'm a respected correspondent with an American news agency. As soon as they hear—"

"They'll disown you," Smith said. "What's the phrase? 'Locally hired trash'? You can fool the locals, Angel, with the blue eyes and fair skin and the accent. But not one of your own. So cut the shit, why don't you? We both know you're little better than a drifter." I fell silent. He knew my game as well as I did.

Smith stood, and he and Lugo Alvarado clucked their tongues for a minute as they stared down at me. Then they went out into the hallway, and I heard them whispering in Spanish. I knew they didn't much care whether I heard them or not. Smith's Spanish was quite good.

"No," Smith said. "No, we can't do that. He is, after all, a journalist. You heard him screaming. It won't take that much anyway."

"Hey," I shouted. I was nearly hysterical. "I have to go to the bathroom, you pricks. Right now. Smith, you gringo pigshit, I have rights. I have to be formally arrested, and then the consul has to involve himself. It's the fucking law."

The faces of Smith and Lugo Alvarado, twin gargoyles, appeared in the doorway.

"As soon as we know what we need to know, you will be formally arrested," Lugo Alvarado said.

"As soon as we know what we need to know, you will have every service the consulate can provide made available to you," said Smith. Then they smiled, and vanished.

In a few minutes two soldiers came and untied my hands and hauled me into the bathroom. When I was finished, they grabbed me and began stripping off my clothes. I tried to fight them, but they were strong young kids, and I was weak from hunger and from the disabling pain in my head. Naked, I was dragged downstairs, where Lugo Alvarado and Smith and several officers were waiting in the living room. The room bristled with guns.

The expressionless soldiers held me by my arms and forced me to face the little crowd of men who sat on Camión's mother's furniture. They all started laughing; it began with a rolling, almost nervous chuckle, and then it gained momentum until it was a roar of laughter that lashed me. Lugo Alvarado was the only one who was not laughing; he was looking down and he seemed sad.

I felt tears wanting to come; I turned my head to the side and fought against them as hard as I'd ever fought against anything. When the laughter had died a little, Lugo Alvarado said, "I hope you don't take this too personally, James. I wouldn't do it to you if I didn't have to." He paused, then said, "Are you sure there is nothing you want to tell us right now?"

I did not trust my voice, so I just shook my head. The soldiers took me into the kitchen, where Major Gallardo was sitting at the table, waiting for me. I started to struggle again, but the soldiers forced me into a chair and lifted my arms and slammed them down onto the tabletop. Then they walked out.

Gallardo was of course clad in full uniform, including a hat, a fact that made me feel insubstantial, almost wraithlike in my pale nakedness. He held a pair of thin leather gloves in one hand. The other hand he raised to the level of my face and then he extended his index finger at me.

"Rules," he said. "You sit here and do not move a muscle. You do not sleep. You get nothing to eat or drink. You keep your hands on the table, with your fingers spread. Until you talk. *¿Comprendes?*"

I nodded, and the hand with the gloves came up and struck them sharply across my face. Those gloves had the bite of a horsewhip.

"I said, no moving," Gallardo reminded me. "You're lucky you're a gringo."

A short while later I heard most of the men in the living room go out the front door. I heard engines start in front of the house. But Lugo Alvarado and Smith remained; they came in from time to time to ask me if I was ready to talk. I always stayed motionless, afraid of being struck by Señor DIM, and they would shake their heads and leave.

I sat like that all night. The pain in my head made my skull heavy and my mind cloudy, but every time I cocked my head to one side or the other, or let it settle toward my chest, he slapped me with the gloves. And usually one of the limp fingers would strike my eye, which would sting and tear, and I would have to fight to keep from lifting my hands to soothe it.

Major Gallardo smoked cigarettes and stared into my eyes. I could not avoid his gaze, so I tried to erase his image before it registered in my mind; I tried to camouflage the ugliness of him with a screen of memories. Strangely I was quite successful at this. I relived the happier times with my friend Tony, and I thought about little Séptimo, and for minutes at a time, I was able to forget that Major Gallardo was even there. Invariably, however, my head would tilt or my arm would twitch, and he would bring me around with a slap of the gloves.

But I would fall easily back into my reverie. I was able to convince myself that nothing much mattered anymore.

Hours passed before dawn came. The light and the birdsong that entered the windows then were an unwelcome distraction; it became more difficult to concentrate. But I battled the light and the sound and I burrowed more deeply into the darkest, quietest corners of myself.

The day wore on; hunger, the pain in my head, cold, the need to use the bathroom, and Major Gallardo's gloves all threatened to drag me back to unacceptable reality. But I fought them off. It pleased me that I seemed to have found an unsuspected talent in myself. Time and time again I saw Tony opening his jacket to release a red rocket of a bird. A living, pulsing bird, the color of blood.

It must have been about noon when Smith and Lugo Alvarado entered the room once again; I stole a glance at them when Gallardo looked up. Lugo Alvarado looked as he always did, but Smith seemed worried. His worry cheered me. Lugo Alvarado carried a cardboard box in his arms.

"Anything?" Lugo Alvarado asked.

Gallardo shook his head. "But he's shaking. That means he'll break any time now."

I noticed for the first time that my skin was quivering under the power of tiny muscles. But I did not feel as if I were ready to break. I felt I could go on for another several hours, perhaps.

"Well," said Lugo Alvarado, "leave him with us for a minute, would you?" Gallardo glared at me, and then he stood and stretched, his knuckles nearly scraping the ceiling, and he left the room.

Lugo Alvarado set the box down on the table in front of me, as if to threaten me with it. I took advantage of Gallardo's absence to yawn and to stretch and rub myself with my hands. Neither Lugo Alvarado nor Smith protested my movement.

"Are you ready, finally, Angel?" asked Lugo Alvarado. "This could go on for days, you know." I found my voice; it was surprisingly strong. From the depths of humiliation, dignity.

"I have nothing to tell, gentlemen. I'm innocent." I looked from one to the other, and Smith surprised me by avoiding my eyes.

Lugo Alvarado set his hands atop the box and let them rest there a moment. Then he opened the box and reached inside; he lifted out a rich fistful of long blond human hair and dropped it on the table. I stared at it uncomprehendingly until he tossed the Polaroid picture of Ronnie Neumon onto the bright swirl of hair. The photograph showed Ronnie sitting in a chair similar to the one in which I myself sat, in a room very much like the kitchen of Camión's mother. His head was shaved to the scalp, and his face was slack, stupid-looking almost. Next to him stood a man in a ski mask who held an electric razor in a gloved hand.

"Jesus," I said. "But he's alive, anyway." It was somehow good to know that Ronnie remained among the living, even if he was a lousy human being.

The two men standing before me exchanged a look. Smith cleared his throat. "There's a letter as well, Mr. Angel," he said.

I could detect no sarcasm in his "Mr. Angel," and I was at once aware that something important had changed. Through many layers of numbness, I felt a flutter of hope. I drew my shoulders back and tried to shrug off my fatigue.

"A letter to whom?" I asked. Smith looked at Lugo Alvarado, who was avoiding his eyes.

"To the Disip," Smith said finally. "From the kidnappers." I stared at him without saying anything. He stuck his hand into the cardboard box and came up with an envelope. He let it fall to the table in front of me and said, "You probably should read it yourself."

My hope grew stronger. I choked back a nervous laugh and warned myself to be careful. Unknown stakes were involved here and I saw a negotiation coming. I had to start bargaining immediately to make sure I got everything I could.

"I'm not going to read that," I said in English. Lugo Alvarado caught the gist, and he glared down at me. Muscles like little frogs squirmed in his jaws.

"Angel," he told me, "you still are in big trouble. You better do as you are told."

"Bullshit," I said, sticking with English. I looked from Lugo Alvarado to Smith and rose halfway from my seat. "I am too tired to read that fucking thing right now. I don't care what it says. I've had the shit beaten out of me, and I've been starved and stripped and pistol-whipped. And it all happened while a representative from the American consulate stood by and did nothing. I'm in no mood for any crap." Tears sprang to my eyes, surprising me. I desperately wanted to read that letter, but I could not let them know it.

"You fucking criminals," I added.

Lugo Alvarado turned away, barely able to control himself. Smith tried to set a hand on my shoulder. I snarled him away.

"Mr. Angel," Smith said. "That letter could be a tremendous help to your case. That's why we want you to look at it, no other reason." I laughed at him.

"Yeah. You're my friend now, right? Helping me out?" I dropped my eyes to the table and said in a softer voice, "You want me to read it, you go out to the cottage and get me one of Camión's bathrobes. After that, you find me a cup of hot coffee. And I want an *arepa*. A yellow-cheese *arepa*." Saliva gushed into my mouth. I was afraid to look up.

I felt their eyes on me. Then Lugo Alvarado stalked into the living room and growled at somebody to get me an *arepa* and a cup of coffee.

I lifted my head and shouted, "A *marrón*. The coffee has to be a *marrón*. *Grande*. With sugar." There was a pause, and then I heard Lugo Alvarado repeat the order, and I smiled.

After I had put on the huge blue terrycloth bathrobe that a soldier brought me and had eaten the *arepa* and drunk my coffee, I slipped the letter from the envelope. I held the small white paper with trembling fingers and devoured the lines of typewritten Spanish with greedy eyes.

Gorillas, it began,

> *We have Ronnie Neumon in a safe place. He will not be harmed unless you do something stupid. You will soon receive a list of the conditions we will require in exchange for his pardon by our revolutionary tribunal.*
>
> *The gringo journalist, Jimmy Angel, is not associated with our revolutionary group and had no knowledge of our plans to arrest this degenerate musician. He was unaware of the revolutionary-group membership of the freedom fighters with whom he was acquainted.*
>
> *We did, however, find him useful for passing information to the public and to the fascist government, and we intend to use him again in the near future. To this end, we suggest that you release him from your affectionate custody and take steps to ensure that his homely face appears on Channel 8 television before eleven o'clock tonight. If you fail to honor this request, not only will you be depriving yourselves of important communications with us, but you will be seriously jeopardizing the continued existence of the vile imperialist monster, Ronnie Neumon.*
>
> *It would be a good idea for Angel to appear on television accompanied by a high police official, preferably Nelson Lugo Alvarado, who would explain to the world that he (Angel) is not a suspect in the kidnapping, and is merely assisting in the case in a selfless and admirable manner.*
>
> *In a day or two we will pass further instructions to you through our conduit, Jimmy Angel.*

It was signed, *The Revolutionary Council of La Gran Colombia.*

The world dissolved in tears of laughter and relief. Packy, as confused a man as he was, was thinking of me. He knew that he and El Camión had left me standing in a deep pit holding a huge bag, and he had remembered to send a ladder. I was saved.

I continued to laugh; I laughed so hard that my body turned to melted butter and I slid from my chair and fell harmlessly to the floor of Camión's mother's kitchen. By then there was no more air left in me to form sound, and I laughed in breathless silence, my stomach cramped into a weary fist.

Smith and Lugo Alvarado stood above me, glowering. Lugo Alvarado reached and tried to grab me by an arm to haul me to my feet, but I pulled away from him.

"You are still in trouble," Lugo Alvarado said, sounding as if he were trying to convince himself.

When I was able to answer, I said, "It's all over, gentlemen. You want my cooperation to get that flaming fool back, there'll have to be some things. Some concessions."

They stared without speaking, so I said, "Packy was telling the truth. I had nothing to do with it." I pushed myself into a sitting position and began to knead my aching gut. "And I want to help." As I said this, I discovered that it was true. I did not want to see Ronnie murdered.

"But I'm not going to let you use me and then hang me out to dry. If everyone is mad enough at me, I'll leave the country when it's over. I'm not going to jail, though." I stuck my hand toward Smith. "Help me up, will you?"

"We might not be able to arrange it," said Lugo Alvarado. I smiled at him.

"While you're trying, I'll be waiting," I said. "Something signed by the president would be acceptable."

Later I dressed in my own clothes, and they took me out of there in Smith's car, a gray Buick. As we drove out toward the smashed gate, I saw a great deal of movement among the fruit trees of the estate; it appeared as though migrant farm workers had moved in and were harvesting the derelict crop. But as I looked, I realized that I knew every one of the fruit pickers. There was Adolfo and his wife and their fat little boys, as well as Lola and her ancient mother, and nearly everyone else who lived on the cul-de-sac. They seemed not to notice our car as they scrambled through the treetops, deft as monkeys, dropping avocados and mangoes into waiting baskets below.

Through the closed, darkly tinted windows of Smith's car, I could hear them laughing. Camión had finally done it; he had given the place up.

When we went out through the gate, I saw little Séptimo standing forlornly in the street in front of my house. His thin arms were crossed behind his back. I waved to him, but he gave no sign that he could see me through the dark glass.

CHAPTER 9

Smith, whose real name turned out to be Sweeney, suddenly could not do enough for me. He rushed me to the Hotel Tamanaco, the most expensive in the country, where he signed me into a suite that was even larger than the one in which Ronnie and Orchid had used the glass-topped table as a sexual aid. He dogged me to my rooms, advising me in fatherly tones that I should have a stiff drink and a good nap before I went before the cameras that night, and then he fixed me a drink with his own hands, pouring the good, golden whiskey over silver ice, just the way I liked it. He told me I had to be hungry, and asked what I wanted. He was right about my hunger, and I said I wanted a big steak, with yucca root instead of potatoes, and a tomato salad. He nodded eagerly, almost teary-eyed with pleasure at being able to serve me. Sipping my drink, I turned away from him and walked to the window. My suite was on the side of the hotel that afforded the best overlook of the city.

Dinner came, and I sat down to enjoy it. Smith-Sweeney stood watching me with his hands folded, and I could not decide whether he was pretending to fawn or was waiting for me to invite him to sit. Either way he was bothering me.

"My head's still killing me, you know," I said. I was not lying. Worry flooded Smith-Sweeney's eyes.

"Yes? That happened before I got there, didn't it? The beating, I mean?" I set down my fork and glared at him; his eyes rolled greasily away.

Finally I said, "I was wondering if you'd get me some pills. I want to do some sleeping, like you suggested."

"Sure," Smith-Sweeney said. "No problem." He began sidling for the door.

"And send someone to my house to pick up some clothes, can you? I can't walk around in this stuff the *guardias* ripped up."

"Absolutely, Jimmy." He had already closed the door when I thought of something important. I got up and opened the door and called into the hallway after him.

"There's a little boy at my house named Séptimo. No one is to frighten him or bother him in any way. In fact they should proba-bly give him a few bolos to buy meals for a couple of days."

"Trust me," Smith-Sweeney shouted over his shoulder. Then he disappeared into the elevator. Muttering to myself, dazed with pain and tiredness, I returned to the suite.

When I had finished my meal and my second drink, I picked up the telephone and called Mickey at the office.

"Jimmy! Jesus! Am I glad to hear from you." There was a slight quaver in Mickey's voice, but other than that, he sounded better than I had expected.

"Well, don't be too glad, Mickey—"

"Shit! You've been missing and I've had to cover this whole thing myself, and the competition is killing us. I haven't slept."

"You haven't slept?"

"No. What, are you shacked up, or drunk, or what? We're both going to get fired." His indignant tone suggested he felt that he was reason itself, while I was insanity incarnate.

"Things have gotten quite complicated," I said. "Let me try to explain them to you."

"Hey, son. I just told you I'm tired. How about coming into the office and explaining things to me here, and then relieving me for a while so I can get some sleep. Now, I've more than held up my end of the bargain, don't you think..."

"You have, Mickey. No question. But the complications I'm talk-ing about will not allow me to work for a while." A few silent seconds passed.

Then: "What?"

"Just what I said." I heard Mickey take a deep breath that sounded like a gasp; he held that breath for a moment, and it crossed my mind that he might be having a coronary. But before I could ask him if he was all right, he let out with a long, deflating, defeated sigh.

"That's it, then," he said.

"What's it? Listen, snap out of it, will you? If you can manage to hold yourself together for a while longer, I have some information that—"

"You know, I'm getting to the point where it doesn't really matter anyway." I immediately suspected one of his emotional ploys, and anger stung me.

"Mickey, it's no use—"

"Remember, Jimmy, remember discussing the fact that the job was the only thing I had left?"

"Yeah. I remember. That was right before we decided there was no love in the world, and that my heart was as black as a lump of tar." My voice was sharp; I was waiting, my trump card poised, for him to finish his play.

"Well, I've been mulling it over, and I don't really think it's true. I've been looking at my priorities here, and I'm starting to realize that this job is no more than it is. Just a goddamn job."

"Really?" A cruel glee was mixing with my anger.

"Sure, Jimmy. And if you can't come in for whatever reason, and I'm stuck here by myself, beating my head against the wall, then maybe the whole thing is just not worth the effort." I laughed at him then.

"You're so full of shit, your eyes are brown."

"Come on, Jimmy . . ."

"What if I told you that you could scoop everybody on this kidnapping story right now?" It took him a moment to answer.

"Oh? Well, that's hardly likely, considering I'm worn out and operating at half speed . . ." But there was interest in his voice; while it was not as much interest as I had expected, it was interest just the same.

"You asked me the other night if I was okay. Well, I'm not okay. I'm in big trouble, Mickey. The reason I can't come in is that I'm personally involved in this kidnapping thing."

"Oh, Jesus." The quaver was back for a moment, but was

quickly crowded away by excitement. "Oh! Jesus! Are you fooling with me, here, Jimmy . . . ?"

"Listen, old man. Better start taking notes." He seemed to realize then that I was telling the awful truth, and his reflexes took over.

"Yeah, Jimmy. Sure." I heard the frantic rustling of papers. "A pencil and a fucking paper. Where's my goddamn head these days?" I could not resist taunting him.

"New priorities, Mickey?"

"If you only knew—" But I was in too much of a hurry now to let him finish.

"Listen," I said. "Are you listening? This is what you can do, okay? This is the scoop. You send an *urgent* that agency correspondent Jimmy Angel is acquainted with some of the members of the kidnap gang and that he is cooperating with police in the investigation. The kidnappers said they are going to pass their demands to the authorities through Jimmy Angel, and those demands will be forthcoming within a couple of days. Mick, this stuff will all be announced on the news late tonight, but you have it first. Now, have you got all that?" Suddenly he was all ears.

"Jesus, Jimmy—"

"You quote fucking General Jorge on this one, Mickey. Highly placed sources who don't want to be identified. Unless there's a leak somewhere else, you'll be the only one with the real shit for a few hours. You'll be a hero."

"You think? Really? But what—"

"Hey," I said. "That's a favor from me to you. It won't do me any good anymore; I've got a feeling I won't be working for the agency once this is over." I was speaking quickly, because I did not know when Smith-Sweeney would come back. There was a pause after I said that, and then Mickey said something that made me think that perhaps some of his ideas about what was important had changed after all.

"Jimmy," he said. "Are you all right? I mean, will you be?" I felt my chin tremble.

"I don't know," I said. "With a little luck, I might come out of it okay."

"Can I help, in any way?"

"Thanks. But right now, everything seems to be in nobody's

hands but my own." I was grateful for his unexpected concern, and at the same time it made me uneasy; it made me suspect I did not have as firm a handle on him as I thought.

"Well, if there is anything, tell me. I've been thinking lately how good you were to my boys, Jimmy. They needed that, then." But just then there came a knock at the door.

"Shit! I have to go. Get your ass in gear, Mickey."

I dropped the phone back onto the cradle, then sat without moving for a moment until I had gathered the strength to answer the door. It was Smith-Sweeney, and as he handed me the box of painkillers, I could tell he was dying to ask who I had been talking to. But his courage did not rise high enough for him to ask me, and I did not volunteer the information. I did not even let him in; I just took the medicine from him and closed the door. Without bothering to read the name of the active ingredient on the package, I swallowed two tablets with a glass of water, decided I was too tired to shower, and fell asleep on the big, soft bed with all my clothes on.

A door near me opened and closed sometime later; I had no idea where that door was or how much time had passed since I last was conscious. It was nighttime again, and, as had happened to me so frequently over the past week, I had no memory of where I had lain down to sleep. Footsteps approached, followed by a hand on the knob of another door that I assumed opened onto my bedroom. DIM Major Gallardo's cruel, bored face appeared in my imagination.

"Who is it?" I shouted. "Get out! I have a gun!"

The door opened; a light went on in the room, blinding me. I saw a hand and the sleeve of a suit coat retreat through the partially opened doorway.

"You don't really, do you?" The voice was uncertain.

"Smith?"

"Sweeney. I brought you some coffee, Mr. Angel." He laughed nervously. "Don't shoot."

I settled back into the bed and took a deep breath. I rubbed my eyes. The headache was still with me, but the pain was flatter. It was the pain of healing rather than of recent injury. The door opened all the way, and Sweeney came in with a cup and saucer from the Tamanaco's china collection.

"Marrón," he said. I took the coffee from him without thanking him; it was an effort not to give in to the reflex, but I thought it was important that I hold on to my anger. It was one of the few things left to me now.

After a moment Sweeney said, "I remembered how you liked it." I nodded.

"Good." I began to sip, staring at the drapes over the windows, and he sat down on the edge of the bed without being invited.

"Feeling all right?" asked Sweeney.

"Okay."

He ran his fingers through his hair, looked at his nails, sighed, and then he said, "Boy, I hope we get this whole thing over with as soon as possible. It's really starting to heat up."

"What do you mean?" He fixed me with a look that was somehow accusatory and apologetic at the same time.

"Someone—your agency, actually—got word out that you were involved in this whole deal and that you were going on the air tonight. Now we've got buzzard problems."

"Buzzards?"

"Newspeople. Flying in from every damn place. Every network from the States is here. Frenchies. Brits. Dutch. They're looking for Ronnie Neumon, they're looking for you, they're looking for anything you've touched or breathed on or slept with in the past year."

I thought of Orchid, and I smiled. I set the coffee on the nightstand. "They would have come anyway, wouldn't they? This is a big story, Sweeney." He looked down.

"Yes, but we wanted more time. We wanted to keep you on ice for a few extra hours, to give the bad guys time to get their demands to you. It's going to be extremely hard for them now, isn't it?" I grinned at him, so he said, "A picture is worth a million, Mr. Angel."

He rose, went to a television on a stand across the room from my bed, and turned it on. A random burst of colored dots, and then, my house. There was a crowd between the television camera and my house; a crowd of uncommonly handsome people, most of them definitely not Venezuelans, who were talking into microphones, swinging cameras this way and that, scribbling in notebooks.

"My dignified brethren," I said. In Spanish I added, "Tigers hunting a tiger."

A line of Metropolitanos stood between the crowd and the house. Two more *pacos* were on the wrought-iron stairs. All the cops looked ill at ease. Then, as I stared at the televised picture, I saw, up in my window behind a white, nearly transparent curtain, the spotted face of little Séptimo. Elbows resting on the back of a chair and fists bunched beneath his chin, Séptimo gazed balefully down upon the commotion. I looked at Sweeney.

"That little boy," I said. "He's being taken care of, isn't he?" Sweeney nodded.

"We took him a sack of groceries. Stuff that isn't too hard to fix. Where'd he come from, anyway?" I did not answer until the living picture of my house vanished and the station cut to a talking head in the studio.

"He's a little angel who fell to earth," I told him. "Just like all the rest of us."

I got up and went to the bathroom, and a minute later I heard Orchid's birdsong voice coming over the tube. She was being interviewed, talking about how she had made friends with Ronnie and what a tragedy his kidnapping was. Then she started talking about me, telling the world that she and I had had a special relationship for a long time.

"Shut it off," I called. Sweeney shut it off.

Later, in the gray Buick, Sweeney said, "We were going to take you to the studio and have you do your thing in privacy. But we now think it would defuse things a bit if you had an open news conference."

I pretended to think for a minute. "All right," I said finally.

Sweeney went on. "Most of the international press are holed up at the Hilton, so that's where we're going. You and Lugo A. will meet the press in a conference room there."

"Right," I said. I looked out into the night.

I never did get inside the Hilton. Right in front of the building itself I encountered a whirlwind of suits and cameras and hairdos and lights and notepads. Uniformed PeTeJotas were trying desperately to clear the Hilton's front drive, but the vicious crowd was overwhelming them. Then someone recognized me, it must have been one of the local journalists, and they closed in around the car, shouting. I was under attack.

With my heart ticking rapidly, almost painfully against my ribs, I pushed open the door against the pressure of bodies and stepped out into the nightmare. Microphones like blunt weapons, like war clubs, came at me then; I winced and averted my head as the crowd forced me back against the car. Lights blinded me and threatened to sear my flesh to the bone. They were barking at me in English and in Spanish, and I could make no sense of the words.

Finally a double column of PeTeJotas in riot gear came pushing its way through to my rescue. They cleared a narrow path, and down that path marched Lugo Alvarado. He looked frightened, and he huddled against the car with me. I caught his eye, and he mouthed the word *coño*.

The PeTeJotas held the tunnel open for a minute more as a Channel h cameraman and light man and a reporter with a microphone came down to stand in front of us.

"Can you move?" said a vexed American voice from somewhere. "Get them out of the way!"

"Favoritism!" screeched a female voice.

The reporter held the microphone to Lugo Alvarado, who cleared his throat and said that authorities had been contacted by the kidnappers, and that conditions for Ronnie Neumon's release were expected to be forthcoming shortly. Señor Jimmy Angel, a distinguished American journalist, had been an unwitting acquaintance of some of the guerrillas and was now helping with the case. The guerrillas had promised to pass their requests to the authorities through the excellent Mr. Angel. The rock star himself, as far as authorities knew, was still alive and in good health.

"What? Louder!" someone shouted.

"In English!" shouted someone else.

The Channel h microphone came at me now. Many more poked at me from out of the crowd. I started in Spanish.

"English!" came the cry. From off to the side, someone kept saying, "Jimmy. Mr. Angel," trying to get my attention.

"Everything the Disip official says is true," I said, staying with the Spanish and looking into the Channel h camera. "I am helping the investigation. And for anyone who is interested, I am free, in good health. I'll be waiting." I knew that somewhere in the city, or at least in Venezuela, Packy's unseen eyes were on me. It was a strange, haunting feeling to realize that. Silently as a prayer, I mouthed his name.

Then I reached behind me and started to open the rear door of the Buick. The newspeople resumed their shouting then, and there was a flurry of motion in the crowd to my right. For an irrational second I thought it was an assassin trying to get close to me. But it was only Humberto Sanabria. He thrust his face out of the crowd, and a moment later an arm snaked out and he grabbed the arm of my coat. His eyes were wild, desperate.

"Jimmy! Give me a telephone number. I need to talk to you."

"I can't." I shook my head at him. This old friend seemed to be looking not at me, but through me. It was unnerving.

Sanabria's lips were white with tension; I thought I saw blood on them. "You have to. You owe me, *huevón*. You owe me."

"No, Sanabria. It's a life—"

"*¡Coño de tu madre!*" The PeTeJotas broke his grasp and were starting to push him away now. "I need this!" he shouted. "You're no friend of mine!"

I squeezed myself into the backseat of the car and sat there shaking. Up in front, on the driver's side, Sweeney was trying to get in. I watched him struggle for a moment before I heard a pounding on the rear window on the opposite side of the car. It was Mickey. I slid over and rolled the window down an inch. Mickey pressed his lips to the gap.

"Jimmy, good news!" he said. He was smiling, but it was the smile of a discouraged salesman that he gave me, and there were dark circles under his eyes. "The company wants to keep us on. Both of us. But you have to get me some information. They'll pay extra for the feature you write when it's over."

Two PeTeJotas grabbed Mickey around the waist and tried to haul him away from the car. He clung stubbornly to the window, and I rolled it down a couple of more inches to ask them to leave him for a minute. The cops turned and started pushing at the rest of the crowd. Just then Carlos the Jackal appeared between the shoulders of the two cops and shot a picture of me with his flash. Sweeney had made it into the car by then, and he started the engine.

274

"Just one minute, Sweeney," I said. I turned back to Mickey, whose skull-like grin seemed frozen on his face.

"I can't, Mick," I said. "I'm a go-between now. I can't let you know what's going on or even where I'm going to be." His grin closed in a bit then. I was horrified to see how badly he was trembling. After a moment Mickey looked down at the ground.

"I was a hero today, Jimmy," he told me. "Just like you said I'd be."

"I knew—" I started to say, but he would not let me interrupt.

"For about twenty minutes I was a hero. About the length of your average *perico* high. But the news rolls on, Jimmy boy, and what will I be tomorrow when they want fresh fodder and I don't have any to feed them?" Guilt and cold helplessness twisted inside me.

"You can get it, just like anyone else. They can't expect you—"

"Oh, Jimmy." Mickey was shaking his nearly hairless head. "*Not* like anyone else. Considering the depth of your, uh, what shall we call it, *investigation*"—he paused to look up and punctuate the word with an ironic smile—"they're going to want something very special."

"Well, give it to them. You can give it to them. You can research—" Mickey stopped me with a choked laugh. Then he stood up and took a step back from Sweeney's car.

"Good-bye, Jim. Be careful, and try not to be a hero. Take it from me, it's not all it's cracked up to be." He began to fade back into the screaming crowd.

"Mickey. Hey, Mick," I shouted. But he disappeared, and then Sweeney turned around to give me an anxious, bug-eyed stare.

"Okay?" he asked. "Okay, Jimmy?"

"Yes," I said. "Okay."

He blew the horn and crept through the crowd, and then the car began to pick up speed. In a minute we were rolling along on the smooth and nearly empty nighttime highway.

Sweeney drove around for a half hour to lose any followers. Then he returned me to the Tamanaco. We went through the back entrance and up a freight elevator to avoid drawing attention. He took me to my suite, where I found my packed suitcases waiting for me.

"Hope everything's there," he said.

"Yeah," I answered. I was still dazed from my conversation with Mickey. Sweeney laid a gentle hand on my arm. I was surprised to find myself feeling grateful for the touch.

"Listen," he said. "You're signed into this suite under the name of Smith. Will you remember that?" I nodded.

"Good. Don't leave your rooms and go walking around; there are some reporters booked in here, and we don't want them to see you. Just use room service, okay?" I nodded again.

He looked at his watch. "Well, I'll stop by in the morning. I just hope those bastards aren't too spooked by all the publicity and can find a way to get their next message to you." He stood blinking at me, his chest rising and falling with nervous breathing. "How do you think they'll do it?"

I shrugged. "A note would be the easiest. Tell the cops to watch my mail."

He nodded and pointed to the writing table. "There's my phone number if you need anything or want to talk to me." He paused to put the *No Molestar* sign on the outside knob of my door before he left.

I took off my shoes and poured myself a drink and sat down in front of that unfailing sedative, the television. I saw about five minutes of the cartoon in which the whale carries the kid to heaven, and then the news came on. The first item was a tape of my chaotic news conference. Lugo Alvarado looked scared; I had expected that. But I was not prepared for how frightened and bewildered I myself looked. The tape showed Sanabria screaming at me, and Mickey speaking to me through the window. It was like reliving a bad dream.

Then the screen brightened, and I saw my house again, in daylight, with reporters in front of it and Metropolitanos on the metal steps. Séptimo's brown face in the window.

I began worrying about Séptimo then. He was surrounded by strangers suddenly and all but imprisoned in a house that was not really his. What must he think?

I turned down the volume of the television and dialed my house. The phone rang a maddening number of times, and then someone took it off the hook. I heard breathing, but no one spoke.

"Timo? Timo? *¿Estás tú?*" There was no answer, only the breathing.

276

"Hablo Jimmy," I said finally.

"Jimmy?" It was Séptimo. "They've been calling all day. Asking for you."

"Who has?"

"Everyone. Hundreds of people. Gringos. Venezuelans."

"Ah. I understand. You don't have to say anything to them, Timo."

"No."

"How are you?"

"Fine." His voice was flat; I thought that perhaps he was angry with me.

"Are you getting enough to eat?"

"They brought food. The *pacos* did. When are you coming home?"

"I can't come home for a while, Séptimo. I don't know when. I'm right in the middle of something." He was silent for a long minute after that. I heard his regular breathing coming through the wires.

Then he said, "Someone else called. After you were on the TV. He said to give you a message."

"A message?" I felt my blood speeding up.

"A message from...Beowulf." He pronounced the English name almost correctly; it seemed that someone had made him practice it.

"Yes? What did he say?"

"He said get a million dollars in a suitcase. Go to Choroní by yourself. No cops."

"Choroní? Are you sure he said Choroní?" Choroní was a village on the western coast that I had visited once.

"Choroní," he said. "Take a room in Choroní and wait for someone to talk to you."

"Is that all he said?"

"Sí."

I sighed. That was the message, then. They had gotten it to me. I felt a wave of relief, and with it a sharp pang of affection for poor little Séptimo. "You're a good boy, Timo," I said. "You're the best boy that I know of in the world."

I had expected him to be delighted with this praise, but I miscalculated. He kept breathing, saying nothing, waiting. His waiting made me nervous, made me feel closed in. I wanted another drink.

"Well, I've got to go, Timo. You'll be all right, won't you?"

There was a wait of half a minute before he said, *"Sí."*

"Good-bye."

"Ciao, Jimmy."

I hung up and went immediately to the minibar. A moment later the phone rang.

"Angel?" It was Lugo Alvarado. "Did the *carajito* give you your phone message?"

"Yes, thank you. Mind telling me where it came from?"

He hesitated a moment. Then he said, *"La misma vaina.* Same old shit. A pay phone in Caracas."

I began to laugh. "Nelson. *Pana,"* I said. "Can you believe it? They're sending me to the beach." Lugo Alvarado left me laughing into the dial tone.

An undercover Disip man wearing jeans and a T-shirt drove me to Choroní in an inconspicuous old Renault station wagon. He chain-smoked and stared straight ahead during the long ride and spoke only twice, when he politely asked if I needed to stop and piss in the weeds. I had drunk a lot of coffee before I left that day, and I took him up on his offer both times. We traveled through farmland and small towns, and despite the worry and risk involved in my errand, the sight of open land and a wide sky in place of pavement and brick was intoxicating. The city caused a chronic compression of the soul, and while stretching my limbs by the roadside, breathing the unsoiled air, I felt physically larger than I ever did in Caracas. I found myself smiling.

To get to Choroní, we drove to Maracay, a fairly flat trip, and then we took the long, slow climb up the coastal mountains that preceded the plunge down through tropical rain forest to the Caribbean Sea. When we were near the sea, we traveled westward through the jungle on a narrow paved road, following the winding course of a river. All along the river we could see dark women washing clothes, and from time to time, high in a tree, we saw clothing hung, not to dry, but as part of some *brujería,* some ritual or ceremony pertaining to a magic that had been brought from the jungles of an older continent.

The road that followed the river led into Choroní and became the main artery through the center of the village until it finally met the shore and bent away, splintering into a warren of narrow back streets. At the point where road met shore, there was a low curving wail of stone and mortar into which were cemented the rusting barrels of ancient cannons. The cannons faced the blue, empty Caribbean. At high tide the water came right up to the bottom of the wall; this was only a scenic point, and not the beach. The real beach lay a quarter of a mile from the town, at the end of a sandy dirt lane that skirted a grove of coconut palms on one side and dense brush and an occasional shack on the other. A shallow stream crossed the lane at one spot, and people driving back to town from the beach would often stop in the middle of this stream and swing their legs out of their cars to wash the sand from their feet.

Choroní was a village of houses and of little else; even the two small grocery stores and the tiny hardware store occupied the front rooms of private homes. The houses were of smooth concrete and were painted in pastel shades with roofs of red tile or corrugated steel. The side wall of one house was often connected to the side wall of the next; the green of one home would flow soothingly into the pink of another, which would in turn melt harmoniously into blue on the other side. There was not a proper restaurant in the entire town. The eating places were almost all located beneath wooden *ramadas* attached to shacks containing a refrigerator and a stove, although some of the bars that sat within dark concrete cubbyholes would often serve food as well. You could get fish, very fresh, cooked with head, tail, and fins intact, or you could order steak. The fish was always better, and cheaper.

The town possessed one real hotel that had very few rooms. When these rooms were filled, visitors had to seek lodging in the spare quarters of Choroní families. By renting rooms, many families earned money to help them get through the times when fishing was poor.

It was late afternoon when the Disip man let me out beside the town's tiny church. As I stood, stretching and admiring the church, the cop got out and opened the back of the Renault and removed my two suitcases. One suitcase was my own hard plastic one, and the other was a battered leather piece of luggage that

279

contained and concealed a smaller aluminum case. The metal suit-case held one million dollars; this sum had been assembled in a matter of hours by Ronnie's people, who considered the ransom figure to be a bargain on the order of a department store Blue Light Special. I had inspected the money myself, riffling the stacks of bills with trembling fingers.

A Jeep Cherokee passed the parked Renault and pulled into an unpaved lane within sight of the church. The driver killed his en-gine and then pretended to study a road map, all the while watch-ing me in his rearview mirror. This was another nameless Disip man, the officer who was responsible for keeping an eye on the money while I circulated in town. I had been told that he would be the only cop with me in Choroní, aside from the locals. I did not believe that for a minute.

I picked up my two suitcases, nodded at my driver, who only stared stonily at me, and walked down into the lane and past the Cherokee. The Disip man in the Jeep, who was short and thin, with a black mustache that he constantly stroked, observed me over the top of his map. I lifted my sunglasses and winked at him as I walked by; he looked startled for a moment, turning his head to the left and the right to see if there was anyone nearby who might have seen my signal, and when he saw there wasn't, he gave me a cool nod. I smiled and continued down the unpaved side street carrying the two suitcases. I had packed little in the way of clothes, and the suitcase with the money was by far the heavier of the two. I was listing to my million-dollar side.

The houses on this dirt lane all sat far back from the street, each of them hidden and defended from the street by either a pastel-painted concrete wall or a wrought-iron fence thatched with an anarchic tangle of rosebushes and other vines. I saw several houses with signs out front indicating that a room was for rent within, but they did not give me the right feeling, and I passed them by. I felt the questioning eyes of the Disip man on my back as I continued my weary trudge down the street.

Finally I found one house that had that certain feeling to it, and I stopped in front of it to set my suitcases down and rest for a min-ute. The wall around this house had been less recently painted than most of the others, with green paint lying in chips on the dust of the street. The twin wooden doors set into the wall were sagging badly on rusted hinges, incapable of closing properly. The Room for Rent sign was written in pencil on dark cardboard, and I could tell it had hung from the door for a long time.

After checking to make sure no one but the Disip man was watching me, I put my hands on top of the wall, boosted myself high enough to peer over the top of it, and dug my toes into the concrete to hold me there. I saw a dark, overgrown courtyard of hard-packed earth and bushes and tall rubber trees. I saw a main house with a patio that was lit by the dim flicker of a TV set, and I saw a smaller concrete cubicle the size of a single room across the courtyard from the house. The darkness and shabbiness of the place gave me a warm feeling deep in the pit of my stomach; I imagined it was the same feeling a rodent got when it discovered a dark and particularly well-hidden burrow. I hoped that there were at least two spare rooms in the house; I had been told not to hole up anywhere where there was not at least one more room to let.

I jumped down and knocked on the old wood of the double doors, and when there was no answer, I called. I saw movement through the generous gap between the doors then; I pressed my eye to that gap and made out the figure of a person who was shuffling toward me. The person got closer, and I saw that it was a woman. An old, lame woman with a body like a loosely packed sack of flour beneath her baggy blue housedress and stringy gray hair shot through with white in places. I drew back from the space between the doors, and a moment later she reached those doors and pressed her own face to them to peer out at me with suspicion.

"¿Sí?" By the sloppy way she spoke that one word, I knew she was probably missing most of her teeth.

When I asked about the room, she unhooked the piece of wire that held the two doors together and led me silently through the blighted garden to the cubicle across from her patio. She pushed open the thin wooden door and turned on the bare bulb of the ceiling light, revealing a cell-like, windowless room with walls, ceiling and floor of gray concrete and a wooden cot covered with a moth-eaten blanket that stood pressed against the wall.

"*Treinta bolivares*," she said. I had to fight off a suffocating feeling of gloom that settled on me.

"Thirty? Are there two rooms? Is there another room?"

"Hay otro cuarto," she admitted, her desiccated face betraying no thought or emotion, barely betraying life. She was not bothered by the fact that I did not lift my sunglasses for her; she was indifferent. She led me across the courtyard to a door in the cement wall at the end of her patio that opened onto the second room for rent. This room was just like the other, except that it had more cobwebs, and more light filtered through the roof of rusty corrugated steel. The door was almost directly across from the door to the first room, a fact that made the setup nearly perfect.

"I like the other room," I told her. "The first room." She nodded and held out a gnarled hand that could as easily have belonged to an old man, and I reached for my wallet. "How many live here?" I asked her as I drew out a twenty and a ten.

"Yo solamente." I nodded and handed her the money. I felt the need to draw some sort of human response from her. Humor was impossible; pain seemed the easiest.

"Your husband, was he a fisherman?" But she merely pointed toward the back wall of her property, where stood a small, self-explanatory wooden building.

"The bathroom is there," she said. "The shower is next to it, on the outside. There is no hot water." Then she turned away and stepped onto her patio. On worn, rubber-soled slippers she moved up the patio to a gray couch and sat down before the cold blue flame of her television.

I went to my cubicle and stashed the suitcase containing the money under the cot. I opened the other suitcase on the cot and I took out my bathing suit and put it on, then dropped my rubber sandals onto the floor and stepped into them. Carrying a towel and a bar of soap and a bottle of shampoo, I walked self-consciously down to the outhouse.

The outhouse contained a flush toilet and a small, dirty sink. Without pulling down my bathing suit, I took a seat on the toilet and sat there for a long while, thinking. Now that I was here, weaned finally from the soothing motion of the journey and the comforting hum of the Renault's tires, I had begun to tremble. I felt strangely displaced within my own skin; I felt feverish, almost delirious. A million dollars in a suitcase under my bed. Payment for kidnappers. It seemed all wrong; the world had reversed its poles. I knew I was not cut out for this, and I saw myself as being at once comical and absurd. And doomed. The whole thing suddenly seemed to make about as much sense as shooting an astronaut to the sun. I held my face in my hands, and I shook.

After a time I spotted a huge spider in that dirty bathroom. It was a female, a hairy wolf spider nearly as big as my fist, and she clung to one of the upper corners of the little chamber. She was watchful, but perfectly still, and I saw that she clutched a white sacful of eggs to her abdomen. I knew that if I tried to touch her, she would slash me with burning fangs. But I was not frightened of her. She was something to focus on in my disorientation, and after a minute I found myself trying to imagine how I appeared as seen through a spider's multiple, unblinking eyes.

I told myself then that Ronnie Neumon needed my protection. It was in my power to protect him as it was in no one else's power. I was not doomed; I had power. I had a mission of humanity. I smiled in the direction of the spider and felt at peace.

I found the showerhead outside the bathroom, attached to a narrow pipe that ran up the side of the building. I opened the single spigot and stood in the mud beneath the cold sprinkle of water. I soaped myself and rinsed off, then started to wash my hair.

The Disip man came into the shabby courtyard while I was showering. I heard him inquiring about the price of the room, asking how many people lived in the house. I knew he would approve when he heard it was just the old *señora* by herself. I heard him ask her if she would please take the Room for Rent sign off the outside door, because he was not feeling well and did not want to be disturbed by drunken *Caraqueños* stumbling in during the middle of the night, and I almost laughed aloud.

After the shower I went back into my cubicle and dressed and dried my hair. Then I put on my disguise, which consisted of my dark glasses and a New York Mets baseball cap, and opened the door with the intention of heading out to dinner. The Disip man sat in his room with the door open. He was sitting on his cot, stripped to the waist, a paperback book in his hands. Beside him was his pillow. He was looking at me over the top of the book. I stepped back into my room so that the old woman would not see me, and I gave the Disip man a low wave. He stared at me for half a minute and finally responded by setting aside his pillow, lifting the machine pistol that rested beneath it, and brandishing it in mock salute. This weapon was no Brazilian-made Saturday-night special; it was an authentic Uzi, easily recognizable by its efficient rectangular silhouette. The Disip man smiled, rehid the weapon, and looked back down at his book. I walked out through the twin wooden doors and into the street.

Twilight was closing in as I strolled down the middle of the main street of Choroní. The town seemed full of men who could have been police agents and other men who could have been guerrillas. I felt them looking at me, and I did not care. People were out on their porches, the men drinking beer, the women scolding the children. Just as I came abreast of one of the houses, an argument broke out in front of it. The porch was crowded with children, and a man began shouting at one of the little boys as a woman stood in the open doorway, watching and twisting her apron in her hands. After a minute the man reached to the floor and picked up a piece of wood that looked like a broken bit of a broom handle; he grabbed the boy by the arm and began beating him on the backs of the legs. As I stood, transfixed, the beating went on and on and on, discipline quickly turning to indecency, to brutality. The man was smiling, but in his eyes there was both anger and helplessness. The boy screamed, "*¡Ay! ¡Ay! ¡Ay!*" with each stroke, but he did not cry; he tried manfully not to cry.

Finally a point was reached where I had to step in, to at least say something to the man. But just as I was making up my mind to move, a crowd of young men sitting on a porch across the street began to shout. "*¡Epa!*" they said, "*¡Epa!*" standing in a group finally to glare at the man. He continued for a minute; not stopping immediately was a matter of pride, of honor even. Then, when pride and honor had finally been satisfied, he tossed aside the stick and went into the house, pushing past the woman.

The little boy bolted from the porch. He went past me, a dark whirlwind of thin, churning limbs, and he dashed into a narrow alley between two houses on the other side of the street and disappeared.

My feeling of peace was shattered. It had proven illusory. I was a coward, helpless and unworthy. I walked to a fairly clean, well-lighted fish shack and sat down at a flimsy metal table. I was trembling again. A fat *criolla* came over and told me the *sancocho* was very good today. So I ordered a Polar and drank it with the good fish soup.

Later I wandered the streets in my disguise, asking where I could get a bottle of a local concoction called *guarapita*. Someone eventually directed me to a house at the end of an alley. Instead of a back wall, this house had a rusty wire fence, and a black dog came up, barking, as I approached. The little house was dark, but in a minute an old man in pajamas and bare feet came out to the fence. He nodded when I told him what I needed, and he went back to the house for a moment and returned with the bottle. The moon was nearly full, and the old man held the bottle against the sky to show me the pale yellow color of his cane-liquor-and-passion-fruit brew.

"It's the best *guarapita* in the country," he told me. He seemed to like me, and when I handed him the money, he said, "Tomorrow night there will be a party. There will be dancing to the drums. Plenty of *guarapita* then. Free." I thanked him, even smiled for him, and I left.

I walked out to the beach. I could hear guitars and singing and laughing above the crash of the surf, and I saw three or four bonfires burning fiercely on the sand. Blankets were scattered here and there in the darkness, and on them lay lovers entwined.

I picked out a private spot, and I sat. The moon seemed huge above the water, cold with dark clouds scudding across its face. The water all the way out to the barely seen horizon had a luminescence to it. I stared out at the water and the moon and I drank.

I awoke in the heat of late morning with a heavy head and a trampled tongue. The burning sweetness of *guarapita* hung about me in the dense air. I swung my feet to the concrete floor of my little cell; a sharp pain pierced my head and nausea swept through me. I stayed as still as I could while I waited for my sense of balance to return.

Drinking. As I huddled, shivering and sick, I had a sudden luminous revelation, a clear remembrance and vision of all the recent mornings I had awakened with the feeling of having been poisoned. Many mornings; as I looked over my shoulder at a month's time, I saw those mornings growing closer together the nearer to me they got, until they began to touch, back to back, in the last weeks of my life.

It was disturbing, this discovery, because of what it seemed to tell me about myself, and because some action, some change, seemed called for.

But it was also annoying to have such thoughts at such a time; it seemed silly in fact. If I were about to die a violent death, which was at least a possibility, I might as well be an alcoholic as not. I made a hasty promise to myself to review my drinking behavior once I got back to Caracas, and not to think about it until then. Then I tried to push it out of my mind. But every time I turned my head, the shooting pain reminded me.

Slowly I stepped into a pair of pants and went out the creaking wooden door of my room. The Disip agent was lying on his cot with his door open; he lifted the back of his hand at me without looking up from the book he balanced on his chest. As I turned away from him, I thought I saw him give me the finger in the American fashion, but I looked back, and his hand was resting on the bed.

I used the toilet and washed up in the sink. The spider was still there, both her position and her posture unchanged. I wondered whether she could yet feel the new lives stirring against her.

I put on my hat and my sunglasses and went out into the street. Even in broad daylight there were men in town who looked like police or guerrillas. They worried me more now than they had the night before. It was nearly eleven when I stepped beneath a palm-thatched *ramada* and ordered two eggs and a broiled red snapper. I also asked for coffee and, after a moment's hesitation, a beer.

As I was eating, a woman entered the open-air restaurant and pulled out one of the metal folding chairs on the opposite side of my table and sat down. I dropped my fork and looked up; saw huge dark sunglasses and a wide-brimmed straw hat and a scarf that went around the hat and under the chin. The hair was tucked so completely into the hat that almost none of it was visible. I blinked, and recognized Loren Hart.

"Oh," I said.

We stared at each other for a minute, and then she startled me by bursting into laughter. "Those glasses," she said between screeches. "That hat." I was just about to feel insulted when she calmed down enough to say, "That stubble. Now you know what it feels like."

I thought about that, and I nodded. I was now as much a prisoner of my own face as Loren was of hers, though in a different way. "That's right," I said. "I'm a marked man. How did you find out I was here?"

She turned serious and looked down at the table. "Would you get me a beer? I don't suppose there's anything else."

I ordered the beer, and the girl brought it quickly, pouring some into a short glass for Loren and then going back to the kitchen. I folded my hands in front of me and watched patiently as she took the first sip.

"The police told me," she said finally. "I kept asking them. I don't suppose they ever thought I'd rent a car and come here by myself."

"You didn't tell anybody else?"

"No," she whispered. She hesitated a moment and then shook her head. "I knew enough not to do that. But I just had to come. Hanging around Caracas with those reporters, and everyone. All of them looking at me . . ."

I sat nodding at her, unsure of what to say. I finished my beer and held up the empty bottle. The girl brought another. Finally I said, "It must be hard. I didn't even think of it. About you, I mean. You must . . ." I let my voice trail off. Her chin began to tremble then, and she brought a hand up to cover it. But she shook her head sadly.

"No," she said. "I mean, it is hard, but not for the reason you think. It's the responsibility, is all. I'm responsible for him." I sat blinking at her as I waited, and she said, "Did you spend any time with him? If you did, then you'd probably know what I'm talking about."

"Yes," I said. "I did spend a little time with Ronnie. And I know about responsibility, too." My voice was calm, sympathetic. And I did feel sympathy, along with a rush of excitement that I did my best to hide. Blood made a sound like snare drums in my ears.

Loren Hart took a piece of tissue out of a small purse she held in her lap and pushed her glasses up to wipe her eyes. When she was done, she smiled and studied me with those artless blue eyes before she settled the glasses back into place.

"You seemed so nice that afternoon when you took care of me, Jimmy," she said. "I hope you won't be too nice to tell me if I'm getting in the way. I don't want to spoil the transaction." My throat seemed suddenly thick, and I took a swallow of beer to clear it.

"No," I said. "I'm waiting for some kind of message from them. When I get the message, then you'll have to stay away. Until then I can't see that you're doing any harm." She smiled gratefully.

"Do you know when the message is coming?" I shook my head.

"I just have to be here to wait for it."

"Then we'll kill the time together. Go to the beach and things. It won't seem so horribly long and lonely that way." My throat was closing up again. I took another long gulp of beer and looked away.

"Right," I said. I tried to say something else, but all words abandoned me, and I could think only in crude pictures, like cave drawings or a child's scribbles. I put my hand over my mouth and pretended to cough.

Loren was staying at the only decent hotel in town. After I had finished breakfast, she went back there to change into her bathing suit, and I returned to my cell to get my own. Once inside the *señora*'s courtyard, I moved with the quickness of excitement to shed my clothes and put on my suit and sandals and to throw a towel over my shoulder. The Disip man, ever-vigilant from the open doorway of his room, noticed the change in the rhythm of my movements and gave me a suspicious look. I looked around to make sure the old woman was not watching, and then I waved and smiled at him and went out the double doors and into the street.

Loren and I walked to the beach together. All along the dirt lane to the water and then down half the length of the beach, I saw men looking at us, their eyes at first widening in surprise and disbelief and then narrowing in hunger and envy. Although Loren's face was hidden by the hat and the glasses, the loose terrycloth bathrobe she wore over her modest one-piece bathing suit did almost nothing to disguise the startling perfection of her body. I could not help but smile to myself.

Loren seemed not to notice the stares. Not even when some brassy character hissed at her from behind a car did she pay attention. She was impregnable, and walking with her, escorting her, I felt strong and attractive and desirable. But I was a little nervous as well, nervous about how things would unfold with Loren and about my increased chances of being recognized while I was with her. It would be hard to blend in from now on.

We spread towels and lay on the beach. We lay without talking, listening to the rhythmic violence of the surf. At first the heat melted me and spread me out over the sand like a jellyfish. But then, as often happens beneath a seductive tropical sun, I began to feel a certain glowing disquietude. When it started, the sensation was almost a pleasant one, and I concealed a smirk in the crook of my elbow. After a time, however, there came discomfort and self-consciousness. Loren, during these tribulations, lay on her back with her eyes closed. But there was a smile on her lips that could have been a smile of amusement. Finally, as I found myself edging toward panic, I stood and headed for the pounding water.

"Hey!" Loren called. I looked at her over my shoulder; her head was tilted up, and she was shading her eyes with a hand. "Going in?"

"Yes." I kept my head twisted awkwardly to avoid facing her.

"I'll go." She began climbing to her feet, and I ran and leaped and split the water.

She was a good swimmer. We went out together past the point where most Venezuelan bathers would go. The waves were steep and fast, but we swam far enough from shore that they did not break over us or behind us. We turned our backs to them and rode them like otters. I sensed the eyes of the beach upon us, but in the water I felt graceful and easy, and I smiled. Loren smiled, too, as the sea lifted us and plunged us. Without glasses or hat, with her dark hair wet and droplets glistening on her eyelashes, Loren looked beautiful. But in the water her beauty was not painful to look at. Soon we were laughing.

After a while a lifeguard came strolling along the edge of the beach, and he blew his whistle and motioned us to come in. We pretended to ignore him for a minute or two, and then we began to stroke shoreward until we caught the crest of a wave, and we rode it all the way in. When we finally stood on the sand, the lifeguard, who was short and sun-blackened and much too friendly-looking for his job, told us that the surf here was danger-ous, that the bottom was hard coral and the current was stronger than it seemed, and that people drowned at Choroní all the time. He told us we must never swim out that far again, and we prom-ised him we would not.

When the lifeguard was gone, we giggled. But I felt a little self-conscious and embarrassed; out of the water I was exposed and dripping and nearly naked. I was also as white as coconut meat, and my ridiculous trunks were clinging to me uncomfortably.

As we walked to our towels, a tall, black Venezuelan in faded cutoff jeans came striding toward us from the upper beach. He was carrying something in his hand. By his purposeful gait I could tell that we were his destination; I wondered if he might be my messenger from Packy and the kidnappers, and I felt the water on my skin turn suddenly cold. The young man was sapling thin, but the muscles of his arms and chest and stomach were gracefully, if not heavily, defined. Loren saw him, too, and she stood with me and waited for him, shielding her vulnerable eyes with a delicate hand.

When he got closer, I saw that the thing he carried was a glass bottle of homemade suntan lotion. He held up his bottle and smiled at us, showing strong teeth with a quarter inch of healthy purple gum above and below.

"For *catires* like you," he said, glancing at me before turning appreciative eyes on Loren. "Real coconut oil. Twenty bolivars."

Loren smiled at him, and they began to talk. He possessed a few words of English, and she had some half-remembered high-school Spanish. I went back to my towel and lay down.

I was angry, and at the same time I was experiencing the same insistent problem I'd had before I went swimming. After ten minutes or so Loren came and stretched out next to me, reaching for her sunglasses.

"I love these beach people," she said, her voice light, almost girlish suddenly. "They're so natural. Do you know what I mean, Jimmy?"

"Hmm," I said. I cautioned myself then to keep in mind how very young Loren Hart really was in spite of her surface sophistication; it had been my experience that even the nicest of very young women could often turn fickle or even unfeeling. Following this self-warning, a warning I knew I would soon forget, I pretended to doze.

Later, when we both began to feel the stinging tightness of too much sun, we rose lethargically and walked back to the village. I gave her a brief tour of the town; we went past my dismal lodging and the little church of pastel concrete, and then we parted with a promise to meet for dinner.

For dinner we had red snapper and yucca washed down with cold Polar.

"You wanted Venezuela?" I said. "Here it is."

She smiled and seemed to eat with increased appreciation. We took a long while to eat, and when we were finished, I carried two bottles of beer to the wall that had the cannons cemented into it. We drank and watched the sun slide down into the water, and Loren talked about how badly she wanted to be an actress.

"I mean a real actress," she said, staring almost invisibly at me through the lenses of her dark glasses. "I'd like to do movies."

"I bet you will," I said. I felt suddenly certain that she would do movies and was at once jealous of those movies and of the men who would direct them and of everyone who would watch them. Strangely I no longer felt even a twinge of jealousy toward poor Ronnie Neumon.

"Do you really think so?" The girlishness was in her voice again. "I would give anything." She squeezed her eyes shut, probably turning the backs of her eyelids into movie screens, and her lower lip disappeared between her teeth. I knew I was seeing a bit of the real, unguarded Loren Hart now.

Then, suddenly, she was looking at me again, her cheeks flushed red. "TV," she said, "is not art."

"No," I said.

"It's garbage. I don't delude myself. What I did on the show those three years was garbage. I want to do art; I want to co-star with William Hurt. I want to prove that I'm an actress."

"Yes," I said. "I can see it already. Hurt and Hart."

"I'm obsessing, I know. It is an obsession with me. It's probably difficult for you to understand." Her hands were moving, grasping, seemingly trying to pull words out of the air in front of her. "This person obsessed with doing something outstanding so that people have to recognize her."

I stared silently out to sea. I felt her questioning eyes on me, but I refused to turn in her direction. Finally, after several minutes, she said, "Oh. Of course." She put a hand on my arm and I let her leave it there.

"I didn't mean that you . . ." she said. "I mean, of course, you must want to do something as well. What's wrong with me?"

I looked at her and managed a rueful, self-conscious smile. "Everyone does, you know," I said. "Everyone is that way underneath it all. It's just that so few ever get the chance to show what they can do."

"Yes," she said. "Of course. You're right, Jimmy."

At dusk the drums started. They made a rolling boom that shook your insides and they were so powerful it seemed no matter how far you walked, you would not escape them.

"It sounds like Africa," Loren said, and she looked at me.

"They'll be dancing soon," I said. "Dancing to the drums. When it's dark, we'll go and watch."

The drumming and dancing took place at the spot where the main road entered Choroní. As we approached, we saw a bonfire licking up toward the palm fronds and a crowd of milling human silhouettes set off by the flames. There was a house near the road, and people stood before it in a ragged line, awaiting cups of free *guarapita*.

Loren put a soft hand on my arm and left it there. Her hand was trembling slightly. I smiled down at her, and she took off her sunglasses and hooked them onto the front of her blouse. She returned my smile.

The drummers were two whiplike black teenagers who were naked except for bikini bathing briefs. Their drum was a long, well-seasoned hollow log, and they sat before it on little stools, working it with heavy sticks. They were all concentration; they were in a rhythm trance. Their arms flew, the white drumsticks flashing in the air.

"They're artists, aren't they," Loren said.

I nodded. "I think they are."

The main crowd stood in a wheellike formation. At the hub of the wheel moved the single couple that was allowed to dance. I could see them over the bobbing tops of the people's heads; Loren had to stand on tiptoe. The female dancer was heavy and old and very black. She wore a long, loose skirt, and her big hips moved wildly within that skirt, making the fabric flutter on either side. She was turning in a small, tight circle, twisting first one way and then the other, and her hands were high in the air, making slow, fluid motions above her. She was smiling.

The man with her was old as well; he was skinny and brown, dressed in long pants and a faded dress shirt, and he also was moving his hips to the beat of the drums, moving them not only from side to side, as the woman did, but also moving them aggressively, moving them in and out. The man's dance was a struggle to stay before the woman, to stay facing her, close to her, as she turned first one way and then the other. He danced with his arms stretched outward, nearly touching her sides, as if trying to contain and control her. The woman would dance with him for a minute or so, seeming to surrender to him, their pelvises almost touching and their asses pumping with the speed of a humming-bird's wings. But then, suddenly aloof, she would turn away from him, and he would have to face her again as she twisted left and then right. Their faces gleamed with a sheen of sweat in the firelight.

After a minute, another man charged out of the crowd. He was short and fat, although younger than the male dancer, and he gave the old man a hard shove in the chest. The old man flew backward, but the crowd caught him, everyone gasping *ooh!* at the same time, and they stood him back on his feet. The old man melted through to the outside of the crowd, and soon I saw him walking toward the house that had the *guarapita*.

Loren tugged on my sleeve, and I lowered my ear to her mouth. "Are they supposed to fight?" she asked. "Is that fair?"

I put my mouth to her ear. "It's fair. That's the way it's done."

The fat man and the old woman danced together for a while, and then a plump younger woman stepped into the circle and caught the old woman's eye. The old woman faded back, and the new couple danced. But after a few minutes a stocky, broad-shouldered young man stepped in. He gave the dancer a light tap on the chest; the fat man tried to push him back, and the young pretender shoved him hard then, knocking him almost all the way through the circle. Then he danced.

Loren became possessed by the beat of the drums. She began by moving her feet, then she started shaking her hips, shaking them timidly at first, and then with spirit. Finally she let her hands creep into the air, and she turned to face me, twisting coquettishly from side to side as I tried to look into her eyes.

I let her dance by herself for a while because I was unsure how the crowd would take it. But after a time, when no one seemed to be paying attention, I put my arms out and began self-consciously shuffling around in the dirt in an effort to keep up with her. Loren was a natural for the movement, and she soon had my blood boiling. We smiled at each other as we shook and turned.

Then something hit me. I flew back and landed in the sand and bumped my head against a coconut palm. My teeth clashed together. I looked up, and there was a man dancing with Loren, the same character who had been selling lotion on the beach. Neither of them looked at me. As I watched, the crowd began to drift away from the legitimate dancers and to surround Loren and her new man. They moved well together. They were irresistible.

I tasted blood. I wanted to get up and punch that man right in the face, but when I attempted to climb to my feet, I found that my legs were like rubber. I had to get up slowly.

When I could finally stand, I began walking away from the dancers and the fire and the drummers. And when I had my legs back fully, I ran.

The Disip man was reading one of his paperback books by the dim light of the bare ceiling bulb. As soon as he saw me enter the courtyard, he stood, snatching a shirt off the bed and signaling that he wanted badly to go out for a drink. I flapped a hand at him to assure him the money was safe with me, and then I let myself into my cell and closed the door behind me without turning on the light.

The darkness was comforting. I tossed myself onto the bed and stared upward. A circular belt of memories like a tape loop ran through my mind: hope, humiliation, new hope, new humiliation, newest hope, newest humiliation. I felt the pressure of tears behind my eyes, and yet I took a perverse pleasure in the dismal pattern I had discovered. Could anyone else, after all, have endured my wretched upbringing, my failures, my defeats? I thought at once of little Séptimo, the orphan, and of Packy, the refugee, but I pushed them from my mind immediately and with great irritation. Inside, where it counted, in the soul itself, I was certain I had been scarred more deeply than either of them. And even if I hadn't, I was entitled to enjoy my pain in all its purity without the contamination of comparison.

I decided that I would let myself cry. First, however, I would allow my feelings to build; I would feed them, so that the plunge itself, when it came, would be the longest, most hallucinogenic ride through the depths that I could get for my money.

But then there came a tentative rasping at the door of my room, a sound between a knock and a scratch. I was paralyzed with fright; I wished, suddenly, that I had borrowed a pistol from the Disip man.

"Jimmy?" It was Loren.

"Yeah?" I spoke without thinking. My voice sounded rough, as if I had already cried. The door opened, and I had a brief glimpse of her silhouette before it closed again. The cot sagged as she sat.

"This is a real classy place," she said. There was concern and embarrassment in her disembodied voice.

"It's okay. It has spiders." I could think of nothing else to say, and I silently cursed myself for my stupidity. I was grateful for the darkness.

Loren decided to take it as a joke. "Spiders?" she said, and forced a chuckle. "Jimmy..." Her fingers found my bare arm. They were cool, almost cold. "I would have gone right over to you if I thought you were hurt. Were you? Hurt?"

"No. No, what makes you think that?"

"It's just that you told me that's the way it was done. The pushing. So I thought it was okay. Like a game."

"It is," I said quickly. "It is a game. I'm just a poor loser."

The bed creaked as she stretched out next to me, forcing me against the concrete wall. Her cool hands went behind my head, and she kissed me. I kissed her back and she pressed against me, and an uneasy feeling began to grow in the pit of my stomach. This was Loren Hart. This could not be happening.

She sat up, and I heard her shucking off her clothes. I sat then, too, bumping her shoulder accidentally and excusing myself, and in a panic, I began taking my own clothes off. This was too fast. I had not had time to prepare for it. A man had to be mentally prepared. I was frightened to death that something would go wrong.

I was still wearing my socks when she put her hands on my chest, hands that had become suddenly warm as though by magic, and playfully pushed me back against the bed. My head knocked softly against the concrete wall, and I grunted even though I was not hurt.

"Oh!" Loren said. Then she laughed and fell on top of me. Her hair tumbled down, tickling my neck. I laughed, though not from the tickling of her hair, and we kissed. It was a long kiss, and I began to feel a keen desperation then. I was excited, and I was desperate. I pulled her to me and kissed her harder than I should have, making her draw away from me. I grabbed her and clung to her and ran my hands all over her as if waiting for an answer to my problem to erupt in Braille somewhere on her whispering skin. I was breathing like a bellows, hard and out of control and dry in the throat. Finally I reached and gave myself an inquiring touch. I was cold; it seemed that the coldness that had been in Loren's hands had somehow gone into me. I was even angry with her for a few seconds before I shook away the defensive anger and gave in completely to the shame.

I sat up and stared at the faint border of light around the door. *"Shit,"* I whispered. I felt her hand on my back.

"Come on," she said. "Lie down." She laughed, but the laugh sounded forced to me.

I wanted to listen to her, to let her soothe me. I was in agony to be soothed. But it seemed somehow that by listening, by being comforted, I would be refusing to face my failure. I would be a coward.

"No," I said. "It's the bed." My voice came out in a bizarre croak; my whole body was making fun of me, betraying me. "The bed is too narrow."

I began to put my clothes on.

"Where are you going?" She sounded alarmed now, and guilt kicked up in me. But I continued dressing.

"Listen, Jimmy. You're being silly. Stop this, will you, and lie down here and talk to me."

"I just need some fresh air." I stood and pushed open the door. "I'll be back," I said, and stepped out into the overgrown courtyard.

I wandered down into the town and found the party breaking up. I went up to the house where they had been handing out the *guarapita* and asked if I could buy a bottle. There were two young men there, twin brothers, and they looked me over and said they weren't selling any *guarapita* tonight, but that they would give me some if I was in need. One of them handed me a milk bottle full of yellow brew and asked me to bring the bottle back in the morning. I thanked him and walked to the beach.

The sweet, blank face of the full moon and the indifferent hiss of the waves calmed me some. Nature was a calming thing; you could be a murderer, a rapist, an impotent, and nature wouldn't care; it would treat you the same.

I sat on the cooling sand and drank *guarapita*. There were no guitars tonight; I imagined that everyone was sleeping off the drunkenness of the drum party. The silence suited me.

The moon seemed to gild a straight, bright path over the waves and across the open sea. I had an urge to shed my clothes and to swim that path for as far as it would take me. It wasn't that I wished to drown. It was the swimming I wanted, the brainless motion of kicking feet and churning hands that would send me forward along the golden path and render both thought and feeling unnecessary.

"Jimmy?" Somehow I knew she would find me. But I was calmer now, almost as indifferent as the waves.

"Hi." She sat down next to me but did not touch me. "What are you drinking?"

"*Guarapita*. The same stuff they were drinking..." She picked up the milk bottle and took a slug.

"Good," she said, and handed the bottle to me. I drank. We sat for a long time watching the progress of the moon across the sky.

Finally she shivered and moved closer to me and slid an arm across my back. The hand crept up to the back of my neck, and she tangled her fingers in my hair. "Listen, Jimmy, I want you to do something for me." Her voice was so heartbreakingly husky it made me want to cry.

"I can't..."

"Not that. I just need you to be close. Is that okay? Can we do that?"

We fell to the sand, kissing, and we began undressing one another. "The secret is," she whispered, "this is really my favorite thing anyway."

I was relaxed, because I had only to be there, to hold her, and I began to enjoy myself.

"Wait," she said as we struggled together. "There. That's it. There."

Loren gasped and clung to me and nipped daintily at my shoulder. I became so busy enjoying her excitement that I did not notice the little miracle that happened. But Loren noticed. With hardly a pause she brought us together, and a moment later she was gripping me, pushing hard against the sand with her toes and making little sobbing noises by my ear. Soon I caught up with her.

Later, as we were holding each other, trying to stay warm, I said, "It's not really your favorite thing, is it?"

She laughed so hard she let me go and rolled away.

I was in love with Loren Hart. Love, with its accompanying demonology of delusions.

Loren's hotel room was tiny, but it had a big, old double bed in it, and it was on the second floor, so that we could leave the window blinds open even when morning came. The sun, passing through the blinds, cast bars of white and black over everything. With our bodies striped like zebras, we made love on the big bed.

It was mid-morning when Loren fell asleep. Although we had not slept at all the previous night, it was hard for me to understand how she could just drop off like that. My life had changed, had taken on magical qualities; I had died and come back to life. Loren Hart had made me a hero. And yet here she was, sleeping. It was an ordinary sleep; her breathing was heavy and regular, and her mouth was parted slightly, a silver thread of saliva running from the lowest corner to the pillow.

Stunned by my good fortune, without the sense to be made uneasy by it, I sat and watched her sleep. Over and over I swept her with my eyes, tasting her with my eyes.

After a time I discovered a mole on her. It was her only imperfection, as far as I could tell, and it was well hidden, on the outside of her thigh, just below the side of her ass. If it had been nothing but a birthmark, a discoloration, it would not have bothered me. But it was a regular raised mole, brown and a little scaly, and it was about the size of a quarter and shaped somewhat like a human hand. It had to have been visible when she wore her bathing suit, but I must have been too dazzled to notice it then. Careful not to disturb her, I bent closer and saw that the mole had a couple of dark hairs growing from the center of it. One of the hairs was quite long.

The hairy mole upset me. I don't know why; perhaps my tiredness and the strength of my recent emotions had made me overly sensitive. But the sight of the mole managed to interrupt my worshipful mood.

I still could not sleep, however, and after a time I got dressed, careful to put on my dark glasses and my baseball cap, and I descended to the street.

I sat down to have breakfast in a concrete café. Soon I came close to forgetting about the mole, and my elation returned. I ate breakfast and then I drank a beer, and I joked with all the patrons in the bar. I asked them if they knew any gringo jokes; they shook their heads shyly and said they did not. So I told a gringo joke, and everyone laughed, and then, one by one, they all began to tell their own jokes about efficient, humorless gringos who could not speak Spanish. We had a good time.

After a while, however, I felt like being alone. I bought two bottles of Polar and went out to the seawall. I watched a couple of fishing skiffs go out, and thinking of Loren, I exulted. I felt I had done a great thing.

In the back of my mind, though, there remained the mole. Well into my second bottle of beer, I decided that I would convince Loren to have it removed. Then she would be nearly perfect, although the procedure would likely leave a little scar.

But of course, there was always the chance that I would meet a woman who was perfect on her own, without the necessity of having a mole removed. A better woman; a sexier, more intelligent woman. A poet this time around, perhaps, instead of a TV actress. I had slept with Loren; that proved I possessed magic enough to capture any number of beautiful women. The fear of being tied down with Loren clawed briefly at my heart.

Of course the more rational part of me knew that this entire train of thought was nothing but foolishness and vanity and astonishing conceit. But the latter two qualities were ones that I had never suspected myself of harboring; I was flattered, in fact, to find them inside of me, and I enjoyed them. I lifted my bottle, and staring up into the Caribbean sun, I toasted to myself.

CHAPTER 10

I stayed out in the town until the afternoon sun on the back of my neck began to make me woozy. Then I wandered back to Loren's room. She was still sleeping, her breathing soft as a child's. I crept up to the bed and bent awkwardly over her to kiss her on the temple. She stirred a little and smiled, and I felt a dizzying, disorienting rush of tenderness for her. For a long minute I stood looking down at her, my chest swelling with mingled awe and pride. Finally I stole back out of the room.

My earlier, foolish thoughts about the mole were forgotten. I went back to the *señora*'s house, where I found the Disip man sitting shirtless on a wooden chair in the courtyard and reading an adult comic book that contained photographs instead of cartoons. The back of the chair was broken, so that it served for little more than a stool. The Disip man's face bristled with black whiskers, three days of whiskers, and as I came in, he glared openly at me, undoubtedly angry that I had gone off the night before and left the money untended. He probably also blamed me for the tardiness of the expected messenger. I shrugged.

The *señora* was back by the outhouse, sweeping. As she swept the tan, hard-packed dirt in front of the little building, she raised a thin cloud of dust that surrounded her and obscured her lumpy features, making her look like a toiling ghost. I badly wanted a shower, and it irritated me to see her working so near the unen-

300

closed showerhead. I did not want her sad, milky eyes upon me while I stood in my bathing suit, washing my hair with my own eyes squeezed tightly shut. The thought of it made me shudder.

But my craving for cleanliness was so great that finally I put on my still-damp bathing suit and my rubber sandals and grabbed a towel. I decided that I would walk to the shower and stand there waiting until she took the hint and cleared out.

When I reached her, the old woman lifted her eyes only slightly, lifted them to the level of my bare navel and then lowered them once again to her work. The broom hissed rhythmically against the hard earth, dragging in a meager pile of leaves and small, broken sticks. The *señora* wore a sleeveless dress, and with each swing of the broom, the loose skin of her bare arms flapped like the wattles of an old hen. Something about that hanging, wrinkled arm skin enraged me. Perhaps it was a child's rage and revulsion against all things ugly and feeble and old. I was ready to growl at the *señora*, to ask her if she could please return to watching her soap operas until I had taken my shower.

But then I saw the can of bug spray. It was a popular American brand, with dark cartoons of different insect pests lying belly-up all over it. The can of poison was sitting on the ground next to the outhouse, the cap of it nowhere in sight. And from behind it stuck two hairy legs like a pair of black pipe cleaners. With a feeling of tragedy in my heart, I walked over and lifted the can aside.

It was the spider, my spider, and she was lying unmoving, with her back against the dirt, the white egg sac still glued to her underside.

"*¿Qué fea, no?*" It was the old woman, become suddenly talkative. I looked at her, and her eyes had a shine to them. She had stopped her sweeping, was leaning on her broom. She was excited about the size, and what she perceived to be the ugliness of, the spider.

"Not ugly," I told her. "She was beautiful the way she . . ."

But the *señora* did not listen. She was too eager to share her adventure. The killing of the spider had undoubtedly been the most exciting thing to happen to her in the past several weeks.

"She jumped at me," the old woman said. She reached toward me with one of her gnarled hands, two fingers hooked to represent a spider's fangs. "She was on the wall, and I sprayed her, and

301

she jumped. I had to hit her with the broom." She lifted the broom then and reenacted the kill, the flaccid skin above her elbows shaking wildly. While she was still moving, dancing, smiling for me now even, with a couple of yellow teeth gleaming at the back of her lopsided mouth, I had a sudden vision of this hag as a young girl, reenacting her tiny tragedies and triumphs before appreciative parents and young friends. Her friends would have gasped and giggled; her parents would have hugged her and stroked her dark hair. Now that she was old and had killed what she saw as a dangerous beast in her bathroom, there was no one to tell about it but a stranger, a foreigner. Part of the sadness I felt for the maternal spider went out to the old woman then.

"¿Fea, qué no?" the old woman asked again. But the light was already fading from her eyes; she had seen my sadness and mistaken it for something else. Boredom perhaps.

"Fea," I agreed finally. There was really nothing else to say.

I went to the side of the outhouse where the shower was located and turned it on. I stepped beneath the trickle of cool water and immediately felt tears wanting to come. Tiredness had suddenly caught up with me, and it covered me like the splashing water. I forced a laugh through the tiredness and the unshed tears; I laughed at Jimmy Angel, who had stayed up all night and made love to a beautiful woman and had gotten drunk and was now ready to cry over a dead spider and a desiccated crone. Still, though, despite the laughter, a feeling of uneasiness pricked me inside. When I closed my eyes to wash my hair, I saw the spider crouching in her corner, fangs out, ready to spring.

After I finished my shower and went around past the door of the outhouse, I found that the old woman, the broom, the pile of trash, and the spider were gone. As I walked up to my room, I saw the señora disappearing out the crooked doors of the courtyard with a wicker basket hanging from one arm. She would surely tell everyone she met on the street about her pitiful conquest of the expectant wolf spider.

The Disip man was standing in his room settling a small semiautomatic pistol into the waistband of his bathing suit. Just before I closed the door to my room, I saw him slipping on a loose Hawaiian shirt to hide the gun.

I knew I should sleep. But there was no way I could rest until I had gone over and seen Loren again and reassured myself that she was there and real and that she belonged to me, or at least that a part of her did. I had pulled my clothes on over a still-damp body and was combing my hair when there came a soft knock at the door. Expecting the Disip man, I pushed open the door and confronted a man in a ski mask.

In the first moment, I felt he could not be real, and I almost laughed. Then I froze, fear like spider venom paralyzing me. When I tried to speak, my throat was too dry for words. He snapped me out of it, though.

"*Huevón*," he whispered. "*La plata*." He wore a revolver in his belt in the exact place where the Disip man had stuck his semi-automatic.

"*Allí*," I told him, eager to help, to be rid of him, and I pointed beneath the bed. The guerrilla pushed me aside and took an anxious step forward. But then he stopped, suspecting a trick.

"Drag it out of there. *Rápido*."

I did as he asked, throwing the heavy suitcase onto the bed. My own movements seemed remote to me now; it was as if my consciousness had crept back into a corner of my skull and was peeking out like a child hiding in a closet.

"Open it."

I unzipped the old leather suitcase, drew out the shining metal one beneath it, and popped it open. The stacks of bills, enough dollars to enrich several lives. I looked at him; from that hiding place within me I watched his eyes grow wide. Then he nodded.

"Okay. Bring it."

"*Bring* it?"

"Hurry up."

He waited for me to step out into the courtyard. Then he drew his weapon and gave me a gentle shove in the small of my back to start me toward the doors. I slid my eyes at the Disip man's room, but his door was closed, and he was not in sight.

A van waited in the street. It was a battered old Ford van, a van for delivering fish, and it was pale green with the words *Pescados de Barquísimeto* painted in black on the sides. One of the rear doors was open, and the guerrilla herded me over to it, and I stepped up inside. There were no windows, and the back of the van was separated from the cab by a wall of plywood paneling. The back of the truck was dark and smelled strongly of old fish.

The guerrilla climbed in behind me and slammed the door. "Sit down," he said. I felt around and located the wooden bench that ran along the side wall of the truck and I sat, holding the suitcase with the money between my legs.

The man in the mask sat on another bench opposite me, and he thumped the floor twice with his foot. The loudness of the thumping startled me. Then we began to move.

We traveled that way for about forty-five minutes. Toward the end the ride got very bumpy; I was twice thrown from the wooden seat to the hard steel floor, and once the metal suitcase fell over as I was picking myself up and mashed my fingers. I swore out loud. During all this the guerrilla sat silently on his side of the truck. He made no move to help me as I thrashed on the damp floor. He did not speak, and he did not fall from his bench. He seemed as balanced as a cat on the wooden seat. I felt his eyes upon me in the dark.

Finally the van braked to a stop and the rumble and shudder of the engine died. Silence. The guerrilla stood and opened one of the double doors at the back and stuck his head out warily before leaping to the ground and motioning me to follow.

I stepped out, also wary, the handle of the suitcase slippery with my sweat. The truck was parked on a deeply rutted road in the rain forest. The sun seemed far away as it shone down through tall trees wrapped and hung with parasitic vines.

I took in the jungle, drank it in, as the guerrilla pulled the suitcase from my hand and laid it on the uneven surface of the road. Another masked guerrilla appeared, the driver apparently, and the two men opened the suitcase and then knelt and began counting the money. They ignored me as they worked, counting aloud, their bowed backs turned to me.

And then I saw Packy. He was standing off in the jungle about twenty yards behind the truck; he was so still and so thin, thinner than I had seen him, that I had not noticed him earlier. I glanced down at the two preoccupied soldiers of revolution, and I walked toward him. Packy, as soon as he saw me move, also began to walk. He moved out toward the road, his feet whispering in dead, brittle leaves, and when he reached the road, he turned and came toward me.

When we were a little farther than an arm's length apart, we both stopped, as if by prearrangement. From behind me came a gleeful laugh, but neither of us paid attention.

We stared. Packy had lost weight; it had not been an illusion. His face was narrow, pinched-looking even, and his skin had taken on a waxy pallor. His hair was stringy and lank and hung lifelessly down to the top of his shoulders. His loose-fitting shirt and pants seemed filled with little but air.

"*Coño,*" Packy said, and he smiled a secretive smile. He seemed to have found something different about me as well.

"*Coño,*" I agreed, and returned his smile. Then, suddenly, we had trouble meeting each other's eyes.

"Packy, what happened?" I asked. Then I realized that under the circumstances, the question was broad enough to be confusing. "I mean, are you sick?"

"Sick?" Packy echoed. He studied the toes of his running shoes. "No. Not sick. Tired. And afraid."

"Jesus. Why did you—?" But he looked up now and stopped me with a warning smile. I could tell he was not ready to talk about it.

"But you," he said. "Are you all right? It must have been rough before our message got through."

I studied him. By some illusion, he seemed to have gotten shorter as well as frailer. I had a sudden vision of him lying in a golden field with the forward edge of a rumbling tank tread inches from his head; the memory was as clear as if I had been there myself.

"Nothing," I said finally. "Nothing. They held me prisoner for a day, that's all. Then your message came. But it was a good thing it came." I was suddenly overwhelmed by a mixture of gratitude for the message and shame at my own weakness. I felt my chin tremble, and I ran a quick hand over my face to stop it.

"Remember how," Packy said, his voice rising, "remember how we serenaded Adolfo that night to show him who was boss?"

I started laughing then, and Packy joined me. "That fat bastard," I said. Our laughter increased.

"The stupid brute," Packy said. We grabbed our sides and shook. Our faces reddened and tears began to leak from the corners of our eyes.

"The asshole," I gasped. Packy stamped his feet and bobbed from his thin waist in appreciation. The laughter was entirely out of proportion to the joke, and we knew it, but we couldn't seem to stop.

When it was over and we were panting to catch our breaths, I said, "I finally got fed up with him, you know. The night that Ronnie Neumon disappeared, I went to his house with a bunch of coins in a sock and caved in his damn stomach with it." Packy looked at me. "Dropped him right in the street," I said, my voice growing softer.

But somehow this was not funny. Packy did not even question me about it. He turned his head to watch a tropical finch dodging tree trunks as it flitted through the forest. When the bird was gone, he looked at me with eyes full of tiredness and pain.

"I made a mistake," he said. He stood looking at me as if expecting me to say something, but I was afraid the wrong word would discourage him. So I just nodded.

"I wanted revolution," Packy continued. "I wanted revolution to make Chile free again. I was ready to die for that. But I wasn't in Chile. I was here." His eyes were lonely. Pleading, almost. I nodded again.

"I met El Camión and he introduced me to Venezuelans who wanted to make revolution here. At first I was on the outside. I thought I would learn things that would be helpful in Chile, you know, but then I started doing little favors for them, and then bigger favors, and then with regularity I was helping move contraband in and out of the house of El Camión's mother."

Packy paused to draw a cigarette and a tiny box of matches from his top pocket. He lit the cigarette and dropped the match to the ground, where it sent up a wisp of smoke from among dead leaves before it died.

"Before I knew it, I was an important part of their operation in Caracas. They counted on me. Do you know how seductive that is, to be counted on?"

"I know," I said. He gave me a slow, sad smile, and I nodded at him and smiled back.

Packy breathed a jet of white smoke into the jungle air. "But nothing was too bad until the *gorilas* blew Rojas away and Mosca came to raise hell in Caracas. Then I was caught up in some bad action, and I couldn't get out. I almost had no choice, I was in so deep. Because if you back out of something like that, you're a traitor, you know. It was the same thing when it came down to Ronnie Neumon."

I felt compelled to speak now. "So you really didn't even want to be involved . . ."

"Well," said Packy, "let's say that much of the time I didn't want to be involved, and now I wish I hadn't been involved at all."

"But at least part of the time . . ."

Packy smiled a sad smile. "It's hard not to see the world all in black and white, Jimmy. You get caught up, and then revolution in Chile becomes revolution here, becomes revolution everywhere."

Packy flicked an ash in the direction of the dropped match. He watched the ash fly, and when it landed, he kept his eyes on the ground. "But I'm not really much of a revolutionary. At least as far as Venezuela is concerned. And you know something? Mosca and most of his friends are not really revolutionaries at all."

"What do you mean?"

"*Pana*, Mosca is a guerrilla because it's what he knows how to do. He's a professional at it. It's got very little to do with politics. He won't lay down arms because he would never make it managing a department store in Caracas."

We laughed then. But Packy quickly became serious again.

"And then the really dedicated revolutionaries, you have to watch out for them. I've been doing a lot of thinking, and I think they're usually no better than gorillas like the *militares* in Chile," he said. "The leftists, *pana*, the real leftists want to tear everything to the ground and build according to some perfect blueprint they think they have, and they'll smash anybody who gets in the way. And the right wants to kill anyone who won't agree that the existing system is perfect. It's all arrogance. Arrogance is killing everyone."

I was reduced once again to nodding. But Packy put on a cheerful face and reached over to brush my arm with his fingertips. "You know, I don't do *perico* anymore, Jimmy."

"No?" I said, allowing skepticism to come out in my voice. "You were such a fiend for it. What happened?"

"Well," he said, "I figured out I was using the stuff to whip myself into a frenzy over some things I had doubts about."

"And you gave it up just like that?"

"It's never just like that. But from now on, I'm trying to live in a way that keeps me from needing it."

One of the hooded men shouted at Packy. "*Ya*," the man said. "*Vámonos.*"

We both looked back and watched the guerrilla who had come into my *pensión* as he tossed the suitcase into the back of the truck and jumped in after it. The arm of the other man stuck from the driver's side window. I felt a sickening, falling feeling. I was going to lose Packy, soon. He began talking quickly.

"Did you ever figure out the Croaker, Jimmy?"

"I got the tape. Camión left me a tape."

"He's got a voice, hasn't he?" said Packy. "Don't you think he's got great range?" I laughed now, and Packy laughed with me. He went on with the story like a boy describing a prank.

"At first it was almost like a joke," he said. "We had just met you and we found out you worked in news, and that you lived near Camión. So when we needed to get some information over, we decided to call you." I shook my head in amazement.

"Then," said Packy, "when the thing worked so well and you proved so reliable, we made you the main outlet for things we wanted to say. Being the Croaker became an important job for El Camión. And you were one of us for a time, whether you knew it or not."

We laughed some more. Our laughter had an edge of desperation to it now. Then I said, "How is El Camión? What is he up to?" Packy became serious. He dropped his voice to a near whisper.

"He is unhappy," Packy said. "He's a Venezuelan, and he still believes very much in the revolution. I don't know if he ever told you about the unknown soldier..."

"He did. But this kidnapping, the money, it's a triumph. Why is he unhappy?"

"It is," Packy said. "But he's idealistic, and he's becoming disillusioned. He's starting to see how Mosca and the others see the revolution. He now sees that the revolution itself has become less important to them than the preparing for it, the discussing of it, the gathering of money for it. He sees that they look upon it as a thing to be lived rather than won."

"Poor Camión," I said.

The driver craned his masked head out the window. "Chile," he shouted. "*Ya, pues.*"

Packy waved at the driver and kept talking. I began to miss him already, even though he was still in front of me. I thought of Tony, my friend.

"The gringo *huevón*, Ronnie Neumon, is already in Caracas," he

308

said. "He's locked in the trunk of a car. When we call and say we have all the money, they'll let him out."

"He's not hurt?"

"No, *pana*. He's a *marico*, though. Crying and begging the whole time."

"Really?" I thought of Loren, and I was pleased to hear that.

"Yes. You didn't do that with the Disip, did you? I know you enough to know that you didn't." I thought carefully.

"No," I said. "I don't think that I did. Not much of it, anyway."

"*¡Chileno, coño de tu madre!*" Packy ignored the driver.

"Things are very hot in Venezuela right now," he said. "They're going to be looking for us. El Camión and the rest of the Venezuelans are going off into Colombia for a while, until everything cools down. They've got some strong connections there. I'll be with them for a few weeks, then I'll make my way back to Chile."

"Chile? Packy, you can't go back there."

"I will. I'm taking home a share of this dirty gringo money, and I'm going to try to use it to do some good." A groan worked its way out of me.

"Good? What good? Bombs and guns? Haven't you already seen what that turns into?" He shook his head.

"Not that shit. Not anymore. I have to believe there's a way of doing things without hurting anybody. Maybe it's stupid, but it's the only thing that keeps me going."

"*¡Chi-le!*"

"*¡Ya voy!*" Packy shouted. The truck engine started. His eyes darted to the truck and then back to me. "By doing that, by using the money, maybe I can make this kidnapping have some meaning after all. And those two bank guards . . ."

"We're leaving!" the driver shouted. He put the truck in gear and began to roll slowly up the dirt road.

Packy's eyes were wide and desperate; he still had things to tell me.

"I was there, you know, when you saw us," Packy said. "With a mask on. Even though it was Mosca who shot him, how do you think I can make up for . . ." He stepped forward suddenly and hugged me. His arms around me felt terribly thin. I hugged him back.

"Jesus," I said.

"I love you very much, *pana*," he said. "Take care, and be happy."

Before I could say anything to him, before I could tell him that I loved him, too, he pushed away from me and turned and began sprinting after the moving fish truck. I watched as he caught up with it, opened the door on the passenger's side, and jumped in. Then, after the door had slammed, I watched the truck until it rolled out of sight, kicking red dust high into the jungle air as it went.

It took me two hours to walk down to the paved road. Almost as soon as my feet hit the blacktop, a couple of uniformed Disip men in a two-toned Plymouth stopped and picked me up. They took me into a Choroní that had been transformed during my absence, had filled with police cars and military vehicles. As soon as the Plymouth came to a stop, two men appeared at my window. One man was my pal from the *pensión,* the other was one of the tourists who had laughed at my gringo joke. The tourist was wearing a shoulder holster with a black semiautomatic pistol in it. He was not laughing now.

"What happened?" the tourist said. I bumped him with the door and stepped out of the car.

"The money is delivered."

"Where?"

"On a dirt road. In the forest. You'll have to get me a map." He snapped his fingers at my friend the guard, and the guard turned and trotted off.

"And the gringo?"

"He's in Caracas already, and he'll be freed as soon as they can make a phone call."

"What were they driving?"

"Green van, *Pescados de Barquísimeto* on the side." The cop pulled out a notebook and began scribbling. Then the other man returned, and there were suddenly four *pacos,* two of them in uniform, spreading a map across the hood of the car. I took a pencil from the head man and, saying a silent prayer for Packy, I drew a line at right angles to the road near where the Disip men had found me.

"There's a dirt road," I said. "It's not marked here; you'll have to look for it. Now I'm going to sit down and have a beer." I started to turn away, but the tourist-cop grabbed my arm and spun me around. He glared at me.

"You're certain," he said, "that these were the right people? The kidnappers?"

"Absolutely." I stared him down, and he let me go then. I wandered over to a nearby fish shack and sat. I was exhausted, and shaking all over.

The beer was cold and good. But a bitter dryness like the dryness and bitterness of ashes ran from my tongue all the way down my throat and into my stomach, and the beer could not wash it away. As I drank, I heard the distant throbbing of a helicopter.

Then Loren was sitting across from me at the rickety little table. Her hair was stuffed up under the straw hat, and her eyes were hidden behind the dark glasses. There was something awful about those glasses now; I looked hard, but I could make out no detail of the real, vulnerable, human eyes behind them the way I sometimes could when the light fell across the lenses just right. The glasses seemed suddenly to endow Loren with the compound eyes of a heartless insect.

We stared at each other for a long minute. Loren's mouth was expressionless, and as I looked at her, I felt my stomach sliding down like a setting sun. I remembered my thoughts about her birthmark, and I tasted regret. Those thoughts made me deserve what was about to happen to me.

Slowly I reached for her glasses. She sat unmoving, watching the slow uncoiling of my arm for a moment, and then she put out a perfect hand and pressed my fingers to the tabletop. Her chin trembled and I thought she would cry, but then she composed herself.

"Where's my husband?" she asked in her husky whisper. I looked down.

"Safe," I told her. "He's in Caracas. They told me they'd let him go soon."

Loren said nothing, but she left her hand over mine. I drained my beer and hissed more loudly than was necessary at the waiter, who was standing close by, and I violently waved my empty bottle in the air.

"We could . . ." I began, my voice choked with hopelessness. But then I stopped.

"I suppose I've got to go back there," she said.

My beer came and I poured it slowly, waiting for my courage to rise so that I could once again attack the windmill. I drank and cleared my throat.

"We could explain it to Ronnie." I kept my eyes away from her. "I'd go with you. We'd both explain. Of course he'd probably hit me again." I was shaken by soft coughs of laughter.

"Jimmy," Loren said. "Come on." I bobbed my head in a clown-like manner and concentrated on not looking stricken.

"Yeah," I said. "I know."

"I mean, in another life we could probably be good together." In another life. I began to wish that she would just shut up and stand up and walk away. I would have walked away myself, but I was afraid I would not be able to move with the grace the moment called for. I didn't want to get up and go lurching away with a broken heart.

Loren sighed. I let my chin rest on my chest and played with my beer glass, turning it around and around on the tabletop.

"We're sad people, aren't we?" Loren said. I looked up at her, startled. "I mean the whole race of us, don't you think? We've got love and sex and practicality all tangled together so badly that I don't think we'll ever sort it out. Do you, Jimmy?"

"I don't know what you mean," I said. "I don't think it was just sex."

"That's *just* what I mean," she said. "Sometimes they're almost the same thing, and sometimes they're not. And then practicality comes along and makes the whole question pointless to begin with."

"Practicality?" I was starting to feel a little anger, and the anger pulled me from my dismal mood.

Caught in the grip of her idea, somewhat consoled by it apparently, Loren seemed less sad as well.

"In other words, what would we do, Jimmy? Live in Caracas on your wire-service salary?"

"There are lots of things."

"You know it wouldn't work. You know I need to get into movies; it's the only thing for me. Ronnie's a tremendous asshole, but that hardly even matters. What matters is that when I'm with him, I've got the visibility I need to get what I want."

My anger was fermenting to bitterness now. The bitterness was good; it let me take secret delight in my thoughts about the birthmark. I looked up and tried to smile and managed a grimace. "Money makes the world go round," I said.

Loren looked surprised and bit her lip. "It's not money, Jimmy," she said. "I hope you don't think that."

"No, I guess not," I said.

"It's a need."

"Yes."

"It's what I need."

"A need," I said, and bobbed my head. "A need."

Later, after she had packed and I helped her carry her suitcases out to the rented BMW, she stood on her toes and kissed me. Then she got into the car and started the engine and drove up the road without looking back. The tires of her car, rolling on the cracked and sandy pavement, left a faint haze hanging in the air long after she had disappeared from view.

Suddenly everything was over. Police and townspeople ignored me as they went about their work. But instead of the deep sensation of relief I had expected, all I felt was a dark and crushing sense of finality. Of course my rueful thoughts of Loren and her not unanticipated desertion contributed greatly to my gloom, but my mood contained another, larger component as well. I had, after all, led the world for a few days, and now the world had shoved me aside and was going on without me.

There were no buses out of Choroní until the next day, and I did not feel like asking any cops for a ride. I ate a tasteless meal, then went back to my room and slept fitfully through the evening and was wide awake by dawn.

In the morning, after I packed my things, I walked down to the beach to throw a stone in the water. Then I caught the bus back to Caracas.

The bus driver had his radio tuned to a salsa station, and he kept it turned up loud. When the news came on, I learned that Ronnie Neumon, the rock star, had been found wandering dazed and hairless but nonetheless safe on a side street in Petare. The forces of national security were doing everything possible to apprehend his kidnappers.

The newscaster did not mention my name. And although I was

no longer wearing my sunglasses and hat, the people on the bus either did not recognize me or did not care.

When the bus stopped at the Nuevo Circo station in Caracas, the first thing I did was to walk into a restaurant and grab a pay phone. I intended to dial the agency's number, but I found myself picking out the numbers to my home telephone instead. The phone rang twelve or thirteen times, and I began to get worried, but then someone picked up and stood listening.

"Timo?" I said. "Séptimo?"

"Jimmy? *¿Estás tú?*" I laughed. I felt myself aching to see him suddenly.

"Yes, it's me, *pana*. How are you?" Séptimo paused.

"*Bien*," he said finally.

"Have you been eating?"

"*Sí*. The *pacos* brought so much. They went away this morning and didn't come back."

"The police are gone? Good."

"Jimmy?" I waited. The phone line crackled in anticipation. "Where were you?"

"I was at the shore. In Choroní." The line crackled between us for a few seconds more.

Then Séptimo said, "I would like to see the shore sometime."

"You've never been?"

"No."

"Not even over the mountain to La Guaira?"

"*Nunca*." I was startled, but then I realized I had nothing to be startled about. He was just a child, a very poor child.

"Well, maybe we'll go," I said. "I don't think I'll be working at the agency anymore, so I'll have time." A strange thickness was beginning to invade my throat. "Or maybe we'll go down to the jungle. Would you like that? We'll go see the big waterfall."

"The waterfall!" he said. There was excitement in his voice. But then he became wary. "That might be good," he said. "I don't know."

"Listen, I've got some more calls to make. I'll be home in about an hour."

"*Ciao*," Séptimo said, and he hung up before I could say anything else.

I called the office, and a gringo stranger answered.

"Angel?" he said, and laughed. "Jesus, are *you* a legend. Of course you know you're not working here anymore?"

"Yeah, I kind of guessed that," I said.

"Not only that, but agents from the immigration and naturalization came by here looking for you today. They appeared to be more than willing to stamp you an exit visa."

"Let me talk to Mickey, will you?"

"Calderón? He's gone too. New York sent me to replace him."

"Fired?"

"Fired. Listen, I'm looking for some down-and-out but literate Yankee boy to help me out here. If you know anyone like that, send him along, will you?"

"Yeah," I told him. "Hold your breath." I hung up on him and dialed Mickey's number. I let it go beyond twenty rings, but there was no answer. So I jumped into a passing *por puesto* and headed toward Altamira through the strangled late-afternoon traffic.

I imagined that I would find Mickey reduced to a despairing shadow by the loss of his job. Yet my feelings about the prospect of encountering him this way were not entirely feelings of dread; caring for Mickey, reviving him, would give me a purpose while I tried to decide what to do next.

In the lobby of Mickey's building I was startled to run into Lulu, the Mexican whore from Mickey's club. She was leaving just as I arrived, and she frowned deeply when our eyes met. I caught my breath as I noticed the dusky-purple color of her blouse; I wondered if she were in mourning.

"How's Mickey?" I asked.

"The same," she told me, still frowning. Then she stepped around me and went out the door.

I hurried to Mickey's floor, found his door open, and nearly tripped over a collection of suitcases as I rushed inside.

"Hello?" I shouted. "Anybody here?" I heard footsteps at the top of the stairs and half-expected to see a priest or a doctor. But it was Mickey himself who appeared on the stairway, a long, plump suit bag in his hand.

"Shit, Jimmy," he said. "You son of a bitch." His voice sounded weary. He was clean-shaven, and he wore dark pants with a sharp crease in them, as well as a white shirt and a tie. I was too surprised to speak for a moment.

Then I said, "I saw Lulu. In the lobby." He slung the suit bag over his shoulder and started down the stairs.

"She's pissed. She wants to go to Buenos Aires."

"Buenos Aires? You found them, then?" I thought of Floyd and Nestor, and I felt a momentary flash of relief before the cold panic rolled through me. Mickey crossed the living room and stopped just as he seemed about to walk right through me.

"We're both shit-canned, you know," he said.

"I know. I called the office."

"And it's your fault. First you got wrapped up with those guerrillas and then you wouldn't give me the information." I shook my head.

"I couldn't help it. If you thought about it, you'd realize it."

"New York was awful pissed off."

"They're always pissed off."

"This time they had a *right*. How professional is that, to get personally involved?"

I was becoming angry now. "Mickey, I didn't know I was involved until it was too late. And by that time a guy's life was in my hands. What do you want? What the fuck do they want from me?"

I thought he would keep the argument rolling, as was his habit. But unexpectedly he lifted a hand and set it on my shoulder. He smiled a sad smile.

"It doesn't matter anyway, Jimmy boy. I'm just upset for you, that's all. For your future. I'd probably be on my way out of here, no matter what."

"Yeah, you were telling me." My icy fear of abandonment returned. "When, anyway?" But Mickey was already on his way to the kitchen.

"Whiskey and water okay?"

"Just whiskey. And ice." He soon returned with a couple of drinks.

"Sit here on the couch with me," he said. I obeyed at once; there was a renewed dignity to Mickey that seemed to demand obedience. He lifted his glass as if to propose a toast.

"The world," said Mickey, "is a shitbox of pain."

"It is," I agreed without even thinking. "It is indeed a shitbox of pain." We drank and looked at each other, and then we were laughing. Tears of laughter came to Mickey's tired eyes; he grabbed me and hugged me, and I hugged him back. A moment later he was serious again.

"I leave tonight."

"Oh." I set down my glass.

"I told you she'd get in touch with me. She needs money." I picked up my glass and took a couple of long swallows of whiskey. It was beginning to seem difficult to take in enough air to fill my lungs.

"But how will you live with her again? After all that happened?" He looked at the floor and gave a low, humorless chuckle.

"Well, I won't. I won't live with her. Truth is, I don't give a damn about her anymore." Mickey lifted his eyes to me and smiled.

"It's my boys. My Nestor and Floyd. I've got to be near them. I've been here thinking and thinking, Jimmy, and the conclusion I've reached is that if there's a true love in my life, it's those boys." As he spoke, I pictured their faces clearly. I found myself nodding.

"They're good boys," I agreed, my voice thick.

"They are. They are. I just wish I realized it sooner, before I got caught up in all kinds of other meaningless concerns. I hope it's not too late."

"It's not," I quickly assured him. "It's not," I said, unable to meet his eyes. "Because they understand things. They understand more than either of us knows." I shot him a quick, pained glance. "You're doing the right thing."

For a few minutes, as we pondered the undisputable rightness of Mickey's decision, there was no sound between us other than the rattling of ice in our glasses. Finally Mickey said, "Whatever job I get down there will be all right with me. And how about you? You'll be okay, won't you, Jimmy?" I gave him a bright, false smile.

"Me? Sure. I mean, I don't know what I'm going to do yet, but I'll be okay." He nodded.

"Well, take a piece of advice from the old man."

"One of many," I said.

"I know you're alone right now, but that probably won't always be the case. The thing is to try not to love anybody who's not worthy of it."

"There's a trick," I said, attempting humor.

"But when you've got somebody who's worthy, somebody who really worries about you, take care of them. There isn't anything else that's very important." I said nothing. Mickey studied me for a time before saying, "You want another drink?"

"No. I better get out of here and let you pack." I set down my glass and stood.

"Jimmy. You'll be okay, Jimmy boy."

"I know," I said. "Say hi to those boys for me, Mick."

"No, really. I'm sure of it." His eyes followed me as I moved toward the door.

"Mickey. I know."

I went into a quiet bar off Altamira and had a couple of drinks. The hour for me to meet Séptimo came and went, but I did not consider myself in any shape to go home. After the third or fourth whiskey over ice, I went to another bar and continued my drinking. But this second bar was too cheerful for my mood, and I soon left it and began wandering the streets.

The problem was that not only had I just emerged from one of the most turbulent episodes of my life to find myself suddenly without a friend or a lover or even a job, but the entire path I had been following for most of my years seemed somehow to have come to its end, leaving me no better off in any way than I had ever been. So that while I had successfully forged my way through certain hazards of the spirit, mind, and body and had arrived safely at this particular destination, the arrival itself held so little meaning and carried so little promise that it left me feeling like a singularly unconnected bit of blowing dust that finds itself trapped in a windy corner, and I had not a clue from anyone or anything as to where I next should go, or how I should conduct myself along the way.

Or so I thought.

I wandered into a few more bars that night, but I was too restless to sit in any one place for long, and after a whiskey or two I would always stand and take to the streets again. Finally as dawn approached, it became impossible to find a place to drink, and my feet remained in mindless motion. I was tireless in my bewilderment, and I believe I would have kept walking deep into the afternoon if an accident had not befallen me.

As I was passing through a canyon formed by tall apartment buildings, so deep in reflection that I all but ignored the glow of the new morning sky, the air around me suddenly became filled with a faint hissing like the whispering of wings. There followed a thunderous *crack* that seemed to come from inside my own head, and then I found myself stretched out comfortably with my cheek resting against the sidewalk.

I moaned and stirred and thought about going back to sleep, but a pain in my head brought me around, and I slowly pulled myself into a sitting position. It was then that I saw the shattered wooden birdcage sitting next to me on the sidewalk. A tiny red finch lay unmoving among smashed bars like broken toothpicks.

In a moment I felt a creeping wetness, and I touched the back of my head; my hand came away sticky with blood. I saw that the cage was heavy enough to have split my skull if it had met me with anything more than a glancing corner or an edge, and a thrill of useless fright ran through me. But soon the little bird twitched and began to flutter, legs kicking and wings flapping as it fought to regain control of its muscles, and I knew then that it was alive, and I realized that by breaking its fall from one of the high balconies, I had probably kept it from being killed. I touched my still-bleeding wound and carried the blood on my fingers and held it before my eyes. I smiled then; it pleased me to think that it had been my broken skin, my blood, the thickness of my skull, that had saved that tiny life.

As carefully as I could, I reached through sharp broken bars and brought the red finch out. I held him in my hand, warming him, and for a moment I considered carrying him home in my pocket as a gift for Séptimo. But the bird shortly gave signs of wanting his freedom, and an old voice came into my head and told me to let him go. The rim of the sun had by then risen above the tops of the hills; when I opened my hand, the bird sat on my finger for a minute, regarding me with a liquid eye before finally taking off on quick-stroking wings to head right for that arc of fire. For as long as I could see him, my heart went with him, lifting high above the city.

I decided then that I would go home, and I would gather up little Séptimo and take him to see Angel Falls. Afterward I would take him back with me to the States or, better yet, to somewhere fresh, someplace like Brazil perhaps.

We'd roll together, Séptimo and I. I would feed him and make him feel protected, and he would help me drive away that awful unconnectedness that a lone adult can feel. And in rolling, maybe we would gather up a woman along the way, a good, kind woman as yet unpoisoned by the world. And maybe we wouldn't. Perhaps it would always be just the two of us; in pondering this, I realized that it probably did not matter quite as much as I had always thought.

Sometimes the most important things remain long overlooked because of their simplicity. I caught the first *por puesto* of the new day and I rode it home.